Praise for Linwood Barclay

'Barclay has a fine ear for dialogue, especially in scenes with Zack and his family, and his expert blend of humour and suspense make this a well-constructed, often witty mystery that's sure to please'   *Publishers Weekly*

'A suspense master'   Stephen King

'Delightful characters and a clever plot created with thoughtful and skilled writing'   *Washington Times*

'Very funny yet suspenseful . . . An hilarious mystery'
Wall Street Journal

'Humour, realistic characters, a jaunty first-person narration, and fast pacing make for an enjoyable read'   *Booklist*

'Some days, all you really want is for someone to tell you a wicked-good story. Linwood Barclay answers the reader's perpetual prayer'   *New York Times*

Linwood Barclay is the multi-million copy international bestselling author of many critically acclaimed novels, including the Richard & Judy Summer Read winner and number one bestseller *No Time for Goodbye*. He lives near Toronto with his wife where they raised two children and is a former columnist for the *Toronto Star*.

To find out more about Linwood and his books, follow him on Twitter @linwood_barclay or Facebook /linwoodbarclay/ or visit his website www.linwood barclay.com

Also by Linwood Barclay

Bad News

LINWOOD BARCLAY

An Orion paperback

First published in the USA in 2007
First published in Great Britain in 2017
by Orion Books
an imprint of The Orion Publishing Group Ltd,
Carmelite House, 50 Victoria Embankment
London EC4Y 0DZ

An Hachette UK company

1 3 5 7 9 10 8 6 4 2

Copyright © Barclay Perspectives Inc. 2007

The moral right of Linwood Barclay to be identified as the author
of this work has been asserted in accordance with
the Copyright, Designs and Patents Act 1988.

A CIP catalogue record for this book
is available from the British Library.

ISBN 978 0 7528 8316 8

Printed and bound in Great Britain by Clays Ltd, St Ives plc

Typeset by Born Group

www.orionbooks.co.uk

For Neetha

*Miranda heard noises coming from the bottom of the stairs.
They were back. If they find me here, she thought, I'll
end up dead, just like the others.*

*It had to be them, downstairs in the bar. It was after hours,
after all. Everyone else had cleared out. The Kickstart had
been closed, the girls had been sent home. They'd be coming
upstairs any moment now to finish up their business. It would
be quite the day for them. Sell some beer, some drugs on the
side, get a bunch of guys laid, figure out what to do with
three bodies.*

*Oh yeah, they'd kill her. Well, maybe not Leo. Chances
were he wouldn't kill her. Gary would be the one to actually
kill her. But Leo, he wouldn't do anything to stop it. He
always let Gary take the lead in these things.* I'll end up
as dead as the others, *Miranda thought.*

If I don't get out of here right now.

The others hadn't been dead long.

*Only minutes, she guessed, although it seemed much
longer. It was true what they said, Miranda thought, about
things slowing down. Maybe that's why, in the movies,
when something terribly dramatic was happening, they ran
it in slow motion. Not just because it was a neat effect, but
because it was a reflection of human experience. Maybe your
brain had to play tricks with time, give you a chance to*

absorb what the hell was happening so you could figure out how to deal with it.

Miranda felt as though she'd been in this room with the three dead men for some time now. But maybe it hadn't even been minutes. Maybe it had only been a few seconds. She wasn't sure. She wondered whether she might be slipping into shock.

All she knew for certain was that they were dead. All you had to do was look at them. Sprawled out across the floor, not stirring, their shirts and pants soaked with blood.

Payne, dead. Eldridge, dead. Zane, dead.

And only moments before, all alive.

Eldridge had been the last to die. He'd hung on long enough to look into her eyes and say, 'Gary . . . He'll kill you . . .'

She hardly needed the warning.

Even as she'd heard Gary and Leo at the bottom of the stairs, she'd tried to pull herself together, to think. Focus, she thought. Focus.

For a moment, she wondered whether she could talk her way out of it. Tell Gary he didn't have to worry about her, let her walk and she'd never breathe a word of the things he'd done, not even that he'd killed the only man she'd ever really loved.

Yeah, right. That was a plan.

She poked her head out the door and into the dingy hallway. To the left, the stairs. The smell of stale beer, human sweat, and cigarettes wafted up. To the right, at the end of the hallway, a window that opened onto the fire escape.

Miranda grabbed her bag and ran for the window, pushed up on it. It didn't want to budge.

The voices were getting closer. Maybe halfway up. She could hear their footsteps. She pushed harder on the stuck

2

window, and it rose an inch, just enough for her to slip her fingers under it. She put everything she had into lifting it, opened it wide enough to get one leg out and planted on the rusted metal grating. Then she swung her body through, her other leg.

She caught a glimpse of them entering the far end of the hallway as she pressed herself against the building's cold brick wall. And then, as if willing herself to be weightless, she descended the metal stairs without a sound, and when she reached the bottom, ran off into the night.

She knew she'd have to get away and never come back. She couldn't go to the police. They wouldn't help, wouldn't guarantee her safety. Gary always found a way.

She was on her own. She'd have to disappear. She'd have to make it so no one ever found her.

Because she knew he'd be looking. And she knew he'd never give up.

ONE

'You have to empty all the change out of your pockets,' the uniformed woman told me. 'And I need your wallet.'

For a second, I thought about making a joke. Maybe, under less stressful circumstances, I might have. A visit to a prison under normal conditions – does anyone visit a prison under normal conditions? – would have been stressful enough. But my reasons for being here were far from normal. And there wasn't anything normal about the guy sitting in the pickup truck, out in the prison parking lot, waiting for me to do what I'd come here to do.

If I'd just been here doing a story for the *Metropolitan*, when the female guard asked for my wallet I might have said, *What is this, a stickup? They don't pay you enough?* And then I would have laughed. Ha-ha.

But there was nothing to suggest that this woman, black, mid-forties, built like a safe, wearing a shiny black belt with a riot stick attached, was feeling all that jocular herself. Maybe working in a prison does that to you. You didn't have to be an inmate to feel the oppressiveness of the place.

I'd already put my cell phone in the plastic tray she'd given me. 'Okay, I can see how change would set off this thing,' I said, nodding at the security portal, like those ones they have at the airport, that I'd have to walk through to get any further into the prison. 'But why do I have to give you my wallet?'

'You can't take any money into the prison,' the woman said sternly. 'You're not allowed to give money to the inmates.' For just a moment, her hand rested on her riot stick. Honestly, I think it was an unconscious gesture, not intended to send a message, but I got one just the same. *Don't give me a hard time.* That was the message I got.

I am not a big fan of getting whacked in the head with a riot stick. But at that moment, honestly, it's hard to imagine how it could have made things any worse than they already were.

I'd never been in a prison before, let alone a women's prison, and I'd only been at this one for about five minutes, and already I was pretty certain it was not a nice place to be. I got that impression as I approached the main entrance. I walked up to a ten-foot chain-link fence looped at the top with barbed wire, and pressed a button on a small speaker mounted next to the gate.

'Hello?'

A voice, no doubt coming from the building fifty feet beyond the gate, crackled, 'Name?'

'Uh, Walker?' Like I wasn't really sure. 'Zack Walker?'

Then, nothing. I stood by the gate a good ten seconds, wondering whether I wasn't on the list even though I'd phoned the lawyer – he was supposed to have pulled some strings, called in favors, name your cliché, to get me in here. But then there was a buzzing sound, which was my signal to push the gate wide. I glanced up at the surveillance cameras as I walked up to the main building, which, without the fencing and barbed wire, might have passed for a community college. Once inside, I approached the counter, where I encountered the humorless guard with the riot stick.

'So,' I said, trying to make conversation and forget how grave the situation was while I fumbled around for my wallet, seemingly forgetting that it was in my right back pocket, where it has been since I was fifteen, 'is this where Martha Stewart did her time?'

Nothing.

Wallet out, I glanced into it, counted seven dollars, before dropping it into the tray with my cell phone. Seven dollars. Then, from the front pockets of my jeans, I dug out fifty-seven cents. How much would $7.57 buy in prison? How many smokes? Wasn't that what everyone wanted money for in prison? Smokes?

The guard slapped a short, stubby key with a square of orange plastic at the end onto the counter, then pointed to a bank of airport-type lockers against the far wall. 'You can put your stuff in there,' she said. I took my tray of belongings, found the locker that matched the number on the key, and stowed it. I had to print my name in a book, then sign next to it, put down the time of my arrival. They ran a wand over me after I stepped through the security door, making sure I wasn't sneaking in with any weapons.

If only I had a weapon. I wouldn't have to be here now.

Once inside I was directed to a room full of carrels, like you might find in a university library, where students could do their work in private. But this carrel faced onto another one, the two separated by a sheet of glass. Each side had a phone, or at least the handset. No keypad. You didn't dial out for pizza from here.

Just like in the movies.

Another guard, also a woman, said something behind me. 'Everything okay here?' I must have jumped. 'Just chill,' she said, smiling. Then she looked beyond me. 'Hey, you're set to go.'

I nodded, swallowed, turned back to look at the glass, and there she was, coming through the door of the room I was looking into. My friend Trixie Snelling.

Another female guard directed her to the chair on the other side of the piece of glass. She sat down, and I got my first look at her since her arrest.

I must have been expecting to see her in an orange prison jumpsuit or something, because I did a bit of a double take when she showed up in jeans (minus the belt), a pullover Gap shirt, and sneakers. Trixie, with her jet black hair, dark eyes, and trim figure, could turn heads no matter what she wore. She certainly had no trouble holding someone's attention when, whip in hand, she donned her leather corset and boots, but that was when she was on the clock. Outside of work, even in a pair of sweats, there was no getting around the fact that she was a beautiful and alluring woman.

But I could see that a couple of days in jail had already taken a toll on her. She was without her usual make-up and her eyes were tired, her dark hair less full. I guessed she'd been managing on a lot less sleep than usual.

No surprise there.

Trixie had been a friend – and just a friend – for a few years now. We'd lived a couple of doors down from her when we still had our house in suburban Oakwood. I was working from home back then, and Trixie was operating a home-based business as well. I was naive enough, at first, to think it was accounting. I was not, at the time, a person who was very good at picking up the signals, and there were plenty of them – think of immense, flashing billboards – to indicate that Trixie was not making a living doing people's tax returns.

We'd already established a friendship when I learned the true nature of Trixie's business, and for reasons I can't totally explain, we remained friends. I'm not exactly the kind of person who befriends people who live on the edge of the law.

It's not that I think I'm better than them. It's just that I'm the kind of guy who panics if he hasn't paid his parking ticket on time. Or I would be, if I weren't the kind of person who runs back to the meter five minutes ahead of time to plug in a few more nickels.

Trixie tried to smile as she reached for the phone, but she had to know that this was more than a social visit. There had been some frantic calls in the last hour to allow this face-to-face meeting.

'Zack, Jesus, what are you doing here?'

'Hi, Trixie,' I said.

'I get this message, my lawyer's setting up a meeting with you, very urgent. What's going on?'

Her lawyer wouldn't have been able to tell her. I hadn't been able to tell him. I'd had to convince him that he had to let me see his client without revealing why. If Trixie wanted to tell him what I'd had to say, afterwards, that was her call.

It couldn't be mine.

'I have some things to tell you,' I said, 'but I need you to remain cool when I do.'

'What?'

'Are you listening? You have to stay calm and listen to what I have to say.'

Her eyes were darting nervously about. No matter how bad she might think what I was going to tell her was, it was going to be worse.

'Okay,' she said. 'What is it?'

'It's bad,' I said, lowering my voice as I spoke into the receiver. 'They've got her.'

The look in Trixie's eyes told me there was no need to be more specific. She knew exactly who I was talking about.

Of course, I'm getting a bit ahead of myself here. There were a whole lot of things that led up to this point.

And a whole lot that happened after.

Maybe I should back up a bit.

TWO

'I need twenty bucks,' said Paul, our seventeen-year-old.

Sarah and I were at the kitchen table, the dirty dinner dishes cleared but still sitting next to the sink, waiting to be dealt with. We had poured ourselves some wine. Sarah had brought home a bottle of Beringer and we had filled our glasses to the top when our son popped his head in.

'What for?' Sarah asked after a large slurp of white zinfandel.

'Just stuff,' Paul said. 'We might go to the movies or something.'

'A movie isn't twenty bucks,' I said. 'Yet.'

Paul sighed. 'Popcorn? You want me to watch a movie without popcorn?'

I looked at Sarah. She said, 'I wouldn't be able to sleep if that happened.'

I said, 'Didn't I give you twenty bucks a couple of days ago?'

Another sigh. 'It was *three* days ago.'

'Okay,' I said. 'So it was three days ago. Where did that twenty dollars go?'

'Screw it, never mind,' Paul said, and withdrew.

'Hang on a second, pal,' I said, and was starting to get up from my chair when Sarah reached over and grabbed my arm.

'Sit down,' she said. 'Let him go.' I settled back into the chair. 'Have some more wine.' She topped up my glass. 'He's just being a D.H.' Parental shorthand for dickhead.

'No kidding,' I said. Paul's in his last year of high school, and he's a pretty good kid, all things considered. But sometimes, I just wanted to ground him for a month or two, only at someone else's house.

I sipped my wine.

'Not like that,' Sarah said. 'You're drinking like a girl. Here, watch me.' She tipped back her nearly full glass, polished it off in four swallows. She put the glass back down, said, 'Hit me.'

I filled it.

'We need to do this more often,' Sarah said. 'It's been kind of stressful around here lately, in case you hadn't noticed.'

No kidding. I'd been home only a couple of days, having returned from my father's fishing camp, where, not to understate it or anything, all hell had broken loose. It was the third time in as many years that I'd found myself in a pickle – now there's a word for it – for which I had no training, and where I was in way over my head.

I had promised Sarah, and myself, that no more would I allow myself to get sucked into dangerous situations, not that I had wanted it to happen those other times. I wasn't cut out for it. I was, and am, a writer of so-so science fiction novels, paying the bills writing features for the *Metropolitan* newspaper, where Sarah is, depending on the day, my editor. At a large daily newspaper, you can get chewed out by so many people higher up the food chain than yourself that it's hard to narrow down the bosses to whom you report to just one person.

'Yeah,' I said, 'very stressful. But he doesn't make it any easier, acting like that. And I swear, he's hitting me up for ten, twenty bucks every day, it seems. And it's just entertainment. Renting movies, seeing movies, buying video games. I don't spend what he does on enter—'

'Drink,' Sarah said.

I obeyed. 'Do we have another bottle of this stuff?' I asked. Sarah nodded. 'Where's Angie tonight?'

Angie was in her second year at Mackenzie University, but since the school was in the city, and we lived in that city, she was not in residence.

'Class,' Sarah said. 'Evening lecture or something.'

'I hardly ever see her around here. Sometimes I don't even think she comes home every night.'

'She has a boyfriend,' Sarah said. The comment hung in the air for a while, which gave me time to consider its implications. 'And she's nearly twenty,' Sarah said. 'If she boarded at university, if she'd gone clear across the country somewhere, you'd never know when she came home and when she didn't.'

I finished off my glass, got up, and went to the fridge. 'Where's the other bottle?'

'It's in there, just look,' Sarah said. 'Did I tell you about the foreign editor thing?'

'What foreign editor thing?'

'They posted it. They need a new foreign editor. Garth's going to the editorial board, where he can write "on the one hand this, on the other hand that".'

'Are you sure there's another bottle?'

'Do I have to come over there myself and embarrass you?'

'Look, I'm either going blind or there's no wine in here at – hang on, here it is. Okay, so, you want that job?'

'It's a step up from features editor. More staff, bigger stories, a larger budget to watch over.'

'More headaches.'

'It's a good step for me. If I ever want Magnuson's job.' Bertrand Magnuson, the managing editor, who gave every indication that he was barely tolerating me. I'd gotten some big stories since joining the *Metropolitan*, but they'd had a way of falling into my lap. That didn't count, in Magnuson's book.

'You want that job?' I asked. 'Magnuson's?'

'Eventually, why not? The paper's never had a woman managing editor, has it?'

'I don't think so.'

'There's only one little problem,' Sarah said.

'What's that?'

'I find it hard keeping all those foreign countries straight. All those -stan places.'

'That could be a problem,' I said, rooting through the drawer for the corkscrew.

'What are you doing?'

'Where's the fucking corkscrew?'

'It's here on the table, Sherlock.'

I sat back down, went to work opening the bottle. Sarah said, 'You're going to have to help me. Quiz me on foreign events. I've been working with the Metro file so long, I don't know what's going on anyplace in the world other than this city.'

'Hitler's dead,' I said. 'And Maggie Thatcher? Not a prime minister anymore. Oh, and there was that guy? The one who walked on the moon? The moon counts as foreign, right?'

'You'll help me?' She wanted me to be serious for a moment.

'I will help you.'

Sarah watched as I refilled our glasses. Then she asked, 'When are you seeing Trixie?'

'We're having coffee tomorrow,' I said.

'What's her problem?' Sarah asked.

'I don't know. I called her up after I got back from Dad's place. You know we'd had this lunch, she was about to tell me something when I got that call that something had happened to my father, so she never got into it. So when I called her after I got back, she said she was in some kind of trouble. She didn't want to go into it over the phone.'

'What do you think it could be?'

I shrugged. 'No idea.'

'I mean, what could she possibly need your help with? What kind of problem could a professional dominatrix have that would require your expertise?' She gave that a moment. 'You're no good at knots.'

'I told you, I don't know. I must have insights in areas even we don't know about.'

Sarah held up her wine glass and peered at me, as if she was looking at me through the rose-colored zinfandel. 'Why are you friends with her?'

I pursed my lips. 'I guess because she helped me out a couple of years back when we got into that trouble in Oakwood. I got to know her before I knew what she really does for a living. I don't know. We just hit it off, I guess. Does it bother you? That we're friends?'

'Bother me? I don't think so. I mean, aside from the fact that she's stunningly beautiful and knows how

14

to fulfill every man's deepest, darkest fantasy, I don't see any reason to feel threatened by her.' She smiled. I started to say something, but she stopped me. 'It's okay. I know you, and I'm not worried about you. I know what we have.'

I smiled softly.

'But I think I understand what it is you like about Trixie,' Sarah said.

'What?'

'She's dangerous.'

'Come on.'

'No, that's it, I'm convinced. You've lived your whole life being safe, playing it safe, locking the doors at night, always changing the batteries in the smoke detectors, making sure the knives don't point up in the dishwasher. You know what you're like.'

I said nothing. My obsessions were well documented.

'But knowing Trixie, this woman with her dark side, who ties men up in her basement and spanks them for money, just knowing a person like this, even if all you do is meet her for coffee once in a while, this is your way of flirting with danger. Makes you feel that you're not so incredibly conservative.'

'That's what you think.'

Sarah leaned forwards across the kitchen table. 'That's what I know.'

'I think you're full of shit,' I said to her.

'Really.' She finished off another glass. 'You know what I was thinking I'd like to do?'

'No, what were you thinking you'd like to do?'

'I was thinking I would like to take you upstairs and fuck your brains out, that's what I was thinking I'd like to do.'

I felt a stirring inside me, and cleared my throat. 'I think, if that's what you want to do, you should go right ahead and do it. I would not want to stand in your way.'

'So like, can I have twenty bucks or not?'

Paul had reappeared. We both spun our heads around, and I don't know about Sarah, but I could feel my brain moving about half a second slower than my cranium.

'Uh,' I said, wondering whether Paul had heard the last part of our conversation, 'we vote no.'

Sarah slowly turned her head back to look at me. 'When did we have that vote?'

'We're going to have it right now. All those in favor of giving Paul twenty bucks, raise your hands.' Neither Sarah nor I raised our hands. 'It's settled, then. You have been turned down.'

'Aw, come on. There's a bunch of us, we're going to the movies.'

'Have you given any consideration,' Sarah said, speaking slowly so as not to slur her words, 'to finding a part-time job someplace, instead of hitting us up for spending money all the time?'

'I second the motion,' I said.

Paul definitely looked pissed. 'I thought you guys said I shouldn't get a job because it would interfere with my homework. That's what you said. Didn't you say that?'

'I believe you may be correct,' I said, 'but, seeing as how you don't do any homework now, I can't see where it would make any particular difference. It just means that instead of going to a movie or playing video games, you'd be making some money.'

'I don't believe this,' Paul said. 'Fuck, what kind of job am I going to get?'

'We look forward to finding out with great antici-pation,' I said.

Paul raised his hands in frustration, then let them fall to his side. 'I guess I'll just hang out here then,' he said. 'Maybe there's a game on.'

I glanced at Sarah just as Sarah glanced at me. For Sarah's recently announced plan to be acted upon, it would be better if we had the house to ourselves.

'Okay,' I said slowly, reaching for my wallet. 'I'll tell you what I'm going to do. I'll give you twenty bucks if you promise that tomorrow you'll start looking for some sort of part-time job.'

Paul strode across the kitchen, snatched the twenty I was holding up in my hand, and said, 'Deal. I'll be some goddamn sorry-ass burger flipper if that's what you want.' And he was out the door again in a shot.

I waited for it to swing shut, for the dust to settle, and then said to Sarah, 'I'm beginning to think we need to crack down on the kids' language.'

Sarah shook her head sadly. 'That fucking ship has sailed,' she said. 'I think you have failed to set a good example.'

She got up from the table, reached out for my hand, and started leading me to the stairs.

'What did they used to call Myanmar?' I asked her.

'Burma,' Sarah replied.

'I think that's right,' I said.

Sarah, not even waiting until we'd reached the second floor, was unbuttoning her blouse as she scaled the stairs.

'Dangerous,' I said, following her. 'You're the one who's dangerous.'

THREE

I was settling back in at my desk at the *Metropolitan*, having just returned from the cafeteria with a coffee, when I caught a whiff of something unpleasant behind me. That could mean only one of two things. Either one of the photogs had just returned from covering a drowning in the sewers, or our top police reporter was in the vicinity.

Without turning around, I said, 'What is it, Dick?' Slowly, I spun my computer chair around to look at him.

'How did you know it was me?' he asked. Dick Colby is not only the paper's best crime reporter, he's also its most odiferous. His fellow staffers are unsure whether it's that he fails to bathe, or to do his laundry, or possibly a combination of the two. He lives alone. I don't know whether he's ever been married, but I couldn't imagine a wife sending him out into the world this way. He's a gruff, slightly overweight, prematurely graying creature in his late forties, and I didn't know whether he was aware that most everyone referred to him, behind his back at any rate, as 'Cheese Dick.'

'Sixth sense,' I said. I'd taken a deep breath before turning around and was slowly exhaling as I spoke. 'You want something?'

'Your notes on the Wickens thing. Phone numbers, stuff like that. I need them.'

This request so took me by surprise that I breathed in suddenly, then coughed. 'What the fuck are you talking about?' I said.

'I'm taking over the story,' Colby said. Just like that. As Paul might say, *Hold on, Captain Butter-Me-Up*.

'Oh, you just decided, "Hey, I think I'd like that story," and thought you'd come over here and I'd hand it to you?'

Colby offered me a pitying smile. 'Shit, you haven't been told, have you?'

'Told what?'

'Maybe you should talk to your wifey,' Colby said. 'After you've done that, you can give me your notes.'

The blood was rushing to my head. I wanted to grab Colby by the neck and strangle him, but I also knew that if I got that close to him I might pass out. My stories on the Wickenses, a family of Timothy McVeigh-worshipping crazies whose plan to kill dozens, if not hundreds, of people had blown up in their faces, if you will, had run in the paper over the last couple of days. They had rented a farmhouse on my father's property, and I'd gotten to know them, in the last week, somewhat more intimately than I could have ever wanted.

'I don't believe this,' I said, getting out of my chair and heading straight for Sarah's glass-walled office.

She was on the phone as I strode in and stood on the other side of her desk. 'What's this about Colby taking the Wickens story?'

'Can I call you back?' Sarah said. She hung up the phone. 'What?'

'Cheese Dick says he's getting the Wickens story. Why the hell would he think he was getting the Wickens story?'

'Fuck,' Sarah said. 'That fucking asshole.'

'So it's not true?'

'Noooo,' Sarah said, stretching out the word and shaking her head slowly in exasperation. 'I mean, yes. It's true.'

'Are you kidding me?'

'It wasn't my decision.'

'Whose decision was it?'

Sarah tipped her head northwards, in the direction of Bertrand Magnuson's office.

'Magnuson pulled me off the Wickens story? I *got* the Wickens story. We played it up huge. It was my story. I'm *part* of that story.'

'I think that's why Magnuson's pulling you off it. Look, everyone knows you did a great job on it. Fantastic story. Award material. Pulitzer stuff. But Magnuson feels, you know, that you kind of, how do I put this . . .'

'Lucked into it?' I said.

Sarah screwed up her face. 'Maybe.'

'I would hardly call it luck, having a run-in with that bunch.'

'You think I don't agree? You think I'd call it lucky, what happened to you up there?' She took a breath. 'But the managing editor feels that it might be more appropriate that for the follow-up stories, like whether the Wickenses were part of a larger movement, other crimes that they might have been responsible for, that that's the kind of thing that Dick is better equipped to handle, what with his contacts in law enforcement and all.'

I stared at her. Sarah broke away, pretended to be looking for something on her desk. She was in management mode and couldn't bring herself to look me in the eye.

'Did you make a case for me?' I asked. 'When Magnuson made this decision?'

Sarah swallowed. 'Sure I did.'

'How hard?'

She paused. 'Pretty hard.'

'It's the foreign editor thing, isn't it? You don't want to piss off Magnuson because you're going for this new job and it's his call.'

'That's bullshit. That's bullshit and you know it.'

I didn't say anything.

'Look, it's not fair, but the fact is, Colby, for all his faults and aromas, has great contacts. He's very experienced with this sort of thing, it's not like his background is in—' She stopped herself.

'In what, Sarah?' My eyebrows went up, questioning. 'Writing science fiction novels? His background's a little more respectable? Is that what you were going to say?'

She deflated. 'No, that's not what I was going to say. I was going to say city hall, and photography. That's what most of your newspaper experience has been about.'

I stood there another five seconds, then turned and walked out. 'Zack,' Sarah called out. 'Zack, please.'

I put my notes about the Wickens story and all relevant phone numbers into the computer and e-mailed everything to Cheese Dick. Then I grabbed my jacket, slipped it on, and started making my way out of the newsroom.

'Hey,' Dick said as I passed within shouting distance of his desk. I kept on walking. 'Hey, Walker!' I stopped, looked over at him. 'I need to talk to you for a sec.'

I took my time walking over to him. 'I sent you the stuff,' I said.

'Yeah, I see that. Thanks. So Sarah, she explained it to you?'

I nodded.

'It's not personal,' Colby said smugly, enjoying immensely just how personal it actually was. 'I'm just more suited to this sort of assignment. When you stumble into something, like you did, it's okay to write the first-person story, you know, what happened to you, but after that, it's really my area, you know? I mean, you don't see me trying to cover a *Star Trek* convention, do you?'

I found myself thinking about what constituted justifiable homicide. My definition of 'justifiable' might, I feared, differ from the justice system's, so I decided not to act on an impulse to grab Colby's keyboard and beat him to death with it.

'Anything else?' I asked.

'Actually, yeah,' Colby said, looking for a piece of paper on his cluttered desk. 'Where is it . . . where the fuck is it? . . . Okay, here it is. Since I'm doing you a favor, taking this story off your hands, maybe you could do this one for me. You'd have to get moving, though. It's in an hour.'

'You've got to be fucking kidding me.'

'Good story, man, could really use your touch. And if you don't want it, it just means I'm going to have to go over to Assignment and tell them you didn't want it and they'll have to pull somebody off somethin' else to do it and then they'll figure you're some kind of fucking prima donna or something.'

'Give it to me,' I said. It was in Colby's own handwriting, some notes he'd taken. I could make out

22

'police union' and 'stun gun' and a time and location. 'What is this?'

'It's a demo. Some new kind of stun gun. The cops would like to have them; the police board's been saying no fucking way. So this guy who sells them is putting on a performance, just for some members of the police union. Some cops, they might decide to buy one, even though stun guns haven't been approved for use. They figure it's better to take heat for using one of those, blasting a guy with a few thousand volts and seeing him get up again, than face Internal Affairs after pulling their regular guns and killing a guy. Photo desk already knows about it.'

'All right,' I said. 'I'll do it.' I was pissed, and felt like walking out of the building and not coming back, but I didn't want to get a reputation as an asshole, either. Or for those who already thought I was one, a bigger asshole.

'Great,' Colby said, handing me his notes. 'Feel your way carefully, though. I heard about this on the Q.T. from a cop. The union may not be crazy about you being there. The board won't like it when they hear the cops have been looking at these things.'

The demo was scheduled for 11 a.m. I was still planning to meet Trixie Snelling at 1 p.m., at a coffee shop only a few blocks from police headquarters. She was making a trip in from Oakwood to see me, and I didn't want to have to cancel on her. I didn't think there'd be a problem.

On my way out of the building, I passed Magnuson's office. The door was open partway, and I could see the miserable bastard sitting at his desk, no doubt plotting ways to ruin other people's lives as much as he seemed intent on ruining mine.

'What makes this stun gun different from previous models, and what makes it the perfect tool for any properly equipped law enforcement body today, is its simplicity,' said the man who had been introduced as Mr Merker. 'Other stun gun models use two wires that are propelled from the weapon to the target. Once the gun has been fired, you must rewind the wires and replace the gas cartridge within the weapon that, basically, exploded when you pulled the trigger. So, you get one shot, then you have to reload. It's a bit like being a Minuteman with his musket.'

There were a few chuckles among the roughly two dozen cops who'd dropped by this meeting room in the police board's offices to see what was going on. A couple of them were clutching crudely produced flyers headlined 'Stun Gun Sale, Demo.'

Lesley Carroll, the *Metropolitan* photographer who'd accompanied me to this event, and I had encountered a bit of trouble getting in. A cop at the door said it was for union members only, and I'd told him, as politely as possible, that if he didn't let me in, my story would have to say that the police had held a secret meeting to consider whether to arm themselves with stun guns, and that might send the message that the police were acting as though they had no police board, or public, to answer to. If he let me in, I argued, readers would see that the police weren't trying to pull any fast ones, but were hoping to open a debate on the issue of whether officers should be issued these non-lethal weapons.

The cop thought about it. 'Fine.'

Once inside, Lesley, who was in her early twenties and interning with the paper, hoping to get hired on staff in a few months, said, 'Nice one.'

Merker, a lean man with closely cropped black hair, pointed chin, and piercing eyes, waved what looked like a plastic toy gun in his hand as he performed for the officers in an open area at the front of the room. The floor had been covered with gym mats, which suggested to me that a demonstration of some kind was imminent.

The gun in Merker's hand looked as though it had been drawn by a cartoonist, with fatter, exaggerated edges.

'But with the Dropper,' he said, 'instead of two wires coming out, two highly concentrated streams of highly conductive liquid come out. Each stream contains a different charge, if you will, and when they connect with the target, fifty thousand volts are discharged, completely interrupting the ability of the brain to send any messages to the body.'

Someone in the audience quipped, 'Maybe that's what happened to the chief.' More chuckling. Disputes between the chief of police and the rank and file were legendary.

'Because,' Merker continued, 'there are no wires to rewind, no gas cartridges to replace, it means that you can fire the gun more than once. Three times, to be exact. The unit needs no time between the first and second, and second and third shots to recharge or be rewinded, what have you. You can fire off three stun shots as quickly as you can pull the trigger. Now, this is not the first liquid stun gun, but is the first to come in a handheld, manageable size.'

There was some murmuring among the police officers, about two-thirds of them male. A woman spoke up. 'What about if we drop somebody with one of these? Is there any chance they'll die? And if they don't, are there any lasting effects? 'Cause, like, I don't want to get my ass sued off.'

'I wouldn't want anybody hurting that ass of yours,' a male cop said, and everyone laughed, including the female cop.

Merker shook his head confidently. 'The subject is instantly incapacitated, for several seconds, as his central nervous system collapses, but within about fifteen or twenty seconds, he starts recovering. Allow me to demonstrate.'

This caused even more murmuring, this time a bit on the agitated side, as if the police officers in the room were worried that they might be volunteered for a demonstration. But then, to everyone's collective relief, a tall, lumbering, round-shouldered man in the first row got to his feet and approached Merker.

'I'd like you to meet my associate, Mr Edgars. He is, as you can see, a big, strapping individual, 240 pounds, six foot four. It would take a lot to stop someone like him. Even an officer armed with a conventional weapon would feel unnerved if someone like Mr Edgars was charging him.'

Edgars grinned. Somewhat stupidly, I thought. He had a kind of 'gentle giant' quality about him.

'But not only will the Dropper drop Mr Edgars, it will leave him unharmed. Leo,' he said, addressing Edgars by what was evidently his first name, 'you've been shot with the Dropper, in demonstrations such as this, how many times now?'

Leo Edgars said, 'Uh, I guess, I think . . . I don't remember exactly, Gary.'

Before any nervous laughter could erupt, Gary Merker said, in the tone of a carnival barker, 'Twenty-seven times! That's how many! Leo has been shot twenty-seven times and yet remains undamaged in any way whatsoever.'

Leo grinned, again. 'Actually, Gary, I believe it's twenty-seven times.'

There were some nervous chuckles. There was the sense among all of us, I think, that Merker's assistant was a bit of a dim bulb who could benefit from a few more volts.

Merker smiled along with everyone else and then did something funny with his nose. He twitched it, pulled on it a couple of times between thumb and index finger. He turned away from the audience for a second to conduct some bit of nasal maintenance, then faced front again and said, 'The Dropper is an ideal tool for dealing with, for example, mental patients. A hardened criminal, a rapist, a bank robber, you don't lose too much sleep shooting one of those types even if they never get up again. But a, you know, nutcase who can't help being the way he is, that doesn't deserve a death sentence.'

Some cops exchanged awkward glances.

'Now, Leo, you pretend to be a mental patient coming at me, with a knife, perhaps.'

Lesley had slipped away a few moments earlier and was off to the side, ready with her camera.

'Sure.' Leo took a few steps back, paused, put his fingers to his temples for a second, as if getting himself in the moment, and then he charged.

'Ahhh!' he shouted. 'I'm crazy!'

Lesley was taking pictures as Gary Merker raised his Dropper stun gun and fired.

The streams of water were so small, and came out so quickly, that I almost didn't see them. But the results were immediately apparent. There was a brief crackling noise as they hit Leo, and his body went into an immediate spasm, dropping instantly. Lesley moved in for a better shot. Given Leo's size, there was quite a 'fwump!' when he hit the mat. Everyone recoiled, wondering whether Gary had just murdered his associate and we would all be called upon as witnesses.

'You see!' said Merker. 'Instant capitulation! And if I wanted to, I'd be able to shoot again immediately!'

Leo just lay there. Lesley got off a couple more shots.

'Uh,' said the woman cop who'd asked a question earlier, 'is he okay?'

Leo was still not moving.

'Leo!' Merker shouted.

His face still pressed into the mat, Leo said, 'Errr.'

'He just needs another minute,' Merker said. Slowly, Leo moved one of his arms, then another, and then he was slowly moving up onto his knees as most of his audience held their breath. With care, he got back onto his feet and dusted himself off.

Everyone, myself included, applauded. We were just relieved, I think, that he wasn't dead.

'Of course,' Merker said, continuing his sales pitch, 'during the period when he was down, law officers would have been able to cuff Leo, to subdue him. All you need is a few seconds to bring a suspect under control.' Merker walked over to Leo, put a hand on his shoulder while Lesley got an 'after' shot. Merker gave her an annoyed look. 'So, that's twenty-eight times now. How are you feeling?'

'Absolutely,' Leo said.

A uniformed cop, a tall black man, stepped forward. 'Mr Merker, I'm the president of this police association, and we have a board that's very hesitant about the use of these sorts of weapons. Has it been the experience of many other large city police departments that while stun guns are designed to be used in special circumstances to stop a suspect without actually killing him, once police have them, they start using them indiscriminately on suspects? Because their use is not fatal, officers aren't just using them on dangerous psychiatric patients. Aren't they using them on everyone from kids playing hooky to jaywalkers?'

It was an interesting comment, given who it was coming from. The police union head seemed pretty skeptical.

Merker was rubbing his nose again, one nostril in particular, like something inside there was really annoying him. He set his eyes on the questioner, almost accusingly. 'Well, I guess if you're saying that you think your own members aren't responsible enough to handle these things . . . well, then I guess you've got a problem.' There was some grumbling in the crowd, and I wasn't sure whether it was directed at Merker or the union president. 'Listen, I'm just here selling the hardware. I can give you guys good deals on these if you're interested. If you don't want them for yourselves, maybe you'd like to buy them for members of your family.'

Lesley was back beside me. 'Got some awesome shots,' she said. 'Did you see that guy go down?'

I nodded. 'I thought he was dead there for a second.'

Three or four cops approached Merker after he finished his pitch, but I didn't see anyone buying anything. As long as the stun guns were not being approved by the police commission, the cops would have to be buying them out of their own pocket.

'What if I could save you another fifty bucks?' I heard Merker tell one officer, but he still had no takers.

We found ourselves standing behind Gary Merker and his associate Leo Edgars at the elevator a couple of minutes later.

Merker turned and pointed to me. 'You're not a cop.'

'We're with the *Metropolitan*,' I said, and offered a hand. Merker didn't even look at it. 'We came to cover your demonstration.'

'I didn't know the press was going to be here,' he said. 'I don't think you should be doing a story about this.'

I shrugged. 'That's really not up to you,' I said. 'The police let us in.'

'Come on, Gary,' said Leo, who was in the elevator and holding the door open. 'I'm starving. You know gettin' electrocuted makes me really hungry.'

Gary Merker was still steamed and shook his head in anger and frustration. Before getting on the elevator, he slipped a finger in and out of his nose at lightning speed, then flicked it at me. 'That's what I think of your fucking story,' he said.

The elevator doors closed. Lesley Carroll looked stunned. 'Welcome to the newspaper biz,' I said to her.

FOUR

'I've had better days,' I told Trixie, who'd just been foolish enough to ask me how things were going. So I told her.

'Have you talked to Sarah since this morning?' Trixie asked.

'No,' I said. 'She tried me on my cell but I didn't answer it.'

'That's mature.'

'I'm just pissed, okay? And I know it's not her fault. It was Magnuson's call. He put her in an impossible spot.' I shook my head, looked into my crème caramel decaf lattacino thingie. I had no idea what it was. Trixie offered to buy when we met at the Starbucks, and I'd told her to surprise me. We'd grabbed a small table in the back corner and had snared a couple of comfy, leather-covered chairs.

'And we had such a nice time last night,' I said, more to myself than Trixie.

'What, did you go out or something?'

'No, no, we stayed in. Cost me twenty bucks, though.'

'Really? Sarah makes you pay for it? That's actually a very reasonable price, you know, and if there were any extras, it was a real bargain.' She grinned slyly at me. She was looking particularly fetching today, in a black cowl-neck sweater, black jeans and boots, her black hair pulled back into a ponytail.

I ignored all that and said, 'She's got this interview coming up, for foreign editor, and it's Magnuson's decision, so she probably didn't feel she could come to my defense. Figured Magnuson would accuse her of not being objective.'

'Because she sleeps with the reporter in question. For twenty bucks.'

'The money actually went to Paul,' I said.

Trixie raised an eyebrow. 'Now that's too kinky, even for me.'

I took a sip of my drink. I didn't know what it was, but it was sweet, and pretty good. 'Anyway, look, these are my problems, not yours. When we spoke on the phone, you said you were in some kind of trouble.'

'Yeah, well, I did, didn't I.'

'Sarah was wondering what kind of trouble you could be in that would bring you to call me. You need more chaos in your life? If that's what you want, then I'm definitely your guy.'

Trixie smiled. 'Sarah's tough on you, you know.'

I went into self-deprecation mode and shrugged. 'Look at what she has to put up with,' I said.

'I could put up with you,' she said, without a hint of sarcasm.

'So come on,' I said. 'What's up?'

She took a breath. 'I figure, what with you being the only person I know who works in journalism, that maybe you could advise me on how to proceed.'

'How to proceed with what?'

'How to proceed with keeping some asshole from writing a story about me.'

'What asshole would that be?'

Trixie hauled her purse, a good-sized one, onto her lap and started rooting around. First, she pulled out a stack of mail and put it on our table so that she could better see what she had in there. 'Just give me a minute,' she said. 'I have a post office box, get as little mail as possible delivered to my home.' I noticed what looked like a Visa bill, possibly a property tax notice from the town of Oakwood, something from a car company labeled 'Important: Recall Notice,' and a number of what appeared to be personal letters, none with return addresses.

I lightly thumbed them. 'Fan mail?'

'Hmm?' Trixie said. 'Oh, sometimes men write to me ahead of time, tell me what they want. They don't want anything showing up in the "sent messages" in their Outlook Express, if you know what I mean, in case the wife happens to read it.'

'Sure.'

She saw the recall envelope for, it seemed, the first time. 'Oh shit, not another. Never buy a German luxury car, at least not a GF300. I thought the GF stood for "goes fast." Now I think it's for "get fixed." It's been recalled for the fuel injection, a power seat, cruise control glitches. Who's got time to get all those things fixed? Open that, see what it's for while I try to find this thing.'

I opened the envelope, pulled out the paperwork. 'Let me see here. Uh, okay, you've got extra-sensitive air bag sensors. Slightest hit on the front bumper can set them—'

'Here it is.' Trixie slapped a newspaper clipping onto the table, then scooped all her mail back into the purse.

I picked up the clipping. It was a column, with a guy's head shot, and a name in bold caps: 'MARTIN BENSON.'

The headline read, 'Council Misses Boat on Harbor Review.'

'Something about the Oakwood harbor? What do you have to do with that?' I asked.

'Nothing. I don't care about the story. I just wanted you to see who the asshole was.'

'Martin Benson.'

'Yeah.'

'What paper is this from?'

'The *Suburban*.'

Oakwood's local, community newspaper. Light on news but heavy on inserted ads, it was delivered free to most of the town's households.

'I don't remember this guy from when we lived there,' I said. When we had a house in Oakwood, I'd at least turn the pages of the *Suburban* before dropping it into the recycling bin.

'He's a new guy. Trying to make a name for himself. By fucking me over.'

'Why don't you start at the beginning.'

'Okay, this Benson guy, he hears through the grape-vine what kind of business I might be operating in my home.'

'You mean, like, a house of pleasure and pain.'

'I offer pain. But some people do find that pleasing.'

'Where do you think he heard about it?'

Trixie shrugged. 'Any number of people know. Clients. Former neighbors.' She gave me a look.

'Not guilty,' I said.

'He did a piece on Roger Carpington. He's already out, you know. Maybe he told him something off the record, like, "Hey, you know what goes on in your supposedly respectable neighborhood?" '

Carpington was a former Oakwood town councillor who'd lost his position after being convicted of accepting money to vote the right way on a housing development. Carpington had never been a client of Trixie's, as far as I knew, but the man who'd been paying him off had been. He might have told Carpington about his recreational activities before having the life squeezed out of him by a python. (Hey, it's a long story.)

'But the thing is,' Trixie went on, 'it doesn't fucking much matter where he found out. The fact is, he suspects something.'

'Okay, so how do you know that?'

'He called me, says he wants to interview me. I say, what about? He says he's doing a column about Oakwood's kinkier side, thinks I might be able to help him out with that.'

'Maybe he doesn't want to write about you. Maybe he just wants a freebie.'

'Yeah, well, if I thought strapping him down and giving him forty whacks would keep him quiet, I'd do it. But I think he's the real deal. He wants to do a story.'

'What did you tell him?'

'I said I had no idea what he was talking about and hung up.'

I had some more latte-thingie. 'So did that take care of it?'

Trixie shook her head. 'He calls again, says he'd like to do the story even if I remained anonymous. So he can still do his story about kinky suburbanites. So I tell him again, I've got nothing to say. Then, after that, there's a car hanging around the street, a little Corolla or something, the sort of car a guy working for a paper like the *Suburban* could afford. I see it enough times that I start to get suspicious, so I decide to go out there, see who it is, ask him what he's doing. As I get close to the car, I recognize him from his picture in the paper.'

She displayed the clipping, pointed to Benson's face.

'I'm about to ask him what the fuck he's up to, and he starts to hold up his phone, and I'm sure it's one of those goddamn camera phones, so I put my hands up over my face and run back inside the house.'

'Well,' I said, 'I'm sure that didn't look suspicious.'

'So I've had to cancel all my appointments. I can't have clients coming to the house, having their picture taken, running the risk of it showing up in the paper. I haven't spanked a guy in over a week.' She spoke like someone who'd recently given up smoking.

I shook my head. 'So just lay low for a while, then. He can't spend all his time parked out front of your house. He'll give up after a while, go on to something else.'

'I'm not so sure. I wish I knew someone who could scare the shit out of him, but you never know with journalists.' She looked at me and smiled. 'Sometimes, when they're threatened, they're more determined than ever to write their story. It's like the only way to stop them is to kill them.'

I guess I was supposed to laugh at that, but when I didn't, Trixie said, 'That was a joke.'

'I know. It's just, I don't really know what you want me to do, Trixie. Maybe you'll actually have to make a respectable living for a while as an accountant. I mean, you are good at it. You know everything there is to know about balancing the books.'

'Or making them appear to balance even if they don't,' Trixie said, like she was remembering something that happened a long time ago. 'And by the way,' she said, 'thanks for not judging.'

'Huh?'

' "A respectable living," I believe you said. That I might want to consider one, for a while.'

'Trixie, don't try to guilt trip me. You operate outside the law. Like most places, Oakwood has laws against prostitu—'

Trixie jabbed a finger at me. 'I am not a hooker, Zack. I do not fuck these men. They don't get so much as a handjob from me.' She became very serious. 'I do not cross that line. I provide them with an entertaining, fantasy-like environment.'

'Okay, but you might have a difficult time persuading the authorities of that.'

Trixie shook her head in frustration, then leaned forwards in her leather chair, which drew me in as well.

'What I was thinking,' she said, 'was that you could talk to him.'

'What?'

'Just, you know, have a little conversation with him. You're a reporter with a big city newspaper. He probably wants to get on at a place like the *Metropolitan*. You could tell him no one gives a shit about two-bit stories like this, that if he really wants to make the jump to the big time, he needs to go after city hall. Politicians on the take, bad cops, that kind of thing. Not some woman trying to make a living.'

'Trixie,' I said. 'Look, you're my friend. I'd help you any way I can. But you can't ask me to do this. I can't, as a reporter for one paper, try to talk a reporter for another paper out of doing his job. I can't begin to count the number of ethical violations. There's just no way, I can't, I'm sorry, I really am.'

She looked into my eyes. 'I thought you'd be willing to help me.'

'I don't want you to be in trouble, but what you're asking me to do could get me in trouble at the *Metropolitan*, where, evidently, the boss already has it in for me. Imagine if he heard I was trying to persuade some community newspaper columnist not to write about a dominatrix.'

Trixie said nothing. Something caught her eye, and she looked to the front of the Starbucks. A leather-jacketed guy with a heavy beard and sunglasses strolled in. Outside, I could see a big motorcycle, a Harley-Davidson or something like that with raised handlebars, parked up close to the door.

Trixie shrunk back into the chair, turned and looked away.

'What?' I said. 'What is it? You know that guy.'

'No, I don't.'

'Then what's the problem? It's just some biker or biker wannabe. He's not bothering anyone.'

'It's nothing. You know what, Zack, don't worry about anything.' Her voice had turned snippy. 'I'll just handle my own problems myself.'

She was trying to make me feel guilty, so I decided to repeat what I thought was sound advice.

'Really, just lay low,' I said. 'This Martin Benson guy will finally go on to something else, and then you can get back to doing what it is that you do.'

Trixie, her shoulder still turned to the front of the coffee shop, folded up the clipping and shoved it down into her purse. The biker already had his coffee in hand and was heading out the front door. 'There, he's gone,' I said.

Trixie relaxed, but only slightly. She slung the strap of her purse over her shoulder.

'You do not understand, Zack. I cannot have my picture in the newspaper. Not any newspaper. Not even a piece of asswipe like the *Suburban*. They may be small, but they still have an online edition too, you know. They run my picture and it's all over the Internet.'

'I can't imagine anyone outside of Oakwood is reading the *Suburban* online,' I said, trying to calm her.

'I can't take that chance. I can't have my mug shot showing up anyplace.'

'Mug shot?' I said. 'Why do you call your own picture a mug shot?'

Trixie blinked. 'Figure of speech,' she said.

He would come in to see her at night, supposedly to tuck her in.

But Miranda, with some tips from her older sister, Claire, figured out a way to deal with this. She would tuck the covers in as tightly as possible on both sides, then crawl atop the bed and slide under the sheet and bedspread from the top.

Once she was there, she felt trapped, like a leftover sandwich Saran-Wrapped to a plate, but secure as well, because any attempts her father might make to touch his fifteen-year-old girl could not be disguised as inadvertent. He was very good at accidentally brushing his hand across her private places when getting her ready for bed. But those supposedly innocent touches weren't possible when she had herself so tightly cocooned. That, and pretending to already be asleep, tended to thwart his efforts, most of the time.

Sometimes Miranda almost wished he'd be more blatant. She wished he could be as direct with his perversions as he was with his violence. He made no attempt at excuses when he took out his belt to punish her or her sister for some perceived misbehavior. At those moments, she could scream back, run out of the house.

But when he slunk into her room at night, he would hide behind pitiful slyness. He'd camouflage baser motives with apologies about losing his temper. But she knew he felt no regrets over that. If only he'd just admit that he'd come in to check on her progress at turning into a woman, that he wanted a form of intimacy he knew to be inappropriate. Then maybe she could react, holler at him to leave her alone. But his feigned innocence always gave him an excuse. 'You're just sensitive,' he'd say. 'What, a father can't give his little girl a hug?'

And there was no use trying to talk to her mother about this. She numbed herself with scotch, cigarettes, and television, but mostly scotch. What chance was there that she would come to the defense of her daughters when she wouldn't defend herself against her husband's bursts of outrage and backhanded slaps?

It was older sister Claire she turned to. It was Claire with whom she shared her secrets. It was Claire who told her how to cope.

And it was Claire who begged her to leave with her. But Miranda said, 'You're eighteen. If you go, they can't make you come back. I'm just fifteen. He'd call the police. They'd bring me back.'

'I wouldn't let them,' Claire said.

But as much as Miranda admired, worshipped, her sister, she didn't believe she had those powers. She wasn't strong enough to protect her against her father and the authorities.

One night, it was Claire who came in to see her. Miranda pulled the sheets about her tightly, but when she heard her sister whisper her name, she relaxed.

'I'm going.' Claire said.

'Where? What do you mean?' Miranda asked.

'I'm leaving. Now. I'm not coming back.'

Miranda felt her heart in her throat. 'Don't go,' she whispered.

'I can't stay here another night.' There were tears in Claire's eyes. 'Come with us.'

41

'I have a math test tomorrow,' Miranda said. Math was probably the only thing that gave her any sense of accomplishment, the only thing she was really good at. Her father was good at telling her she was pretty much useless, and it rankled him when she came home with perfect math marks, proving him wrong. 'It's worth fifteen percent,' she protested.

'Jesus, forget your math test. I'm talking about getting out of here!'

'Shhh!' Miranda said. She didn't want her father coming in, taking the belt to the both of them.

'They're asleep,' Claire said. 'He's passed out, they're both passed out.'

'Where's your stuff? How can you just leave?'

Claire's bags — and that's what they were, bags — were all packed. They were already at the end of the drive. Her boyfriend, Don, was going to pick her up.

'Where will you go?' Miranda asked.

'Anywhere. Any place that's not here,' Claire said. 'If I stay here any longer, I'll kill him. Please come. Don says it's okay.'

Miranda liked Don. He was a nice boy. Not like most of the others. Claire was lucky to have found someone like that.

Miranda sat up in bed. She looked at her dresser, wondered what she would use to carry her clothes. She didn't even have a suitcase. They had never gone on a vacation. They'd never been anywhere. She could put some clothes in some paper bags. Two or three would probably do it. A couple pairs of jeans, a couple of tops, some underwear. She could get a job, make money, and buy some other clothes, maybe from a secondhand shop, maybe—

No, she couldn't do it. She couldn't run away. She was only fifteen. As horrible as home was, it was still a haven. She knew bad things happened here, but she knew what the bad things were. If she ran off with Claire, what different bad things might happen? Would they be worse than the things she had to deal with now?

'I can't do it,' Miranda said.

'I can't just leave you here,' Claire said. Her eyes were moist with tears.

'Just go.'

Outside, they could hear a car coming to a stop. Claire glanced out the window, and the tears running down her cheeks glistened in the moonlight. It was Don. He was putting Claire's paper bags of belongings into the trunk.

Claire threw her arms around her sister, and they were both crying now.

'Soon,' Miranda said. 'I'll try to leave soon.'

Claire sniffed, wiped her nose with her sleeve. 'I'll help you. Whatever you need, anything, I'll help you. I will always help you, no matter what.'

'I love you,' Miranda said.

'I love you too,' Claire said, and then she slipped out of the room.

Miranda watched from the window as Claire ran down to the road. Don threw his arms around her, opened the passenger door of his old Camaro for her, and then they drove off into the night.

Miranda did not cry long. You're on your own, she told herself. Start getting used to it.

FIVE

Back at the office, I banged out the stun gun story after first placing a couple of calls, one to the chair of the police commission to see what her reaction was to officers meeting with a guy who was selling stun guns when such weapons were not approved for use.

'Go on the Net and read up on these things,' she advised.

A number of stories came out of Florida. A disabled man in line at a theme park, disgruntled because he's had to wait so long, gets zapped with a stun gun by a security guard. A twelve-year-old girl, skipping school, is located by authorities hanging out at a swimming pool, smoking. When she tries to run away, she's stun-gunned. A father who gets hold of one illegally uses it to keep his three kids in line. An off-duty cop pulls out his stun gun and shoots a buddy who'd just beat him at poker.

Just for a moment, I imagined the advantages a stun gun might offer an exasperated parent. And I recalled a comment Sarah once made, upon hearing a radio newscaster say, 'Police do not understand why the mother of three small children snapped and wiped out her entire family.' She said, 'Well, there's your answer. She's the mother of three small children.'

So I threw a bit of stuff from the Net into the story, put a '-30-' on the end, and sent it on to the cityside basket with a note that there were photos with it. I felt someone behind me, but I was sure this time that it was not Dick Colby. Especially when a pair of hands fell softly onto my shoulders.

'I tried to call you,' Sarah said.

'I must have been in a bad zone,' I said.

'Bullshit,' she whispered. 'I'm sorry about this morning.'

I didn't say anything.

'I'm still finding this hard, being the person who you most often have to report to.'

'It's fine, don't worry about it.'

'Listen, if I get the foreign editor thing, we won't have these kinds of problems, unless you get posted to Beijing or Baghdad or something.'

'If you could get me sent there now, maybe it wouldn't be as urgent to become the foreign editor.'

I felt her hands lightly squeeze my neck. 'Don't think I haven't thought of it.'

I waited a moment, and then said, 'There's something I want to ask you.'

Sarah's hands stopped moving. I could sense her wariness. 'What?'

'Can you name two German political parties?'

Her fingers tensed. 'Okay, hang on. There's a couple that sound very much alike. There's the Christian Democratic Union, and the Social Democratic Party.'

'Correct. Now, a bonus question. Can you name a third German political party?'

Sarah was hunting in some inner recess of her brain. 'Well, there's the Green Party, right?'

'That's correct. You've won what's behind Zipper Number One.' I reached up and touched one of her hands. Sarah laced her fingers into mine.

'We okay?' she asked. I nodded. Then, 'Did you see Trixie?'

'Yeah. She had a problem I couldn't help her with.'

'What was it?'

'I can tell you all about it later, but I can say that it involved a violation of journalistic ethics. I think she was pissed.'

'So she didn't ask you to run away with her?'

'I suspect she was working up to it, but when I turned her down on the other thing, I think she abandoned the idea.'

Sarah had things to do. I was pretty much done for the day, but there were some things niggling at me that I wanted to look into before I left the building.

I knew I couldn't do what Trixie'd asked of me, to try to scare another reporter off his story, but I was feeling uncomfortable with the way we'd left things. Trixie, who'd never worked in journalism and probably didn't fully understand how impossible her request was, had left our meeting feeling betrayed. She'd thought we were friends, and no doubt believed I'd let her down.

It's not that I was unsympathetic. I could understand why Trixie wouldn't want any publicity for her business. She was probably getting all she needed now. Word of mouth, as they say, is everything. When you're the best dominatrix in the burbs, your reputation gets out there. You hardly need your picture in the local paper telling the world how you make your living.

But Trixie's concerns about her picture running in the paper seemed to go beyond how it might disrupt her livelihood. She seemed terrified by the repercussions of Martin Benson running, as Trixie called it, her 'mug shot' in the *Suburban*.

Was Trixie on the run from the authorities? Had she been on some episode of *America's Most Wanted* that I'd missed? And what was to account for her skittishness when that biker came into the Starbucks?

I typed 'Trixie Snelling' on the Google page. The only thing that came back was a reference to a woman by that name who, at the beginning of the last century, married a man who wrote a cantata for a church in England. I didn't think that was my Trixie. Next I tried a Yahoo 'people search' and came up with a big fat zero. I tried Google and Yahoo again, this time with the name 'Trixie Snell,' who, I learned, was a character in the 1933 movie called *Sensation Hunters* that featured a young Walter Brennan as a stuttering waiter. But I didn't learn anything more useful than that.

I went into the paper's library and checked our own database. It would find any story the *Metropolitan*, or any other major North American newspaper, had run with the name Trixie Snelling. I figured, if police were looking for her, her name could have been mentioned at some point.

But I came up with nothing. Which seemed, on the face of it, to be a good thing.

I returned to the newsroom, found an Oakwood phone book on the shelf where we kept directories from all over the country – even though more and more of them were online – and looked up Snelling. Nothing. I guess all that proved was that Trixie had an unlisted number.

Of course, if the police were looking for Trixie, and given her line of work it was not beyond the realm of possibility that they might be, chances were pretty good she was not using the same name today that she was using when she'd originally come to their attention.

If she'd come to their attention at all.

Maybe she'd come to the attention of someone other than the police.

Whoever might be looking for her was going to have a hard time finding her, at least if they looked for her under the name I'd always known her by. Because, using the most conventional resources at my disposal, it appeared that no one by the name of Trixie Snelling had ever actually existed.

I was home before Sarah and started throwing something together for dinner. I concluded, from the presence of the backpack full of books by the front door and the absence of Paul, that he had preceded me home and gone back out again. Clearly, not to the library to work on an assignment.

I had some pasta on the counter and was looking in the fridge for a half-full jar of spaghetti sauce when Angie came into the kitchen. I felt the same thing I always felt when I saw her – that I had the most beautiful daughter in the world, and I'd be a fool to think I could take any of the credit.

'Hey, stranger,' I said. 'I can't remember the last time I saw you.' She hugged me and I gave her a kiss on the cheek. 'You here for dinner?'

'What are we having?'

I love this question, the one that says, *Hey, there's nothing like getting together with family, so long as you're serving something decent.*

'Spaghetti,' I said.

'Don't worry about me,' Angie said. 'I'll grab something somewhere. I've got to go back downtown tonight for a lecture anyway.'

She blew threw the kitchen like a twister, there one moment, up the stairs the next. I heard the front door open, a new storm system approaching.

'Well, I hope you're happy now,' Paul said, forcing me out of the way as he reached into the fridge for a can of Coke.

'Happy about what?' I asked.

'I got a job. Just like you and Mom wanted. I won't have to be bugging you for money anymore.'

'That's fantastic!' I said. 'About the job, not the money thing. When did this happen?'

'This afternoon. After school. I went by this place, they needed help, they had, like, this sign in the window, I applied, I got it. You want to hear how the interview went? I go, "I'd like to inquire about your job?" And they go, "You start tomorrow."' He scowled.

'Where's the job?'

'That place over on Welk? Burger Crisp?'

'Burger Crisp? What do they serve, burnt burgers?'

'I know, it's a fucking stupid name. The "Crisp" is supposed to refer to the fries, but I guess they didn't want to call it Burger and Crispy Fries, so they called it Burger Crisp. These are the people I'm going to be working for, who can't even come up with a non-sucking name for their establishment.'

'Well,' I said, putting on my positive face, 'this is clearly a cause for celebration, then.'

Paul rolled his eyes. 'This is my new life, flipping burgers, scraping grease, and I have to wear a frickin' paper hat over my hair that makes me look like some guy who couldn't make it into the retard academy. And the woman who runs this place, she's like Greek or Russian or Turkish or something and looks like if she stood in front of a moving tank she'd total it. And she's got these two twin daughters who help her run the place, look like they could be playing for the NFL. If they fell over, they wouldn't be any shorter.'

'So,' I said, struggling to maintain my cheerfulness, 'when do you start?'

'Tomorrow, after school,' Paul said. 'Unless I blow my brains out tonight.' He shook his head, unable to believe something this horrible could happen to him. 'When my grades start to go down, it's not going to be my fault.'

'Why don't you go share your news with Angie,' I said. 'She just got home.'

I figured, with so much joy in the house, why not spread it around?

Paul trudged upstairs, his every step shaking the house right down to the foundation.

The phone rang. 'Hello?' I said.

'It's all set up,' Trixie said. 'We've got a sit-down with Martin Benson to talk some sense into him. Tomorrow. One o'clock.'

SIX

Trixie told me the location – Pluto's, an Oakwood diner that featured neither delisted planets nor Disney characters in its décor – before I could voice my objections. By the time I was able to get the words 'Trixie, there's no way' out of my mouth, she'd hung up. I called back but she didn't answer, so I left a message: 'Trixie, I can't meet you and this Benson guy. Maybe if you gave me some idea why this has freaked you out so, I could help you with some sort of alternative, but I can't talk a fellow reporter out of – Oh fuck, just call me back.'

Paul had come back downstairs and was in the kitchen, looking in the fridge for something to snack on. 'I heard you saying to Mom the other day that we swear too much. Like, look in the mirror, Dad.' He found a processed-cheese slice, peeled the cellophane wrapper off, folded it in half, downed it in two bites, walked out.

Trixie did not call back. Not during dinner, not that entire evening. I left two more messages asking her to call.

So I had to decide whether she'd gone out and wasn't there to take my calls, or was ignoring me. She likely had caller ID, so I placed one call using

Paul's cell phone, which he'd left on the table by the front door, and still she didn't answer, which convinced me that she wasn't home. I only hoped Paul didn't hit Redial and find himself connected with a dominatrix.

After dinner, while we were clearing the table, Sarah said, 'So what, exactly, did Trixie want today? You said something at work about journalistic ethics?'

I shrugged, like it was no big deal, doing my best to cover the fact that Trixie's actions were very much on my mind. 'Oh, there's some reporter, for the *Suburban*, wants to do a story on her, and she was asking my advice.'

'What kind of story? About what she does for a living?'

'I guess. Kink in the burbs, that kind of thing.'

'So what was she asking you? Whether to do it or not?'

'Yeah, sort of. I think she's a bit uncomfortable with it.'

Sarah snorted. 'Well, considering that what she does is, to the best of my knowledge, against the law, I can see that.'

'Anyway,' I said, wanting to move on, 'it's her decision. Whatever she wants to do, doesn't matter to me.'

Sarah gave me a look. 'She's not dragging you into some sort of trouble, is she?'

'Trouble? Are you kidding? Do I look like someone who needs any more trouble? Haven't I had enough trouble lately?'

'You haven't forgotten your promise, have you?' Sarah said.

'Promise?'

'The one you made? Just a few days ago? When you got back from your dad's place? That you weren't going to get into any of these ridiculous messes again? Where you end up, Jesus Christ almighty, where you end up nearly getting yourself killed?'

I finished drying off a dish and threw the dish towel over my shoulder and turned and held Sarah by the shoulders. 'The last thing in the world I want to do is get into any more situations where I, or anyone in this family, is put at risk. If anyone understands how unsuited I am to that sort of thing, to taking on the frickin' forces of evil, believe me, it's me.'

Sarah eyed me warily before slipping her arms around me. She rested her head on my chest. 'Okay,' she said. Then, more softly, 'Okay.'

I tried Trixie again in the morning, from my desk at the *Metropolitan*. She picked up.

'I tried to get you last night,' I said. 'You weren't answering.'

'I was out. And besides, if I can't risk clients coming to the house, what's the point of answering the phone? Why? Everything okay?'

'I can't make it today. I can't meet with you and Martin Benson.'

'But Zack, it's already set up. How's it going to look if you're a no-show? Isn't that going to make him even more suspicious?'

'You've told him I'm coming? That I, personally, am going to be there?'

'I sort of hinted that there might be a surprise guest,' Trixie said. I didn't say anything for a moment, so

Trixie continued, 'Zack, I know I'm putting you in a bit of a bind here, no pun intended, but this is really important to me. Remember that night you came to me, with that ledger in hand, asking me to figure it out while those nutcases were hunting you down?'

'I remember,' I said.

'So I'm calling in a favor. Just talk to the guy. Look, Zack, there's more at stake here than you realize.'

'I wish you'd tell me.'

There was a pause on the other end of the line. 'I wish I could. Maybe, sometime, I can. But for now, I'm asking you to take this on faith.'

I swallowed. Shit. 'I'll be there,' I said, and hung up.

'You'll be where?'

I looked over my shoulder. Sarah. 'What?' I said.

'You got something on the go? Because I was just going to give you something.' She was standing there with a piece of paper in her hand.

'Sure, what is it?'

'But if you've got another story, I can hand this off to someone else.'

'No, no, let me have it.'

'Okay, well, it's just some city hall budget thing. The bureau's a bit short-staffed this week, so we're helping out. It's about the proposed Windsor Street bridge project over Mackenzie Creek. The way it is now, you have to go all the way down to Broad, or up to Milner, and the neighborhood has been asking for a bridge for years and every year when they prepare the budget the money gets put in but at the last minute gets taken out.'

'Yeah sure, I can do that.' I took the sheet from her that had some contact numbers on it and an earlier story someone at the city hall bureau had done.

'What's the other thing you got?' Sarah asked.

'Oh, just someone calling about a *Star Trek* convention. There's going to be one here, next spring, they wanted to send me some stuff on it, because of my books. That guy, the one who played Picard's nemesis, Q? That guy? I think he's coming, they want to know if we're going to want to interview him.'

'Okay,' Sarah said. 'You just better check with Entertainment. They find out you're interviewing some TV star, they're going to have a shit fit.' She glanced up at one of the many wall clocks, all set at different times depending on the world locale they were supposed to represent. It was midafternoon in London. It would be nice to be there, hanging out in some pub, right about now. 'I've got to go to the morning meeting. You know how Magnuson is when you show up late at these things.'

'How's the foreign editor thing going?'

'Interview's in a couple of days,' Sarah said. 'Tonight you can drill me on the difference between Shiites and Sunnis. I don't think I understand it any better than Bush does.'

'Sure,' I said, forcing a smile. I wasn't a particularly good liar, and I was afraid she wouldn't buy the *Star Trek* thing. But it helped that she had a lot on her mind.

I could make some calls on the bridge story, get the interviews done, I figured, before heading out to Oakwood.

A couple of hours later, I slipped out of the office, got in our Virtue, a hybrid car that I'd bought in a police auction a couple of years ago, and did the twenty-minute drive out of downtown to the suburbs of Oakwood. I headed south off the highway, towards the lake, and found a parking spot along the main street, just down from Pluto's.

Pluto's, while ignoring the solar system and animated characters, is done up with enough fifties-style kitsch on the walls that you're supposed to think the place has been around the last forty years. The only problem with that is, in a suburban community like Oakwood, nothing's that old. So you plaster the walls with Elvis movie posters, put in a jukebox that doesn't actually work, and line the window ledges with antique Grape Nehi, and no one's the wiser.

But I seemed to recall that they made a pretty decent breakfast of eggs and sausages, and a respectable turkey club at lunchtime, and by the time I arrived I was ready for something to eat.

The place wasn't that busy, and I quickly scanned the tables. I didn't see any sign of Trixie, but there was a guy sitting in a booth by the window who looked remotely like the logo shot that went with Martin Benson's column in the *Suburban*, so I tentatively approached. He was probably in his early forties, balding, thirty or forty pounds overweight, wearing a sports jacket that was just slightly too small for him.

When I hesitated by his table, he looked at me, his face apprehensive, almost fearful.

'Martin Benson?' I said.

He nodded, attempted to stand, but he was caught under the table and could only manage to get halfway up. 'Yeah,' he said, extending a hand. I shook it. It was damp.

'Zack Walker,' I said, letting go of his hand and sliding in across from him.

'Why does that name ring a bell?' he asked cautiously, settling back into the booth.

I smiled. 'I, uh, I've written a few sci-fi books. And my byline runs occasionally in the *Metropolitan*. I write features, stuff like that, but not a column. I don't get a head shot in the paper like you do.'

Benson nodded. 'That's where I've seen the name. In the paper. I don't read science fiction. Mostly I read literary fiction.'

I just smiled.

'So,' he said. 'Where's Ms Snelling?'

'I guess she'll be here any time now,' I said. 'Why don't we get some coffee while we wait.' I signaled the waitress, asked for two coffees. 'Have you had the turkey club here? It's good, lots of real, roasted turkey, not that processed stuff.'

Benson nodded again. 'I was worried you might be some sort of tough guy. You know, scare me into backing off my story.'

I laughed nervously. 'If there's anything I'm not, it's a tough guy.'

'But you do want me to back off the story, right?' He leaned a little closer across the table. 'That's why you're here.'

'No, no,' I protested as two porcelain mugs of coffee were placed in front of us. 'Of course not.' I looked around, checking the front door of Pluto's. 'Where the hell is she?' I glanced at my watch. Trixie was seven minutes late. Why was she seven minutes late to her own meeting?

'So what's your connection to Ms Snelling, then?' Benson asked. 'You a relative? She a friend? Or,' and he paused a moment here, 'are you a client?'

I nearly spat out a mouthful of coffee. 'No, gosh no, we're just, we used to be, this was a couple of years ago, we were neighbors. We – that's me and the family – lived a couple of doors down, but we've moved back downtown since then. You might have heard about what happened, there was a bit of a kerfuffle.'

'No,' said Benson. 'I only got to the *Suburban* a year ago. Came here from Buffalo.'

'Oh yeah, wings,' I said. 'Love those wings.'

Martin Benson stared, thrilled that his former home was reduced to an appetizer.

He said, 'You do know what she does for a living.'

I hesitated. 'What is it you think she does for a living?'

'I think she runs a sex business. I think she's a hooker, a very high-end hooker that caters to very specific tastes.'

'I certainly wouldn't know anything about that.'

'Then why did you nearly choke on your coffee when I asked whether you were one of her clients?'

'Look, I, I'm pretty sure Ms Snelling – where the hell is she, anyway? – is not a prostitute. She does not have sexual relations with her customers.'

'Where have I heard that phrase before?' Benson asked. 'When I asked whether you were a relative or a friend or a client, I forgot one. Are you her pimp?'

I guess my jaw dropped, and I stared at him in open-mouthed astonishment for a moment, before I had the sense to close it. Twice I started to say something, and each time, a chuckle got in the way. 'You have no idea,' I said, 'how totally ridiculous that comment is.'

'Is it? Then you tell me, why are you here?'

'First of all, let's go back to this hooker thing. Far as I know, Trixie – Ms Snelling – does not offer sexual services. But you know what, you'd be better asking her about that yourself once she gets here.'

The waitress had reappeared, notepad at the ready. 'You gentlemen ready to order?' she asked.

'We're still waiting for someone,' I said. She nodded and withdrew.

Now Benson was looking at his own watch. 'Pretty late.'

'I'm sure she'll be along any—' The cell phone in my jacket pocket rang and vibrated. 'Hang on,' I said, taking out the phone and flipping it open. 'Hello?'

'How's it going?' Trixie asked.

'Where the hell are you?' I said. Benson's eyebrows went up. 'We're here, in Pluto's, waiting.'

'Yeah, I know. I watched you go in. I'm parked up the street, reading your newspaper.'

I couldn't stop myself from looking out the window, which, of course, tipped Benson off to do the same.

'How long have you been there?' I asked.

'I don't know, half hour maybe. Have you steered him off this thing yet?'

'Trixie, we were sort of waiting for you.'

'I won't be able to make it,' she said. 'You know what that fat fucker will do, soon as I walk in or sit down, he's going to take my picture. Why do you think he showed up? He wants a nice shot to run with his story.'

I slid out of the booth, held up an index finger to Benson to indicate I'd be back in one minute, and moved a few booths away before I continued my conversation.

'He thinks I'm your fucking pimp,' I said.

Trixie laughed. 'Now that's rich.'

59

'Look, I came out here for a meeting, a meeting that I thought you were going to attend. You don't show. Trixie, you're my friend, but you're fucking me around.'

'Okay, go back and tell him I'll come in if he gives you his camera phone.'

'Jesus, what if he says he hasn't got it on him? Do you want me to frisk him?' Trixie was quiet. Finally, I said, 'I'll see what I can do. Call me back in five.'

I slid back into the booth. 'That was Ms Snelling,' I said. 'She's, she's afraid that if she comes in here, you're going to take her picture.'

Benson said nothing.

'So. I think she'd be willing to come in if you let me hold on to your camera phone while she joins us.'

Benson ran his tongue over his lips. 'So let me see if I understand this. You, a reporter for the *Metropolitan*, want to take from me, a reporter for the *Suburban*, my camera phone, in case I want to use it to do my job. Is that what's going on?'

I had to admit that it sounded bad when he put it that way.

'You know what?' Benson said. 'You fucking reporters, you work for these big fucking dailies, you have no respect for what a guy like me does for a smaller paper like the *Suburban*. You think we're some kind of joke, don't you? That we just exist to wrap around a bunch of advertising flyers, that we don't care about journalism, that we don't care about what we do.'

I said nothing.

'Well, I may work for a small neighborhood rag, Mr Walker, but when I hear that a woman is running some sort of sex dungeon in the middle of our community,

I think that's a story, and I'm not going to let some smartass hot-shit city writer try to warn me off it.'

'What have I said?' I said. 'Have I threatened you? Have I tried to get you off this story?'

'Here's what I don't get. Why aren't *you* writing about Trixie Snelling? Any reporter worth his salt would be taking a run at this.'

'She's a friend,' I said. 'She—'

Benson pushed his coffee cup aside. 'We're done here,' he said, shifting his weight across the seat and getting out. 'See ya later.'

My cell rang as he walked out the door. I reached into my pocket, flipped it open.

'Zack,' Trixie said, 'I'm reading this story of yours in the paper, about these guys trying to get the cops to buy stun guns. Jesus Christ, Zack, do you have any idea who these guys are?'

'Trixie,' I said, 'I don't give a rat's ass who they are. The meeting here is finished. Benson's walked out. You set me up. Thanks a fuck of a lot.' I slapped the phone shut and went back downtown.

One day he went too far.

Miranda was in the kitchen, making an after-school snack. It hadn't been a good day. The guidance counselor wanted a word with her. Brought her in for a meeting. He said he'd tried to reach her mother, to discuss her school performance, but wasn't having any luck when he phoned the house.

Miranda thought, Good luck. Mom's there, but she's probably watching Family Feud and getting smashed.

'Then I tried calling your father at work,' he said.

Oh no, Miranda thought.

'And he was very helpful. Good to talk to. Says you just haven't been pulling your weight. He knows you could do better if you just put in some effort. You stand to lose your year,' the guidance counselor told her. 'You're failing all of your subjects, with the exception of math. You're a natural at math. Why can't you bring that sort of effort to your other subjects, huh, Miranda? What's the problem? Is it drugs? Are you getting into drugs, Miranda?'

No, she wanted to tell him. My mom's a drunk and my dad wants to get into my pants. And you think I should give a flying fuck about how I'm doing at school?

Except for math. I like numbers, Miranda thought. At least there's some order there. Some predictability. You don't wake up someday and find out that somebody decided fuck it, we're making two plus two equal five.

So she went home, dumped her backpack at the door, opened the cupboard and looked for something to eat. Her mother was sitting in the living room, a Camel in one hand and a scotch in the other, watching One Miserable Life to Live *or* As the Fucking World Turns. *Didn't say anything when Miranda came in the door. It was nothing short of a miracle that there was some peanut butter. The Wonder bread was probably a week old, but Miranda managed to find a slice or two without green spots on them, and dropped them into the toaster.*

That's when he came in the door. He was early. He didn't usually get home from the plant until after six.

'Well, look who's here,' he said. 'I got a call about you today.'

Miranda ignored him, stared at the toaster, watched the tiny elements inside glow red as they browned her slices of stale, white bread.

'Your guidance counselor says you're flunking everything except math. Here's what I don't get. Why do you even try at math? Why don't you be a total fuckup, instead of a 95 per cent fuckup? It's like you can't even get that right.'

No wonder he was angry. She'd been blocking her door with a chair every night for weeks. Sometimes, during the day, he'd take the chair out, and she'd have to find one and take it to her room right before bedtime.

'Hey,' he said, slapping her ass, but not too hard, so it was almost a pat. 'I'm talking to you here.'

She didn't know she was going to do it. It just happened. She doesn't even know how she had the presence of mind to first yank the plug from the wall. But once she'd done that, she reached her fingers into the two slots of the toaster. Her fingers would have been burned worse than they were

63

had the two slices of bread not been there. She jammed her fingers in, almost like it was a rectangular bowling ball, and came around swinging.

Swinging hard.

The toaster caught him just above the right eye, and the connection of metal against bone made a hell of a noise. The move was so unexpected, so out of the blue, he didn't have time to bring his arms up, but he had them up when she came at him a second time. The toaster bounced off his arm, and Miranda was thrown slightly off balance, staggered up against the counter.

The blood was pouring out of her father's head and through his fingers as he put his hand up to the wound.

'Jesus!' he shouted, staggering back himself. 'Jesus!'

Miranda's mother came into the room, looked at her husband, at the bloody toaster still in her daughter's hand, and shouted, 'He's your father! How dare you! This man is your father!'

She ran out of the kitchen. She ran out of the house. She didn't even have time to pack her things in a paper bag.

SEVEN

Three times on my way back into the city, Trixie tried to phone me on her cell. When I got back to my desk at the paper, the light on my phone was flashing. I hadn't even checked the message yet when the phone rang. I picked up.

'Zack,' Trixie said, 'I'm sorry about what happened with Benson. Really, I'm sorry about that. But forget about that for now. Those guys, those two in your story. They didn't always sell stun guns, these guys. They—'

I felt Sarah standing behind me. 'I gotta go,' I said, and hung up. I turned around. ' 'Sup?'

She nodded her head toward Magnuson's office. 'He wants to see us,' she said, and she didn't look happy.

'Both of us?'

'Apparently.'

'What's it about? Is he going to apologize for dragging me off the Wickens story and giving it to that asshole Colby?'

'I don't think so,' Sarah said. 'I don't think that "sorry" is part of Magnuson's vocabulary.'

I got up, made sure my shirt was well tucked in, and followed Sarah to the far corner of the newsroom, where the managing editor's corner office looked out over the city.

Even though we could see him in there, sitting at his desk, we didn't walk right in. Sarah told his secretary we had arrived, as if that were not immediately evident, and she buzzed him. Through the door, we watched him watching us as he picked up his phone. 'Send them in,' we heard him say into the phone.

His secretary said, 'He'll see you now.'

We went in. I had a bad feeling.

'Ah, the Walkers,' he said, not getting up to greet us. That seemed like a bad sign to me. 'Take a seat,' he said. I would have felt better had he said, 'Please, be seated.'

We sat down. Magnuson said, 'I didn't bring you in here because you happen to be married to one another. I brought both of you in because I wanted to speak with you, Mr Walker, and seeing as how Sarah is your editor, this will impact her as well.' He stared at both of us for a while, but mostly at me.

'I have an old friend,' he said suddenly, 'name of Blair Wentworth. We used to work together, as reporters, long ago. Used to get drunk together on a regular basis too. Once, when he'd had a little bit too much one night in the bar, we got into a heated debate about whether Jimmy Carter really had a peanut farm, or whether it was just a load of bullshit, so we walked out, got in a cab, and asked to be taken to Plains, Georgia. Well, that was several hundred, if not thousands, of miles away, and the cabby had some reservations, but we said not to worry, we were newspapermen, and we had expense accounts. Instead of driving us to Georgia, he drove us back to our paper and dropped us off at the front door before we made complete asses of ourselves. If I could find that cabby today, I'd give him a job here. Doing what, I don't know, but he clearly had more sense than some of the people who work for me here now.'

I blinked.

'Anyway, Blair decided to go off in another direction. He was a pretty business-minded individual, got into community newspapers, worked his way up to publisher of one of them. The *Suburban*, out in Oakwood. You might have heard of it.'

Oh God.

'We keep in touch, Blair and I, so when something comes across his desk that troubles him, he gives me a call. And I just now got off the phone with him. It was a very interesting call, the most amazing thing. Do you have any idea, Mr Walker, what it might have been about?'

Sarah turned to look at me.

'Yes,' I said as evenly as I could. 'I have a pretty good idea.'

'What is it, Zack?' Sarah asked.

'Why don't you tell her, Mr Walker.'

I cleared my throat. 'I was out to Oakwood for lunch — well, actually, I never had any lunch, come to think of it, only a coffee. Which probably explains why I'm feeling a little light-headed all of a sudden. Edgy. I could use a bite to eat.'

'Zack.'

'I had lunch with Martin Benson, who writes a column for the *Suburban*. I think he may have been left with the impression that I was trying to get him to scrap doing a story on Trixie, which is not at all the case.'

Sarah was speechless. Magnuson was good enough to fill the silence.

'Blair says this Benson fellow told him that you wanted him to surrender his camera phone so he wouldn't take a picture of this, this woman known as Trixie, who, I understand, has a rather unorthodox line of work.'

'She was, yes, that's sort of true, but she was very frightened that he was going to take her picture and run it in the paper.'

'That's what journalists do,' Magnuson said. 'We take pictures of people we want to do stories on, and we put them in the paper, whether they like it much or not. I'll bet you Sarah could explain the whole concept to you if you're not all that familiar with it.'

'That's who called you, isn't it?' Sarah said. 'There was no call about a *Star Trek* convention.'

Magnuson's bushy eyebrows went up a notch.

'Yes,' I said. 'I mean, no, there was no call about a *Star Trek* convention.' I was starting to feel that I'd be lucky to cover anything as newsworthy as a *Star Trek* convention in the future.

'It's one thing to try to outsmart the competition when we're trying to get a story that we want just as much as they do,' Magnuson said. 'One time, when I was based in Washington, there was this little runt-nosed jackass from the paper out on the coast, doesn't matter which one, kept shadowing me, figuring he had a better chance snooping on me and my sources than trying to cultivate any of his own. So I'm on a pay phone, and I know he's just around the corner, but he doesn't know that I know, and I ask for Rewrite, tell them I got a hell of a story about a particular congressman who was found dressed in women's clothes in a whorehouse, and off he dashed. Then I told

Rewrite we had to start again. Our paper didn't have a story about a congressman found dressed in women's clothes in a whorehouse, but his did.' He sniffed. 'Never followed me around again after that.'

I laughed.

'Shut up,' Magnuson said. 'You've got nothing to laugh about. What you did isn't the same as what I did. You tried to steer Benson off a story to protect a friend.'

'I didn't—'

'I can't fire you outright,' Magnuson said. 'That would involve the newspaper guild, and hearings, and back and forth and who needs that shit anyway. So instead, you can remain a reporter.'

I knew it was too soon to think I'd dodged a bullet.

'But not for city. Tomorrow, you start in the homes section.'

I was dumbstruck. Surely, firing would have been more humane.

Sarah, as well, could find no words. She looked back and forth between me and the managing editor.

'I'll see what I can do about getting someone else for you,' Magnuson told her. 'I don't want you to have to run that department shorthanded, because, I can tell you right now, you're going to be running that department for the foreseeable future.'

He turned back to look at something on his computer, and it was clear that we were being dismissed.

I'd been busted down to the homes section.

Sarah wasn't going to become the foreign editor.

It didn't matter anymore what Myanmar used to be.

EIGHT

'Actually, we're not the "homes" section,' the 'not-the-homes' section editor told me. 'We're "Home!" That's the way we did the masthead when the paper had its redesign a few years ago.'

The Home! editor was a short woman named Frieda, and as she stood next to me while I sat at my new desk, we were almost at eye level. She wore a bright orange dress that seemed to be humming, like a trans-former. She was pointing to the masthead on a copy of the Home! section spread out on my desk. The letters H-O-M-E, in brilliant blue, followed by an equally bold exclamation mark.

'I came up with that,' she said proudly. 'You know how, when someone comes into your house, a member of your family, they shout "I'm home!" Well, my thinking was, we take the last part of that sentence and turn it into the name of the section. It's the punctua-tion at the end, that dramatic exclamation mark, that makes it, I think. It's what separates our home section from home sections in other papers. It's what gives this section its punch, its vitality. I think we have the best home section anywhere, and it sure is nice you're going to be able to work for it.'

She smiled.

I thought, *If I could find a home tall enough to get the job done, I'd throw myself off the roof and kill myself.*

'Of course,' said Frieda, 'I understand that coming here wasn't totally your idea – Mr Magnuson explained that to me – but I think you're going to find working here very fulfilling. We do a lot of important stories here, and you should know that Home! is one of the biggest revenue producers for the paper. We have advertisers lined up to get into our pages, and many weeks we have to turn them away. There simply isn't any more space for them. The presses can't handle a section that big. Did you know that?'

'Wow,' I said. 'I did not know that.'

'I've had this story idea percolating for a while, and haven't had anyone free to do it, but now that you're here, I'd like to give it to you, because you have the kind of skills, I think, to run with it.'

I steeled myself.

'Linoleum,' Frieda said. 'There are so many angles, I'm thinking along the lines of a series, not just one article. What advances are being made, scuff resistance, design choices, whether the linoleum is being made here or whether we're going overseas to get it. Is this country hanging on to its linoleum jobs, or giving them away to Mexico?'

'So it would have a political angle,' I said.

Frieda nodded enthusiastically. 'I can see you're thinking already. That's great. Listen, why don't I leave you to it, if you have any questions you can ask, and don't forget that at three, we traditionally have a little biscuit break.'

I glanced up at the clock. 'Gee, six hours,' I said. 'I may not be able to wait.'

Frieda smiled and touched my arm before departing. I sighed and slumped in my chair. I was more than depressed. I was tired. I'd barely slept the night before. And not just because Sarah wasn't speaking to me. There'd been a wild electrical storm around midnight. Flashes of lightning filled our bedroom with light, just long enough to see Sarah's back turned to me. The wind came out, and I lay awake wondering whether any of the stately old oaks that surrounded the house would come crashing through the roof. Briefly, the power went out – the wired-in smoke detector chirped once, and when I glanced at the digital clock radio, it was flashing 12:00.

According to the morning news, some parts of the city had lost power, some for several hours. A great many limbs and a few entire trees had come down, taking power lines with them. But when I looked out in the morning, all I saw were a few twigs and short branches scattered across the yard and the street.

'That was some storm,' I said in the morning, trying to make conversation while I poured Sarah her coffee. She said nothing.

'Look,' I said, 'I know I've fucked up, big-time, but it's not like Magnuson made it out to be. I wasn't trying to keep that guy from doing his story, I had no intention of doing that, and I'd said to Trixie that—'

'Just what did you say to Trixie?' Sarah said. It was the first time I'd heard her voice in maybe eighteen hours. 'What do the two of you talk about? When you have your little lunches, your little meetings, your rendezvous?'

' "Rendezvous"?' I said. 'Why not "tryst"? There's a word we don't hear much anymore.'

'It's a tryst?'

'Listen, I had lunch with her the other day, she told me she had this problem, I told her I couldn't help her out with it.'

'Is that how you weren't helping her out with it? Going back out there to talk to that reporter, to get him to give up his camera?'

'All I did was tell him Trixie was afraid to come into the diner unless he gave up the camera. He'd been trying to sneak a pic of her and—'

Sarah, screaming: 'And what do you care! So what if he does! What is that to you? Since when did you become her protector?'

Her voice echoed off the kitchen walls.

I didn't say anything for a moment. Then, 'You're right. It's her problem. It's not my problem.' I paused. 'It's not our problem.'

Sarah took one last glaring look at me, then turned and went back upstairs to get ready for work. The coffee I'd poured for her sat neglected on the counter.

Angie, who'd been coming down the stairs as Sarah was going up, appeared. 'I don't know what you did, Dad,' she said, 'but it must have been bad, even by your standards.'

I was ready with something sarcastic, then said, 'Yeah. It was.'

And as I sat in my new! desk! in! the! Home! section, I tried to sort out which was the worst of my crimes. It hadn't been getting myself demoted to one of the paper's soft sections, and it hadn't been nixing Sarah's chances at becoming foreign editor, although that one was up there.

It was the fact that I hadn't been honest with her. I hadn't told Sarah what Trixie had asked of me. I hadn't told her I'd agreed to at least meet with Trixie and Martin Benson.

The way Sarah must have seen it was, if I hadn't disclosed the details of that conversation with Trixie, what other conversations with her had I failed to fill her in on?

Once, a couple of years ago, when I'd made a joke that I was not having an affair with someone, Sarah had laughed. It was the one thing she knew she'd never have to worry about, she said. I could never pull it off, I'd have too guilty a conscience, my face would betray me when I attempted a lie.

Plus there was the part about my loving Sarah more than any other woman in the world.

But I'd crossed a line somewhere, and was over it before I'd realized it. My marriage to Sarah meant a lot more to me than my friendship with Trixie. And if that meant distancing myself from her, then that's what I'd have to—

My phone rang.

Did the *Metropolitan* switchboard already know I was here, and not out in the newsroom?

'Walker,' I said, picking up.

'It's happened,' Trixie said.

'What?'

'My picture. It's in the paper. Fucking amazing picture too. Must have been shot with a telephoto. No camera phone shot.'

'I don't know what to say.'

'Maybe you could tell me why your paper shot it?'

'What? What are you talking about?'

'There's this little line, under the picture.'

'A photo credit,' I said.

74

'Whatever. It says, "Special to the *Suburban* by Lesley Carroll, slash, *The Metropolitan*." She must have been parked up the street from the house, took my picture as I was going from the car to the house. I'm fucked.'

Lesley Carroll took the picture? One of our photogs? I thought about it for a moment, and it started to make sense. Magnuson tells his old buddy Blair, *Hey, our Walker guy messed with your guy over a picture of this woman? Leave it with us. We'll get you a picture. We'll send one of our people. We've got shooters who've been to Iraq and back. Think we can't get a shot of this, what's her name? Trixie Snelling? We've got this young intern, eager to make a name for herself as a photographer. You can bet she'll get you your picture. Consider it our way of saying we're sorry.*

That's how it must have gone.

'I'm sorry, Trixie. I really am.'

'This couldn't happen at a worse time. With those guys in town, trying to sell stun guns.'

'Trixie, I have to go.'

'Didn't you check those guys out? Didn't I tell you to?'

'Trixie, I'm sorry.'

And I ended the call.

For a while, Miranda was your basic street kid. Stopped going to school, gravitated to the big city, hung around teen drop-in shelters, slept someplace different every night, got a bucket and a squeegee and tried to make some money cleaning people's windshields. Most of them, they pretended not to see you when you tried to make eye contact. If you could catch their eye, wave the squeegee, smile nice, make them realize you weren't some crazy crackhead or something, they might give you the nod, let you clean their window, they'd give you a couple quarters, maybe a buck if you were lucky. But mostly they ignored you, or waved you away, or told you 'Fuck off, you miserable cocksucking whore, go get a real job like everybody else.'

But she still made a good buck. She got to where she could guess who'd let her squeegee and who wouldn't. She did better with men, not so good with lady drivers. She figured, maybe the men are less intimidated. 'You dumb ass,' one of her coworkers said. 'You wonder why you do okay with the guys? Look at you. Leaning over their window with those knockers? That one guy, he drove around the block, didn't you notice you did his window twice in five minutes? Shit, you look like that, what are you cleaning fucking windshields for? You could be making a fortune doing something else.'

'I'm not hooking,' Miranda said.

76

'Who said anything about hooking? You're like a dancer, leaping between those cars. Go on stage, dance around, shake 'em. Beats cleaning somebody's windshield when it's ten below.'

Miranda had never really thought of herself as good-looking. Compliments weren't exactly handed out back home. Somebody told her there was a bar up in Canborough where they were looking for strippers. She should check it out, they said.

It wasn't exactly what she wanted to do, but she was tired of working outside and freezing her ass off. She could have landed on Claire's doorstep, but she had a decent life with Don. Miranda didn't feel right barging in on it. They were living above a pizza place somewhere, sleeping on a pull-out couch in a one-room apartment. She had some secretary-type job, he'd lined up something at the Ford plant. You could make good money there. Someday, he said, they'd get a nice house out in the country.

Miranda was happy for Claire, happy that she had a boyfriend who loved her. They were probably going to get married, that's what Claire had told her. Miranda didn't want to mess that up. She had to try to make it on her own. She'd been put down all her life, but she still had pride. She wouldn't allow her parents to steal that from her.

'You can stay with us,' Claire told her. 'Really.'

But Miranda said no, don't worry, she had plans.

Going to Canborough and trying out to be a stripper, that was her plan.

She hitchhiked up there, carrying everything she had in a backpack she'd found in a secondhand store. Got herself cleaned up in the washroom of a McDonald's. Someone must have told, because just as she was finishing up, this short woman in a brown uniform and name tag that said 'Lulu' came in, said, 'This ain't the Y, sweetie. Scram.'

Then she went to the Kickstart. 'Heard you're looking for dancers,' she said.

'You done any dancing?' This was some short, nasty-looking fellow who kept sticking his finger up his nose.

'Sure,' she said. 'But, you know, not on an actual stage or anything.'

'Let's see 'em.'

'What?'

Rolled his eyes. 'Jesus, you come in, want to be a dancer, you don't know what I'm talking about when I say "Let's see 'em"?'

So she showed 'em.

'Whoa,' he said. 'Not bad. Rack like that, we got other ways you can make money too. Upstairs. Nice chunk of change to be had.'

'I don't think so,' Miranda said. 'I'll just dance.'

'Suit yourself,' he said. 'But when you see the other girls pulling down major bucks, you'll be begging me, you wait and see.'

And then, almost as an afterthought, he said, 'What's your name?'

Miranda had already thought about this part. 'Candace,' she said.

NINE

Sarah sent me an e-mail.

'Working late. Will grab something to eat on the way home. S.'

She wasn't more than seventy or eighty feet away from me, in her office, but she decided to send me a message rather than walk over and just tell me. True, she couldn't actually see me at my desk the way she could when I was working in the newsroom. I was now down the hall and around the corner, working in Home! But honestly, was this what Bill Gates had in mind? That the greatest technological advances in history would be used to make it possible for people who were within shouting range of one another to not speak face-to-face?

I clicked on 'Reply' and started to write something and then couldn't decide what. Finally I opted to say nothing and canceled my reply. Sarah had plenty of reasons to be angry with me, but her e-mail pissed me off. If she had something to say, she could damn well find her way Home! and say it.

'How's the linoleum thing coming?' Frieda asked, passing by my desk, being extremely cheerful.

'Frieda,' I said, 'you only gave it to me an hour ago. Is it a fast-breaking linoleum story? Is page one looking for it?'

She looked hurt. Her face fell. I instantly felt like a shit.

'I'm sorry,' she said. 'I was only asking.'

This was the difference between working in the newsroom, where sarcasm and angry outbursts are the norm, and toiling away in Home! or travel (called 'Away!' at the *Metropolitan*) or our new shopping section ('Spend!'). It was more like a typical office back here. Someone made tea. A card got sent around for everyone to sign when it was someone's birthday. People were friendly, sociable, decent to one another.

I had to get out of here.

'I'm sorry,' I said. 'Really, I'm sorry, Frieda. I was just being a dick.'

Her eyebrows jumped. I guess people didn't refer to themselves as 'dicks' around here, either.

She left before I could say anything else to offend her.

I went online, looked for some contacts in the flooring industry who could fill me in on the latest developments in linoleum, and as I did so, this sense of hopelessness washed over me. How could it have come to this? It had only been days since I'd written a major piece for the paper about this gang of nutcases who'd planned to set off a bomb at a small-town parade. It was page one, above the fold. The TV stations picked it up.

I was golden.

But that was how it was in the newspaper business. You were only as good as your next story. So what if you got a big exclusive on Thursday. What are you going to do for us Friday?

I had the feeling that someone or something was pressing down hard on me as I sat in the chair. My shoulders were sagging so hard, it's like they were dragging me down to the floor. I had a shit assignment, my wife was only communicating with me by e-mail, and I'd just been mean to Frieda, perhaps the sweetest woman in the entire building.

I jotted down some contact numbers on my scratch pad, but I couldn't bring myself to pick up the phone and make a call. For reasons I cannot explain, I found myself unable to focus on linoleum. There was something else nagging at me.

I grabbed a copy of yesterday's paper from one of the recycling bins and found my story about the stun gun salesmen.

Why was Trixie going on about them?

I found their names and scribbled them down on my pad. I decided to start with the one who'd done most of the talking before the assembled officers, Gary Merker. I Googled him. There weren't many. One was a radio DJ somewhere out west in Arizona. There was a picture of him, along with the other station personalities. Young guy, very thin, bald, wire-rimmed glasses, big smile. Definitely not the guy who'd done the stun gun presentation. Another was a financial consultant up in Maine. No picture. There was a phone number, so I called.

'Hello? Merker Financial.' A woman.

'Is Gary in?'

'Just a moment.'

Some dead air. Then: 'Merker?'

'Hi,' I said. Frieda was looking over at me, turned away when I saw her checking on me. 'Is this Gary Merker?'

'Yes. Can I help you?'

81

'I'm looking for the Gary Merker who's got some of those new Dropper stun guns for sale. Would that be you?'

'No, sorry. Stun guns? You got the wrong guy, pal.'

I offered my apologies and hung up.

Only one Gary Merker came up when I did a search on the paper's database. This Merker showed up in a story that evidently had run in the *Metropolitan* five years earlier, with a Dick Colby byline, no less. It was datelined Canborough, and the headline read, 'Three Slain in Biker Massacre.'

Canborough was a city of about sixty thousand, maybe a hundred miles west. It was a college town; the Canborough River ran through it north to south. The college was the main thing that had kept the town alive after the auto parts plant closed down seven years ago, the jobs all having gone to Mexico. I had done a book signing up there once, when my first science fiction novel, *Missionary*, had come out. Two hundred miles, round trip, sold three copies. The store owner couldn't look me in the eye when it was over.

The story read: 'Canborough may be on the verge of a biker gang war after three members of the Slots, a local gang that makes its money off drugs and prostitution, as well as some legitimate businesses, were shot to death above their own tavern, the Kickstart.'

The story went on to say: 'Dead are Eldridge Smith, 29, Payne Fletcher, 26, and Zane Heighton, 25. All the victims were said to be known to police. All were fatally shot, and while police hinted there was something distinctive about the manner in which the executions were conducted, they would not provide further details.'

I started to imagine things. Were they shot in the mouth? Did someone stick a gun in their ears and blow their brains out? Were they lined up in front of each other, and one bullet passed through the lot of them?

That one seemed a bit unlikely. Unless it was a really, really, big bullet. Despite having held, and even fired, a gun in the last couple of years, and having had the misfortune to have been around some, I still knew very little about them, and that was just fine, thank you very much.

The story continued: 'The Kickstart is a well-known local watering hole that also features adult entertainment. The shootings occurred shortly after the close of business hours, and the women employed as exotic dancers were not believed to have been there at the time. The Slots own the Kickstart, and were believed to have been counting the receipts in the upstairs office when the incident occurred.'

Out of the corner of my eye, I caught Frieda sneaking another look at me. I waggled my fingers at her.

'Canborough Police say there are three or four small gangs operating in the region, and while none of them is a large operation, they are responsible, collectively, for much of the area's drug trade. In the past, each gang had carved out a portion of the market for itself, not stepping on the others' toes, but that now appears to be over.

'The question now may be who is left in the Slots to retaliate. The gang's reputed leader, Gary Merker, 30, who is also said to be the manager of the Kickstart, was not present when the three members of his gang were killed. Nor was another member, Leonard Edgars, 29.'

I glanced back at my story. It appeared that I had found the right Gary Merker. His associate, the one who'd been zapped with fifty thousand volts, was Leo Edgars.

What were two surviving members of a small biker gang that ran drugs and prostitutes doing peddling stun guns?

And what business was it of Trixie's?

'I thought maybe you would like a coffee,' Frieda said. 'But I didn't know what you take in it.'

I jumped. 'Oh, sure,' I said. 'That would be nice. Cream and sugar.'

'What's that you're reading about?' she asked. She was scanning the Colby story, probably wondering why she wasn't seeing the word 'linoleum' anywhere.

'Gang shooting,' I said. 'I was thinking, an interesting way into the feature would be, what kinds of linoleum are most resistant to bullets and blood stains.'

Frieda was getting downright scared.

I forced myself to call a couple of flooring experts, just to keep Frieda from setting security on me, and when it was cookie time in the afternoon, I updated her on my progress. I asked her if she knew, for example, that linoleum had been invented in 1863, in England, by Frederick Walton, who had come up with the word by taking the Latin names for flax, which is *linum*, and oil, which is *oleum*, and putting them together. She did not, and seemed absolutely fascinated, offering me another Peek Frean.

I'd had no further communications from Sarah, and I'd sent nothing to her. If she could get something to eat on the way home, then I didn't see why I couldn't do the same. I managed to sneak out of Home! a little after four, and as I was heading out of the parking lot in our Virtue, I remembered that Paul was going to be working at his new job after school today. I thought maybe it might cheer me up to see Paul gainfully employed, and get myself a cheeseburger and fries. We never knew whether Angie would be home for dinner, so I didn't feel any obligation to get home and make sure there was something on the table for her when she returned from Mackenzie University.

I wheeled into the oil-stained parking lot of Burger Crisp. The lot was about half full, and there was trash spilling out the tops of trash containers that looked sticky with old soda. Flies buzzed around the opening.

The squat, square building, all glass up front, looked as though it might have been; in a previous life, a doughnut franchise. There was a row of tables along the front window, then down the right side, in an L shape. At the left end of the long aluminum counter was a cash register, and above it a menu made out of little black plastic letters that fit, crookedly, into grooves on a white background. Written in marker, on a sheet of cardboard and taped to the wall, was the special: 'Ch'burger/fries/Coke/$5.49.'

At the cash register must have been the woman Paul said could stand in front of a moving tank and total it. She appeared, in a word, formidable. She was shorter than I, but standing there behind the cash register, she seemed rooted like an oak. Stocky, fridge-like, with thick fleshy arms that hinted at considerable muscle underneath. Slavic looking, late fifties, early sixties maybe, gray hair pinned back, a severe, weathered face devoid of anything you might call make-up, deep creases running down from her nose on both sides of her mouth, and piercing black eyes.

She fixed them on me and said, 'What want?'

Some kind of accent, Russian, Turkish, Croatian, I had absolutely no idea. 'The special,' I said, looking around, wondering where Paul might be. 'The cheeseburger special.' There were people sitting on swivel chairs bolted to the floors, eating burgers, dipping fries into tiny containers of ketchup, off chipped Formica tables.

'Here or go away?' she said, her words clipped as if each one were chopped off at the end with a butcher's knife. For a moment, I thought she was asking me to leave.

'Uh, to go,' I said. I thought the ambiance at home might be better, although the way things were these days, probably not by much.

I handed her a ten. She dug her short, thick fingers with chipped nails into the cash register tray and handed me my change.

'Thanks,' I said with my usual charm. She didn't even look at me.

Next to the register the counter was raised up, and it was like a salad bar in reverse. Before me, behind glass, were the toppings. Pickles, onions, relish, tomato, hot peppers. Two identical-looking women – these had to be the twins Paul had mentioned – were working shoulder to shoulder. They were younger, but not necessarily more attractive, versions of the woman who'd taken my money. Large, soft and doughy looking, with arms like hams. They both had their blonde hair streaked with black, pulled back and tied into short ponytails.

They were being handed burgers fresh off the grill, asking customers how they wanted them garnished. That's when I spotted Paul, standing at the grill, flipping burgers, living his life's dream.

'Hey,' I said.

He didn't hear me the first time, so focused was he on his job. He had a huge apron, which years ago might have been white, tied around his waist, a white cap pulled down over his hair.

'Hey!' I said, again, and Paul looked over, and his eyes went wide and his mouth opened.

'Dad?'

I just smiled and waved. He was working, and I didn't want to interrupt him. I just wanted him to know that I was there.

He didn't look at all happy to see me. But that's the way it is with kids. They're always embarrassed when their parents show up. Make an appearance at their place of employment, and they want the ground to open up and swallow them whole. I thought it was too bad I hadn't worn something stupid, maybe a ball cap on backwards, to make Paul's humiliation complete.

One of the twins had grabbed a cheese-covered patty off the grill and slipped it into a bun. 'Whatcha want on it?' she asked me.

I started pointing to toppings. 'Hold the onion,' I said.

'Peppers?'

'Sure, a couple.'

I watched her pile everything on, then put the burger, with some fries, into a takeout Styrofoam container.

'Dad, what are you doing here?' Paul was standing next to me, up very close.

'Jeez, hi,' I said. I looked to see who was on the grill. Another kid about Paul's age had filled in for him. 'So how's it going?'

'Why are you here?' he asked again.

'I'm getting some dinner, okay? Is that a problem?'

'Dad, you can't eat here.'

I shook my head. 'What, did I embarrass you? All I said was "Hey." If they had a drive-through window, I'd do that, you wouldn't even have to know I was here at all.'

'Dad, just . . .' He pulled me aside, away from the counter and towards the door. 'Just don't eat here.'

'What *is* your problem?' I said, shaking his arm off me. 'I just wanted to show an interest, for Christ's sake.'

'No, Dad, you don't get it,' he whispered. 'You can't eat here. You can't eat this stuff.'

I glanced down at my foam box and then back at him. 'What, you're watching my diet for me now? If I want to have fast food once in a while, I'll have it. I had a cholesterol test six months ago and I'm fine, thanks for asking.'

'That's not what I'm talking about,' Paul whispered. 'This place is a fucking death trap. The meat's bad. I've been burning everyone's burger all day, making sure it's really cooked, just in case.'

'The meat's bad? What, why?'

'You know that big thunderstorm last night? Well, the power went off here, and the freezer was off for hours, didn't even come back on till, like, just before lunchtime, I guess, and everything had thawed out. The burgers had been at room temp for ages.'

I swallowed. 'Are you serious?'

Paul looked over my shoulder. 'You could get, like, cheeseburger disease from eating this. I can't talk to you anymore. They might figure out what I'm telling you. Just don't eat this, Dad. I don't want you to fucking die on me.' He paused a moment. 'I think the fries are okay, though. They're actually pretty good.'

He turned to go back to his post and this time *I* grabbed *his* arm. 'Wait a second. Are you telling me, all these people here, they're eating potentially contaminated food?'

Paul shrugged. 'Yeah, they are. But they're not my dad.'

'Paul, cheeseburg – hamburger disease can kill people. It's that *E. coli* virus or whatever. You can't mess around with that. If these people are eating this stuff, they've got to be told. Has anyone been sick yet?'

'Some guy came in a while ago, said he got a bad burger at lunch, felt like he was gonna puke. He talked to Conan over there,' he nodded towards the woman on the register, 'and she practically threw him out the door. She's a fucking linebacker.'

I swallowed hard. My mouth was starting to feel very dry. Paul could see that I was pondering what to do.

'What?' he said. 'What are you thinking?'

There was an elderly couple at one table, cutting a burger in half with a plastic knife. At the next table, a guy who looked like some sort of city worker, orange vest and jeans, hard hat on the seat next to him, chowing down on a double burger. And then, two tables over from him, a mother with two small children. She was unwrapping the foil covering on burgers for each of them.

'Kids,' I said, to myself as much as to Paul.

He looked around. 'What?' he said.

'Kids can die,' I said. 'They can die from hamburger disease. It can cause kidney failure.'

Paul's eyes were getting wild with panic. 'Jesus, Dad, what are you going to do?'

I was feeling pretty panicked myself. What, exactly, *was* I planning to do?

And then I just acted, without even thinking. I took a few steps over to the mother feeding her kids, bent down, and said to her quietly, 'Don't give them that.'

She looked at me, pulled back in surprise. 'Excuse me?'

Paul, behind me, said, 'Dad, what the hell are you—'

'The burgers,' I said, ignoring him. 'Don't let them eat the burgers. They had a power failure here. There might be a risk of *E. coli* and—'

'Oh my God,' she said, reaching across the table and grabbing the burgers out of her children's hands.

'Mouuum!' one whimpered angrily.

The guy in the orange vest turned around, looked at me. 'What did you say?'

'I just, I heard, the burgers, they may not be safe to eat,' I whispered urgently.

'Fuck,' he said.

The mother whirled around. 'Do you mind?' She nodded towards her small children.

The guy in the vest turned around and tapped the older woman, the one sharing a burger with her elderly husband, and whispered something to her. He pointed at me, and when the woman caught my eye, I nodded.

'Dad,' Paul said.

'Thank you so much for telling me,' the mother said. 'We come here all the time, although the kids usually want to go to McDonald's for a Happy Meal and—'

'Dad,' Paul said.

'You see,' I told her, 'my son just got a job here, and he was telling me that—'

'Dad,' Paul said.

Finally I turned around. The woman from behind the register was standing there, glowering at me.

'What you saying?' she asked. I noticed that, hanging from her right arm, was a baseball bat.

'What's wrong, Ma?' asked the twin who'd put the toppings on my burger.

I tried to remain calm, nonconfrontational. 'I had heard, I understand that your freezer went out. For several hours.' Tried not to make it sound like an accusation, more like a statement of fact.

'What you know about my freezer?'

'It's just that, if the meat had been thawed for some time, there's a risk that it could be contaminated. And I understand there's already been one man who'd eaten here at lunch—'

She raised the bat. 'Where you hear this?' She turned those black eyes on Paul. 'You tell him this?'

Paul's voice squeaked. 'This is my dad.'

Eyes back to me. 'You get out.' She brought up the bat, ready to swing, just as her two daughters started coming around the counter.

'I'll have to call the health department,' I said, trying to stand my ground but knowing I was a moment away from bolting.

'Go ahead and fucking call them,' said the twin. 'See what happens, Mr Big Asshole.'

There wasn't anyone in the restaurant who couldn't hear what was going on. No one was eating. People were getting up, leaving their unfinished burgers on their trays, not bothering to dump them into the trash.

Ma's eyes bored into mine. 'You go or I smash your fucking head in.' And then, to Paul, 'You, you fired.'

He peeled off his hat, untied his apron, and tossed them over the back of a swivel chair. We both backed our way out and said nothing to each other until we were safely in the car and driving down the street. Blood was pounding in my ears.

'Way to go, Dad,' Paul said. 'You just lost me my first job.'

Eldon wasn't like the others. The others, well, they were like her father. Pigs, basically. Always with the jokes. Tit jokes. Ass jokes. Any kind of sex joke. You're a stripper, people can say whatever they want to you. Even if you're not a whore, you're a whore. Grabbing your butt when they walked by, pressing themselves up against you at the bar, all hard under their jeans, even when you're back in your regular clothes. What did she expect, exactly? The place was run by a bunch of biker types. You wanted a bunch of gentlemen? Go work someplace else, lady.

Eldon, he was one of them, but he wasn't one of them. Didn't even have an actual motorcycle. Had this old Toyota, the guys made jokes about him. He always treated Miranda, eighteen now, like a lady. Thought her name was Candace, though. He was the only one called her that. Everyone else called her Candy. Let's have a lick of Candy, they said. I'd love to eat Candy, they said.

So dumb, she thought, coming up with a name like that. Thought it sounded like a good name for a stripper when she applied for the job. Stupid.

But Eldon, he called her Candace, talked to her like a person. Asked what she wanted to do with her life, like he knew she was destined for something better than wrapping herself around a pole for a bunch of horny drunks.

93

'I like numbers,' she said. 'Maybe, like, something financial. Planning, or accounting, doing people's books for them. I look around here, they're wasting so much money. They could be saving a lot.'

'No shit?' he said.

'They have a course, at the college?' she said. 'I'm going to see if I can take it, learn more stuff. I don't like the dancing.'

'Yeah, you're good though. You bring the people in.'

'They'd come in and watch anyone does what I do.'

'You should do what you want to do. You're smart. No offense, but you're too smart to be up there doing that, you know?'

She told him that Gary, the guy who ran the Kickstart, he kept pushing her to work upstairs, where lots of the other dancers made extra money on their backs, or their knees.

'That's not right, him pushing you like that,' Eldon said. 'Not right at all.'

He had a nice smile. Not huge. Just the corners of his mouth coming up, like he wasn't just smiling, but he was thinking about why he was smiling. He did odd jobs for Gary, dope runs up from the city, upkeep on the Kickstart. The heavy-duty stuff, like when someone from the other gang in town started cutting in on your territory, and you had to go out and teach somebody a lesson, beat the shit out of somebody, blow up a car, that kind of thing, Eldon gave that a pass. Let Zane do it. Or Eldridge. They were fucking crazy. They were made for that kind of work.

Eldon thought it was great that Candace was going to take a course to better herself. 'You got a car? If you don't, I could drive you up to the college in my Toyota, you could check it out, this financial stuff. On days that you have a class, I could take you there, bring you back, we could get something to eat after.'

So he drove her up. She didn't have the marks, or the money, to enroll full-time, but she was able to take a couple of courses. She was a natural. She'd dress real plain, bulky sweaters, try to look like someone else, in case some of the male students recognized her from stripping at the Kickstart. Eldon would come by when her course was over and drive her home. 'Stop here,' she'd say along the way. 'I gotta go in and buy the new issue of Money.'

She said to Gary – they called him Pick behind his back sometimes but not to his face – he could save some money by changing around some of the bartending shifts, he had too many people during the slow parts of the day, she could draw up a better schedule?

'The fuck you talking about?' he said. She explained it to him. He said, 'Shit, you're right.'

She had other suggestions for him, how he could negotiate better deals with his restaurant suppliers, how the girls upstairs could charge more for certain things some guys really liked. What the hell, as long as she didn't have to do it. She told him how he could be putting his money from prostitution, and the cash from dispensing dope, in legit investments, make it look like it came through the Kickstart legally.

'How you know all this shit?' Gary wanted to know. She shrugged. 'I like this stuff.'

'Math,' Gary said, shaking his head. 'I don't get it.'

And he didn't. Miranda figured that if he had to rely on profits from a legitimate business, he'd go tits up in no time. It was only because the markup on drugs was so high, the profits on prostitution so huge, that he managed to keep his head above water.

'You're amazing,' Eldon said. 'I'm gonna talk to Gary, see if he'll put you in the office full-time, you won't have to take your clothes off anymore.'

95

She took them off for him, though. He wasn't the first man she'd ever slept with. But he was the first she slept with more than once. Was this what it was like for her sister and Don? How many men were there out there who weren't total assholes? Had she and Claire found the only two?

Claire phoned her. Their dad had come out of a bar, looked the wrong way crossing the street, got flattened by a tractor-trailer hauling pigs to a plant where they'd be turned into bacon.

No shit. She had to laugh.

TEN

When we got home, I went straight for the phone book, hunting down the number for the city health department. I was rattled and having a hard time finding which section of the book it would be in.

'I just want it on the record,' Paul said, 'that I did actually get a job, and that I lost it through no fault of my own. Okay?'

I found it under the listings for municipal government departments, then dialed the number. And got a recording. The offices were closed for the day. So who did you call when a health emergency occurred after business hours?

'So, like, do you expect me to get another job now? Are you and Mom going to gang up on me again?'

The fire department? The police?

'And what do you want me to do with this?' Paul asked. He was holding the Styrofoam container that contained my cheeseburger and fries. When I didn't immediately answer him, he opened the cabinet door under the kitchen sink, where we keep the garbage bin.

'No!' I shouted. 'We may need it for, I don't know, evidence, to give the health department. Put it in the fridge.'

Paul screwed up his face. 'What if somebody eats it?'

I opened the kitchen drawer where we keep all the odds and ends we didn't know what to do with, like keys to unknown locks, bread bag clips, and batteries we aren't sure are dead or still have a bit of juice in them, and picked out a thick-point Sharpie marker. I tossed it to Paul and said, 'Put a note on it.'

I watched him write on the top of the white box, in big capital letters, 'EAT THIS AND DIE – PAUL.' Then he put it on a middle shelf of the fridge, near the back.

I found a non-emergency number for the police, not wanting to tie up a 911 line with a call about a potential food hazard that might keep a call about a house fire from getting through. I was bounced from desk to desk, getting the same message at every stop. Not our job. Call the health inspection office in the morning.

'Shit,' I said.

Paul said, 'What's for dinner?'

I didn't tell Sarah about the episode at Burger Crisp. I was responsible for enough chaos that she already knew about, I couldn't see the sense in piling it on. I asked Paul if he'd mind keeping his mother out of the loop, at least for now, about what had transpired, or how, exactly, he lost his job. 'If your mother asks why you're not going to work,' I said, 'just tell her they hired somebody else instead.' Paul knew Sarah was mad at me, and he didn't want to make things any more tense around the house, so he said okay. His conscience wasn't the slightest bit disturbed by participating in a lie. This was troubling, but given the circumstances, I was also grateful.

'But that place,' he said, 'it was really weird to work there. There were these people dropping by, at the back door, and they weren't dropping off buns or meat or frozen fries or any shit like that. They'd drop off packages, and then later, someone else would come by and pick up the packages. And Mrs Gorkin, the lady who ran the place? She didn't think this was weird or anything.'

It sounded as though I'd gotten him out of there just in time.

The following morning, after another frosty evening with Sarah, I put in a call to the city's health inspection department from my desk in the Home! section. I got, much to my surprise and in clear violation of my preconceptions about civil servants, a woman who said if I gave her enough details, she could probably find the health inspector responsible for the part of the city where Burger Crisp was located. I waited, hearing her tap away on a keyboard in the background, and then, 'That would be Brian Sandler. Let me put you through to his extension.'

A few seconds, a ring, and then, 'Sandler.'

I identified myself, told him I was calling from the *Metropolitan* but left it a bit murky as to whether this was a personal call or he was being interviewed for a story, and quickly told him what had transpired the evening before. Said at least one person, according to my son, who worked there, had come back to the restaurant complaining of food poisoning. That the owner, and her daughters, were not particularly open to discussing any possible problems with the menu. There was the matter of the baseball bat, for example.

'That all seems kind of amazing,' said Brian Sandler. 'I know the place you're speaking of, that's Mrs Gorkin's place, she runs it with her girls. Any time I've been in there, it's always seemed pretty shipshape to me.'

I thought about the overflowing trash cans, the general appearance of the joint. Even before finding out there might be an actual health problem, the place looked a bit dodgy. If Paul hadn't been working there, I doubt I'd have gone in. And now there was this other stuff, this business of dropping off packages, other people picking them up.

'Seriously?' I said.

'I'm looking at their file here, and they have a passing grade, Mr Walker. I've been in there personally. Nice people.'

'Mrs Gorkin?'

'You mentioned your son works there?'

'Well, not anymore. Not since yesterday.'

'Maybe you need to look into that. Getting fired, he might have had an ax to grind, you know?'

'No no, you see, that happened after the other thing. Look, we saved some food from there, so that you could test it. We put it in our fridge as soon as we got back home and—'

'I tell you what. I'm heading out this morning, and I'll drop in, see how things are at Burger Crisp and I'll get back to you.'

'Fine,' I said, and gave him my number. 'Could you call me this afternoon and let me know what you find out?'

'I'll get back to you,' Sandler said, in what I thought was a pretty noncommittal way, and hung up.

That's when I realized Frieda was standing behind me.

'How's it going?' she asked. 'With the feature?'

I sighed. 'It's coming along. Look, I've had a few things going on I just needed to deal with, but don't worry, you'll get your story.'

'Because the thing is,' Frieda said, almost wincing, like it was hurting her to tell me this, 'they want, well, I think Mr Magnuson wants me to do a performance review on you. To see how you're doing here.'

'A performance review. Frieda, it's my second day on the job. How on earth can you be expected to assess my work for a performance review? I haven't turned in a single story to you yet.'

'Well, that's certainly true. But if Mr Magnuson wants me to do it, I'm not going to tell him no. But I don't want you to feel under any pressure. This would be a chance not only for me to tell you how you're doing, but a chance to tell me how you feel things are going, whether you have any issues you want to raise, any goals, that kind of thing.'

'My issue would be that this paper is totally fucking me over at the moment, Frieda,' I said. She blinked. I continued, 'I've gotten some great stories for this paper, but Magnuson feels that because they sort of fell into my lap, or more accurately, because I stumbled into some deep shit a couple of times, I don't really deserve any credit. And then some dip-shit reporter from a two-bit paper in the burbs figures he can give his career a shot by sabotaging mine – may he get trapped in a Wal-Mart cave-in, the son of a bitch – and now I'm sent to the exclamation point section, working with you, no offense, because this is the first newspaper department I've worked in where you get cookies in the afternoon, but this is not really where I want to be, so when you do your performance review, in the part where it talks about attitude, you could put down that mine could be categorized as,' and I thought a moment, 'miffed.' I smiled. 'Yes, fucking miffed.'

Frieda's mouth was half open. Finally, it occurred to her to close it, and she said, 'It's true. You really are an asshole.'

I tried to think of something to say, but Frieda's comeback seemed so out of character that I was struck dumb. We seemed engaged in a staring contest when, thankfully, my phone rang.

'I better get this,' I said. Frieda walked off and I grabbed the receiver. 'Walker,' I said.

'It's me,' Trixie said. 'I called to apologize.'

'Yeah, well,' I said.

'I haven't been totally honest with you.'

'I kind of figured that.'

'I'm not going to ask anything else of you. I was wrong to put you in an awkward position. I took advantage of our friendship.'

I said nothing.

'This has been a tough time for me. I just hope no one saw that picture in the paper.' She paused. 'No one that matters. But I think he's still snooping around. Benson, that is.'

'I remember,' I said.

'I'm calling from my cell. I've been out of town the last day, I'm getting back to Oakwood early this afternoon. I'd like to tell you what's going on.'

'Go ahead.'

'Not on the phone. Can you come out to the house? At one-thirty?'

I paused. 'Here's the thing, Trixie. Things are not very good right now with Sarah. Personally, and professionally. My dust-up with Martin Benson got me moved out of the newsroom and cost Sarah a promotion. You follow that trail back and it leads to you.'

'I'm sorry. I don't blame you for being pissed.'

'Look, I value our friendship too, but it's kind of interfering with my marriage these days. Sometimes I think Sarah has the idea that we've got something going on.'

Although it might have been slightly humiliating had Trixie laughed then, it also would have been comforting. Instead, she was silent.

'You still there?' I said.

'This'll be the last time,' Trixie said. 'I want to tell you everything. I think you should know everything. I feel like,' she seemed to be catching her breath, 'I feel like I have to tell somebody. And you're one of the few people I actually trust.'

I sighed, closed my eyes. I felt, suddenly, very tired. There seemed to be so much going on. My troubles with Sarah. My career in a shambles. Losing Paul his job. And now Trixie wanted to unburden herself to me. I didn't know whether I had the energy.

'Zack?'

'Yeah,' I said. 'What time did you say, one-thirty?'

'That's perfect,' she said. 'I should be back home by then.'

I arrived around 1:25 p.m. Trixie's nondescript two-story brick house was two doors down from our old place, the one Sarah and I and the kids had lived in during our suburban interlude. I wondered who lived there now, and how much they knew about what had happened in that house.

There was no car in Trixie's driveway, no sign of her GF300 on the street. Perhaps I had beat her home from wherever she happened to be coming from. I parked in the drive, rang the bell, got no answer, and got back into my car.

Trixie pulled into the drive ten minutes later.

'Sorry,' she said, getting out of her car. 'There was a truck rollover on the expressway.'

'No problem,' I said. 'I only got here a couple minutes ago.'

She was in jeans and a silk blouse, and her high heels clicked on the pavement and flagstone as she approached the front door, keys out. She put the key in the dead-bolt lock, turned it, and cocked her head to one side.

'That's funny,' she said. 'It didn't feel like the bolt went back.'

'That happens with me sometimes,' I said. 'You can't tell whether you unlocked it or whether it was already unlocked.'

She opened the door, somewhat warily, and stepped inside. I followed. Trixie had a kind of Crate & Barrel look going on throughout the first floor, and the tasteful decorations gave no hint of the 'early dungeon' décor of the basement. She headed straight for the kitchen, all white cupboards and aluminum trim with skylights filling the room with light. She tossed her purse onto the countertop, where there was a copy of the *Suburban*. She handed it to me.

'Check it out,' she said.

It was a pretty good picture of her. Striding from her car to a coffee shop. The wind blowing her hair back so you could get a good look at her face. And under the pic, Lesley Carroll's photo credit.

'Shit,' I said, putting down the paper. I didn't bother to read Martin Benson's accompanying story, which speculated about just what sort of activities this woman engaged in in the fine, morally upright town of Oakwood.

'I'll start some coffee,' she said. She opened the freezer, hunted around. 'Can you do me a favor? I keep my tins of coffee in the freezer, keeps it fresher longer, but there's none in here. There's probably some in the fridge downstairs, in the freezer compartment? You want to grab that while I get some cups out?'

'The basement?' I said.

Trixie flashed a smile at me. 'You're a big boy. You go past the rack, around the corner, there's the second fridge. I've got decaf and regular, take your pick.'

'The rack?'

Now she sighed, hands on hips, looking at me like I was six. 'Fine,' she said. 'I'll go.'

'No,' I said, already turning for the door to the basement. 'I can do this.'

I flicked on the light at the top of the broad-loomed stairs and descended into Trixie's pleasure palace – or torture chamber. Pleasure and torture seemed so closely linked in Trixie's world, it was difficult to know what terminology to use.

It had been a long time since I'd been down here. And the last time had not been as a client, but to rescue one who'd been strapped in a bit too snugly to one of Trixie's restraint devices, a huge wooden X with straps at all the far points.

I found another switch at the bottom of the stairs to light up the whole room, and there was the wall adorned with straps and belts and whips, the kind of stuff that a naive individual like myself might have first thought would be used to secure camping gear to the roof of a car. But then, once you saw the collection of silver and fur-lined handcuffs hanging there, it started to dawn on you that this stuff was not intended for a trip to Yellowstone Park.

The room looked pretty much as it had on my last visit, except this time, the guy strapped to the big X wasn't doing any struggling.

He was dead.

I froze when I saw him. Stripped to the waist, arms and legs secured, throat cut, blood everywhere.

Martin Benson.

ELEVEN

'Did you find it?' Trixie shouted from upstairs. She must have been wondering why it was taking me so long to find a tin of coffee in a fridge. 'You're not playing with my toys, are you?'

'No,' I said, unable to take my eyes off Benson. I don't exactly have a medical degree, but I was as sure as I could be that there was no urgency to check for a pulse, to get the paramedics here pronto. Martin Benson looked very, very dead.

His head was tilted to the right, resting on his shoulder. The gash in his neck appeared to run right under his thick chin, but with his head slumped slightly forwards, it was difficult to tell. But that was where the blood started, and there was a lot of it, smeared across his oversized torso, blackening his trousers, on the floor.

Over in the corner, I saw a shirt and jacket and tie, presumably his.

I think I might have thrown up if I hadn't heard Trixie coming down the steps. I whirled around, saw her long legs appear first, then the rest of her. 'What *has* caught your interest down here, Za—'

Her jaw dropped, and then she screamed.

I ran to her, held on to her, pulled her towards me

so she wouldn't have to look. 'Oh my God!' she said. 'Oh God oh God oh God!'

She broke away from me, approached Martin Benson slowly. 'Oh God, it's him,' she said. 'The guy. The son of a bitch from the paper.'

'Yeah,' I said slowly. 'It's him.'

She took another tentative step towards him, reaching out.

'Don't touch anything,' I said. 'Just leave everything the way it is.' I looked away again, took a couple of deep breaths. 'I'll go call the police.'

'Look,' Trixie said, pulling herself together. 'There's a note.'

A piece of paper was rolled up and tucked into one of the closed handcuffs hanging from the wall display. She slid it out.

'Trixie, you shouldn't be touching that. The police will want it, they'll want to check it for fingerprints, they'll—'

Trixie unrolled the sheet, looked at what was written on it, and went very white. She whispered, 'They've found me.'

'Who?' I said. 'Who's found you?'

'Someone must have seen the photo and told them. They've got friends everywhere.' There was panic in her voice.

'What does it say?' I asked her. 'Show me the note.'

But she had already folded it and put it in the front pocket of her jeans. She stood a moment, breathing out slowly, pulling herself together.

'You're going to have to help me,' she said.

'Help you what?'

'We have to get rid of the body.'

Perhaps, if I weren't still in some sort of shock at discovering a dead guy in Trixie's basement, a guy that Trixie would probably have been happy to see dead a few days earlier, I might have been able to laugh at her suggestion. But I was too numb for that. Instead, very slowly, I said, 'Trixie, we have to call the police. And we have to call them right now.'

She took a step towards me. 'You don't understand. There are things I have to do. Things I have to sort out. I don't have time to waste talking to the police. I can't get involved with them. I've got some plastic in the garage, we could wrap him up, find someplace to dump him—'

'Trixie!'

I guess she was unaccustomed to hearing me raise my voice, to actually shout. Her eyes danced for a second, and she focused on me as though seeing me for the first time.

'Trixie, we are not hiding the body. You're not hiding it, and I'm not helping you. You have to tell me what the hell is going on. Who's done this? Who did this to Benson?' I paused a moment. 'You didn't do it, did you?'

'You think I'm capable of this? Of *this*?' Her arm flung out in the direction of Benson. 'You don't know me better than to think I would do something like that?'

'There seems to be a lot I don't know about you, Trixie. Like what's written on that note. Why you were so scared for your picture to show up in the paper. Why those guys selling stun guns put you on edge. Does this have something to do with Canborough, Trixie? Something that happened five years ago?'

She blinked.

'Is this all related to three bikers getting killed? Did you see something that night, Trixie? Are you on the run? Are you some kind of a witness?'

'What have you been doing? Have you been checking up on me? What gives you the right to start poking into my personal affairs and—'

'Trixie, forget about that. We have to call the police. They can protect you. They can get whoever did this to Benson, they can make it so you don't have to be on the run.'

Trixie appeared to be weighing her options. 'Maybe you're right,' she said. 'I can't keep living this way.'

I smiled. 'Okay. Let's go upstairs. I'll make the call if you want.'

'Maybe you should,' she said, and reached out for my hand.

It happened so fast, I never had a chance to react.

As she slapped a cuff around my right wrist, she pulled my body towards her, yanking my right arm forwards towards the base of the stair handrail, onto which she snapped the matching cuff.

Thrown off balance, I shouted, 'Jesus Christ! Trixie, what the hell are you doing?'

She jumped back, afraid that I might try to grab her with my free arm. I yanked my right arm and the handcuffs jangled, cut into my wrist. The handrail held firm. I shook it several times, unable to believe my predicament. When I looked back at Trixie, she was holding a second pair of cuffs.

'I'm going to toss these to you,' she said, 'and I want you to put them on your other wrist, then put the other cuff on the railing.'

'What?'

'I need to be able to get by you on the stairs, Zack. I can't trust that you won't try to hang on to me.' She tossed the cuffs and they landed by my foot.

'I'm not putting them on,' I said.

Without saying a word, Trixie disappeared around the corner where I guess the fridge that held the coffee was, and returned a moment later with a gun in her hand.

'Trixie, you wouldn't.'

'You're probably right, Zack, but I'm in a rather desperate situation at the moment, and I don't think you should test me.' She raised the gun and pointed it at me.

I stared at her a good ten seconds, then bent down, picked up the cuff with my left hand, moved it close to my right hand, which I used to apply half the cuff. Then I slipped the other cuff around the railing and closed it.

'I need to hear it close,' Trixie said. I squeezed it, and she heard the telltale click. 'That's good.' She produced two keys from her jeans. 'I'm going to leave these right on the table here, so that when someone comes to rescue you, you'll be able to get those off right away. And promise me you won't start yelling your head off as soon as I leave here. I need some time to get away. If you're going to yell, I'm going to have to leave you gagged.' She nodded at some red balls attached to straps that were hanging on the wall with the other S&M equipment.

'That won't be necessary,' I said quietly.

Still holding the gun, she came up close to me. 'Where are your car keys?'

'What?'

'Zack, just tell me where they are.'

'Front pants pocket,' I said, and Trixie came alongside me and slid her slender fingers down into the pocket of my jeans as I once again tested the cuffs on the railing.

'Don't worry,' she said. 'I'm only going after your keys.' She found them, gave them a shake. 'I'll just take the car keys, not your house keys. I figure they know what kind of car I've got, so it's better if I get a running start in yours. You can have my car. I'll leave you my set on the kitchen counter.'

'Trixie, you're making a big mistake. Let me help you through this.'

'I need help, that's for sure,' she said. 'But not the kind I think you're up to.' She leaned in close to me, her face so close to mine I could feel her breath. 'I know I keep telling you this, Zack, but I'm really sorry about everything. Maybe someday I can make it up to you.'

And she leaned in and kissed me, placed her mouth squarely on mine, slipped a hand behind my head so I couldn't try to pull away. She moved her lips over mine for a second or more, pulled away, leaned in to me again for a small, follow-up peck, and smiled sadly at the shocked expression I guess was on my face.

'Sarah's a very lucky gal,' she said, and climbed to the top of the stairs. 'Don't worry, I'll make sure someone comes and finds you.'

'Trixie,' I said, one last time. 'Just tell me. Why are you doing this?'

She paused, looked at me very seriously for a moment, and said, 'I'm not going to let them get my little girl.'

And then she was gone.

She was late.

A couple of days, Miranda didn't worry. Took note of it, but didn't panic or anything. But then it was a week. Ten days. Now it was time to panic. She went to the drugstore and came home with a pregnancy test. Went into the bathroom, closed the door.

'What's up, Candace?' Eldon said. 'You seem funny.'

She came out a few minutes later. 'You've knocked me up,' she said.

'Huh?' he said.

'I'm gonna have a kid,' Miranda said. She had no idea what he would do. Storm out, maybe? Start screaming? Accuse her of fucking up her birth control? She thought maybe he'd hit her. That's the sort of thing her dad did when she said something that upset him. Just whacked her upside the head. Eldon had never hit her, but there was always a first time. There always had to be a first time when a guy you thought loved you took a swing at you.

He said, 'You think it's a girl?'

She said, 'What?'

'A girl. You think it's a girl? Because, you're so beautiful, if it's a girl, she'll be beautiful too.'

The guy was full of surprises.

Gary had already been letting her split her time between the stage and the office upstairs. He'd turned over the books

113

to her, but once in a while, a girl would take off sick, Gary'd tell her, 'Go downstairs and do some bump and grind. If we didn't have the ol' bump and grind goin' on, there'd be no books to balance.' Like Miranda should be grateful he was giving her a chance to take her clothes off because it gave her money to count upstairs later.

But once she started showing, well, that was it. Nobody wanted to drink their beer watching some chick who was knocked up.

So in a way, it all worked out okay. Sort of.

But in the back of her mind, Miranda was thinking about the kind of world she was going to bring this baby into. She hadn't known, for several years now, a particularly respectable life. Not like her sister, Claire. She and Don had gotten married, they had a decent apartment now, not some place over a pizza joint. She had her secretary job, he had his job at Ford. Not that they'd have to worry that much about bringing any kid into the world. Claire couldn't have kids, it turned out.

How crazy. Claire's home was the perfect one in which to raise a child, but she couldn't have one.

And I'm the one who's pregnant, thought Miranda. Working in a bar with strippers and hookers and dope dealers.

I need my head read.

But she did have a man in her life. Eldon seemed excited about the idea of becoming a father. She would talk to him – she still had not told him that her real name was not Candace – about getting some sort of new life. Of leaving the Kickstart. Of getting respectable jobs. Of making a proper home for their baby.

'Yeah,' he would say. 'That sounds like a good idea. Maybe I should start looking for something else,' he said.

114

'Maybe I should take some courses too. You know what I've always been interested in? Electrical work. Wiring.'

'Electricians make a fortune,' Miranda said.

So she worked all the time in the upstairs office, doing the finances, turning dirty money into clean. It was a gift, no doubt about it.

And then one day, sitting upstairs at the computer, she knew this was it. She phoned down to the bar, asked for Eldon. 'This is it,' she said.

It was a girl.

Her name was Katie.

TWELVE

The moment I heard the front door close, I yanked on the cuffs. The stair railing didn't budge but the cuffs cut sharply into my wrists and I winced from the pain. Already I could feel my fingers starting to go numb from reduced circulation. Outside, I could hear the door of my Virtue hybrid car open and close. The vehicle was so quiet, I didn't hear it start or back out of the drive and pull away.

I hadn't heard Trixie make any phone calls from upstairs, but I had to hope, certainly if I couldn't get free on my own, that she'd keep her word and send someone to rescue me. The handcuff keys were on a table only ten feet away, but they might as well have been in the next town for all the good they did me now.

I glanced in the direction of Martin Benson, not wanting to look at him, yet not able to take my eyes off him. The slice across his neck was a macabre grin. *Look what happens when you mess with me*, it seemed to be saying. I tried not to think about what might happen if the person or persons who did that decided to return before I could get myself out of these handcuffs and the hell out of this house.

Rather than yank on the railing with the cuffs again and make my wrists even more sore, I put my hands directly on the railing and pulled. If I could pry it off the wall and drag it just ten feet, I could reach the keys and get out of here. I pulled once, and nothing. Clearly, the screws that held the hardware to the wall had been sunk into studs and not just drywall. I tried again, really putting my back into it this time, still without success. I cursed under my breath.

Even if I could free myself, it wasn't necessarily my plan to run. I'd feel a lot safer than I did now as long as I had the freedom to move around. If Trixie wanted to make a break for it, well, that was her decision. Evidently she had her reasons, one of which had just been revealed to me.

'I'm not going to let them get my little girl.'

Just when I thought there was so little I knew about Trixie, I found myself realizing there was even more I did not know. Not long after I'd first met her, I'd asked her whether she had children, and she had said no.

While Trixie might have had her reasons to flee before the police arrived, I couldn't see myself following suit. I had to stay and explain this as best I could. Chances were I wouldn't even need to call the police. They were probably on the way now, or at least would be soon. Once Trixie felt she had enough of a head start, I was reasonably confident that she'd let them know about me, and Benson.

So I would explain this to the police as best I could. That was the Zack Walker way. You bring in the authorities. You extricate yourself from the situation and let the professionals take over.

Not that that had always been my approach. There was that one time, when I found myself in a situation where I figured I was the most likely suspect in a homicide, that I did not pick up the phone and immediately call police. There were extenuating circumstances.

But surely that wasn't the case this time. I would not be the prime suspect this time. What possible reason would I have to want Martin Benson—

Hold on.

I started to work it out in my head.

What would Martin Benson's editor have to say when the police interviewed him? *He was investigating this dominatrix*, the editor would say. *Must have been ruffling some feathers too, because some writer from the* Metropolitan *tried to talk him out of it. The M.E. there's an old friend of mine. Told him all about it.*

And then the police would talk to Magnuson. And then they'd want to have another interview with me.

So you tried to warn Benson off a story, the police would say, *and when he didn't go along with it, he ratted you out, and you got demoted.*

I couldn't be sure the cops would use the word 'ratted', but I figured that would be about the gist of it.

Maybe it made more sense to stop fighting with the railing. Maybe it made more sense to stay handcuffed until the police arrived. How likely a suspect was I when I was left handcuffed at a murder scene? I was a victim too, although I had to admit I'd gotten off a little bit better than Martin Benson.

Of course, the only problem was, we hadn't both been victimized by the same person. Being handcuffed by Trixie would no doubt lead police to suspect that she was also responsible for Martin Benson's murder.

Trixie did, after all, have some familiarity with the apparatus to which Benson was secured.

What a fucking mess.

I twisted my right hand around to look at my watch. Coming up on 2:30 p.m. Trixie had been gone at least half an hour, maybe more. Just how far away was she planning to get before she called someone to rescue me?

It hadn't occurred to me then that she might actually have called someone right after leaving the house. That she might have called someone who would need thirty minutes or more to get here.

Finally, around 2:45, there was a hard knock at the door.

'Down here!' I shouted.

Another knock.

'Hey!' I shouted. 'In the basement!'

I thought I heard the door open, and then a voice, tentatively, called out, 'Hello?'

I think, of all the people Trixie could have called, Sarah would definitely have been my last choice.

I went to say something but the words caught in my throat for a moment. I guess, for a fleeting instant, for nothing more than a millisecond, I must have thought I could keep Sarah from finding me handcuffed in Trixie's basement only a few feet away from a dead guy strapped to a cross with his throat cut open. But it only took the briefest of moments to realize there was no way out for me that didn't include immense dollops of shame and mortification.

'Sarah!' I shouted.

'Zack?' Sarah sounded scared, 'Zack! Where are you?'

'Just listen to me first, okay? Okay? Just stop and listen!'

'Zack, what's happened? Are you okay? Where are you?'

'Sarah, *stop*! Are you stopped?'

A pause from upstairs. 'Okay, yes. I'm not moving. Zack, Trixie phoned. She told me to come out here, that something had happened and—'

'Sarah! Listen to me!'

'Okay.'

'First of all, I'm okay. I'm going to need your help, but before you come downstairs, I have to prepare you for what you're going to see.'

'Oh my God. Don't tell me you're trapped in some sort of leather thing. You've been coming to Trixie, paying her to—'

'No, Sarah. Please just listen and don't interrupt. I'm not hurt, but I am handcuffed to the stair railing and I need you to get the keys.'

Even from where I stood, I could hear her intake of breath upstairs.

'But Sarah, what I have to tell you is, I'm not exactly alone down here.' I took a breath of my own. 'I'm down here in the midst of a . . . I'm in a crime scene, Sarah.'

'A crime scene.'

'A man has been killed, he's been murdered, and I'm down here with his body.' I paused. 'It's very, very . . . bad.'

From Sarah, almost a whisper: 'Who is it, Zack?'

'Martin Benson. The reporter from the *Suburban*. Somebody's . . . oh man.'

'Tell me you're okay.'

'I'm okay. Are you ready?'

Sarah paused a second before she said, 'I'm ready.'

And then she appeared at the doorway at the top of the stairs, assessing my situation in a glance. She came down the steps slowly, and as she was able to see more of the room, she saw Benson at the far end of it.

'Dear God,' she said. She stayed on the last step, next to me, as if putting a foot on the floor would be an admission that what she was seeing was really true.

'The keys are right there,' I said softly, nodding at the table a few feet away. 'If you give them to me, I can get these off and call the police.'

'Zack, his throat's been slit clear across.'

'I know. The keys. Hand me the keys.'

She was holding it together fairly well, considering. She'd been a police reporter back in her early days and had seen the odd corpse here and there. Usually after the police had arrived.

She looked at the keys on the table. She'd have to put both feet on the floor to get there. As if she were putting her toe into icy cold water, she came down the last step and approached the table hesitantly. She delicately picked up the keys in her fingers, turned, and handed them to me.

'Your wrists are bruised,' she said as I struggled to work the keys into the openings. It took a minute or more for me to get the cuffs off my wrists. I didn't bother to remove them from the railings. Perhaps, if they stayed there, it would bolster my version of events when the police arrived.

'Come on,' I said, leading Sarah up the stairs. 'Let's get out of here.'

I took her into the kitchen, where sunlight was streaming through the blinds and down through a skylight. Sarah slipped her arms around me and hugged me tight.

'I didn't know what to think,' she said, starting to cry. 'Trixie called, all mysterious, said you were in some trouble at her house, that she'd had to take your car, that she was very sorry, but that I should get out here as fast as possible.'

I put my arms around my wife, held her tight.

'I'm glad she called you. And I'm sorry you had to see what's happened here.'

She pulled back, looked into my face, put a hand on each of my cheeks. 'What's going on, Zack? What's happened?'

And then something caught her eye, something on my lip, and then she moved her left thumb over and rubbed at the corner of my mouth, then glanced at her thumb.

She stared at it for a moment, as though transfixed, then looked at me and said, 'The police. You better call the police.' Then she turned and walked away.

I realized then what she'd found on her thumb was lipstick.

THIRTEEN

Two blue and white cabs with uniformed officers arrived first. Sarah and I were waiting outside, leaning on her Camry. I had the keys to Trixie's German sedan in my pocket, as well as the copy of the *Suburban* from the kitchen counter that had her picture in it. Sarah had her arms folded in front of her, and whenever I shifted my butt along the fender towards her, she moved away.

'I know what you're thinking, and you're wrong,' I said.

'Stay away from me,' Sarah said quietly.

The uniforms, as I suspected, kept their interrogations to a minimum and set about making sure the crime scene was secure, well aware that the more senior detectives would be along shortly to conduct the investigation.

An unmarked car parked at the end of the drive and a short, squat man in his late fifties, dressed in a dark suit and black fedora, got out. Who the hell wore fedoras anymore? And then I recalled that I knew at least one detective who did, and that was Detective Flint, from the Oakwood Police Department, whom I knew from my earlier troubles in this neighborhood.

Halfway up the drive he stopped, looked at Trixie's house, then scanned two doors over to take in the house Sarah and I and the kids once lived in. Even with his eyes narrowing, it was possible to read them. *I've been here before*, he was thinking.

And then he looked at me and smiled to himself, as if everything was starting to make sense. 'Well, well,' he said. 'Mr Walker. We meet again.'

'Detective Flint,' I said, trying to smile but not quite pulling it off.

'And you would be?' he said, turning to Sarah. I noticed that when I introduced her as my wife she hardly swelled with pride.

'Hello, Mrs Walker. I'm going to want to talk to both of you, but individually.' He called over one of the uniforms. 'Why don't you show Mr and Mrs Walker to separate cars so that they can rest comfortably while I check things out in there.'

He disappeared into the house. Sarah and I were put into the back seat of different cruisers. I could see her from mine, but she wasn't looking over in my direction. I couldn't resist trying the door handle, to see whether it would open, and it did not. I sat there, feeling like a criminal, and feeling even greater shame that Sarah was being put through the same ordeal. It was about ten minutes before Flint reappeared. He got into the back of Sarah's car first, questioned her for at least fifteen minutes before he got out and settled in next to me. Even though he appeared to be done with Sarah, she had not yet been allowed out of her cruiser.

Flint shifted in the seat, got comfortable, and asked to see my wrists.

'Ouch,' he said empathetically, inspecting the bruises from the handcuffs. 'That part checks out.'

He got out his notebook, clicked his ballpoint a few times, made some scribbles. 'Where's Trixie Snelling gone?' he asked.

'I don't know,' I said.

'You don't know, or you won't tell me?'

'I honestly don't know. She said something about trying to find her little girl. I'm guessing she means her daughter.'

'Where's her daughter?'

'I didn't even know, until she said that, that she might have a daughter. So I have no idea where she might be.'

'Hmm.' He made some notes. 'I understand that you know the deceased.'

'Yes.' I cleared my throat. 'Martin Benson. A columnist for the *Suburban*.'

'Yeah, I've read him now and again. Saw his big exposé on suburban kink, a dominatrix in the neighborhood. Lordy lordy.'

'There was a picture,' I said.

'Yeah, I saw that. She was dressed in her civilian clothes, though,' Flint mused. 'I guess, if they'd got a picture of her on the job, they couldn't even have run it. Family newspaper and all that.'

'I guess,' I said. 'Listen, should I have a lawyer?'

'I don't know,' Flint said, scratching his prominent nose. 'You think you should have a lawyer?'

'I haven't done anything wrong.' I paused. 'Stupid, maybe, but not wrong. That's why I called the police.'

Flint grunted. 'When did you get here?'

'I guess, around one-thirty. I got here before Trixie.'

'She wasn't already home?'

'No, she'd been away somewhere, I don't know where, and we arranged to meet here at that time.'

'So both of you went into the house at the same time.'

'That's right.' I remembered something. 'As we were going into the house, Trixie thought maybe the door was already unlocked, but she wasn't sure. You know how, sometimes, you turn the deadbolt, but it'll still turn even if it's not in the lock position?'

Flint shrugged. I went through the rest of it with him, how I'd gone into the basement for some coffee and found Benson. That Trixie came downstairs wondering what had happened to me, screamed, found a note, started to panic. That she handcuffed me to the railing and took off in my car. That she called Sarah at work to rescue me.

'Hmm,' Flint said. 'So what were you meeting her here for . . .?' He leaned in a little closer, as if there were someone else in the car he didn't want to over-hear. 'You can tell me. Nice-looking lady, I gather. Your wife might not understand, but I would.'

I swallowed. 'It wasn't like that. Trixie and I were friends, from when we used to live on the street. She helped me out when I was in trouble, with that other mess.'

Flint nodded, remembering.

'She'd been having trouble lately with the local paper, and wanted my help with it, and I told her there really wasn't anything I could do, and then she set up this meeting between me and Benson – I thought she was going to be there but she bailed – thinking I'd try to talk him out of taking her picture, but I explained to her I couldn't do that. But there was a huge misunder-standing, with Benson, and it got me in a lot of trouble at work. I was pretty pissed with her. But she called, said she was going to come clean, tell me what kind of trouble she was in, and I agreed to come out and see her, one last time, to hear her side of the story.' I shook my head. 'Good call.'

'So you weren't having a sexual relationship with Ms Snelling?' Flint asked.

'No.'

'You weren't one of her clients? You didn't get those marks on your wrist some other way? You weren't coming out here, paying her to do some things for you your wife's just not too crazy about?' He smiled, like we were just a couple of guys, talking. 'Look, it happens. You're married awhile, you have the kids, the wife's just not into it like she used to be, and her idea of kinky is doing it with the lights on.'

'Don't speak about my wife that way,' I said.

Flint's eyebrows went up. 'My apologies. That was rude. I was just speaking generally. But you didn't answer my question. Were you paying her? Were you hiring her for one of her little sessions?'

'No.'

Flint kept going over the same ground, again and again. What time I got there, what I'd been doing before my arrival, where Trixie might have gone, did she have any family that I knew of, who might have done this to Benson, whether I'd noticed anyone else around the house. My earlier meeting with Benson, how it had gone wrong, my subsequent demotion at the *Metropolitan*.

I was getting a headache.

'So both you and Ms Snelling, you had really good reasons to be angry with Martin Benson,' Detective Flint said.

I thought about that. 'The thing is, the damage had already been done,' I said. 'The paper got the picture they wanted, they ran it. I think that's when things started to totally unravel for Trixie. Someone saw that picture, tipped off someone who'd been trying to find her, and they tracked her down to this house. It was the thing she'd been worried about from the beginning.'

'And what was Martin Benson doing here in the first place?'

It was a good question. 'Maybe he was in the wrong place at the wrong time. Maybe he was trying to get more dirt on Trixie, and the guys who came to get her found him instead.'

Flint's lips pursed out, considering it.

'Or,' he said, tipping his fedora back an inch and exposing the top of his white forehead, 'it could be a whole lot simpler than that.'

'What do you mean?'

Flint took a long breath. 'She invited Benson over. She offered him a little demo of what she does for a living. Told him, "What the hey, you know what I do, you might as well get the tour." Gets him strapped down to that cross thing. Then she kills him.' He ran his index finger quickly across his throat. I shook my head, but Flint continued. 'She leaves. She drives around for a while. Calls you. Tells you she's been out of town, whatever. Arranges to meet you at her place. Makes sure she arrives after you do so you get the idea she's been away, hasn't been home for a while. She does this thing at the door, like maybe there's something wrong with the lock, plants the idea with you that maybe someone broke in. You go inside, everything seems fine, she finds a reason to send you downstairs to get something, the coffee you said. You go down, you find the body. She comes down, acts all surprised. I'll bet she screamed just right, huh? Made it seem like she was seeing Benson's dead body for the first time.'

'No,' I said. 'It wasn't an act.'

'Oh, it was an act,' Flint said. 'A command performance, just for you.'

'I think you're wrong.'

'And the beauty of it is, not only does she have you convinced that she didn't know anything about it, she's set it up perfectly, making you her alibi. You're here before she arrives. So how can it be her? She wasn't even here. And you're the one who can testify to that fact. And how shocked she was at finding some guy who's bled to death in her torture chamber.'

Flint adjusted his hat. 'She used you to try to get Benson to back off. And now she's using you to cover up the fact that she murdered him.'

I was going to tell him no one more time, that he had it all wrong. But I wasn't sure I could say it with complete confidence.

FOURTEEN

When he was done with me, Flint let us both go. Sarah got in her Camry and drove off without saying a word. She either didn't care whether I got back to the city, or assumed that I would be taking Trixie's car, since I had the keys to it.

I didn't know whether Flint was going to want Trixie's car for his investigation. I couldn't see why, since the murder hadn't taken place in it. If it were peppered with incriminating evidence, she'd hardly have left it behind and taken mine.

When I was in the back of the police car, Flint had asked me for a full description of my Virtue, including plate number, which I happened to know, since I'm good with licenses, phone numbers, and the like. He was on his cell right away, passing on the description.

The thing was, I needed wheels. It would probably be easier to take the car and say sorry later, if I had to, than ask Flint for permission to drive off in it now.

I got into the front seat of the GF300, settling into the leather upholstery. One glance at the dash told me this was a more complicated vehicle than my Virtue. A multitude of buttons and switches, including about a dozen on the steering wheel itself, and a tiny screen in the middle of the dash that had to be some sort of navigation system. Turn on the car, and a map showing the car's exact location would probably pop up.

There were some bits of paper in a recessed tray between the seats, what looked like gas receipts, a car wash ticket. Impulsively, I grabbed them and slid them into my jacket pocket, then started looking for the ignition so I could slip the key in and get on my way.

There was a sharp rapping on the driver's window and I jerked my head around to see a very annoyed Flint looking at me through the glass.

I fumbled around, looking for the power window button. Flint, tired of waiting, opened the door and said, 'What the hell you think you're doing?'

'Heading back into the city,' I said.

'Not in this car you're not,' he said. 'Get out.'

I did as I was told, handed the keys to Flint. 'But Trixie took my car. She said I could use hers.'

'Oh, gee,' said Flint, putting the keys in his pocket, shrugging elaborately. 'If it's okay with her, then I guess it's fine.' He shook his head in disgust. 'Do you really work at a newspaper? Have you ever even seen a crime show on TV?'

'I guess your forensic people have to go over the car,' I said.

Flint smiled. 'You can catch a train back downtown. There's a station only half a mile from here. I'll have one of my people give you a lift.'

It was almost an hour before I got back to the paper. I figured Sarah had returned to the office, and I felt I had no choice but to follow her there. There was still some shit left to hit the fan and land on me, and I figured it was going to happen somewhere in the vicinity of Magnuson's office.

I wanted to head straight to Sarah's office, to try to make her understand the bizarre set of circumstances that had brought us to this point, to ask her to forgive me for the stupid things I'd managed to get myself into lately, and most of all, to tell her that I loved her more than anything in the world.

But I didn't have the nerve.

Instead, I wandered over to my new desk in Home!

'You missed cookie time,' Frieda said when I walked past her desk. I glanced at the clock and saw that it was nearly five. 'Where have you been all day?'

I sighed, too tired and too depressed for any sort of smart answer. 'I don't think you're going to have to worry about me around here for much longer,' I told her, dropping into my computer chair. The red message light on my phone was flashing.

'What are you talking about?' Frieda said.

'The clock's ticking,' I said. 'It's only a matter of time before Magnuson suspends me, or fires me outright. I just hope he doesn't fire Sarah too. None of this is her fault.'

Frieda wheeled over a chair and sat close to me. 'I don't think I've ever known anybody in this much trouble.'

I smiled weakly. 'Me neither.'

'Is there anything I can do?' Her concern seemed genuine, and I felt badly for all of my sarcastic outbursts the last couple of days.

I shook my head. 'I imagine I'll be out of here before I can finish your linoleum story.'

She looked sad. 'And you were doing so well with it. Finding out where the word comes from and everything. That was real initiative.'

'Yeah, well.' My phone rang. I looked at it tiredly and figured, with all that was happening, I'd better answer it. It could be Flint, or one of the kids. Part of me wanted it to be Trixie, telling me where she could be found, that she would wait there for the police to arrive. And there was part of me that didn't ever want to hear from her again.

Frieda excused herself as I reached for the receiver. 'Walker,' I said.

'Hi, Mr Walker. Brian Sandler here.'

I shook my head. Who? 'Hi,' I said. 'I'm sorry, who did you say you were?'

'Sandler? City health department? You called me this morning about an incident at Burger Crisp? I left you a couple of messages.'

It took a moment for me to put it all together. 'Oh yeah, right, of course,' I said, glancing at the flashing red light on my phone. 'I'm sorry. It's been kind of a long day.'

'Anyway, I just wanted to put your mind at ease. Everything's fine.'

'What do you mean?'

'I paid a visit today, after your call this morning, to Burger Crisp and spoke with Mrs Gorkin, and her daughters, Gavrilla and Ludmilla, and I was satisfied that everything was in order.'

Godzilla and what?

'But how could that be? Their freezer was off for hours, my son Paul said at least one customer returned to the store feeling sick and—'

'I understand your son was fired from Burger Crisp. Or he quit.'

'I told you that this morning. That he quit, was fired, after this incident.'

'That's not how the Gorkins explain it,' Sandler said, a hint of condescension in his voice.

'What are you talking about?'

'Mrs Gorkin says they'd already fired your son, that he wasn't doing a very good job, couldn't get the hang of it, and that then the two of you came back making all sorts of wild accusations.'

Anger swept over me like a hot wind. 'That's total bullshit, Mr Sandler,' I said. 'My son was working, flipping burgers on the grill, when I came in and he told me what was going on. He wanted to keep me from eating my meal. He was scared for me.'

'Well, I'm sorry, Mr Walker, but your story doesn't jibe with theirs.'

'Or their story doesn't jibe with mine. You really think I'd call the health department with a pack of lies just to get even for something, which didn't even happen?'

'I don't know, Mr Walker.'

'Look, did you test the food? Isn't there something you can do, take it into a lab and dissect the microbes or count the bacteria or something and determine whether it's contaminated?'

'Of course. But I didn't see any need in this case.'

'Are you serious? Okay, look, we've got an entire meal from Burger Crisp in our fridge. I could bring it down to you, you could have it tested, you'd know then whether the Gherkins—'

'Gorkins.'

'Sure. You'd know then whether they're telling the truth.'

'Mr Walker, I've taken this as far as I can. I don't think there's anything here for you,' and he hesitated, 'or your paper to get involved in.'

'Is that what you're worried about?' I asked. 'You're worried that I, or someone else here at the paper, might be planning to do a story on this?'

'I never said nor implied that,' Sandler said. 'The paper is welcome to do whatever story it wants, but there's none here, and I don't think the *Metropolitan* would like to find itself the subject of a million-dollar libel suit.'

'Oh, that's good. I haven't written a single word yet, and already you're threatening me with a lawsuit.'

'It wouldn't just be me,' Sandler said. 'I'm sure the Gorkins would do whatever they had to do to protect their reputation and their livelihood.'

My hot wave of anger had turned into a chill. I was pretty sure I'd just been threatened, and with more than just a lawsuit.

'I'm just going to go out on a limb here,' I said, 'and ask you how much Mrs Gorkin pays you to look the other way. It's probably a lot quicker, and cheaper, to pay off an inspector than bring an establishment up to standard, am I right?'

Sandler's response was slow and measured. 'I'd be very careful about throwing around those sorts of allegations, Mr Walker. I think the smartest thing you could do would be to let this go. There's nothing there. Am I making myself clear?'

'Oh yeah,' I said. 'It's becoming very clear.'

'Thanks very much, Mr Walker, for bringing this to the health department's attention,' he said formally. 'And watch your back.'

He hung up.

I replaced the receiver feeling numb. I dialed in for my messages, and both had been from Sandler, asking me to call him. The son of a bitch had threatened me. And he'd more or less passed on a threat from Mrs Gorkin and her daughters as well.

What else could possibly go wrong today—

'Zack?' I turned around in my chair. It was Frieda. She gave me a pained smile. 'Mr Magnuson's secretary just called. He'd like to see you in his office.'

I could feel everyone's eyes on me as I walked through the newsroom. Word spreads fast. The city desk would have already been tipped to a murder in Oakwood, and chances were that if Dick Colby had been on the phone to Detective Flint, he might already know of my involvement. All I needed, as I took my last steps toward Magnuson's door, was someone to announce, 'Dead man walking!'

Sarah was already there. Her eyes were red, and there was a wadded tissue in her fist.

'Mr Walker,' Magnuson greeted me from behind his desk. 'I was trying to recall the last time one of my reporters found himself handcuffed in a hooker's basement next to a man who'd had his throat slit. And you know something? Nothing comes to mind.'

'Yes, sir, I don't suppose it does.'

'I'm suspending you, effective immediately, with pay, which is mighty generous of me if I do say so myself, while the police and the courts and the CIA and the Masons and the Shriners for all I know sort this fucking mess out. I'm also putting Colby on it, see what he can learn. Call the guild, file a grievance, I don't much care. But when you walk out of this office, keep on walking until you hit the street.'

I thought, considering everything, that I had gotten off easy. I was expecting to be fired outright. Or, possibly, shot.

'Of course, this leaves Frieda short someone once again,' Magnuson mused. 'You were barely there long enough to warm a chair,' he said, looking at me. 'But fortunately, I can solve her personnel problems imme-diately. Sarah, you can report to her tomorrow.'

Sarah was dumbstruck. 'Sir?'

'Is that a problem?' he asked.

'Mr Magnuson, with all due respect, not only do I not feel I should be punished for any of my husband's alleged misbehaviors, but I'm in a different job classifi-cation. I'm an editor. You're proposing moving me to a lower job classification, to a feature-writing position. You can't do that.'

Magnuson said nothing for a moment, then a sense of calm came over him that was nothing short of chilling. 'Ms Walker,' he said, 'I can do anything.'

He swiveled his chair around so that he could work on his computer, and it was clear that we'd been dismissed. Once outside his door, Sarah burst into tears.

'I can't believe this,' she said. She stormed off towards the center of the newsroom. I almost had to run to keep up with her.

'Honey,' I said to her, 'I'm so sorry. That was totally unfair. Not what he did to me, but what he did to you.' I reached out, touched her arm, but she yanked it away. There wasn't anyone in the room who was still looking at their screens. 'You should go to the guild, you should fight this—'

She shook her head and waved her hands at me in a fit of rage. 'Shut up! Just shut up! Just shut the fuck up and leave me alone!'

The newsroom was dead silent. Sarah turned away from me and headed for the elevators. I took the stairs down to the parking lot. By the time I got there, Sarah's car was gone.

'No, no, Candace, hold it like this,' Eldon said. He molded Miranda's hand around the gun. 'There, doesn't that feel better?'

'Yeah, I think so.'

They were out in the country. He'd lined the top of a split-rail fence with half a dozen empty Campbell's asparagus soup tins. Eldon liked asparagus soup. 'Okay, just squeeze the trigger. Just look at your target and your arms will know what to do.'

She squeezed. Blam. God, what a feeling. Thrilling and terrifying at the same time. Would have been even better if she'd hit the can.

She glanced back at Eldon's Toyota parked on the shoulder of the gravel township road, saw six-month-old Katie through the open back window, buckled into her safety seat, gnawing on a red plastic ring. Miranda waved.

'Okay, try again, but relax a bit this time. Don't think so much about aiming, just look at your target, concentrate on it, don't concentrate on your arms or your hands or anything. You're just one with the gun.'

'Jesus, you're getting all philosophical on me.' She squeezed again. Blam. Ting! A can flew off the fence. 'I did it! I don't believe it!'

'Yes!' Eldon said, giving her a hug. 'Awesome!'

It didn't take long until she could hit a can about half the time. Not bad, Eldon said, considering how small the can was and how far away she was standing. 'If it was a moose,' he said, 'you'd have no problem. And really, how often do you see a little can walking through the woods, anyway?'

She went to hand him the gun when they were finished, but he said, 'No, it's yours. I got it for you. You keep it. You know how to use it now. It's small. It'll fit in your handbag.'

Well, she didn't want to carry it in her handbag. She was too frightened by what it could do. She couldn't imagine using it on anything but a tin can. And there was the baby. It wasn't safe, having guns around with a baby in the house.

But she didn't tell him all that. She kissed him and thanked him. He wanted to do the right thing for her. He just wanted her to be safe. Things had been kind of crazy the last few months, and he wanted her to have some protection. But he was her protection. She didn't want to have to carry a gun around in her purse.

There was a war on, and Eldon was feeling pretty tense. Not just because of the skirmishes between the Slots, who owned the Kickstart and were led by Gary, and the Comets from across town. The battle over hookers and drugs would have been enough to keep someone awake at night. But Eldon was troubled by how ineffective a leader Gary was. Gary needed to take bold action. He needed to make it clear to the Comets, once and for all, that the Slots were in charge.

But Gary wasn't a planner. He was ruled by impulses, often reckless ones. A Molotov cocktail had been tossed through the window of the Kickstart, starting a small fire. Luckily, it was after hours, no one got killed. But Eldon couldn't stop thinking about what might have happened if Candace had been there. If the fire had spread upstairs, to the office, where she often worked late into the night adding up the receipts, doing the books.

She could have been killed, those motherfuckers.

The Comets were sending a warning, that they were moving in. They had to send a message back.

Eldon, who'd been content up to now to let Zane and Eldridge and Payne handle the more violent stuff, pressed Gary to take a stand. Run a tractor-trailer through their clubhouse, he said. Find their homes and blow them up. Go nuclear on them.

Gary couldn't decide quite what to do. He wanted to do something, but wasn't sure what.

So one day, he's driving around town late one night in his big four-wheel-drive pickup, he sees one of the Comets out and about in his mint, red 1970 Dodge Super Bee, hood scoop, bumblebee racing stripe, the whole deal. Grant Delmonico, a minor player in the Comets, but still one of them. So Gary follows him, figures maybe an opportunity will present itself.

Grant's coming up to a railroad crossing, lights flashing, big freight coming in from the west, couple of massive SD40s linked together. Gary comes up along behind, truck sitting up high, headlights shining into Grant's car.

The crossing has no gate. Gary gets an idea. He drops the truck into low gear, shoves the Super Bee right into a passing tank car. The train took hold of the front of the car, dragged it down the track, mangled it all to shit. Some mess. Grant was toast.

Gary was pretty proud of himself when he got back to the Kickstart, telling the boys. Eldon said it was bush league. Grant was small potatoes. And would the Comets even get the message? For all anyone knew, the dumb ass just drove into the side of the train.

Not long after, one of their own, some hanger-on by the name of Sebastian, never really one of the crew but did some go-fering for them, gets beaten to death behind a butcher shop.

What are you gonna do? Eldon asked Gary. 'That's what I asked him, right in front of everyone else,' Eldon told Miranda on their way back into town from shooting practice. ' "What the fuck are you gonna do now?" '

'Not in front of Katie,' Miranda said. 'What do you want her first word to be?'

A week later, she found out what Gary had decided to do.

There was a knock at the door around midnight. She'd gotten home early from the Kickstart, relieved the elderly woman from down the hall of their apartment building who often looked after Katie, who was fussy. Teething, she figured. Miranda was cradling her in her arms, walking her around the apartment, trying to settle her down.

'Police,' someone said.

There was hardly anything left of the Toyota, the officer told her. The train hit it at nearly sixty miles per hour, carried it down the track well over a mile. They'd need her to come in and identify this Eldon Swain person, at least those parts of him that were left.

FIFTEEN

'So, what's the plan, Stan?' Angie asked me.

It was hard not to smile. It was perhaps the first time I'd allowed the corners of my mouth to go up since coming home several hours earlier from the *Metropolitan*. Although there had been no 'family meeting' to fill in Angie and her brother Paul on what had happened, it didn't take long for them to put it all together. I'd told Paul a couple of things, Angie had spoken to her mother, then the kids compared notes, went back to me and Sarah individually to try to fill in some of the gaps, and they more or less had it. They'd been so good at information gathering, I couldn't help but wonder whether they didn't have a more promising future in the newspaper business than Sarah or I, certainly the way things were at the moment.

Paul, freed of work obligations by me, had gone off to a friend's house, and Sarah had vanished as well, telling Angie she had errands to run at the mall. I doubted that. She just didn't want to have to keep avoiding me in the house. She needed more space. We hadn't said a word to each other since Sarah blasted me in the middle of the newsroom for everyone to hear. I wished I could have been one of the people in the audience, rather than one of the featured players,

It would have been the greatest bit of office gossip to chew on in years.

Now I was sitting at the kitchen table, a cup of coffee in front of me, staring at the wall.

I had fucked up, and didn't know what to do.

Then Angie came in, sat down across from me with a cup of coffee of her own, and asked her question.

'I don't really have a plan,' I said.

Angie stirred her coffee, took out the spoon, and licked it. She and I had been through a pretty traumatic set of circumstances a little over a year ago, and that shared experience had given us a special kind of bond since. She'd grown up a hell of a lot since then. She was in her second year at Mackenzie University, and taking, among other things, some psychology courses. But it hadn't been her classes that had given her insights into human relationships. She had an instinctive feel about those.

'This is not what it's supposed to be like around here,' Angie said.

'Yeah,' I said.

'Has it ever been this bad between you and Mom?' she asked.

I thought a moment, shook my head. 'No. That thing, a couple of years ago, with the purse?'

Angie nodded. It was not an easily forgettable episode in our lives.

'That was dumb, but your mom forgave me. And I've tried to be a better person since then, not such a know-it-all, not telling everyone how to live their lives. Trying to keep a lid on the anxieties.'

Angie nodded. 'We've noticed. You've been doing not too badly.'

I smiled again. God, she was beautiful, this girl of mine. 'Thanks for noticing. But I let myself get dragged into something where I didn't belong, and it's blown up big-time.'

'Where do you think Trixie is?' Angie asked. 'She's really got a daughter?'

'So she said, just before she took off. I guess, wherever her daughter is, that's where she's going to go.'

Angie knew Trixie. Of course, she'd met her when we used to be neighbors, but Angie had also consulted Trixie, given her area of expertise, for some background on at least one of her psych courses. 'I think she'd be a good mom,' she said.

My eyebrows went up. 'You think?'

'She's a nice person. Like, just because she does what she does doesn't mean she can't be a nice person. I mean, you're the one who's her friend and everything.'

I sighed. 'Look where it's got me.'

She reached out and touched my hand. 'You always get in trouble because you care. You care about us, and you care about your friends. Maybe a bit too much, sometimes.'

I smiled. 'How'd you get to be so smart?'

Angie smiled. 'Mom.'

'I think she thinks I had something going on with Trixie. She left some lipstick when she kissed me, when I was handcuffed to the railing. I wasn't really in a position to resist.'

Angie said, 'I wonder if all the other girls have these kinds of chats with their dads.'

'I don't, you know. Have something going on with Trixie.'

'I know. I know you'd never do that to Mom.' She paused. 'Or to me and Paul.'

I took a sip of cold coffee. 'I don't know what to do now. I'm suspended, Mom's been demoted. The cops, Detective Flint, they're probably wondering whether I really do have anything to do with Martin Benson's death. Trixie's run off with my car.'

'Too bad you weren't able to get hers,' Angie said. 'It's a lot nicer than ours.'

'Yeah, well, the police are probably going over it for hidden bloodstains, hairs, you know the drill, you've seen *CSI*. But Trixie showed up at the house after Benson was killed. I don't think they're going to find anything.'

Angie got up and went looking for cookies. 'I need an Oreo or I'll die,' she said. She found the bag in the pantry and brought it back to the table. 'So who do you think killed that guy? He wrote for the Oakwood paper, right?'

'Yeah. And I don't know. But I'm wondering if it has something to do with a couple of guys I actually ran into just the other day. Trying to sell the cops stun guns. When Trixie saw the story in the paper about them, she freaked out.'

'Why?'

'I don't know. It may be related to something that happened in Canborough a few years ago. Some biker types who got murdered in a stripper bar.'

'You know that school trip I went on, back in high school, to Quebec City?' Angie asked.

'I think so, yeah.'

'One night, we went to this club where they had male strippers. I put a five right into this guy's thong. I never had so much fun in my life.'

I pictured it, then tried not to. 'How many other things have you done that I really don't want to know about?'

Angie appeared thoughtful. 'Seven,' she said. 'No, eight.'

I gave her a look.

Angie said, 'So, this Canborough thing, are you going to check that out?'

I blinked. 'I don't know. I was sort of thinking about it, in the back of my mind.'

'In the back of your mind,' Angie said. She took the lid off an Oreo, scraped off some filling with her teeth. 'Exactly what kind of journalist are you, Dad?'

'Up until today, I was the paper's top linoleum expert,' I said with mock pride. 'Checking out what happened in Canborough might help me figure out where Trixie went.'

'We could get our car back,' Angie said brightly, as though being down a car were the biggest crisis facing our family at the moment.

'That's true,' I said. 'You know,' I added, 'I might have a clue.'

Angie's eyebrows went up. 'I love clues,' she said.

I got up and found my jacket in the front hall closet and dug out the receipts I'd snatched from Trixie's GF300 seconds before Flint had ordered me out of it.

'Where did you get these?' Angie asked, and I told her. She took them from me, went back into the kitchen where we could look at them under better light.

'What are they?' I asked.

Angie glanced at the first one. 'A receipt here, for service, like an oil change or something? It's for a place in Oakwood.'

That didn't sound very helpful.

'And here's one for a dry cleaner, also in Oakwood, another for a coffee at a drive-through, hang on, it's one not far from where we used to live. Hang on, this one looks interesting.'

It was a gas receipt, from a place called Sammi's Gas Station, with an address in a place called Groverton.

'Where the hell is Groverton?' I said.

Angie shrugged and went to the front hall closet where we keep, on the top shelf, highway maps, old phone books, and scarves no one wears anymore. She was back in a few minutes with an old map, torn around the edges, which she opened onto the kitchen table. 'Who folded this up last time?' she asked, dealing with unnaturally folded creases. I found the index and ran my fingers down to the Gs.

'Groverton. L-7.' I found the box where the L and 7 intersected. 'Here it is.'

It was a small town, about a hundred or more miles east of Canborough. Pretty much in the middle of nowhere.

'Hmm,' I said.

'What?' Angie asked.

'Well, I could ask some questions in Canborough on my way to Groverton.'

'That's my dad,' said Angie.

SIXTEEN

I made myself a mental list of things to do.

First, I wanted to know what made Trixie run, what she was mixed up in, who'd killed Martin Benson. I thought maybe, if I could get the answers to some of those questions, it might mitigate the damage caused by my getting mixed up in this whole mess in the first place.

Second, I wanted to get my job back, and get Sarah out of Home! She was about to have her first day with Frieda. I could just imagine Sarah's reaction when Frieda passed over to her what I'd managed to get done so far on the linoleum story.

And finally, I had to repair things between Sarah and me. I thought that if I could accomplish the other things on my list, this last and most important thing on it would fall into place.

A trip to Canborough and Groverton, I hoped, might help me accomplish a few of my goals.

Once Sarah had left for work, I put in a call to a local car rental agency and reserved a sedan. I told them I'd probably need it a couple of days. I just didn't know whether one day out of the city would be enough to do everything I might need to do, so I grabbed an over-night bag from the closet and tossed it onto the bed. I had saved packing until Sarah was gone so I wouldn't have to answer any questions about what I might be up to, assuming, of course, that she would even have asked me. Even though we'd slept in the same bed the night before, and been in the kitchen at the same time grabbing some breakfast, we had not spoken.

I didn't want to give her the wrong idea, seeing me pack a bag. She might think I wasn't coming back. No sense getting her hopes up.

I tossed a couple of pairs of socks and boxers into the case. I must have been in the bathroom, my head full of the sounds of brush scrubbing teeth, when Sarah returned to the house and came upstairs.

She was standing in the bedroom, staring at the open case on the bed, when I came out of the bathroom. She looked at me, bewildered.

'I forgot my watch,' she said.

'You won't need it in the home section,' I said, trying to sound apologetic. 'Deadlines are somewhat ethereal. Although Frieda's fairly rigid about cookie time. You won't want to miss that.'

Her eyes went back to the overnight bag. 'You're going away?'

'Uh,' I said. 'I was just throwing in a few things—'

'Maybe that's a good idea,' Sarah said.

'Huh?'

'I mean, maybe we do need a bit of time. Apart, I mean.'

'You see, I was actually—'

'Where are you going to stay? Are you going to go back up to your father's place? He might be happy to see you. You know, spend some time without all that other stuff hanging over you.'

'Uh, no, I'm not going to see him.'

'I can't imagine Lawrence Jones would let you move in with him,' Sarah said softly. 'Even for the short term.'

'No, I don't imagine he would,' I said, feeling a growing emptiness. My detective friend Lawrence, he liked his world well ordered. I would be a piece of paper not lining up with the edge of his desk.

'Have you told the kids?' Sarah asked.

'The thing is, Sarah,' I said, 'I wasn't actually leaving. I was just figuring to be away overnight, maybe two nights at the most, sorting out some things. But not actually leaving. But now maybe I should get a bigger suitcase, take a few extra things, if that's what you'd like.'

She started to speak, stopped, opened her mouth again, closed it. Finally, 'I just figured, when I saw you packing . . .'

I looked into Sarah's eyes and said, 'I would never leave you.' I paused. 'Unless you didn't want me here.'

Sarah broke eye contact, saw her watch on the bedside table. She went over, picked it up, slipped it over her wrist, concentrating on the task, making more out of it than she needed to. But it only takes so long to put on a watch. Finally she said, 'Where are you going?'

'I'm going to try to figure out what's going on. I'm heading to Canborough, and then on to some place called Groverton.'

'So you're helping Trixie,' she said quietly.

'Maybe,' I said. 'And maybe not. All I want to do now is find out the truth. I've been suspended from work, handcuffed next to a corpse, and implicated in a murder. And' – I shrugged – 'now that I don't have a job to go to, it's important to keep busy.'

She still wouldn't look at me. 'I used to laugh when the suggestion of you having an affair came up. The idea that someone like you, someone as nervous as you, someone whose emotions and anxieties are so close to the surface, could pull it off.' She took a tissue from the box next to her bed and appeared to be dabbing at her eyes. 'Now, I don't know anymore.'

'The lipstick,' I said.

Sarah froze, said nothing.

I couldn't tell her that I'd already explained this to Angie. 'It was when I was handcuffed,' I said. 'Trixie gave me a kiss goodbye, before she ran off, with my car, leaving me there to be found by you. Maybe she thought it was the least she could do for the trouble she'd caused me.'

I knew I wasn't being totally honest here, at least not about how I had perceived Trixie's kiss. It had seemed like more, on her part, than a simple kiss of apology, or goodbye.

And I didn't quite know what to make of that.

'Everything started to go wrong when you decided we should move to Oakwood,' Sarah said. 'You got into that trouble, you met Trixie. If you'd never moved us out there, you never would have met her. And you wouldn't be in this mess you're in now, and I wouldn't be heading in to my first day in the home section, having been humiliated in front of the entire newsroom.'

There was that.

'Yeah,' I said. 'I can see how you might put it together that way. But I need to follow this through now. I can't just sit here.'

She turned around, her eyes red, her make-up smeared. 'I think I liked it better when you were home, writing your books.'

I nodded. 'It's when I'm allowed to go out into the world that I start getting into trouble,' I conceded. I thought maybe she would laugh at that, but there was nothing. I took a breath, and asked, 'Do you want me to pack a bigger bag?'

Sarah bit her lip, looked out the window. She lowered her head, glanced at her watch, and said, 'I'm going to be late for work.' She sniffed. 'One doesn't like to be late the first day of a new job.' She had to move right by me to get out of the room, and as she passed she reached out and touched my arm for just a moment. 'Be careful,' she said.

I listened to her go down the stairs and out the door, then, feeling almost dizzy and with a lump in my throat, dropped onto the edge of the bed. She hadn't told me to pack a bigger bag, but she hadn't told me not to. I had to make this right. I had to climb back out of this hole, to—

The phone rang.

I glanced at the digital readout, didn't recognize the number, and picked up. 'Hello?'

'Mr Walker? Zack Walker?'

I thought I knew the voice, but wasn't sure. 'Yes?'

'I'm sorry for calling you at home, but when I called the *Metropolitan*, they said you were on leave or something. But there was only one Z. Walker in the phone book, so I took a shot.'

'Who's this?'

'Brian Sandler. From the city health department.'

Sandler? I suddenly felt my guard go up. The last time we'd spoken, he'd implied any number of threats. 'What is it?'

'I – I need to talk to you.'

'About what?'

'I think I may have crossed some sort of line when I was talking to you yesterday. I think you might have taken what I said as a threat.'

I wondered what sort of game he was playing here. 'Okay,' I said.

'Look, I think I'm ready to talk. I need to tell someone what's going on.'

'Talk about what? What's going on?'

'I can't talk to you about it on the phone. Could you meet me someplace?'

I shoved a pair of rolled-up socks that I'd tossed onto the bed into my bag. 'I'm heading out of town for a day or two,' I said.

'When are you leaving?'

'Pretty soon.'

'I could meet you in the next hour. You know Bayside Park?'

'Sure,' I said. I hadn't even picked up my rental car yet. I might have to grab a cab if I was going to meet him within the hour.

'I'll be in a blue Pontiac. In the parking lot that faces the lake.'

I was curious, and thought, What the hell. 'Okay. In an hour.'

'Don't bring anyone with you.'

'What is this, Sandler? Are you setting me up for something?'

'God no, just do it, okay?'

I ran my hand across the bedspread, feeling the texture of it on my fingers. 'An hour,' I said, hung up, and instantly wondered whether I had done the right thing.

What if this was some kind of trap? What if Sandler was setting me up for a meeting with Mrs Gorkin and her charming daughters? Maybe they planned to rearrange my face, fit me with concrete overshoes, or even worse, make me eat one of their burgers.

Was it smart to go into something like this alone?

I walked down the hall to my study, where, if I still wrote science fiction novels, I'd be writing them. It would be nice, I thought, to be doing that again. How much more relaxing it would be spending my days imagining encounters with multi-eyed, acid-spewing aliens than dealing with real-life thugs.

I found my address book and opened it to *J*, found the phone number I was looking for, and dialed.

'Jones,' said a voice after the third ring.

'Lawrence,' I said.

'Zack, I'll be damned,' said Lawrence. 'How ya doin'?'

'Well, I'm thinking that I might be in a situation where I'm in over my head.'

'Well,' said Lawrence. 'There's a surprise.'

Of course, Gary denied having anything to do with Eldon's death. Shocked, he was. Simply shocked. But Miranda was pretty good at spotting liars. She'd had one for a father. When Gary said, 'I can't imagine what happened. How could he not see that train coming?', it was just like when her father would say, 'I was just tucking you in, sweetheart, don't make a federal case out of it.'

And there was what the police had told her. That the engineer, up in the cab of the diesel that took Eldon's Toyota for its harrowing trip down the track, said he'd seen a pickup behind the car, that he could have sworn the truck rammed the car, shoved it right onto the tracks just before the impact.

The police already suspected Gary'd had something to do with that other gang member whose Super Bee got pushed into the side of a moving train. So they figured this for a retaliation, a tit-for-tat kind of thing. Give them a taste of their own medicine.

'That must be what happened, Candy,' Gary said, when Miranda told him the theory the cops were working on. 'A revenge thing. Although, still, it might have been an accident. You never know, right? Crazy shit happens sometimes.'

'It's just funny,' Miranda said, trying to keep the sarcasm out of her voice. 'Eldon dying just like that other guy.'

'Yeah, well,' said Gary.

The thing was, if the other gang had killed Eldon, why didn't Gary want to launch some sort of counterattack? Even Payne and the others were puzzling over that one. 'It's time to be reasonable,' Gary said. 'We need to come to some sort of a whatchamacallit, an accommodation.'

Accommodation my ass, *Miranda thought.*

She could have gone to the cops with her suspicions. That detective, Cherry was his name, he'd been around asking questions, but he didn't seem to be getting anywhere. She could talk to him, tell him, Yeah, Gary did that other guy, but he did Eldon too, because he was getting too uppity, too big for his britches. Followed him around until he could do him the same way he did Grant Delmonico.

She could have done that. She could have gone to the cops.

But she decided not to. She decided on another course of action.

The tough part would be pretending to get over it. Pretending to believe Gary's version of events. Pretending to accept Gary's argument that retaliation was not the wisest course of action.

Pretending to go along.

But you did what you had to do.

So she kept on working at the Kickstart. Managing the money. The legit and the not so legit. Moving it here, moving it there.

Moving it to a few new places.

It wasn't even all that difficult. Phony invoices worked best. You drew up a fake bill, you paid it. Except the fake company didn't exactly have a bank account. But you did.

Once she had enough, she'd be gone. Just wouldn't come to work one day. She'd take Katie and off they'd go, with more than enough cash to start new lives, with new names, in a new location.

She was doing it for Katie.

This was no kind of world in which to raise a little girl. In a world full of drugs and strippers and hookers and bikers who shoved people into the front of trains. She was going to get out.

And when she did, she was going to rip off this miserable fucker for everything she could.

Except one night, before she had all that she needed, there was a problem. A situation that made it very difficult to go on pretending.

It was after hours at the Kickstart. Katie was with the sitter. Miranda was counting receipts from the night, doing what she always did. And working some new financial magic, shaving off a bit of money into this account here, that account there. Gary, he couldn't count his own fingers and toes if his life depended on it.

They're all in the upstairs office, Miranda at her computer, the guys sitting around drinking. The girls – not just the strippers and waitresses from downstairs, but the ones giving blowjobs upstairs as well – have all gone home.

Eldridge and Zane, they're drunk. Payne's catching up. Gary's there too, and his dimwitted friend Leo, the one he treats like a little brother. All a bit giddy. Made a lot of money tonight. There's piles of cash on the tables. Some obscure Doobie Brothers song, 'I Cheat the Hangman', playing on the radio.

Payne comes over and grabs her by the arm, pulls her out of the chair, starts dancing with her. She says, 'No thanks, really,' but then he's got her pushed up against the wall, his mouth pressed up against her ear, saying, 'It must be tough, huh, Candy? Eldon gone, no one to meet your needs,' and then everyone's hootin' and hollerin' and turning up the music and then she's on the floor and she can't stop them and they're holding her down and someone says, 'Whoa, remember these? Haven't seen these since you were onstage, what the fuck we got you up here doing the books for?' And they go one after the other, all except Leo, who's off in the corner, sounds like maybe he's whimpering, until finally Gary tells him to go downstairs, have a piece of pie or something. The Doobie Brothers sing, 'The rain that fell upon my stone, Like tears you cry I shared alone.'

Afterwards, they're very quiet. Someone says maybe they should get Candy a cab.

The next day, she doesn't come to work. She hurts.

The day after that, Gary comes by the apartment. She comes to the door holding Katie. He's got a 'Come Back to Work Soon!' card he bought at the drugstore, and there's cash in the envelope. It's $110. This is the part Miranda can't figure out. A hundred, maybe, but what's the extra ten for?

He says the guys are sorry, they got carried away, but they really need her back soon, you know? She's so good and all. But if she wants, take an extra day. He won't dock her pay or anything.

And she goes back.

And works with them.

And pretends to get over it.

Because she's not done yet.

Not by a long shot.

SEVENTEEN

I put my toiletries into my bag, zipped it up, and bounced down the stairs. I had a lot on my agenda. Grab a cab to meet Sandler of the health department, hit the car rental agency, drive to Canborough to see what I could learn there, then head further east to Groverton. I was doing a last-minute check. Cell phone? Check. A map? Check. The photo of Trixie from the *Suburban?* Check. A bit of cash? I checked my wallet. Forty-eight dollars. Check.

I had a go for lift-off.

I slung the strap of the bag over my shoulder, opened the front door to leave, and came face-to-face with Detective Flint.

He had his fist suspended in midair, or mid-knock, and I guess we both surprised each other, taking half a step back.

'Detective Flint,' I said, catching my breath.

He smiled kindly, lifted his fedora a tenth of an inch in greeting, and set it back on his head. I looked over his shoulder, and there, at the curb, was Trixie's GF300. A man got out the driver's side, walked halfway across the yard and tossed the keys to Flint, got into the passenger side of an unmarked car parked in front of it.

'What's going on?' I asked.

'We're done with it,' he said, tipping his head towards Trixie's car. 'Forensics went over it, didn't find a thing. She took your wheels, so go ahead and use hers.' He dangled the keys in front of me and I took them warily.

'Thanks,' I said, pocketing them. 'That's very thoughtful of you.'

'Don't go thinking I made a special trip. I have more questions. First one being, you taking a trip?' His eyes were on my overnight bag.

'Uh, just an overnighter, I suspect,' I said.

'Little vacation?'

'No, it's for an assignment. An out-of-town assignment, a feature I'm doing,' I said.

Flint nodded. 'You mind if I come in?'

'No, of course not,' I said, admitting him to the house and tossing my bag onto the floor as we eased into the small living room at the front of the house. Flint, clearly a man of manners and breeding, took off his hat once inside, and held it in his right hand by the brim.

'What sort of assignment?' he asked.

'Well, actually,' I said, 'I can't really discuss assignments I might be working on for the paper, with the police. I'd have to speak to my editor about that.'

'The reason I'm asking is, it's my understanding that you've been suspended.' He gave me that friendly smile again. I said nothing. 'So I don't understand how you could be going off to do an assignment for the paper if you're not actually working for the paper at the moment.'

I was starting to sweat. Flint didn't even have me under the hot lights in an interrogation room yet. I was here in my own home, and I could feel beads of perspiration on my forehead. I could see how bad this looked. Found with a dead guy one day, discovered hitting the road with bag packed the next.

'I talked to some people where you work – well, where you worked,' Flint said. He tossed his hat onto the couch so that he could reach into his jacket for his notebook. He turned over a couple of pages, squinted to get a better look at his own handwriting. 'You know a woman named Frieda, I think it is?'

'Yes,' I said.

'She runs the housing section at the paper?'

'Home,' I said, without the exclamation mark. Flint would have wondered what was wrong with me had I shouted it at him.

'You got moved there, according to Mr, hang on . . . Mr Magnuson?'

'That's right.'

'Yeah, I had a little chat with him. You got moved out of your feature-writing job because of this difficulty with Mr Benson, the deceased, this business about trying to get him not to write about Ms Snelling.'

'That was his interpretation. I never told him not to write about her.'

'Yeah, well, unfortunately, it's kind of hard to ask him about that at the moment.' I felt a droplet of sweat run down my neck and under my shirt collar. 'So,' Flint continued, 'you went to work for Frieda, and she said things didn't work out very well there.'

'Not really. But I didn't have much of a chance to settle in.'

'She told me you were upset about a lot of things, including your troubles with Mr Benson. She said, and just hang on a second here, I wrote this down. Okay, here it is. She said you referred to him as a "dipshit" reporter. Does that sound right?'

I swallowed. 'It does sound like something I might have said.'

'And that you also said you'd be happy if he got caught in a, hang on, got caught in a "Wal-Mart cave-in." Does that sound like something you said?'

'I was,' I said carefully, 'a bit upset.'

Flint nodded again. 'I guess you were. I mean, who wouldn't be, right? Benson, he complains to his boss, his boss is an old friend of your boss, they get talking, and you get demoted.'

'That's pretty much what happened.' I happened to glance at the clock on the mantel. I had forty minutes to get to my meeting with Sandler. At least now I had transportation.

'I see you looking at the clock there,' Flint said. 'Am I holding you up from something?'

'No, that's fine.'

'So tell me again, where are you off to? It's clearly not an assignment. I guess you sort of lied to me about that, what with you being suspended and all.'

'My wife and I,' I said, 'we're having a bit of a rough time. We need a bit of space.'

Flint frowned. 'That's too bad. My wife and I, we've had our ups and downs too, over the years. Kind of goes with the territory, this kind of job, you know? Long hours, working nights, that kind of thing. But we worked through it.'

'That's nice,' I said.

'So what would make you imagine a Wal-Mart cave-in?'

Flint was giving me a case of mental whiplash. 'I don't know,' I said. 'I just have that kind of mind, I guess.'

'Creative,' Flint said, helping.

'I suppose.'

'Because I remember, you write science fiction books, right?'

'I have. Not lately. My last one was a sequel to *Missionary*, but it didn't get a whole lot of attention. That, and getting back into a mortgage, since we moved back downtown from Oakwood, meant getting a job at the *Metropolitan*.'

'That's a shame, not being able to realize your goals and all.'

Don't let him mess with your head, I told myself. *Just let it go.* 'Sure,' I said.

'I mean, not that you aren't doing okay. A good job with a big paper, until, well, yesterday, when you got suspended. They still paying you while you're suspended?'

'Yes. At least, I think so.'

'You got a union?'

'Yes.'

'You should talk to them.'

'I probably should. There's been so much going on, I haven't really had a moment to think about it.'

'So you really don't think your friend, Ms Snelling, had anything to do with Mr Benson's death?'

It was like watching a one-man ping-pong game. Flint had the ball moving so fast I could barely keep track of it.

'I, I don't think so,' I said. 'I mean, even if Trixie had wanted to kill Benson, the time to do it would have been before his story and the picture of her ran in the paper.'

'What do you suppose he was doing there?'

'I don't know. Maybe he was looking for an even better story. An exclusive on Trixie's basement.'

Flint gave a satisfied nod, like this was his line of thinking too. I tried not to be obvious as I took another look at the clock.

'You sure you don't have to be someplace?' Flint asked.

'No,' I said. 'It's fine.' God, I'd barely glanced at it.

'So, that's quite the basement Ms Snelling has,' Flint said.

'I suppose,' I said. 'I think, if I had that kind of space in my basement, I'd build a model train layout.'

Flint actually chuckled. 'Yeah, I love those. With the flashing signals, the crossings that come down. Did Ms Snelling ever do anything to you in that basement of hers?'

'No. You asked me this before. We're friends, that's all.'

'Some friend. Leaving you handcuffed in the same room with a corpse and all. You got any extra friends like that I could have?'

'I guess she had her reasons.'

'You ever check out all the equipment she has in that basement? Straps and whips and all that stuff?'

'I certainly saw it hanging on the walls, but it's not like I did an inventory.'

'Some men, they get off on being tortured, spanked, that sort of thing.'

I said nothing.

'But you wonder, how far would some guys like for Ms Snelling to go?'

'I don't think anyone would want to have his throat slit, if that's what you're asking.'

'No,' Flint said, his voice drifting off. 'What I was wondering was, would anyone ever want to be electrocuted?'

'Excuse me?'

'You know, shocked. Have a few volts shot through their system.'

I shook my head. 'I can't imagine anyone getting their jollies that way.'

'Well, me neither. But I was wondering whether you ever noticed, did Ms Snelling have a stun gun?'

'What?'

'A stun gun. You know, the kind some police forces have. You shoot a guy, you put fifty thousand volts into him, tends to slow him down a bit.'

'No,' I said. 'I never saw anything like that. What makes you ask?'

'Well, you see,' Flint said, 'we found something interesting on Mr Benson's body. Looked like a couple of bee stings at first. Right on his torso, just to the left of the navel, these two spots, a few inches apart.'

'Maybe he'd been stung.'

Flint shook his head. 'No, no trace of any sort of bee venom in his bloodstream. No, these looked like the marks that are left when someone gets zapped with a stun gun.'

'Really.'

'Yeah. See, what I'm thinking is, maybe Ms Snelling, or maybe somebody else if we accept your version, that she didn't do this, zapped Mr Benson with a stun gun, and while he was incapacitated, strapped him to that big wooden cross, and finally cut his throat open.'

I tried to make some sense of this. 'Don't you think, if Trixie had done this, she wouldn't have had to use a stun gun on him? She could have lured him onto the device, promised him a bit of fun, made a game out of it, but then, once she had him strapped down, killed him. That's if she'd done it. But someone else, someone who wasn't into the whole role-playing thing, they'd have to use a stun gun on him first to get him up there.'

'They?'

'A couple of days ago, these two guys, they did a presentation for the city police, not Oakwood, not your department, but downtown, of this new kind of stun gun. Wanted to get the cops to buy a bunch of them. I did a story on it, for the paper. When Trixie saw the story, saw a picture of these guys, she freaked out. Like they were the very ones she'd never want to see her picture in the paper. And then her picture runs, and now there's a dead guy in her basement, and you say he was shot with a stun gun.'

Flint scratched his forehead. 'That's quite a story. Here's another one. Martin Benson came to Ms Snelling's house, still determined to get the whole story on kinky sex in the suburbs, wants to see her basement, maybe he actually breaks into the house to get a look at it. He's a moralistic son of a bitch, and would never be persuaded to get on that cross for entertainment purposes. Ms Snelling has a stun gun on the premises, uses it on Mr Benson, straps him down and kills him.'

'I don't think so,' I said. I nodded in the direction of Trixie's car. 'I take it you searched that for a stun gun.'

'That we did,' said Flint. 'No such luck.'

Flint flipped his notebook closed and slipped it into his pocket. 'Well, I can see you have places to go, people to see,' he said, picking up his hat and putting it on.

'Sure,' I said.

We both went outside, and I locked the front door behind me.

'You have a nice little time away, and I hope things work out with your wife,' Flint said. 'She seems like a real nice lady. Too bad about her getting busted down a rank or two at work too.'

There seemed nothing he didn't know.

'You got a cell phone number where I can reach you if I need to?' Flint got out his notebook and wrote down the number I gave him.

'You have a nice day now,' Flint said, walking down to the curb and getting into his unmarked car.

EIGHTEEN

I swung Trixie's car into Bayside Park ten minutes later than I'd promised to get there. The heavily treed park was on a high parcel of land overlooking our Great Lake, and when I pulled up alongside a nondescript silver Buick, the view beyond my windshield was blue-gray to the horizon line. There was a light wind, and some chop on the water, and a freighter was moving slowly from west to east, heading back up the seaway.

I didn't see Lawrence, or his car – neither the Jag nor the old clunker he used for surveillance – anyplace. He'd promised to be here, keeping a watch on things, in case anything unexpected happened.

Where the hell was he?

I glanced over at the Buick, and Brian Sandler got out and opened the passenger door of my GF300. I hastily grabbed my overnight bag and wrestled it over the center console and into the back seat.

'You're late,' Sandler said, clearly agitated. 'I thought you'd decided not to come, that something had happened.'

'Sorry,' I said. 'The police dropped by.'

'Jesus!' Sandler said. 'You didn't talk to the police about this, did you? I didn't tell you to go and call them.'

'Calm down,' I said. 'It had nothing to do with this.'

'Oh, okay,' Sandler said. It was enough to know it wasn't about him, and I was just as pleased not to have to explain it to him. 'I don't know about getting the police involved. I figure, if it comes out in the press, all at once like, then maybe I'll be safe. There'll be no point in them going after me then.'

'Mr Sandler, what are you talking about?'

'You weren't followed or anything, were you?'

'For Christ's sake, no! You wanted a meeting. I'm here. And I've got a lot of other places to be today. What do you want to tell me?'

He sat still in the plush leather seat, pulling himself together, staring out at the lake but not really seeing it.

'The city health department,' he said. 'It's all . . . it's all fucked up.'

'Tell me what you're talking about.'

'Payoffs, threats, deals being made to look the other way. You got no idea.' He took a breath. 'I want to state, for the record, here and now, that I have never taken a bribe. Not one penny. Nothing. No free tickets to baseball or hockey games, no free dinners, nothing. But I'm not going to let my family get hurt. No job is worth that. I don't care if they put me in jail. I'm not going to let something happen to my family. I got two kids, Mr Walker. My daughter is five, and my son is thirteen. I'm not going to let anyone hurt them, but I can't go on like this, either.'

'Okay, just calm down. Just tell me what's going on.'

'Are you taping this? Is there a tape recorder in this car?' He looked around the interior. 'Fuck, reporters at the *Metropolitan* must do okay. What's a car like this cost? These are even more than Beemers, aren't they?'

'It's not my car,' I said. 'And no, you're not being taped. But if you're about to tell me something important, I'd like to take some notes. Is that okay with you?'

'Yeah, sure, take some notes. That's okay.'

I reached into the back for the overnight bag. I'd tossed a reporter's notebook in the top before leaving. I grabbed it, folded back the cover, and pulled a fine-point from my jacket pocket.

'Shoot,' I said.

'Not all, but there's a bunch of businesses in the city, restaurants, a lot of these people that run them, they're pretty well connected. Some of them, they've moved here in recent years from Europe, the old Soviet Union and other places, they don't leave all their old ways behind. They don't have a lot of time for rules and regulations, they don't much like inspectors coming in, telling them what to do, insisting they spend money on proper equipment, pest extermination, stuff like that. Their way of dealing with this is, you give somebody some money, they go away.'

'So that's what they're doing? Buying people off?'

'Some. It's cheaper to put a couple hundred bucks into somebody's pocket than spend a thousand upgrading your kitchen. Or get him a hooker for the night. Or put a case of liquor in his trunk.'

'And what about those who won't take a payoff?'

'They say things to you like "We know where you live. We know where your wife shops for groceries. We know the route your kids walk to go to school. Fuck with us," they say, "and we'll fuck with you." '

'What about Mrs Gorkin?' I asked.

'That woman,' he said, 'she scares the shit out of me. Her and those two girls of hers. They're like robots or something. They're not what you'd call very feminine, you know? About as sexy as cement trucks. She sends them out to do something and they do it, no questions asked.'

'Did she threaten you?'

'First time I go into her place, I tell her I see mouse droppings, she's going to have to do something about that, the bathroom's a mess, the grill isn't properly cleaned. I find at least a dozen health violations. I could probably have shut the place down. I'm wondering, why didn't my boss do something about this place? He used to have the same territory as me, then he gets made a supervisor, I inherit the territory.'

'What's his name?' I asked.

'Frank. Frank Ellinger.'

'Okay.' I was scribbling madly.

'So I've got a list for Mrs Gorkin. Tell her she's got to do these things. She's "No, we no do dat." I say, "What?" She says, talk to my boss, he'll explain things to me. But first, she says, her girls will explain it to me first. And the two of them grab hold of me. This is, like, midafternoon, there are no customers. Mrs Gorkin goes and closes the door, puts up a Closed sign, comes back, and the one of her girls, Ludmilla or Gavrilla – who knows, you can't tell them apart – she's got her hand around my mouth, holding one hand behind my back, and her sister, she holds my hand over the deep fryer.'

I stopped writing.

'The oil, I can feel the heat from it, and my hand's still a good six inches away. And then she starts moving my hand closer. She gets hold of my index finger, wraps her hand – her hand's the size of a fucking catcher's mitt – around the rest of my fist.' He demonstrated, holding his right hand so only one finger protruded. 'And she moves my finger toward the hot oil, like she's going to dip it in.'

'God,' I said.

'And she's saying, "In the oil, Ma?" Like, she's taking directions every step of the way. And Momma says, "Maybe just the tip." This bitch, she takes the very tip of my finger and touches it to the oil, and pulls away.' He paused. 'My fucking finger sizzled.'

I wrote down 'finger sizzled'.

'So then she pulls my finger away, but the two of them are still holding me, and Mrs Gorkin, she comes around, stands in front me, must be a good foot shorter than I am, and she wags a finger in my face and says, "Next time, we put your whole arm in. Or we cut off your dick and drop it in and serve it to somebody as a hot dog." She says, "You understand?" And all I can do is nod, her fucking daughter still has her hand over my mouth. And then she says, "After we cook your dick, we go find your wife, we cut off her tits, and we cook them too. And your kids, because some people, they like their meat extra tender." '

He was shaking. He reached into his pocket, pulled out a tissue, and wiped his nose.

I finished writing and looked at him.

'Did you talk to your supervisor?' I said. 'This Frank Ellinger guy?'

'Yeah,' Brian Sandler said, pulling himself together. 'I told him I'd been to see the Gorkins. He says, "Hey, you can cut them some slack. They're just trying to make a go of it here." If I looked after them, they'd look after me. I said to him, "They tried to fry my fucking finger." And you know what he says?'

'What?'

'He says be glad that's all they fried. But the thing is, it's not just the Gorkins. They're connected with some other places, run by their Russian or whatever friends. They do all other kinds of shit on the side. Drugs, I'm pretty sure. It's like a dropoff point or something. A shipment comes in, they leave it with the Gorkins, someone else comes to pick it up. They figure, they have this legit business, the burger joint, makes them look less suspicious, since people are coming in and out all the time anyway.'

'How many others in the department are being threatened or taking bribes?'

'I don't know. I don't want to talk about it with anyone. But this other guy I work with, Harry? He's been buying all this hot-shit electronic stuff the last few months. Gadgets. Going out, partying, new clothes. We don't make that kind of money. He didn't used to have it. Now he does.'

'What about the cops?'

Sandler craned his neck around, checking the parking lot for strange cars. 'I've thought about it. But what if they start checking around, can't prove anything? What's going to happen to me then? The Gorkins figure out it was me, or Frank rats me out to them, what happens? But if there's a story in the paper, if you guys can blow the lid off this all at once, the city, the mayor and council, they'll have to take action. They'll demand an investigation. It'll all be out there, in the public. They won't be able to do anything to me then, or to my family. Right? And then, the cops will have to protect me. Won't they?'

'Probably,' I said.

'Can you do this story?'

'I think so.' I decided not to tell Sandler that I was not, technically, a reporter at the moment.

'What do you mean, you think so?'

'I mean, yes. This can be done. Why are you telling me all this? As opposed to some other reporter.'

'When you called, about your son, and the incident at Burger Crisp, I figured it was only a matter of time before the shit hit the fan. I want to get out in front of this. I don't want to be dragged down by it. I'd rather be the guy who blew the whistle than get caught in this with everybody else.'

I asked him a few more questions. Names and dates, as many specific details as I could pull out of him. Plus where I could reach him.

'You gotta be really careful how you go about asking questions,' he said. 'I don't want anyone knowing where all this came from, not before the story hits the paper.'

'I understand.' I paused. 'Does your wife know what's happening?'

Sandler shook his head. 'I'm too ashamed. Maybe, when it comes out, it'll give me some of my pride back, and then I can tell her.' He looked at his watch. 'I gotta go.'

'Listen,' I said, 'I have a couple of other things I have to deal with first.' I was thinking of my trip to Canborough and beyond. 'But in a day or so, I'll start looking into this.'

Unburdened, he said thank you, asked me for an e-mail address, which he wrote down, then slipped out of my car and back into his Buick. The tires of his car crunched the gravel and he backed out, turned around, and drove out of Bayside Park.

I sat there, a plan taking shape in my mind, a plan that could get me, and Sarah, our rightful jobs back. If I had a story about rampant corruption in the health department, about restaurant owners offering bribes, making death threats, I'd—

The passenger door opened abruptly. Before I could even think, I'd shouted, 'Jesus!'

Lawrence Jones settled in next to me. 'You always that jumpy when a black man gets in your car?' He pulled the door shut, looked at what I was driving. 'Wow. This makes my Jag look like a piece of shit.'

NINETEEN

'Where were you?' I asked.

'What do you mean, where was I?' Lawrence said. 'I was *hiding*. Did you want me to sit on the hood of your car?'

I waved at him dismissively. 'Okay, you're brilliant. But thanks for keeping a watch on things.'

Lawrence Jones shrugged. 'Everything looked pretty harmless. You hardly needed me around. From where I was watching, the guy appeared to be doing a bit of blubbering. They seem a lot less threatening when they're blubbering.'

'He unloaded,' I said. 'Sorry if I dragged you out here for nothing.'

Another shrug. 'Whatever. I only had to cancel some highly lucrative corporate surveillance stuff to do this.'

Lawrence was looking, as usual, trim and fit and immaculately turned out. Even to hide in the bushes and keep a watch over me, he wore perfectly tailored black slacks, leather shoes, and a dark green windbreaker with a Hugo Boss emblem stitched to the collar. This one outfit was worth more than everything in my closet.

I've known Lawrence a couple of years now. I was doing a feature on a day in the life of a private detective, and Lawrence, a former cop who'd gone out on his own, had agreed to let me tag along with him. That encounter turned into much more trouble than either of us ever expected, and nearly left my new friend dead. Lawrence credits me with saving his life. Not because I warded off his attackers. I just showed up in time to get him to the hospital before he lost his last drop of blood.

And more recently, he'd been there for me, and my father, when my dad was having a bit of trouble with his neighbors.

'I'm starting to worry that I'm becoming a nuisance,' I said.

'Becoming?' Lawrence said.

I smiled. 'You got time for a coffee? I'm buying.'

'I'd rather you bought me lunch,' he said. 'You mess up my day and think you can make it all better with a coffee?'

He had to go back and get his car, so we agreed to rendezvous at a nearby diner. He ordered an open-faced roast beef sandwich and mashed potatoes, smothered in gravy. With coffee. I got a BLT with extra mayo.

'So,' Lawrence said, 'you keeping out of trouble?'

How could you not laugh?

I gave him the quickest possible summary. Trixie missing. Body in basement. Me handcuffed next to it. The Flint investigation. Possibly a couple of stun gun-selling bikers on Trixie's tail. It appeared that she had a daughter she'd never told us about. Me suspended from the paper. Sarah demoted. Wasn't sure she still wanted me around the house. Paul fired from his job. Nasty Russian ladies putting people's fingers into deep fryers.

'Other than that,' I said, 'things are pretty good.'

Lawrence's expression never changed the whole time. He kept eating his roast beef and mashed potatoes.

Finally he put down his fork, picked up his napkin, and daintily dabbed at the corners of his mouth.

'Aren't you going to ask how I'm doing?' he asked.

I waited a moment. 'How are things with you?' I asked.

He shrugged. 'Pretty good. Kent and I are still off and on.' Kent, who owned a restaurant in the city, and Lawrence had been seeing each other for a couple of years. 'Work is good. Fairly steady. Like I said, I've got some corporate stuff. They throw money around like nobody else.' He waved the waitress over for a coffee refill.

He sipped some, ran his tongue around the inside of his mouth, and said, 'You are seriously fucked up.'

'Yes.'

Lawrence shook his head back and forth sadly. 'Even by your standards, you are seriously fucked up.'

'Yes,' I said again. 'I can see why you're a topnotch investigator. You size things up right away.'

Lawrence put another forkful of mashed potatoes into his mouth. 'You need any help?'

'I don't want to impose,' I said.

Lawrence grinned. 'Really, if you run into some trouble, give me a shout.' The grin faded. 'I've told you this before, so I won't get all mushy on you. But every day I'm around, since that night, I owe to you. You're annoying, kind of a pain in the ass, but if you need me to cover your back, I'm there.'

I allowed the corner of my mouth to go up a notch. 'You're not going to hug me, are you?' I asked.

Lawrence shoveled in some roast beef.

'Ewww,' he said.

★

After lunch, I got on the road to Canborough. I figured I could be there by midafternoon. I didn't expect to find Trixie there, but I thought I might learn more about what it was that prompted her to disappear.

Canborough first came into view as I came over the hill on Highway 17, a couple of church spires, a water tower poking up through the trees. It was a small city, and there had been attempts of late to revive and trendy up the downtown, which had taken a hit after the local auto parts factory shut down a few years back. But Canborough still had other, lesser, industries to keep it going, plus a college on the north side of town, and there were some year-round tourist dollars it could count on. The river that ran through the center connected with a few nearby lakes that were crowded with cottages and, in the winter, there was skiing.

I'd been up here a few times, not just for that disastrous book signing for one of my SF novels. (When you've had the sort of book signings I've had, you start to feel that the modifier 'disastrous' is implied.) A few years ago, Sarah and I had been invited for a weekend at another couple's cottage, and we'd driven into Canborough to shop and wander around.

I drove straight into the downtown, and decided not to look for a place to stay right away. First of all, I didn't know for sure that I'd learn enough to keep me from continuing on to Groverton, and second, some of the places where I hoped to get information might be closed in another hour or two.

The public library was my first stop.

I'd been able to find a story or two in the *Metropolitan*'s database about the biker massacre, but I figured the local paper would have more about what happened before, and after, that incident.

The library, an old brick building flanked by modern glass additions, sat across from a wooded park. I found a place on a side street to leave my car, walked back to the library, and approached the information desk. A wiry young woman told me the library had the *Canborough Times* on computer going back six years, and if I knew what I was looking for, it could be found pretty quickly.

She set me up at a terminal, showed me how to operate their system, and set me loose. 'If you need anything, just ask,' she said sweetly.

I conducted a number of searches using a variety of keywords, in particular 'Gary Merker' and 'Leonard Edgars'. Also 'Kickstart', the hotel where the three bikers had been shot to death. And 'Slots', the name of the gang Merker and Edgars supposedly belonged to.

And of course, 'Trixie Snelling.'

That last one brought up absolutely nothing.

But the other entries produced a wealth of stories.

Going back six or seven years, there were at least two gangs known to local police. Neither on the scale of Hell's Angels or Satan's Choice or any number of other major biker gangs, although they were believed to have some loose affiliations with the larger organizations. One, which was run by Gary Merker, current stun gun merchandiser, was known as 'the Slots'. The other group went by 'the Comets', which had a very fifties ring to it.

The Slots had maybe half a dozen to a dozen real members, and maybe another dozen hangers-on. Not a lot of people, but enough to bring in drugs from the big city and across the border and market them to the locals. Merker, also known as Pick, and his crew made enough money from illegal activities to acquire a controlling interest in a local bar, Paddy's, which they renamed the Kickstart. They made some changes. The entertainment, which up to then included not much more than darts and a wall-mounted television to watch games, now included strippers. The small stage, which had occasionally featured a local country-and-western or blues singer, now featured a pole. Some of the girls who wrapped themselves around it were not opposed to providing more personal performances in the rooms upstairs.

The Comets had similar business interests, although not an actual establishment like the Kickstart. They owned a large house on the city's outskirts, which they'd fortified with concrete blocks to discourage drive-by shooters. They'd had a few, presumably members of the Slots who didn't approve of attempts by the Comets to muscle in on the drug and prostitution trade. The Comets offered drugs, and had a small stable of hookers they could send to clients' houses, or put into rooms in the city's seedier hotels. But the Slots had a distinct advantage by running the Kickstart. As a semi-respectable business, they were able to attract large numbers of the public and, once they had a pitcher of beer in front of them, spread the word that other services were available, for a price.

Some notable events:

June 18, 2001: One of the Comets, Grant Delmonico, was sitting in his old Dodge Super Bee at a country railroad crossing, the kind where there are only flashing lights, no gates. He was alone, according to police.

Delmonico was on a long list of suspects after a Molotov cocktail was pitched through the window of the Kickstart the previous week, a little message to the Slots to back off on the drug trade, leave some business for them. The fire was contained quickly, and the bar was only out of business for ten days.

The Slots had put out the word that they weren't going to take this shit, even though the police told them they would look into it.

What police figure happened was this: A truck came up behind Delmonico, a four-wheel-drive job, with plenty of traction, and shoved his Dodge right into the side of a fast-moving westbound freight. There were skid marks on the pavement, indicating Delmonico had stomped on the brakes, tried to hold his classic car in place, but the vehicle was no match for the four-by-four. Once his bumper was caught by the fast-rolling trucks of a tanker car, the Dodge was yanked off the road and dragged down the track, twisting and ripping apart along the way.

Delmonico was dead at the scene.

July 23, 2001: Sebastian Loone, loosely associated with the Slots, is found beaten to death out back of a Canborough butcher shop. This is assumed to be payback for the murder of Delmonico.

July 31, 2001: The Slots suffer another loss. This time, it's the gang's reputed second-in-command, Eldon Swain. The irony is, he dies in nearly the same manner as the Comets' Delmonico, except Swain's car doesn't get pushed into the side of the train. It gets shoved into its path. The engineer was able to see the whole thing pretty clearly from the cab of the diesel, even though the incident happened at night. The headlight beam picked up the car, a small Japanese sedan, waiting at the flashing lights. With the engine only a few yards from the crossing, this big pickup appears out of nowhere, rams the sedan from behind, right in front of the locomotive.

Swain was declared dead at the scene, but they had to gather his various parts together before they could get someone to come look at the body for the purposes of identification.

April 9, 2002: The Kickstart, after hours. Someone bursts into the upstairs back room, where the night's receipts are counted, and shoots Eldridge Smith, Payne Fletcher and Zane Heighton. The shooter disappears, with the money. Gary Merker and Leonard Edgars, who were not in the building at the time, return to find the three men dead. Canborough Police steel themselves for an all-out war against the Comets.

It doesn't happen.

The Comets deny any responsibility for the Kickstart massacre. As if they'd own up to it if they'd done it.

Police speculate that the Slots don't respond because there aren't enough of them left to mount a war. Merker lost his number two man a few months earlier. Now he's lost three more. He hasn't got enough soldiers left to go into battle.

But there are other questions, reading between the lines. Why was it that Merker and Edgars weren't there? Merker, at least, was usually there to check the day's tally. Was it possible he'd cut some deal with the Comets, that he'd set up his friends for some sort of reward from the other side?

It was all speculation. No one really knew what happened. And no one was ever charged in the deaths of the three men.

Nothing I read in the *Canborough Times'* files indicated what was unusual about the manner in which the three men were shot.

People stopped frequenting the Kickstart. Who wanted to grab a beer where you stood a chance of getting your brains blown out? The strippers quit, found work elsewhere. Before long, Merker bailed on the Kickstart, and wasn't much heard from again. He left Canborough.

The Comets, it seemed, assumed control of the drug and prostitution trade in the city.

All interesting stuff, but some big questions remained unanswered for me.

Where did Trixie fit into all this? Why didn't her name even come up? What did she know that had her on the run from Gary Merker? What had she seen?

And there was another question I supposed I had to consider.

What had she done?

Gary was impressed with how you never had to say to Candy, 'Get over it.'

He liked that she got over things so quickly. What a trooper.

Her boyfriend Eldon, the father of her kid, gets himself smacked by an oncoming train, she pulls it together. He and all the other guys except Leo, they get a little out of hand one night, treat her, he had to admit, a bit disrespectfully, and she's back to work a couple of days later.

It must have been the get-well-soon card, he thought. Chicks love cards. He was actually going to bring her flowers too, then, on the way over to her apartment, but he forgot and only got the card, and yet, that seemed to do the trick. He tucked that away for future reference. A card, or flowers, but not necessarily both.

A few months had gone by, and Candy — it was the only name he knew her by — was there pretty much every day, lots of nights too, doing her job. What a fucking relief, letting someone else handle the finances. Those rare times when he'd actually go to a bank machine — not very often, considering there was always plenty of cash around the Kickstart — and take out a hundred, he had to count out those five twenties two, maybe three times, to double-check that he was getting what he was supposed to.

But Candy, she paid the bills, took care of all those invoices, was always on top of things. Never even got that moody. He'd never known a broad didn't get moody.

Miranda figured she deserved a goddamn Oscar. Meryl Streep never had to work this hard at playing a role.

Almost every day after she got home from work, she'd get sick to her stomach. It was eating her up, working day in and day out with these people. With these men who'd raped her. This man who'd killed her Eldon. She'd take a shower, like she was washing the stink of them off her every day.

She was giving herself a year.

Eldon had died the last day of July. She thought, Maybe I can hang in until next August. Or until Gary starts getting suspicious. The dummy accounts, the fake invoices, it was all going very well. By the time she was done, he'd be fucking bankrupt and she'd have enough to start over with Katie someplace else. But if he started getting wise, started asking too many questions, the 'Abort! Abort!' warnings would start sounding in her head. *She had to be ready, in case she had to bail early.*

But so far, so good.

When she started going crazy, when she thought she couldn't stand being in the same building with them one more moment, she used thoughts of revenge to calm herself. She imagined Gary's reaction the day she didn't show up for work, went hunting for her, discovered she and Katie were gone. And then when he figured out what had happened, that she'd ripped him off. Big-time.

Oh, to be the fly on the wall.

He'd be too astonished to remember to stick his finger up his nose.

The other guys, they seemed wary of Gary lately. They could never figure out why he didn't avenge the death of Eldon Swain. It had to be the Comets, right? They had to have done it. But Gary, he wasn't ready to go to war. He was cool with it.

186

Didn't seem like Gary.

Even Leo, who didn't think too hard on anything, asked him one time, 'Don't you miss Eldon? I do. He was always nice to me. When he was going out and I asked him to grab me a burger or something, he'd always do it.'

'He thought he knew everything,' Gary said. 'He thought he was the boss around here. Well, he wasn't. I'm the boss around here.'

Leo pondered that. 'If you're the boss, shouldn't you be getting who done that to Eldon?'

Gary said, 'You want some pizza?'

Leo thought that was a great idea.

Miranda had to be strong. She had to hang in. And she had to be careful not to get too greedy. She had to know when to call it quits. Because if she blew this, she'd be ending up plastered to the front of a train herself.

Katie needed her mommy.

TWENTY

One name kept showing up in all the stories I found about the Slots and the Comets: Michael Cherry, a detective with the Canborough police.

I asked the woman at the information desk where the police station was, and it turned out to be only three blocks south. I left my car where it was and hoofed it. There was a cool breeze coming in from the north, and my sports coat wasn't up to the job of keeping me warm. I put my hands in my pockets and hunched my shoulders up, thinking that would help. It did not.

Unlike the library, the police services building lacked any architectural link to the past. It was a wide gray and black building devoid of personality. I went up to the main desk and asked whether Detective Cherry was in, and if so could I speak with him?

I got lucky. The woman on the desk said he was still in the building and would come out to see me in a few minutes. I kicked around the front lobby, half listened as some woman complained at the desk about a barking dog. Two uniformed cops brought in an unruly drunk.

Then a bearded man in tattered jeans, T-shirt and jean jacket approached me, and I wasn't sure whether this was somebody who'd just been released after appearing in a line up, or Cherry.

'Mr Walker?' he said, extending a hand.

'That's right,' I said. 'Detective Cherry?'

'Yeah. Come on in.'

He led me down a couple of hallways, then into a small office. Cherry dropped into a metal and plastic chair behind a cluttered desk. I glanced at some mug shots on the wall as I sat down opposite him.

'So you're with the *Metropolitan*?' he asked.

I nodded. I didn't see the sense in being specific about my current status with the paper.

'You got some ID?' he asked.

I fished out my laminated *Metropolitan* card and tossed it on Cherry's desk. Fortunately, Magnuson had not thought to make me surrender it. If I were a cop, I'd have had to turn in my shield and my piece, but reporters didn't carry around that much paraphernalia. Cherry glanced at it, tossed it back.

'Long way from home,' he said. 'What brings you up here?'

'The Kickstart shootings,' I said.

'Whoa, that goes back,' he said, sitting up in his chair and leaning forwards across his desk. 'Man, that was something, certainly by this town's standards. A triple gang shooting. Watcha looking into that for?'

'It's kind of complicated,' I said. 'But there might be a connection between those shootings and a recent murder in Oakwood. A columnist with that town's paper got himself killed.'

'Interesting. We were never able to close that one. Had our suspicions, of course, but we never nailed anybody for it.'

'Who was your leading suspect?'

'More like suspects. Those clowns that got killed,

they were part of a small-time biker gang called the Slots. They had a running rivalry with the Comets over drugs, hookers, that kind of thing.' I was nodding. 'Maybe you already know some of this,' he said.

'I did a bit of reading at the library before coming over. I found your name in a lot of the stories. That's what led me here. I guess I'm looking for anything that didn't make the papers, recent developments, that kind of thing.'

'Well, no recent developments. It's an open file, like I said. Couple odd things, though. I was expecting some retaliation after it went down. Figured the Comets would lose a couple guys, maybe their place would get firebombed, something. But it actually got quieter afterwards. Whatever it was, whoever it was, it kind of brought some peace to the situation. In fact, it was relatively peaceful even before that. Few months earlier, another guy from the Kickstart was killed, car got shoved in front of a train, but not much fallout from that either. And it's not like crime stopped after that triple shooting. The Comets, they took over from the Slots, they don't have much competition even to this day.'

'So it worked for them, killing those three,' I said. 'They scared this Gary Merker right out of business.'

Cherry looked thoughtful. 'Yeah, ol' Pick got out of Dodge. It seems to have worked out that way. But I was never sure the Comets were responsible. The thing is – we off the record here for a minute?'

'Sure.' I didn't even have a notepad out.

'We got approval for a slew of wiretaps on the Comets. We got hours and hours of their head guy, Bruce Wingstaff – Wingnut to his detractors – and the rest of his crew, chatting away, and there was never a word about the Kickstart thing, other than being somewhat amazed by it.'

'Maybe they knew they were being listened in on.'

'Well, if they did, then why'd they talk about everything else? Dope deals, busting some guy's knees who didn't pay on time, girls they had working for them. All sorts of shit. But nothing about the Kickstart. I mean, they talked about it, but more along the lines of "I wonder who the fuck killed those motherfucking Slots?"'

'So they were as baffled as everybody else?'

'Seemed that way.'

'What about Merker and his friend Leonard Edgars? They weren't there at the time, didn't get shot.'

'Yeah, there's that,' Cherry said. There was something in his tone, a hint of skepticism.

'What? What are you thinking?'

'Again, this is off-the-record speculation, but I always thought it was convenient that Merker wasn't there. Him and Edgars, who he always treated kind of like a brother. The slow-witted one.'

'So what are you saying? That he had someone hit the place after hours, shoot his three former pals, then make off with the receipts for the day?'

Cherry frowned. 'No, not that. He'd hardly need to hire someone for a job like that. I suspect Merker would have all the requisite skills.'

'You think Merker did it? That he killed three members of his own gang?'

Cherry raised his hands in the air in a gesture of frustration. 'Who knows? It's just one of the things I've been kicking around ever since that night. I wouldn't even be thinking along that line, except there was that other incident, the one I mentioned a moment ago, happened the year before.'

I waited.

'His number two guy.'

'Eldon Swain,' I said.

Michael Cherry made his hand into a gun and shot it at me. 'Bingo. Eldon Swain. Got shoved into the path of a train. He's in the car, truck comes up behind, rams him right into the front of it. Messy.'

'There'd been another, similar incident.'

'Yeah. One of the Comets died that way. Everything about it was the same. Except the first time, it's a guy from one gang, second time it's somebody from another.'

'Okay,' I said.

'We thought Pick – that's the name I always think of first for Merker – looked good for the first one. Then another guy dies, same M.O. Makes you wonder.' He shook his head. 'I wonder where that son of a bitch ended up.'

'He's in the stun gun business,' I said. 'With Edgars.'

'No shit?'

'He just tried to get our cops to buy a bunch of them.'

'Whoa, whoa, hold on,' Cherry said, starting to smile. 'Pick is flogging stun guns to cops?'

I nodded.

'Man, that guy has got balls. So, he's working for a stun gun company?'

'I got the impression he was his own boss. They hit police union meetings. Edgars demonstrates for him. Merker shoots him with the gun, gives Edgars fifty thousand volts. Says he's done it a couple dozen times to him so far.'

'Jesus. That guy wasn't working with a full deck of neurons back when I knew him. What must he be like after getting fried with a stun gun a few times?' Cherry kept shaking his head at the audacity of it all. 'You know, there's something about this that rings a bell someplace . . .' He turned to his computer, started tapping away at some keys. 'There was this heist, about six months ago, this place that's making a new line of stun guns, uses like high-intensity vapor or water or something . . .'

'Yeah,' I said. 'That's what he's selling.'

'Okay, here it is. Like, four dozen of these things were ripped off. In Illinois. There's not a lot of these out there yet. New technology. That'd be a great way to unload them, sell them to cops. Nice way to bring a guy down without having to kill him, avoid a massive investigation. Regular crooks, they'd rather just have guns. It's not like they're going to face Internal Affairs.'

'You don't honestly think,' I said, 'that Merker would try to sell hot stun guns to the police, do you?'

Cherry was smiling ear to ear. 'I'm flattered that you think that no cop would ever buy anything stolen.' He kept grinning. 'This is beautiful. This would be *so* Pick. I mean, really, who'd check? Who'd even think that someone would try to sell stolen goods to a bunch of cops? They buy any?'

'I don't think so. I was covering it for the paper, and Merker got kind of skittish when he found out the press was there. Is it ballsy, selling police stolen goods, or just incredibly stupid?'

'With Pick, it would be a bit of both. One time, he calls us, keep in mind now that at the Kickstart, they're dealing drugs, girls giving blowjobs upstairs, and he's on our ass about people parking illegally out front of his place. Wanted to know what the fuck he was paying taxes for.'

'And tell me, why do they call Gary Merker Pick?'

Cherry smiled. 'Obsessive nose picker, with intense concentration. He could be beating a guy to death with one hand and still have a finger from his other mining away. Don't shake his hand, don't borrow his pen. You don't know where they've been.'

I felt queasy.

'I got another question,' I said. 'Part of the story I'm working on involves tracking down a woman who I think may have had something to do with the Slots, or with Merker.'

'You got a name?'

'Trixie Snelling.'

Cherry's eyebrows came together in thought. 'Doesn't ring any kind of bell.'

'She might not have been going by Snelling then,' I said. 'I don't honestly know.'

'Merker had a lot of girls in and out of the Kickstart. Stripping, hooking, waiting tables. Lot of turnover in a place like that. I don't ever remember a Trixie. What do you know about this woman? You got a picture or anything?'

I took the clipping from the *Suburban* out of my pocket, unfolded it, and put it on his desk. 'She might have looked different then, hair color, that kind of thing.'

Cherry studied the shot, shook his head. 'I don't think so. What can you tell me about her?'

'Last few years, she's lived in Oakwood. Trained in accounting, but actually making a living as a dominatrix. A pretty good living, I think.'

Cherry's eyebrows went way up. 'Really? The whole whips and chains thing?'

'Yeah.'

'Still doesn't ring any kind of bell.'

'She might have had a child. Very young at the time. A little girl.'

'I still got noth . . . A little girl, you say?'

I nodded.

'I seem to recall, I think it was Eldon Swain. I think he may have had a kid. I remember, when he died, there was something about him leaving a baby girl behind.'

'He was married?'

'Don't think so, but yeah, I think he might have had a kid. Maybe with one of the dancers there, I don't know.' He thought a moment. 'You know who might be able to tell you?'

I waited.

'Wingstaff.'

'The head of the Comets?' I said. 'The biker?'

'Yeah. I could give him a call. Get the two of you together. He might know something about this Trixie chick. The two gangs actually knew each other pretty well, before the Slots up and faded away. When they weren't trying to kill each other, they were probably drinking, fucking each other's women.'

I glanced at the clock. Nervously, I said, 'It's the dinner hour. We wouldn't want to disturb him during the dinner hour.' I was pretty relaxed talking to cops, but did I really want to talk to a biker boss?

'Nah, he'll be fine. We're on opposite sides, Bruce and I, but we get along. You'll like him.'

I was not so sure.

Cherry was reaching for the phone, but before he could dial I had one more question.

'There was something, in one of the *Metropolitan* stories I think, hinting that there was something unusual about the manner in which those three guys were shot at the Kickstart.'

'Yeah,' Cherry said, holding the phone in midair. 'We didn't release everything to the press.'

'It's been a while,' I said. 'What was it?'

Cherry shook his head. 'I'd like to tell you, but I'm not sure it would be a good idea at this time.'

'Let me ask you this,' I said, thinking back to the question I felt obliged to consider, even though I didn't believe it was possible.

'Shoot,' Cherry said.

'Do you think a woman could have killed those three club members at the Kickstart?'

Cherry considered a moment before answering. 'Maybe.'

TWENTY-ONE

Detective Cherry got hold of Bruce Wingstaff. I heard only half the conversation, which struck me as surprisingly friendly. 'Okay, so we'll catch up with you there,' Cherry said, and rang off. 'He's good for seven. That gives us a bit of time. You got plans for dinner?'

I said no. 'But I don't want to be any trouble. Like, I don't want you to miss dinner with your wife or anything.'

'No wife, no kids,' Cherry said. 'We'll grab something.'

I followed him out of the building the back way. We were almost to his unmarked Ford sedan when Cherry stopped abruptly and said he had to go back inside and tend to one thing he'd forgotten. I waited in the car and he reappeared about ten minutes later. We drove across town to a run-down-looking building that could have been a small motor repair shop, but was actually a restaurant. The clue was the *Good Eats* neon sign hanging over the doorway. Cherry led me inside, and a cloud of cigarette smoke billowed out as he opened the door. A waitress with big hair, lots of lipstick, and, I had to admit, a rather spectacularly engineered figure smiled at Cherry like he was a regular and showed us to a table.

I waved my hand in the air as Cherry got out some cigarettes.

'This town doesn't have antismoking bylaws?' I asked.

Cherry nodded. 'Sure. We just choose not to enforce them. And Rose, who runs this joint, she pretends not to notice.' He tipped his cigarette pack towards me. 'Smoke?'

'No thanks,' I said, 'I'll just breathe the air. How's the food here?'

'Basic. But good.' The big-haired waitress came over and got close enough to the booth so Cherry could give her a friendly squeeze around the middle. He pushed his head into her breasts. 'How's my honey?' he said.

She smiled. 'They ain't a pillow, Mikey,' she said. 'What'll you have?'

Cherry ordered a cheeseburger with onion rings and I said I'd have the same. When the waitress walked away, Cherry lit up, leaned across the table almost conspiratorially, and said, 'So, you're suspended.'

For a second I thought maybe I'd pretend not to be shocked that he knew this, but I didn't have the stuff to pull that off.

'That's right,' I said.

'I made a call when I went back inside. To your paper, to check you out. And they know you there, no question about it. But evidently you were put on a bit of a leave recently. I don't like it, people don't play straight with me.'

I swallowed, took a sip from my glass of water. 'I haven't told you anything that wasn't the truth.'

Cherry put his index finger in the air. 'Ahh, but, you haven't told me everything. That's a little bit like lying.'

'I'm still on the *Metropolitan* payroll. And with any luck, if I can figure out what happened up here, and find out what happened to Trixie Snelling, I think I might be able to end this suspension.'

'If you're straight with me, then I can be straight with you. And if you're not,' he leaned back in the booth, took a long drag on his cigarette and blew out smoke like he was a steam engine, 'I can kick your ass all the way back to the city.'

'Do you think I could get a beer?' I said.

Cherry waved his waitress over. 'Couple of beers here, hon,' he said. She had the bottles on our table in under two minutes.

I told Cherry everything I could think of. Finding Martin Benson's body, Trixie's disappearance, my being left handcuffed in the basement. Flint's investigation. How Trixie's dragging me into this mess might cost me my career with the paper. That once I'd learned all I could in Canborough, I was off to Groverton, based on no more than a gas station receipt I'd taken from Trixie's car.

'If you find her,' Cherry said, 'you might learn something that could help me with my open file on the Kickstart murders.'

'Maybe,' I said.

He took a swig from the long-neck bottle, wiped his mouth with the back of his hand. 'Are you going to dick around with me anymore?'

'No,' I said.

Our cheeseburgers arrived. They were the size of curling stones, without the handles.

'That's good. Because you seem like a nice guy, and I've set up this thing with Bruce, and it would be a shame to cancel.'

'I appreciate it,' I said.

Cherry worked his hands around the cheeseburger. 'If this doesn't make your heart stop, you'll really enjoy it.'

My heart was still beating when we left, but I was pretty sure I'd come down with a touch of lung cancer. My clothes reeked of cigarette smoke. When we came out into the night air, I sucked in as much of it as I could, feeling as though I'd just emerged from a house fire.

'You need to hang out in more dives,' Cherry said. 'I thought newspaper reporters were a bunch of hard-drinking, heavy-smoking types.'

'That's kind of changed over the years,' I said. 'Now we all own minivans and have to leave work early to get our kids to soccer.'

'Funny you should mention that,' Cherry said.

'What?' I said.

'You'll see.'

Cherry turned into an industrial area on the out skirts of Canborough. He slowed as we passed a low-rise concrete-block building with bars on the windows. Surveillance cameras and spotlights were mounted in several spots just under the eaves. Half a dozen motor-cycles, big ones with sweeping handlebars, were parked out front.

'Clubhouse,' Cherry said. 'This is where the Comets hang out, conduct their business. Some of them even sleep here, pretty much live here.'

'Wingstaff?'

'No. He's got a house in town. Doesn't look like a bunker, but it's still got plenty of surveillance equipment around it.'

I felt a sense of unease sweep over me. 'We're going in here?'

'Huh? No. This is just part of the tour. We're meeting Bruce someplace else.'

Cherry turned around in the gravel lot out front of the clubhouse and headed back into the city's older residential district. We were driving through a neighborhood of traditional Victorian-type homes when we came upon a large park illuminated with floodlamps.

We parked, and as we walked towards the park, we could hear the sounds of children's voices, pounding feet, soft chatter. It was a kids' soccer match, boys about ten years old, kicking the ball back and forth, working their way from one end of the field to the other. Standing along the sidelines, and sitting in a set of wooden bleachers, parents watched and cheered.

'What are we doing here?' I asked.

Cherry ignored me, working his way through the parents. He glanced up the bleachers and started climbing them, a row of seats with each step. Sitting at the top, off to one side, was a large man in his forties, not fat but big, dressed in black jeans and a windbreaker. He was clean-shaven, with dark, neat hair and glasses. A bit Clark Kentish. This, I concluded, could not be the head of a biker gang. Maybe this guy was going to tell us where we could find Wingstaff.

'Hey, Bruce,' Cherry said.

Okay, so I was wrong.

Wingstaff kept his eyes on the field. 'Mike, how's it going?'

'Who's winning?'

'Other side. We're getting our ass kicked. Blake got a goal, though.' His eyes caught something, and he was on his feet. 'Hey!' he shouted. 'Come on!' He sat back down. 'It's not hockey, for Christ's sake. You can't check a guy like that.'

'This is the guy I told you about,' Cherry said. Wingstaff sized me up in half a second and returned his eyes to the field.

'Hi,' I said. 'Thanks for seeing me.'

'Yeah,' he said. 'Anything for Mike here.' His voice dripped with sarcasm. 'You're looking for some woman?'

'That's right. I think, although I don't know for sure, that she might have something to do with Gary Merker, maybe from a few years ago. Or Leonard Edgars.'

'This lady you're looking for got a name?'

'Trixie Snelling.'

Wingstaff was on his feet again. He coned his hands around his mouth and shouted: 'Hey, ref! You wanna borrow my glasses?' He sat back down. 'Name don't mean nothing to me.'

'Maybe she wasn't using that name at the time,' Cherry offered.

'Well, if you don't know what name she might have been using, then I don't know how I can help you. Hey, Blake's got the ball. Come on, come on . . . Ah, fuck. He's got to learn how to hang on to it. He's falling all over himself.'

'Show him the picture,' Cherry prompted me.

It was nighttime, but we were under the spotlights. I got out the picture from the *Suburban* and handed it to Bruce Wingstaff. He looked down, squinted, reached into his pocket for a pair of reading glasses and slid them on.

'Nice looking,' he said. 'But I don't know . . .' He glanced up at the field, looked again at the picture. 'You know who it could be?'

I felt my pulse quicken. 'Who?'

'Well, maybe not, the hair color's not right, but it looks a bit like maybe it could be Candace.'

'Candace?' I said.

'Yeah, what was her last name . . . Shit. She got knocked up by Eldon Swain. Remember him?' He was asking Cherry.

'Oh yeah.'

'Car pushed in front of the train, with him in it?'

'I remember.'

'And I would like to state, once again, that we had nothing to do with that,' Wingstaff said. 'Given half a chance, we mighta, but we didn't.'

'Sure, Bruce,' Cherry said. I was having some difficulty getting used to this, a bike gang leader and a cop having a casual chat, talking about old murders like they were reminiscing about somebody they'd known in high school.

Wingstaff was on his feet again. 'Go, Blake! Go! Go!' I turned and looked at the field. A blond-haired boy was moving up the field, then tripped himself up on the ball, without any interference from an opposing player, and landed on his face.

Wingstaff winced, made a face.

'So you think this woman might be Candace,' I said. 'And that she had a child.'

'Little girl, I think,' Wingstaff said.

'Whatever happened to them?'

He looked up at the stars for a moment, as though the answer could be found in them. 'After those three got shot, I don't remember ever seeing her, or her kid, again. Kid couldn't have been more than a year old at the time, anyway. But come to think of it, she did just seem to disappear. But then, so did a lot of the girls who worked at the Kickstart – they'd come and go – 'cept for those that came to work for me.'

'She was a stripper? Or a prostitute?' I asked.

'Uh, I don't think she did much hooking. Started out dancing, I think, but then she started working in the office. Had a head for figures.' Wingstaff cocked his head at a funny angle, half smiled. 'Fuck, now I remember.'

Cherry and I glanced at each other, then studied Wingstaff.

'After that little massacre, Pick arranged a meeting with me. We had to set it up, careful like, because we figured Pick thought we'd put the hit out on his guys. Found some neutral ground, which actually turned out to be a Starbucks on Elmer Street. Anyway, we had this sit-down, and I expressed my condolences, and I figured he'd be accusing me of offing his boys.'

'But he didn't,' Cherry said.

'Naw, which I thought was kind of interesting. Anyway, he as much as said that he was packing it in, taking Edgars with him. Said it wasn't just the others getting offed. He was broke. Couldn't make his bills, no money in the kitty. But he said to me, if I ever saw Candy, I was to let him know. Like, if she came to work for me, or I just saw her around. He said I owed him that, for letting me take over his share of the market. And that if I saw her, he'd see that I got a little reward on top of that.'

'Really,' I said.

'I think he put the word out to the rest of my guys, and others that he knew, like regular customers at the Kickstart. Said no matter where he ended up, they could reach him through his mom, leave a message with her.'

'Where is she?'

'In town here. Getting kind of on, I suspect. Don't see her out and about. Not what you'd call very motherish.'

'So did you ever see her? Candy?'

Wingstaff shook his head. 'Never did. Never really cared. Got my own problems to take care of.'

'Why do you think he was wanting to find her so bad?' I asked.

'I don't know. Didn't ask, wasn't my problem. But you know, you had the sense that maybe she was something of a liability.'

'A liability?' I said.

'Someone who could tell people things,' Wingstaff said. 'Sometimes you don't want people telling other people things.' He gave Cherry a wink. 'Ain't that so, Mike?'

'Certainly is, Bruce,' Cherry said.

A whistle blew. The soccer game was over.

'That's about all the time I have, gents,' Wingstaff said.

'You come out for your boy's games a lot?' I asked.

'Never miss a one,' he said. 'You have to get the kids involved in things, you know, or they've got too much time on their hands, get themselves into trouble.' He nodded and headed down towards the base of the bleachers.

'You think he's ever killed anybody?' I said quietly to Cherry.

'You mean this week?' the detective replied.

We worked our way down to the field, saw young Blake Wingstaff run over to see his father. His face was muddy from when he'd fallen on the ball.

'We got killed,' the boy said, his face awash with shame. His father, the biker boss, smiled and knelt down and gave his son a friendly rub on the head. You could almost feel him aching to hug the boy, but he didn't want to embarrass him in front of his teammates.

'You done good,' he told him. 'I saw that goal you made.'

'I fell down,' Blake said.

'We all fall down,' Wingstaff said. 'Then we get up, and we keep on playing.'

TWENTY-TWO

'I'd like to drop in on Gary Merker's mother,' I told Cherry as we walked back to his pickup.

'She's a treat and a half,' Cherry said. 'You might want to go in and talk to her alone. I don't think she's very fond of me.'

I glanced over at Cherry as he hit his remote key and unlocked his truck. 'And that would be why?'

Cherry opened his door and waited till I had the passenger side open and was getting in before he said, 'This would be, like, ten years ago, I guess. I had to arrest him once, at home. Hauled his ass out of the kitchen just as he was about to sit down to his momma's lasagna. Stolen cars or something. Guy's eating with one hand, picking his nose with the other. Anyway, he kicks up a fuss as I'm taking him through the living room, and I have to shove him up against the wall, and his forehead, it kind of makes a hole.'

'In the drywall?'

'Yeah. Not a huge one, you know, maybe like a good-sized yam. Like that. He was okay, though. Just the wall that looked like shit.'

We drove about ten minutes and Cherry slowed in front of a small, one-story white house, the only one with an empty garbage can out front, like Mrs Merker never got around to bringing it in after trash pickup. The house, which looked to have been built sixty or more years ago, sagged in the middle. The streetlights were bright enough to reveal shingles that had curled, and rot had settled into the boards around the windows.

'There a Mr Merker?' I asked.

'Naw. Run off when Gary was a little guy. Must have known what the little shit would grow up to be, figured get out while the getting was good. No father–son picnics for those two. See if she's patched the wall. As you go in, it would be on the right side.' He smiled, eager to know.

'Sure,' I said.

'I'll park a ways down the street,' Cherry said. 'You have fun now.'

I got out of the car, and had only taken a step when my cell phone rang. I reached for it, flipped it open, and saw my home number displayed.

'Hello?' I said.

'Hi, Dad.' Angie. 'How's it going?'

'Okay,' I said. 'Finding out some things. How's it going there?'

Angie didn't speak for a moment. 'Mom cries.'

I swallowed. 'Does she say anything?'

'Nothing. Not to me or Paul. She goes into the bedroom, figures we can't hear her, but I stood outside the door, and she was crying.'

'Is she there? Can I talk to her?'

'She went out. She said she had to go to the mall or something, but I think she's probably just driving around. Which, actually, sort of sucks, because I wanted the car tonight. I think she's scared, Dad.'

'Scared?'

'Yeah, like, about a whole bunch of things. I think she's worried about you, about what you might be getting mixed up in, and she's scared her job is falling apart, and I think she's scared that you guys are headed for the dumper.'

I felt a lump in my throat. 'I don't want that to happen.'

'Yeah, well, like, neither do I. And I don't think Paul'd be all that crazy about it either.'

'How is Paul?'

'He's okay, I guess. That reminds me, somethin' kind of weird. This woman came to the door, like, she could have been a football player or something. And there's a car in the drive, there's another one exactly like her behind the wheel, and this really ugly woman in the passenger seat.'

Who the hell would that be? Not Mrs Gorkin and her daughters?

'Anyway, the one that came to the door, she asks is Paul there, and I say no, because he wasn't, right? And so she hands me this envelope, has a hundred bucks in it, and she says, "This is for work," well, actually, she says, "Dis iz for verk." She has this kind of accent, you know?'

'Okay.'

'She tells me to give it to Paul, that he should remember they did the right thing. These were the burger ladies, right?'

'Yeah.' I felt cold, standing outside Mrs Merker's house. 'She didn't threaten you or anything, or say anything about Paul?'

'No, nothing like that. Well, except, she said, tell Paul, he was wrong about the freezer. That the meat was okay.'

I breathed some cool night air in through my nose. 'Honey, if she ever shows up again, or there's any trouble, call the police. Or Lawrence. His number's in my book.'

'Okay. When are you coming home?'

'I don't know. I'm going to stay in Canborough overnight, then head on to the Groverton area in the morning. Maybe tomorrow night, I'll be back.'

'Okay. Be careful?'

'I will, honey.' I thought a moment, and said, 'Tell your mother, when she comes home, that I love her.'

'You tell her, Dad,' Angie said. 'Bye.'

I closed the phone, slipped it back into my jacket, and collected my thoughts before completing my journey to Mrs Merker's door.

I knocked three times. Old flyers advertising sales long since past were littered about the shrubs. There was a dim light, probably from a television, visible through the front door blinds.

I heard a bolt slide back, then the door opened six inches. A wizened old woman, slightly hunched over, peered through the opening over her smudged reading glasses. 'Fuck you want?' she asked.

'Mrs Merker?' I said.

'Who the fuck are you?'

'I don't suppose Gary's around, is he?' I was pretty confident that he wasn't, that this was a good way to break the ice with his mother, but suddenly I felt a wave of panic, that maybe he might actually be there. I didn't feel I was quite ready to speak one-to-one with him yet.

'He hasn't fucking lived here in years,' his mother said. 'What you want him for?'

'Well,' I said, realizing that I was making this up as I went along, 'I was hoping to get a message to him.'

'A message? What fucking message?'

'Could I come in just for a moment? I'm very sorry to bother you, to drop by unannounced this way.' Like maybe, if I'd given her a call, she'd have had a chance to put on a pot of tea for me. Maybe make some scones.

She opened the door wider, and I realized I'd have had to give her a lot of notice if she'd wanted to pick up a bit before company arrived. The room could have been a newspaper-recycling depot. Yellowing papers and magazines were piled high on nearly every available surface, even on the plaid couch. There was a spot opened up, at the end, where Mrs Merker must have been sitting to watch the television, which was tuned in to an old episode of *Fear Factor*.

'I love it when they eat fucking bugs!' she cackled.

'Oh yeah,' I said. 'Those are the best.'

She had her back to me and was headed for what I guessed was the kitchen. 'I'll be back in a second. I was just going for a cracker when you knocked.'

'Sure,' I said.

As she disappeared into the kitchen I glanced at the right wall. About halfway along, there was a large, garish painting of a seaside, in a thick gold frame. It was the kind of art you saw sold out of vans at major metropolitan intersections. Tentatively, I took hold of the bottom corner and tipped the painting away from the wall, peered underneath, and saw the hole in the drywall.

'You a friend of Gary?' she said from the kitchen.

'Well, not real close, but, you know,' I said, letting the picture settle back against the wall.

She reappeared with a red box of saltines, her blue-veined hand rooting through the cellophane to get hold of one. She took one out, bit off half of it. 'I like crackers,' she said. She chewed a few times, crumbs spilling out from the corner of her mouth. 'These are pretty fucking stale.' She tossed the other half in, chewed.

'Have you heard from Gary lately?' I asked.

'Oh, talked to him a few days ago,' she said.

'How's he doing? He get back up this way much?'

'Sometimes, yeah, the little fucker. He does a lot of important business, of course. He was in Chicago not long ago, he was telling me.'

'Love Chicago,' I said.

'So what you say your name was?' Mrs Merker asked, squinting in my general direction.

'Zack,' I said. 'He probably never mentioned me.'

She was thinking. 'I think he mighta. You used to hang out at the Kickstart?'

'Yeah,' I said. 'That was probably me.'

'Well, he's not here.'

'What's he up to?'

'Like I say, he's a businessman. Doesn't run that hotel anymore, doesn't hang out with those motorcycle friends of his, 'cept for Leo, that dumb, pitiful son of a bitch.'

'Yeah, Leo,' I said. 'Edgars.'

'I guess Gary missed having a little brother, so he adopted Leo. When they was handing out brains, that boy was out getting a sandwich.'

'Does he keep in touch with the old gang, the customers?'

Mrs Merker reached into the box for another cracker, shrugged. 'Not too much. One called here the other day, though, wanting to pass on a message.'

'Oh yeah? Who was that?'

Mrs Merker was swallowing some cracker and winced. She coughed, tried to clear her throat. 'Fucking dry cracker,' she muttered, and turned to go back into the kitchen. I listened to the familiar *pish!* of a beer can opening. A moment later she was back in the doorway, tipping back a Bud.

'What?' she asked.

'You say someone called a few days ago for Gary?'

She nodded, took another sip. 'Did you want anything?'

I thought she meant a beer, and shook my head no, I was good.

'No, I mean, why'd you come here?'

'Oh,' I said. 'Well, I'd heard, one of the guys was saying, that there was this girl from the Kickstart, that Gary was always wondering what happened to her, and if we ever heard anything, we should give him a shout, or get in touch with you, and you could pass it on.'

'This about that cunt?' Mrs Merker said. 'Candy?'

I tried to keep the surprise off my face. 'Actually, yeah, I think so,' I said.

'That's what that other boy called about,' she said. 'He called about that cunt too.'

'What did he say?' I asked.

'Said to tell Gary he thought he knew where she was.'

'No kidding?' I said. 'Where was that?'

'Shit,' said Mrs Merker. 'I wrote it down somewhere.' She looked about the room. 'I think I wrote it on a piece of newspaper.'

Terrific.

Of course, I had a pretty good hunch what this caller had said. But if the answer was, indeed, Oakwood, it would mean that things were starting to fall together.

Mrs Merker put beer and crackers on top of a newspaper pile and began wandering the living room, peering at the white edges of various newspaper stacks. 'I scribbled it down someplace, so I could tell Gary when he called. He calls me every couple of days. He don't get home much, but he cares about his mother. I hope you call your mother regular.'

I smiled sadly to myself. 'I would if I could,' I said. 'But I'm in touch with my dad more these days.'

Mrs Merker scoffed at that. 'Gary's fucking father, I hope the son of a bitch is dead someplace and has been for a long time. He was a no-good cocksucking bast— Hang on, here it is, I think.' She pushed her glasses higher up on her nose. 'Yeah, this friend phoned and said to tell Gary that cunt was in Oakwood.'

'Oh yeah,' I said.

'I guess he lives down that way, saw her picture in the paper, remembered Gary was looking for her.'

'Well, that's great,' I said. 'Guess I made this trip here for nothing. I was going to pass on the same information.'

'No harm done,' she said, taking a seat on the small clear spot on the couch. She pointed to the television. 'That crickets they're eating?'

I looked. 'Maybe.' She cackled. I asked, 'So what's Gary been looking for Candace for, anyway? He kind of got a thing for her?'

She let out a laugh. 'Ha! I don't think he'll be dipping his dick in that pussy!'

'Then why does he want to find her?'

'Well, if some bitch stole something from you, wouldn't you want it back?' She looked at me like I was some sort of an idiot.

'So that's why he wants to find her?' I said. 'Because she stole something? Not because, I don't know, for revenge?'

'Revenge?' The old woman cocked her head at an odd angle. 'I suppose. If you stole something from me, I guess I'd want revenge. That what you gettin' at?'

'I was just thinking back to that time. When Gary's three friends got shot.'

'Oh, that,' she said, and waved dismissively. 'He got over that. Only real friend Gary's ever had is that retard Leo.' She turned her attention to the TV, where contestants were working up the nerve to swallow tiny wiggling things. 'For fifty thousand dollars, I'd put anything in my mouth,' she said, and laughed.

She barely noticed as I slipped out the front door and walked down the sidewalk to Cherry's truck. I felt, in some small measure, slightly relieved about what I'd learned.

'Well?' Cherry said as I pulled the door shut.

'Someone, some old friend of Merker's, called his mom, told her to tell her son that this woman he'd been looking for, that her picture had turned up in the newspaper in Oakwood. So he knew where she was, where to look for her. And, I'm just guessing here, he ran into Martin Benson by mistake, and ended up killing him, maybe trying to get some info out of him about Trixie, or Candace, or whoever the hell she really is.'

Cherry waved his hand impatiently. 'I don't mean that shit,' he said. 'Is the hole still in the wall?'

I paused. 'Yes,' I said.

Cherry banged his fist on the steering wheel and let out a whoop. 'Fucking awesome,' he said.

TWENTY-THREE

I got myself a cheap room at a Holiday Inn clone, dumped my bag in the room, and wandered down the hall to the vending machine. I bought a Coke, a bag of Doritos, and a Milky Way. In any given week, I might succumb and treat myself to one trashy snack, but splurging on all three at once seemed to be evidence that I was feeling sorry for myself.

I watched the news without taking in what any of the stories were about, then *Letterman* without laughing at any of the jokes, then turned off the light and tried to get to sleep. I tossed and turned and punched the pillow. I don't sleep well when there's not someone in the bed next to me, and at two in the morning I felt overwhelmed with the notion that there might be a lot of nights like this in my future.

I had too much time to think, and worry, about a great many things.

First, Sarah. I could only hope that by finding out the truth behind this mess I'd been dragged into, and by trying to take control of the situation instead of letting it control me, I might somehow redeem myself.

Then there was Trixie. My quest to find out just what kind of trouble she was in, and what had led her to this point, was motivated by more than a desire to help out a friend. I needed to know, for myself, what the hell I'd been dragged into. And if uncovering that truth brought some aggravation and inconvenience to Trixie, well, if it happened, it happened.

And then there was me. Well, I guess it was already about me. About me and Sarah, about me and the kids, about me and Trixie, about me and my job. As I lay there in the hotel bed, staring at the ceiling, turning to the side and watching the luminous numbers of the digital clock work their way to 3:00 a.m., I hoped that maybe these events, and perhaps the story that city health inspector Brian Sandler detailed for me, would help me win my way back into the newsroom, and liberate Sarah from Home!

I couldn't have known then I'd be happy just to come out of all this with my life.

I woke up at eight-thirty. For me, that's sleeping in. I had a quick shower, dressed, and went to the hotel lobby for breakfast. They'd laid on Special K and Frosted Flakes in sealed, single-serving plastic bowls, muffins, doughnuts, Danishes, coffee and tea. It was self-serve and all-you-can-eat, and a family of four was taking full advantage, stuffing cereal and pastries into bags for the road ahead.

Once in the car, I got out my map and double-checked how I was going to reach Groverton. There was a yellow wooden pencil in the tray between the seats, and I used it like a pointer, tracing the route I would take.

It was a long shot, of course. All I had was a gas receipt leading me there. But it was the best, and only real clue I had. Groverton was farther away than I'd first realized – two hours, and still heading in the direction away from home.

I didn't have much of a game plan for when I reached my destination. I figured I could find the gas station where Trixie got her receipt, but beyond that, I couldn't think of much to do but drive around looking for my car, the one Trixie had fled in. Perhaps, once I got there, other opportunities would present themselves.

As I drove, tuning in Trixie's eight-speaker stereo to a jazz station – my friendship with Lawrence Jones had expanded my musical tastes in the last couple of years – that was playing some Stan Getz, Oscar Peterson, and Diana Krall, I tried to sort out the things I had learned in the last day.

Trixie, if she was the person I'd been hearing about named Candace, or Candy, certainly had a colorful background. She'd come to work at the Kickstart, fallen in love with a man named Swain, who ended up plastered onto the front of a locomotive. She'd had a child. She'd disappeared after three members of the Slots motorcycle gang were murdered at the Kickstart. And the surviving gang leader, Gary Merker, trying to earn a bit of cash selling presumably stolen stun guns, had been putting the word out, for years, that if anyone ever saw her, they were to let his mother know, so that she could pass the message on. And shortly after that happened, Martin Benson was found dead in Trixie's basement dungeon, with two telltale marks on his body indicating that he'd been shot with a stun gun before he'd had his throat slit.

And Merker's charming mother had said that the reason her son wanted to find this Candace so badly was because she'd taken something from him. Something that he wanted to take back from her.

I had a hunch that Merker wanted more from Candace than just something she'd stolen from him. He wanted to take from her the memories of what had transpired the night of that massacre, her memories of what she'd witnessed. And I was guessing Merker would have a permanent way of dealing with a witness.

There'd been that little voice in the back of my mind, wondering whether Trixie might have played any role in the deaths of Merker's gang associates, but his mother's responses seemed to suggest otherwise. Gary seemed to have moved on with his life pretty quickly after the tragedy. 'He got over that,' Mrs Merker had said.

The highway to Groverton was two-lane all the way, and between all my ruminating and the music, the trip went quickly. I passed through some gently rolling hills the last twenty miles or so, and the outskirts of Groverton were marked by a lumber store and, across the street, a tractor dealership. There wasn't much to get excited about once I passed the *Welcome to Groverton* sign advertising a population of 4,500 – maybe twice the size of the closest town to my father's fishing camp north, and west, of here. There were enough locals to justify two grocery stores, half a dozen convenience stores, another lumber operation on the other side of town, and a main street with three traffic lights and about ten blocks of businesses.

It didn't take long to find Sammi's Gas Station, a block past the center of town. Eight self-serve pumps, five do-it-yourself car wash bays, and a kiosk just big enough to hold a cashier, a counter and a rack displaying candy bars, chips and pine-scented car deodorizers.

The car needed gas, so I pulled up to the pump and popped the fuel lid by pulling on a lever on the floor by the front seat. There was a label on the lid advising me to use the high-octane stuff, so I hit the button for super unleaded, shoved the pump into the car, and squeezed the handle.

Rather than pay by credit card at the pump, I went into the kiosk when I was done and handed the short, dark-skinned, East Indian-looking man at the computerized cash register my credit card.

'How you doing?' I said.

He nodded as he swiped my card through the reader. 'You want anything else? Some snacks? I have got the chips and candy bar.'

I passed. I'd had my fill of junk at the hotel. 'I wonder if you could help me, though,' I said. 'Do you recognize this car I'm driving?'

The man peered out the window at it. 'That is a nice car,' he said. 'Very expensive, I am betting, yes?'

'It was in here a few days ago, but there would have been someone else driving it. A woman.' I took the *Suburban* clipping from my jacket pocket, unfolded it, and showed it to the man.

The man shrugged. 'We get many people, mostly from around here, but some passing through too, so I don't know. She is very pretty, though. This woman, she is your wife?'

'No, she's not, but yes, she is pretty. Do you recognize her at all?'

He shook his head. 'No. I am so sorry. I do not.'

'Or the car? I bet you don't get that many cars like that one.'

'Oh, it is a nice car,' he said again. 'You don't see

many like that around here. Most people, they drive pickups or four-times-four. That car, it is no good in snow, right?'

'Well, I don't know. I've never driven it in the winter. So did you see the car here last week?'

'What day was it?' I handed him the receipt I'd found in the car. He glanced at it. 'This was Thursday. See?' He pointed to the numbers at the top of the receipt indicating the date. That would have been the day before Martin Benson was killed. It would have meant Trixie had driven up here probably just for the day, maybe driven back the morning of the day Benson had his throat slit.

'Thursday, I do not work, also Wednesday,' the attendant said. 'That is my weekend, but then, on the real weekend, I work both of those days, the Saturday and the Sunday. I am here from eight in the morning until eight at night. It is a long day. At least I do not get robbed, not like my cousin, who runs a gas station in the city. He's a surgeon.'

'Who would have been here on Thursday?'

'Well, Hector, he would have been here. He is here most days of the Monday to Friday. He is over there, in the car wash bays, getting the change out of the machines. He might have noticed something. He is always looking for, you know, what he calls it, the snatch.'

'Yes, well,' I said. 'If he's always looking for that, then yes, he might have noticed this woman.'

The man beamed, glad to be helpful. 'I have to stay here, but you go find him.'

Hector, a tall, fat, bearded man who looked like he'd be more at home on a pirate ship than maintaining a car wash bay, had opened a locked panel on the self-serve car wash controls and was dumping quarters into a plastic pail. Before he noticed I was there, I saw him grab a small handful of quarters and slip them into his pants pocket.

'Excuse me, Hector?'

I nearly gave him a heart attack. He whirled around, saw me, put his hand to his mouth and coughed nervously. 'What?'

'Are you Hector?' I asked.

'Yeah, I guess. Sure. What can I do for you?' He turned so that I couldn't see his pocket bulging with coins.

'The fellow at the cash register said you might be able to help.'

Hector rolled his eyes, as if his fellow employee was always fobbing things off on him. 'Yeah, what is it?'

'I'm trying to find someone who was in here for gas recently.'

'Oh yeah?' Hector, taking a few steps in my direction, had figured by now that maybe I didn't care about his skimming a few quarters off the top. He'd come close enough to the front of the bay to see the pumps, and I pointed to Trixie's car.

'She would have been driving that vehicle,' I said. 'On Thursday. I have a picture.' I handed him the clipping.

Hector held on to the paper as if it allowed him to touch Trixie directly. 'Whoa, no wonder you're looking for her,' he said, leering. Then he wiped the expression from his face and said, 'She's not your wife, is she?'

'No.'

He smiled and relaxed. 'I didn't want you to think I'd be speaking disrespectfully of your lady or something. But since she's not your wife, I gotta tell ya, that's a fine piece of ass.'

There was a bit of a whiff coming off Hector, and I suspected his involvement with members of the opposite sex was limited to discussing them as lecherously as possible, with other men.

'Oh yeah,' I said. 'That's for sure. Nice-looking lady. Why do you think I'm looking for her?'

Hector grinned. 'I hear ya. She was driving that car?'

'That's right.'

'So, like, how come you're driving it now?'

'Long story,' I said, but decided I could give it a smutty twist to keep Hector interested. 'Let's just say she was happy to provide a few services for the chance to borrow it from me for a while.'

Hector snorted. He pointed to a rusty pickup beyond the kiosk. 'I don't suppose she'd like to borrow that for a weekend?' He laughed, then added, 'Fuck, she could keep it!'

Now we were both a couple of dirty guys having a good laugh.

'So, do you remember seeing her?' I asked, trying to keep things on track.

'Sure, I remember. Don't see a lot of girls like that around here, you know? Be hard to forget her. Black leather coat, these black high-heeled boots. Instant boner material, you know what I'm talking about?' He looked at me to see if I really did know what he was talking about. I nodded. 'She pulled in, pumped the gas herself. I'd of been more than happy to do the pumping myself, if you get my drift.' Another grin.

I forced another smile onto my face. 'You talk to her at all, notice anything? She have anyone in the car with her?'

'Didn't see no one. And I didn't talk to her, neither. She just filled up, was all. I like a girl pumps her own gas.'

'How about when she left? Which way did she drive out?' If she'd been heading back to Oakwood at this point, she'd have probably gone left, or west. If she'd turned right, and gone east, it was anybody's guess where she'd gone.

Hector thought back. 'Actually, she just pulled out and parked across the street and I think she went into that store over there.' He pointed to a children's clothing store with a sign over the window that said *Terri's*. First, Sammi's, then Terri's. The town had a y shortage.

'Did you see her leave after that, notice which way she went?'

Hector shrugged. 'It's not like I hung around to see where she'd go. I'm not like some sort of perv or something.'

'No,' I said. 'Who'd ever think such a thing?'

I thanked Hector, moved my car so it wasn't blocking the pumps, and found a parking spot on the main street. I walked back down to Terri's, surveyed the display window featuring clothes and brightly colored, chunky-looking plastic toys for youngsters. A bell tinkled as I opened the door to go inside, and I browsed the tables until a woman in her mid-thirties with reddish-blonde hair approached.

'May I help you?' Her voice was soft, almost whispery.

'Hi,' I said. I'd never done much of the clothes shopping for Sarah and Paul – didn't even do that much for myself, not without a lot of arm twisting. And my kids certainly weren't of an age anymore where anything in this store would fit them. 'Uh, a friend of mine, he and his wife have just had a baby, and I was thinking I should get them a little something.'

'We have infant clothing at the back of the store. Did they have a girl or a boy?'

'Uh, they had . . .' Come on, you dumb bastard. Just pick one. 'A boy.'

She led me to the back of the shop. 'I think this is the place someone recommended to me,' I said. 'I have a friend who shops here for her daughter, I think.'

The woman cocked her head. She smiled playfully. 'You don't sound too sure. Are you not sure whether she has a daughter, or are you not sure whether it's her daughter, or not sure that she shops here?'

'Where little kids are concerned,' I said, 'the only thing I'm really sure about is that I don't want any more. Our kids are pretty grown up now, and while the little years were wonderful, they're the sort of thing you only want to do once, right?'

Nice blathering. Nice, totally idiotic blathering.

'I suppose,' the woman said. 'Who's your friend, who shops here?'

'Ms Snelling,' I said, gambling that if Trixie had been in here, and if she had given her name, it might have been that one.

The woman shook her head. 'Doesn't ring a bell.'

'She was here last Thursday. Probably getting something for her daughter. About five-four, dark hair, very pretty.' I thought of Hector's description of what she'd been wearing that day. 'Would have probably been wearing a long leather coat, these high-heeled boots.' I thought about showing her the picture of Trixie from the newspaper, but that would put a totally different spin on the nature of my questioning.

'Oh yes, I remember her. But I didn't get her name. She always pays cash.'

'Yes, that sounds like her,' I said. 'Likes to keep those credit card charges down. So she comes in regularly?'

The woman was holding up some sort of jumper thing in blue. It didn't look big enough to hold a shih tzu. 'The odd time, but not very often. But I don't think it could be the same person. She doesn't buy for her own daughter. She likes to buy presents for the Bennets' little girl when she's up this way visiting. I think she must be her aunt or something.'

'Oh, that's right,' I said. 'I meant niece. Not daughter.'

The woman gave me a look, like she thought something funny was going on, but I kept smiling and maintained eye contact, and she seemed to let it go.

'She is just the most adorable little girl. I think her aunt spoils her,' the woman said.

I felt a charge going through me. 'The Bennets, they still have that place down the road a ways?'

'Well, if you call Kelton down the road a ways,' she said. 'How about something like this?' She'd matched the jumper to some booties and socks and the whole outfit looked a bit fussy, to tell you the truth.

'I'm not sure,' I said. 'Last time I dropped in on the Bennets, must be six years or so. Don't think I could find their place if my life depended on it.'

'They're still on County Road 9, can't miss them,' she said. 'Hang on, I think I have her on my mailing list. I could check for you if you'd like.'

I felt an adrenaline rush, but stayed calm. 'I don't want to put you to any trouble.'

'Oh, it's no trouble.' She dug out a book from under the register. 'That's right, County Road 9, just north of Kelton. Would you like their phone number?'

I wasn't sure I needed it, but took it just the same. All I wanted to do now was burst out of the store, check my map, and find County Road 9.

'I'll take this,' I said, pointing to the jumper and booties. I figured that to back out on the sale now would start raising suspicions again.

'Would you like it done up in a gift bag?' she asked.

I said that would be fine. I thought it would take forever, her arranging the tissue paper, scoring the string with the blunt edge of some scissors to make it go all curly, helping me pick out a card.

It was all I could do not to run out of the store. But once I was out the door, I made a mad dash to the car.

TWENTY-FOUR

I got out the map. If I'd had the smarts to figure out the GPS system in Trixie's car, I could have looked up Kelton and County Road 9, but finding it on a piece of paper not only seemed simpler, but a hell of a lot faster.

Using Trixie's pencil, I followed the route west out of Groverton, up to Kelton, which was barely big enough to warrant a dot, then found County Road 9 heading due north from it. I turned the key, heard the engine's powerful but understated roar – not the sort of thing I was used to behind the wheel of my hybrid Virtue – and started heading out of town.

It was only slightly after noon, and I could have used some lunch, but I felt that I was so close to finding Trixie, and to learning what was going on, that I didn't want to stop. But as I drove, I found I wasn't thinking of food anyway. I was burdened with doubts that finding Trixie would actually accomplish all of the things I hoped it would.

She'd already run away from me once. And she'd shown herself capable of taking desperate measures to make sure I didn't come after her. But maybe this time, if we could have a conversation in a less unsettling environment – in other words, without a dead man in the room – she'd be more inclined to tell me what was going on.

It took twenty minutes to reach Kelton, and another twelve seconds to drive through it. A general store, a gas station with pumps from the middle of the previous century, maybe a dozen houses. Motorists were supposed to slow to forty miles per hour driving through, but most, like me, held pretty close to sixty and no one seemed to mind.

County Road 9 wound through farm country. Barns, their boards weathered gray, sat back from the highway, beyond two-story homes likely built seventy to a hundred years ago. At the end of every driveway stood a mailbox, and at some, a small building, phone booth-sized, that could have been outhouses if it weren't for large, window-like openings. These, I realized, were for children to stand in, for shelter, while they waited for school buses on wintry mornings.

I slowed for each mailbox, trying to read the name. Some were painted on crudely, others used those metallic-looking peel-and-stick letters you can buy from the hardware store. For a while, I had a pickup behind me, the driver wondering what I was doing, letting my foot off the gas as I approached each farm's driveway. Finally, catching a break in the oncoming traffic, he gunned past me, giving me the finger.

'Whatever,' I said under my breath. I had other problems.

I'd seen boxes labeled 'Fountain' and 'Verczinski' and 'Walton' and 'Scrunch.' That one gave me pause. Scrunch? I tried to imagine going through life with a name like Scrunch. Maybe that was why they lived out in the country. Fewer people to introduce yourself to.

'Hi, we're the Scrunches.'

'We're a bunch of Scrunches.'

'Packing lunches for the Scrunches.'

I was having so much fun entertaining myself that I drove right past the mailbox marked Bennet.

I actually spotted the name, 'Bennet,' in my rearview mirror. There was no name on the approaching side of the mailbox, so when I glanced into my mirror and saw what appeared to be the right letters, if in the wrong order, I hit the brakes.

Once I had the car pulled over to the shoulder, I scoped out the Bennet house. It sat a good hundred yards back from the road, a two-story brick farmhouse with a porch across the front and down one side. The gravel drive led beyond the house to a barn out back. The land that surrounded the structures didn't appear to be used for growing anything other than tall grass, although the lawn out front of the house was green and well tended.

I backed up, turned into the drive, noticed one of those mini-shelters for bused children. Made of chipboard, it looked unfinished, but new, as though waiting for its first winter. As I rolled past it, gravel made crunching noises under the wide tires of the GF300. As I got closer to the house, I noticed the ass end of an old minivan parked out back. I pulled in next to it, got out, and when I happened to glance into the van, noticed a child's booster seat attached to the second row of seats.

I admired the flowers in the garden, which looked as though it had just been weeded, mounted the two steps up to the porch, walked past some white wicker furniture, and knocked on the front screen door. Leaned up against the house, next to the door, were a garden rake and a small shovel, fresh dirt still clinging to it. Inside the house, I heard movement, and then the main door, beyond the screen, opened.

At first I thought Trixie had done something with her hair.

It was blonde now, instead of black, with some streaks of gray in it. She was wearing jeans, with a denim shirt tucked in, the sleeves rolled up. A wisp of hair hung over her forehead and across one eye, and when she used the back of her wrist to move it away, I could see that I had made a mistake.

This was not Trixie. But her face, the shape of her nose, something about the chin, it almost could have been. But this woman was older. Not by much. Three or four years, maybe, but no more. She was lean, and her forearms, where the sleeves had been rolled up, were ropy and muscular.

'Yes?' the woman said.

'Excuse me,' I said. 'I—'

And I realized I had no cover story worked out. Maybe if I just told the truth.

'Are you Mrs Bennet?' I asked, pointing to the mailbox out front.

I guess, what with her name out there by the road and all, she couldn't see much point in denying it. 'Yes,' she said, hesitantly.

'Mrs Bennet, I'm looking for someone,' I said, my voice full of apology. 'I don't know whether I have the right place, but, uh, I'm looking for a woman by the name of Trixie Snelling.'

Mrs Bennet's eyes seemed to widen, then go back to normal, all in a thousandth of a second.

'I'm sorry, there's no one here by that name,' Mrs Bennet said.

'Well, that's possible,' I said. 'I might have the name wrong. I don't even know that that is her name. It might actually be Candace something. You see, I know her as Trixie, we used to be neighbors, she's a friend of mine, and—'

'Mister,' Mrs Bennet said, starting to close the door, 'I don't know what you're talking about. I'm afraid if you have any more questions, you'll have to talk to my husband.'

I nodded agreeably. 'That would be fine. Could I speak to him please?'

'I'm afraid he's not here right now. You'd have to come back another time.'

From somewhere down the highway, the sound of an approaching truck.

'Mrs Bennet, please, I'm sorry, I haven't even told you my name. I'm Zack—'

'I don't care who you are. You'll have to leave and come back another time. I can't help you. There's no one else here, there's no woman by that name, and I don't know who would have told you such a thing.'

The truck noise was growing louder, and I turned away from Mrs Bennet long enough to see what it was. A school bus. A big, yellow, black-striped school bus. It slowed as it approached the end of the Bennets' driveway.

But it was only just after lunch. Too early for children to be coming home from school. No, wait, not for a kindergarten student. A child who went to school just in the morning, half a day, would be coming home right about now.

'You have to leave,' Mrs Bennet said. She had grown increasingly anxious, like she wanted me gone before I had a chance to see who was going to get off the bus.

But the bus was already stopped, its flashing red lights on. The door opened. A small girl, about five years old, dressed in blue jumper and red tights, her head a mess of tiny blonde curls, a pink backpack dragging at her side, hopped down from the bottom step and landed on the gravel. She turned and waved goodbye to the driver, who waited until he was sure the girl was walking toward her home, and not making some impulsive dash across the highway, before he levered the door shut, threw the bus into first, and drove away.

The girl didn't head straight to the house, but dawdled. Something had caught her eye in the tall grass beyond the drive, and she was stepping into it, reaching down for something, missing it, reaching again.

Mrs Bennet, who'd been about to close the door on me a moment earlier, now opened it, pushed open the screen, and stepped out onto the porch. 'Katie!' she called. 'You get here *now*!'

Katie looked up momentarily, then whatever she'd been trying to catch was trying to make a break for it, and she pounced again. 'Gas hopper!' she shouted.

Mrs Bennet was off the porch now, running up the drive. Katie, alarmed to see Mrs Bennet moving toward her so urgently, must have figured she'd done something wrong, because she stopped going after the grasshopper and stood stock still, awaiting whatever it was Mrs Bennet had in store for her.

But it was protection, not punishment, that was on the woman's mind. She scooped Katie up into her arms, turned and ran back towards the house. As she mounted the porch steps, I opened the screen door so she could run straight inside with the child. Although I only had a glimpse of Katie, there was something about her too that was familiar. She certainly looked as though she could be Mrs Bennet's daughter. But then, Mrs Bennet looked a lot like Trixie Snelling.

From inside, I heard Mrs Bennet say, 'There's soup and a sandwich all ready for you in the kitchen. You go in there and you stay there till I come in.'

'What kind of soup is it?' asked Katie.

'Tomato.'

'What kind of samich?'

'Tuna.'

'Is there cut-up celery in it?'

'No, no celery. I made it just the way you like it.'

'Is Mommy here for lunch?'

Now my eyes went wide for a thousandth of a second.

'You just go in there and eat, okay? I'll be in in a minute.'

This time, rather than talking to me through the screen, Mrs Bennet stepped out onto the porch. 'You're going to have to go, mister,' she said. 'I'm afraid you've got the wrong house.'

'I don't think so,' I said. 'That girl, Katie.' I weighed my words carefully. 'Is she Trixie's daughter?'

Mrs Bennet sighed, shook her head in tiny jerks of exasperation. 'I don't know what the hell you're talking about, mister.'

'I need to talk to Trixie,' I said. 'Even if I have her name wrong, I'm sure you know who I mean.'

'I don't. I have no idea.'

'It's urgent. Look, I was there when they found the body in her basement. The police are looking for her.

I've been suspended from work, my wife's ready to leave me, and I think Trixie at least owes me some sort of explanation about what she's dragged me into. What if you just gave her a message?'

'A message.'

'Look, I could write something down, you give it to her.' I reached into my pocket for a small notebook and pen.

That's when I took my eyes off Mrs Bennet.

When I glanced back up, she had the small shovel in her hand, and she was swinging it, like a baseball bat, for the side of my head.

'Hey, wh—' I shouted, putting an arm up to keep the blade from crashing into my skull.

The wooden handle connected with the bone in my forearm, and the pain shot through me like lightning.

'Shit!' I shouted.

But she was coming at me again, taking another swing, and she had this wild, determined look in her eye that told me she meant business. I jumped back and the shovel whipped past me so quickly I could hear its blade cutting through the air.

When I jumped back, I lost my footing, and fell backwards. My head slammed into a post at the end of a porch railing.

That's when the lights went out.

TWENTY-FIVE

The first thing I became aware of was the voices. A conversation between a man and a woman. It had to be a dream, I thought. It was the sort of conversation one might expect to hear in a nightmare.

'What are we going to do with him?' That was the woman.

'I don't know,' the man said. 'But you did the right thing.'

'It was when he looked at Katie. I got so scared.'

There was a damp earthy smell. Could you smell things in a dream? Probably. At the very least, you could imagine you were smelling something in a dream. But it was more than earth or dirt. Was it hay? Had I smelled enough hay in my life to know for sure?

I tried to wake myself up, to blink my eyes open. But the world remained dark; I couldn't get my lids to move. There was something sticky over them.

'I can't believe you dragged him back into the barn yourself,' the man said.

'I guess I was just going on adrenaline,' she said. Okay, I thought. I know that voice. I'd heard it recently. Just before going to sleep.

No. Not sleep. That was the voice I'd heard just before I'd hit my head on the post. Mrs Bennet. That's who it was.

Speaking of which, fucking hell, the headache I had. The pounding was at its worst at the back of my head, but the whole thing hurt like a son of a bitch. I went to put my hands on my head, but found I could not move them. They were restrained somehow behind me. And I was lying down. I moved my head, ever so slightly, and felt my face rub against cold earth and straw.

'I didn't actually drag him the whole way,' Mrs Bennet said. 'I backed the van up to the porch, dumped him in, then I tied him up. Then I drove him into the barn. I had to work fast while Katie ate her lunch.'

That made sense. That explained why there was tape over my eyes, why I couldn't move my arms. I tried moving my legs, but there wasn't much happening down there either. I was bound at the knees and ankles. And, breathing through my nose, it became apparent that there was a piece of tape across my mouth as well.

'Mmmm,' I said.

'At least he's not dead,' Mrs Bennet said.

'Not yet,' said the man.

I swallowed. This was not good. 'Mmmm,' I said again.

'We can't kill him,' Mrs Bennet said.

I waited for the man to say something along the lines of yes, that was true, they couldn't kill me. But instead, he said nothing.

'If he's working for them,' the man said, 'if we let him go, he'll lead them right here.'

'But what if he isn't?'

'You want to take a chance like that? Is that what you want to do?'

I could hear Mrs Bennet's breathing, like maybe she was on the verge of tears. 'I have to go check on Katie. She can't know what's going on in here.'

'Maybe take her into town or something,' the man said. 'I'll take care of things here.'

'What does that mean? Taking care of things?'

'Jesus, Claire, what the fuck do you want me to do?'

'I don't know, okay? I don't know!'

They both took a moment to calm down. 'Where's the car?' the man asked.

'I got the keys out of his jacket, moved it around back of the barn. You can't see it from the road.'

'It's her car, isn't it?' the man said.

'Yes,' Mrs Bennet said. 'But just because it's her car, that doesn't mean anything.'

'Mmmm,' I said, a little louder this time.

'I knew this was going to happen someday,' the man said. 'From the first day, this sort of thing, it was inevitable. Jesus.'

Mrs Bennet, agitated: 'Why don't you go into the house then, tell Katie you're sorry, this whole thing was a big mistake, but we won't be looking after her anymore. Is that what you want?'

'Jesus, Claire, that's not what I'm saying. I don't want to do that.' His voice went quiet. 'I love her. I love her as my own.' He paused. 'All I want to do is make sure she's safe, and whatever that takes, I'm prepared to do it. For Katie, and for you.'

'Including murder?'

Again, the man had nothing to say. I heard shuffling on the straw floor, the man pacing back and forth, trying to decide what to do.

'Mmmm!' I said, stirring about on the barn floor, trying to roll over.

'Shut up!' the man shouted.

238

'We need to ask him some questions,' Claire Bennet said. 'We need to know why he's here. We need to know if he's a threat or not.'

I tried to nod. 'Hmmm mmm!' I said.

'Of course he's a threat,' the man said. 'If he's here, if he's found us, found Katie, then he's a threat. Because if he can find us, anyone can find us.'

Some more pacing, then footsteps right up next to my head. Someone kneeling next to me.

'I'm gonna ask you some questions,' the man said, his breath hot on my face. 'Okay?'

I nodded. I felt fingers on my cheek, working their way under the tape, and then he ripped it off suddenly.

'Owww!'

It took my mind off how much my head hurt. I moved my jaw around, did a bit of moaning. 'My eyes,' I said. 'Can you take the tape off my eyes? Please?'

'Whaddya think?' he asked Claire Bennet.

'He's already seen me,' she said. 'I guess it's not that big a deal.'

He was working his fingers under the strip that went across my eyes when my cell phone went off.

'Shit,' he said. He stopped taking off the tape. 'Who the hell is that?'

'I don't know,' I said.

'Is it the people you're working for?'

'I'm not working for anyone. The phone, it's in my jacket.' I felt his hands reach in across my chest, fumbling about with my inside pocket. The phone's ring got louder as he brought it out.

He said, 'There's a number showing.' He rhymed it off quickly, the phone ringing in his hand. It was the *Metropolitan*. Sarah, most likely.

'It's my paper,' I said.

'Paper?' the man said. 'A fucking newspaper? You're a reporter?'

'Yes, well, not exactly. I'm suspended. Are you going to answer it for me or not? If they can't get me, they'll wonder what's happened to me.'

Well, maybe. With cell phones, you didn't get someone, you blamed it on the network. Your first assumption was not usually that the person you were trying to reach was bound with duct tape, on the floor of a barn, with some guy who was weighing the pros and cons of whether to kill him.

'Okay,' the man said. 'But one word about where you are, you're a dead man, okay?'

I nodded, heard the phone flip open, felt it pressed up against my ear.

'Hello,' I said.

'Zack?' Sarah. Even in my present situation, I was thrilled to hear her voice.

'Hey, honey,' I said.

'You okay? You sound funny.'

'No, I'm fine,' I said, trying to spit a bit of dirt from between my lips. 'It's good to hear from you.'

'I just, I don't know, I thought I should call.'

'Yeah, well, that's good. It was kind of, you know, awkward yesterday morning.' It was only yesterday, wasn't it? When we'd had our chat in the bedroom, when Sarah had thought I was packing up to leave indefinitely? Unless I'd been unconscious for a day or two and didn't know it yet.

'Yeah, well, yeah,' Sarah said.

'How's it going? How are things, you know, at the paper?'

'Having a wonderful time here with Frieda.' Sarah paused. 'This is the most humiliating thing that's ever happened to me. I mean, there's nothing wrong with being a home writer, okay?'

'Sure,' I said. My duct tape blindfold, at least the half that was still stuck to me, was starting to itch.

'But to get busted down from management and end up here, working for Frieda. Honest to God, she should be running a fucking flower shop.'

'Yeah, well,' I said. In addition to massive headache, having my arms tied behind me was making my shoulders sore as hell.

'Where are you?' Sarah asked.

I felt the man's hand on my neck. Clearly, he was able to make out both sides of the conversation. I was going to say, 'I'm kind of tied up right now,' but it seemed like such a cliché, so I said, 'Canborough? You know Canborough?'

'Okay, I know.'

'Just talking to some people, you know.'

'Listen, Zack, I've been thinking,' Sarah said.

'Okay.'

'And, I don't know, I love you, you know.'

'Okay.'

'I want you to know that. That I love you.'

'Okay.'

'But I need something from you. I need you to understand me.'

'Okay.'

'I want you to understand what I need. And I need some stability. I need some calm.'

'Sure,' I said, feeling the man's grip on my throat relax somewhat. 'I could use some of that too.'

'You seem to have this knack lately, it's like, I don't know, you've become this magnet for trouble,' Sarah said.

'Well,' I said, trying to shift my duct-taped legs, 'maybe a little, sure.'

The man whispered, 'Wrap it up.'

'What was that?' Sarah asked.

'Nothing. I was just saying yeah, a little, about the magnet thing. Attracting trouble.'

'You never used to be like this.'

'It is kind of new, I know. I can't explain it. I think maybe I'm hanging out with the wrong kind of people.'

'Fuck you,' the man whispered.

'Is there someone else there?' Sarah asked.

'No, it's a coffee shop. Just some other people.'

'Anyway, Zack, the thing is, I can't go on this way. I can't take the stress. It's not just hard on me, it's hard on the kids. If you were a cop or something, you know, maybe I could understand, try to live with it. But you're not really cop material.'

'No,' I said, twisting a bit more. 'That's true.'

'Look, I have to go. Frieda's looking for a linoleum update. Maybe we can talk again in a day or so. Think about what I'm saying.'

'Sure, honey,' I said.

'Bye.'

'Bye.'

The man flipped the phone shut. 'That was touching,' he said, and then, without warning, ripped the rest of the tape from my eyes, taking half my eyebrows with it.

I screamed, even more than when he'd ripped the tape off my mouth. Then, as light filled my eyes, I blinked to let them adjust.

242

He was a big guy. Work shirt, John Deere hat, jeans, work boots. Gray stubble, needed a shave.

Claire Bennet stood further back, and she looked taller than I remembered her, although that might have had something to do with the fact that my face was pressed against the barn floor. 'Mrs Bennet,' I said, trying to be cordial. 'And you,' I said, my eyes darting toward the man in the tractor hat, 'are Mr Bennet?'

He nodded slowly. 'Why are you here?'

'I'm looking for Trixie,' I said.

'Who are you?'

'My name's Zack Walker. I used to be Trixie's neighbor, we became friends. Just, you know, friends, nothing more than that. Then we moved away from Oakwood, but Trixie and I, we kept in touch.'

Claire Bennet said, softly, 'She's mentioned him, Don.'

Don Bennet said, 'How do we know that's who you really are?'

'Check my wallet, my driver's license. In my back pocket.'

He rolled me over onto my stomach, wriggled my wallet out of my pants. Suddenly, this all felt a little too intimate. I rolled back over and watched as he opened it up, looked at my various cards. He held my license up, compared the image to the person before him.

'That would have been when I still had eyebrows,' I said.

He tucked my license back into the wallet, set it aside. 'So what do you want with her?'

'She dragged me into this mess. Now I want to know what's going on.'

'How did you get here? What led you to this house?'

'Do you think you could untie me first?'

Don shook his head. 'You answer my questions and then we'll see.'

'A gas station receipt in Trixie's car. It led me as far as Groverton. I asked around, in the kids' clothing store—'

Claire Bennet drew in a sharp breath.

'And that led me up here.'

'It sounds legit, Don,' Claire Bennet said.

'I don't know. I don't trust him. I think I may have to try a little harder to get the truth.'

'This is the truth,' I said.

'Honey,' Don said to his wife, 'you go into the house, make sure Katie's okay.'

'What are you going to do?'

'Just go. Mr Walker and I just need a moment here to talk, alone.'

'Look,' I said, 'I'm not lying to you. This is the God's honest truth I'm telling you here.'

'Okay,' Claire said, turning to leave. 'Just do what you have to do.' And then she left.

'Now it's just us,' Don Bennet said. He took one of his meaty hands, made it into a fist, and pounded it into his other hand.

'Jesus, Don, do I look like some kind of thug? Do I look like—' and I searched for the right word, 'some sort of biker?'

His fist, on its way into his palm again, froze in midair. 'Biker? Why do you say biker?'

'Isn't that who Trixie's on the run from? Some ex-bikers? From Canborough? I figure Trixie must have seen something, that she's been on the run ever since.'

'How do you know this shit?' Don's face was a mask of desperation. 'I need some real answers, pal.'

And he brought the fist back, winding up for a punch I'd never forget.

'Don!'

He whirled around.

'Don! Stop!'

I knew the voice instantly, even before I could see her. As she moved into the barn, she appeared first as a head, then a torso, then legs.

'Jesus, Don, what the hell are you doing?' Trixie asked. 'Don't you know who this is?'

'You know this guy?' he asked her.

'Trixie,' I said.

She cracked a smile at me. 'Well,' she said, 'most recently.'

TWENTY-SIX

We were all sitting around the kitchen table.

Claire had put on some coffee and was thawing a Sara Lee cake from the freezer. 'Maybe I could just put that on my head,' I said, rubbing my noggin where it had hit the post.

'How are you feeling?' she asked.

'Better,' I lied. Getting knocked unconscious wasn't like on TV. As a kid, I'd watch private eye Joe Mannix get knocked out every week, wake up a few minutes later and carry on without taking so much as an aspirin. But there was a sizeable bump on the back of my head, and it pulsed with pain.

'Maybe you should go to the hospital,' Claire said. 'There's a small one in Groverton. You could go there. You might have a concussion, you know.'

'No, no,' I said. 'I think I'm okay.' I paused. 'You got any Tylenol?'

'We'll have to watch you tonight,' Trixie said. 'Wake you up every once in a while, make sure you're okay.'

I gave her a tired look.

'You can't drive back today, Zack,' she said. 'It might not be safe, getting hit in the head and all.' She paused. 'You'll have to sleep here tonight.' She tried to say it neutrally, but her words seemed to carry some extra meaning.

'I hope the couch is okay,' Claire said. 'Miranda's in the guest room.'

'What?' I said, wondering if there was still someone here I'd not met yet. 'Who's Miranda?'

'That's me, Zack,' said the woman I knew as Trixie. 'We might be able to get you something more comfortable than the couch.' And I saw that twinkle in her eye, the one I'd seen shortly after I'd first met her, before I knew how she made her living two doors down from our house in Oakwood.

'So, what's your real name?' I asked. 'You're Trixie, but you're also Miranda, but I think you might also be Candace.'

Her eyebrows went up at the mention of the third name. 'You've been asking around,' she said, impressed. 'But my real name, the one I was born with, is Miranda.'

'Miranda,' I said softly. 'What would you like me to call you?'

She pursed her lips thoughtfully. 'Maybe it'll be easier for you to just keep calling me Trixie.'

'Okay,' I said, 'Trixie.'

Don Bennet, his green tractor hat sitting on the table next to his coffee cup, said, 'Listen, I'm sorry about all this.'

'Sure.'

'You threw a real scare into us. We've always been afraid someone might figure out the connection, come looking for . . . Miranda, or Katie.' The little girl was in the next room, watching cartoons. 'And now, knowing there'd been trouble, we were kind of on edge.'

I took a sip of my coffee. It was hot, and I blew on it. Quietly, I said, 'Would you have done it, Don?'

'Hmmm?'

'Would you have killed me?'

He ran his hand over his mouth, and I could hear his rough palms going across his whiskers like sandpaper. 'Yeah,' he said. 'If I had to do it to protect Katie, yeah, I'd have done it.'

'You ever killed someone before?' I asked.

Don Bennet shook his head very slowly. 'Shit, no.' The question surprised him. 'I'm a machinist. Worked on the Ford line for a while, building vans. Now I work in Groverton, fix tractors.' He took a sip of his coffee. 'I would hope I'd never have to do anything like that. But a man does what he has to do to protect his family.'

Trixie wanted to know how I'd found her. The gas station receipt, I said. From the center console of her GF300.

'Shit, that was pretty careless, wasn't it?' she said, then, worried that Katie might have heard her obscenity, glanced over her shoulder into the living room, where the little girl was flipping the channels. I heard Bart Simpson crack wise.

'Put it back on six!' Claire shouted.

'It's *The Simpins,*' Katie said.

'Your show's on six!' She shook her head. 'She's not watching *The Simpsons* yet.'

Trixie, ignoring the exchange, said, 'I was afraid I'd left some clue on the GPS thing. I've programmed the route to get up here before, but I always delete it from the trip record, to be safe.'

'I haven't even used that thing,' I said. 'I haven't got a clue how it works.'

'Actually, I'm kind of surprised the cops let you take the car.'

'They didn't, at first,' I said. 'But once the forensics people were done with it, they gave it to me.'

Claire was serving the chocolate cake. It was still pretty frozen, and I had to force my fork in, but it was still good. I'd had no lunch, and despite the headache, was ready to eat.

'So,' I said with some formality, looking at Trixie, 'maybe you'd like to tell me what's going on. I mean, I've come all this way and all.'

She smiled at me, reached over and touched my hand. 'Claire's my sister,' she said. Claire, who'd gotten up to put some dishes in the sink, looked at Trixie over her shoulder. 'And Don here is my brother-in-law. And' – she nodded toward the living room – 'you've met Katie. My little girl.'

'You told me, a long time ago,' I said, 'that you didn't have any children.'

'I remember,' she said. 'I guess, first of all, I didn't want you to know. I didn't want anyone to know. I wanted to protect her. And also, a large part of me doesn't feel I deserve to be called a mother.'

Claire, sitting back down, said, 'Miranda.'

'It's true,' Trixie said. 'If I were a good mother, a responsible mother, I wouldn't have had to ask my sister, and her husband here, to raise her.' She gave Don a warm smile and he gave a tired shrug.

'Why are Claire and Don raising Katie?' I asked. 'It's not just because of, you know, your choice of occupation.'

'No,' Trixie said. 'That's not it.'

Everyone was suddenly very quiet. No one stirred coffee or cut cake. The only sound came from the TV in the other room.

'I could never guarantee that Katie would be safe, living with me,' Trixie said. 'I've spent the last four years looking over my shoulder. The men, that man, coming after me, he wouldn't hesitate to hurt Katie to get at me.'

'Are we talking about Gary Merker?' I asked.

'He murdered Katie's father,' she said. 'And he'd like nothing more than to find me, kill me too. And Katie.'

'Why?'

Trixie opened her mouth to speak, but no words came out right away.

'Is it because of that massacre at the Kickstart?' I asked. 'I've talked to the police in Canborough. I know about that night, when the three bikers were shot and killed. And how Merker, and his friend Leo Edgars, somehow managed not to get killed, saying they weren't there at the time. How, after that, Merker bailed on his share of the drugs and prostitution, how he let the Comets run things, take over his share of the market. What happened, Trixie? Did Merker cut some sort of deal with the competition? Wipe out his buddies? Was that easier than trying to get them in on the deal, too? Did you see something? Are you a witness?'

Trixie listened in quiet amazement. She was taken aback at how much I knew, I could tell that by the look on her face.

'Is that why Merker's after you? Because of what you know? And something you took from him?'

Trixie got up, walked over to the row of hangers by the back door, fished something out of a jacket, and came back to the table. It was a piece of paper, folded over. She unfolded it.

'This was the note that was left for me, in the basement, when we found Martin Benson.'

I remembered her finding it, how she wouldn't let me see it.

'It's not all as simple as it seems,' she said, pushing the note across the table to me.

It read:

Dearest Candy or should I say Trixie?

So sorry we missed you bitch. Ran into Mr Benson instead, looking threw your house. He didn't know where you are. He'd of told us if he'd know. Leo's all freaked, and hungry, so we have to go. But we know where you live, right? We'll be coming hack. When we do you better have what you took from me or we'll do you to bitch. I want all of it plus interest. Hows your little mini bitch? I bet shes a cutie. You'll here from us soon.

It wasn't signed, but given that its author had mentioned 'Leo' in the letter, it might as well have been. And just because someone wasn't a master criminal didn't mean he wasn't dangerous.

Reading from the letter, I said, '"I want all of it plus interest."' I looked at Trixie. 'What's that all about?'

She took a long breath. 'I ripped him off,' she said quietly. 'To the tune of about half a million bucks.'

'Are you kidding me?' I said. 'You took five hundred thousand dollars off this guy?'

'Not all at once. A little bit at a time, so he wouldn't notice. It was my going-away money.'

'Is that the only reason he's after you?' I asked, 'Just for the money? It doesn't have anything to do with those three bikers getting shot?'

The Bennets exchanged glances.

'Oh, I think he'd like to talk to me about that too,' Trixie said.

TWENTY-SEVEN

'Sometimes,' Claire said, 'I blame myself.'

'Oh, stop,' said Trixie. 'This has nothing to do with you.'

Claire shook her head, dismissing her sister. 'You taking off with five hundred thousand dollars? Okay, I'm not saying I specifically blame myself for that. But your life. How it's turned out for you. I blame myself for that.'

'Claire, we've been over this before,' Trixie said. Claire sniffed and looked away, and I thought maybe she was going to cry. 'Aww, come on.'

'Don't beat yourself up,' Don told his wife. 'You did what you had to do. You had to protect yourself. You had to get out of that situation.'

'What are you talking about?' I asked. Looking across the table at Claire, I said, 'What do you mean you blame yourself?'

Claire sniffed again, took a deep breath. 'Miranda's my baby sister,' she said, and smiled. 'When you're the big sister, you're supposed to be there, you're supposed to be looking out for the younger one. But I left. Our father was a – he was a monster. And our mother was a drunk. He beat her, he took the belt to us, and . . . that wasn't all.'

'Claire,' Trixie said, reaching across the table to touch her sister's hand.

'When I was eighteen, I got away. I left. I couldn't take any more,' she looked down at the table, took a moment, and raised her head, 'of the night visits. I wasn't going to let him touch me again. I didn't have any money, I didn't have anything, but I knew I had to get away. I figured I'd either kill him or I'd kill myself if I didn't leave. I couldn't count on my mother to protect me. She had her bottle to protect her, and who could blame her. It was the only way she knew how to deal with the pain. The only one who could help me was me. So one night, I packed up what I had, which wasn't much, and at four in the morning, I slipped away and never went back.' She looked at her husband and reached over for his hand. 'Don took me away.'

But then her eyes shifted to Trixie. Her face started cracking. 'And I left without my sister.'

Don slipped his arm around her. 'Come on, honey.'

'If I had taken you with me,' she wept, holding Trixie's hand, Miranda's hand, 'maybe your life, maybe things could have been better for you.'

'I got out too,' Trixie said.

'But not right away. You were only fifteen. You had to live with . . . you had to live with that for almost two more years.'

Claire Bennet grabbed a couple tissues, dabbed at her eyes. 'Every night I thought about you, cried myself to sleep worrying about you, praying that you'd leave too.'

'I did, Claire.'

'But you went from one bad environment to another. Bikers, strip clubs, drugs.'

'As bad as it was, it was better than what I left behind,' Trixie said, although she didn't say it with much conviction. 'I didn't exactly have what you might call a high opinion of myself. I didn't believe I deserved anything good. I felt worthless.' She was holding back tears of her own. 'But something changed when I had Katie.'

'What changed?' I asked.

'I'd seen how Claire had managed to survive, to pull her life together,' Trixie said. 'She met Don, this wonderful, wonderful man.' He couldn't keep himself from blushing. 'They got an apartment, they got a house, and finally they got this house, they have a life. A normal, decent, life. A safe life. And I thought, that's what I want for Katie. I didn't want her to have a life like mine. She was barely a year old when her father died, was murdered, by a man he thought was his friend. These were the people I was associating with, these were the people I was working with day in and day out. And this was the world I was going to bring my daughter up in?

'And so I began to plan my way out. When I started working at the Kickstart, I was dancing. Shit, stripping. That's what I was doing. But I've always had a head for numbers, and gradually I worked my way off the stage and into the room upstairs, showed them I could do a lot more than shake my titties.'

Claire glanced in the direction of the living room, assured herself that Katie was occupied with the television.

Trixie continued, 'Wasn't long before they valued me more for what I could do with their books than what I could do onstage.'

She told me a tale of fraud, setting up dummy accounts, faking invoices, skimming from here and there, covering her tracks, trying to gather together enough money to make a life for herself and Katie.

Claire said, 'You haven't told them what else they did.'

'Claire,' Trixie said, caution in her voice. 'Everything in time.'

'What?' I asked.

'Later,' Trixie said.

'Then, when the thing happened, when the others got killed, I had to get away right away. That night, I disappeared, with Katie.'

'And ended up on our doorstep,' Don said. There was no resentment in his voice, no sense that Trixie was a burden to them.

'She was in trouble,' Claire said. 'It was finally my chance to make things right, to help her out.'

'I asked them to take Katie,' Trixie said, and now it was her turn to tear up. 'I knew that Gary – Pick, we used to call him.'

'I heard,' I said, pointing my index finger towards my nose.

Trixie shook her head at the memory of his personal habits. 'Anyway, I knew Gary would figure out what happened to his money, that he'd be looking for me, that he'd put the word out, that he'd have everyone keeping an eye out for me. I knew Katie'd never be safe with me. And so Claire here, and Don, took her in.'

'Wouldn't Merker have been able to find her here?'

'He never knew me by my real name, Miranda. Miranda Chicoine. When I got hired at the Kickstart, I told them my name was Candace. I don't know, I guess when I applied for a job as a stripper, I didn't want it to be Miranda who was doing it. So while

I was there, I was Candace. When I left, I became someone else. I've always been hiding out from the place I'd last run from. My father wasn't going to find me when I was Candace, like he'd even be looking. And when I didn't want Gary Merker to find me, I became Trixie. But inside, I've always been Miranda.'

'I abandoned Miranda years ago,' Claire said. 'When she turned up with Katie, I couldn't say no. And Don didn't say no, either.'

He rubbed his unshaven face again, shrugged. Don was probably in his early thirties, but he seemed older, and wiser than his years would suggest.

'And that's why I couldn't have my picture in the paper,' Trixie said. 'Worst fears realized and all that.'

'I saw Merker's mother, in Canborough,' I said.

'Isn't she a treat?' Trixie said.

'She said one of Gary's old friends had called him, said he'd seen the picture in the Oakwood paper. She passed the message on.'

'A real darling.'

'About that night,' I said. 'When the three bikers were shot. Did you see Gary do it?'

Trixie hesitated, shook her head. 'No.'

'But he thinks you did? You said he'd be wanting to talk to you about that.'

Trixie was about to say something when Katie ran in, her curly-haired head not reaching the top of the kitchen table. 'I'm hungry,' she said. She sidled up to Trixie and pressed her head into her side.

'It is getting to be dinnertime,' Claire said.

'Are you going to live here now?' Katie asked Trixie.

'Well, sweetheart, I'll stay here as long as I can, but you know I can never stay for a long, long time.'

Katie gave Trixie a squeeze, and then said to me, 'Do you have two moms?'

'No,' I said.

'I do,' Katie said, beaming.

'You're very lucky. I just had the one.'

'Does she come and visit you all the time?'

'Not anymore,' I said.

'Is she dead?' Katie's eyes danced.

'Yes,' I said.

'You must be sad,' Katie said. 'I don't want any of my moms to die.'

No one could think of anything to say to that.

'Are we going to have hamburgers?' Katie asked.

'Chicken,' Claire said.

'Is it with the icky sauce?' Katie asked.

'No. It's the sauce you like.'

'Okay,' Katie said, and ran back into the living room.

I looked at Trixie, and I guess she could sense a question. She said, 'We've told her the truth, at least some of it. That I'm her mother, but I'm the mommy who can only come to visit once in a while. But Claire, even though she's her aunt, is really more like her every day mother, so she calls her that.'

'Okay,' I said. My next question for Trixie I blurted out before I considered its implications: 'If your problems with Merker disappeared, would *you* become her every day mommy?'

Claire's head went up, and I saw something in her face at that moment. Fear, maybe. Fear of giving up a child she'd come to love as if she were her very own, in every way.

'Well,' said Trixie, 'I guess we'll cross that bridge when we come to it. I think, the way my life seems to be going lately, one threat just gets replaced by another. The thing is, I could never be any better a mother to her than my sister has been.'

And some of the fear bled away from Claire's face. Maybe this was best for her, that her sister have a life of uncertainty, so that she could keep raising Katie in relative normalcy.

Trixie tapped my arm. 'Let's you and me take a walk. Claire, you okay for dinner, if I take a walk with Zack?'

'Sure, go ahead. I'll call you when it's ready.'

Trixie motioned for me to follow her out the front door, onto the porch. We leaned against the posts that straddled the steps. I chose the one I'd not whacked my head against. We crossed our arms and looked at each other.

'I'm glad you found me,' Trixie said.

'I'm a regular Sherlock,' I said.

'Didn't even need Lawrence's help,' she said. 'You're good.'

'I hate to call him for everything.'

'Come on.' We went down the steps, walked around the house and towards the barn. As we passed it, I saw my car, the Virtue, parked around back, where it couldn't be seen from the highway.

'That car of yours,' Trixie said, 'has been nothing but a pain in the ass.'

'I'm sorry. I never would have let you steal it had I known. Yours, by the way, has been trouble-free, despite your bundle of recall notices.'

Trixie made a face that said *Go figure*. She pointed to mine and said, 'Sometimes you try to start it, it won't go.'

'It hasn't been doing that for a long time. I thought it was all fixed. I'll have to get it looked at.'

'Good on gas, though,' she said.

Two dirt ruts with a strip of grass down the middle carried on beyond the barn and into the field. I took the left rut, Trixie the right.

'How's Sarah?' she asked.

I grimaced. 'Things could be better.'

'How much of it's my fault?'

I appeared to be doing calculations in my head. 'I was going to say about seventy-five per cent, but that's not fair. The fault is all mine. I have to accept responsibility for the decisions I've made, including those to help you.'

'But those are the ones that have landed you in the doghouse.'

I smiled. 'Pretty much.'

'I've told you more than once that Sarah's lucky to have you, even though, at times, I'd have to concede, you are a bit of an asshole.'

'Yeah, well, all the polling we've done would seem to indicate that.'

We walked a bit further, and I stopped and looked back at the house in the distance, so tranquil.

Reading my mind, Trixie said, 'I wish I could stay here forever.'

I looked up at the sky, and a large bird caught my eye. 'Look at the wingspan on that one,' I said, pointing. 'That's a huge bird.'

'What is it?'

'I think it's a hawk,' I said.

'Looking for field mice, anything else it can find,' Trixie said.

We stood out there a few more moments, not saying anything to each other. Finally, I said, 'You have to come back, you know.'

'You think?' Her response was laced with sarcasm.

'The police, I'm not sure they're convinced you killed Martin Benson. They told me he'd probably been zapped by some sort of stun gun before his neck was slit. We know it was Merker, and we know he's got stun guns. He's been trying to sell them to the cops.'

'Yeah.'

'You've got reasons for your actions. I'm sure, you get a good lawyer, you can work things out.'

'I've got one,' Trixie said. 'Guy named Niles Wagland. He's pretty good.'

'Okay,' I said. 'I mean, look at your situation. You were scared for your daughter's life. Running away, making sure she was safe, it's not totally unreasonable. And there's got to be plenty of evidence against Merker. The note he wrote, for one thing. They'll test it for prints, do handwriting analysis, who knows, but they'll be able to figure out it was him. And once they've got him in custody, they'll reopen those murders in Canborough. The guy'll spend the rest of his life in jail. And then you'll be able to get on with yours.'

'I don't know, Zack. There's a small matter of five hundred thousand dollars.'

'Is Merker going to tell the cops about that? Could he even prove it's his? That you took it?'

'I don't know.'

'Trixie, you can't keep running. From Merker, from the police. You need to face these things, sort them out. You need to do it for Katie.'

Trixie stepped over the grass median and into my rut. 'Maybe,' she said, 'if I could spend my life with someone like you, I'd think about it.'

I said nothing.

'All I've ever known are bad men. My father was a bad man. Even Katie's father – he tried, you know? There was a lot of goodness in him. But he was no poster boy for stability. If he hadn't ended up getting killed by Gary, he'd have died some other way before long. You can't live that kind of life and expect it to go on forever. My sister, she got a good one. But my luck, it doesn't run in that direction.'

'I'm sure there's someone out there for you. Someone who'd treat you right. Treat you with the respect you deserve.'

'What can I really expect, Zack? Look what I do. I'm a step up from a hooker. I torture men. You know why I think I do that?'

Again, I said nothing.

'I think it's my way of taking it out on all the men who've treated me like shit all my life. My father, Merker, the others. When I abuse those men, when I demean them, when I hurt them, I'm getting even.'

'But,' I said, 'they like it.'

'They have their fantasy, and I have mine.'

Back at the house, we could hear Katie laugh about something in the kitchen. Trixie glanced back, and the wind blew a lock of hair across her face. She looked beautiful, but in a more natural, almost innocent way.

'So what about you and Sarah? How bad is it?'

'Not so bad that I've given up on it,' I said. 'I love her.' I took a breath. 'I love her more than I've ever loved anyone else.'

Trixie studied me. 'I've thought about you a lot since I left you in my basement. I'm sorry. I'd like to make it up to you.' She took a step closer, and for a moment, I felt dizzy. 'Did you like it when I kissed you? When you were handcuffed to the railing?'

'It took me somewhat by surprise,' I said. 'A simple peck on the cheek would have sufficed.'

Trixie smiled. 'Always with the joke.' The wind caught her hair again, and she reached up and tucked the lock behind her ear. 'There's something I really need to tell you,' she said.

I had a feeling this was not going to be good. At the very least, it was going to be awkward. Was she going to tell me she loved me? Was she going to ask me to leave Sarah? That seemed unthinkable. She was enticing, Trixie was. No doubt. She was beautiful. Exotic, even. She'd have no trouble fulfilling almost any man's wildest fantasies. I'd be lying if I said none had ever crossed my mind.

But no matter how beautiful, how sexy Trixie might be, there was something she could never be.

She could never be Sarah.

'You don't have to tell me,' I said. 'Whatever it is.'

'No,' Trixie said, her hand reaching up and touching my shirt. 'I think, before we go any further, that you need to know my secret.'

I waited.

'That night,' she said. 'When Zane Heighton, and Eldridge Smith, and Payne Fletcher, when the three of them got shot at the Kickstart?'

'Yes?'

'I saw it happen.'

My mouth felt very dry. 'You saw it?'

'I was there.'

'Then you *are* a witness. If you tell the police what you saw, you can—'

Trixie touched a finger to my lips. 'Zack, you don't understand.'

'What?'

'I killed them, Zack. I killed them all.'

'Where was that place,' Leo wanted to know, 'where we got pizza the other night?'

Sometimes it bugged Gary that, even though the Kickstart served food – some burgers, wings, fries, basic stuff – Leo always wanted to get something to eat from someplace else. The novelty of it, he guessed. The kid could eat, but he never got fat. Just stayed tall and stringy.

'Rocco's,' Gary said.

'Yeah, it was good,' Leo said.

Miranda listened to all this as she counted up the night's receipts. The Kickstart had closed half an hour ago, everyone had gone home, including the girls. Now it was just her, Gary and Leo, and Payne and Eldridge and Zane. Those three – sometimes Miranda thought of them as the Three Musketurds – were getting into the booze again. A good night would do that to them, prompt them to raid the bar's fridge for free beers. And Payne had some coke, and was willing to share.

'We're going out,' Gary said. 'Get some fucking pizza. Anybody want some?'

The others said sure, yeah, bring back lots. Gary and Leo left. Miranda stayed at her desk, working.

She figured this would be the week. She was ready. She had enough put away. About half a mill. It seemed unbelievable, that she'd been able to skim off that much. But so much money went through that joint, and when you didn't pay the legitimate bills, or paid just enough to keep the creditors off your back, and used the money you actually did have to pay invoices that you'd manufactured yourself, well, it all started to add up.

She'd already emptied out most of the accounts where she'd been squirreling away cash. She'd pulled together some fake identification. She'd come up with a new identity, for someone she'd decided to call Trixie.

Miranda was as ready as she'd ever be. She just had to pick her moment. To go when it felt right. Maybe just after a shift that was followed by a couple of days off. She'd have forty-eight hours' lead time before Gary started to clue in to what was going on. By then she'd be far away, already be establishing her new life with her baby daughter. She'd change her hair color, do her make-up differently, whatever she could to distance herself from the woman known as Candace.

The guys were getting a bit rowdy. The hairs went up on the back of Miranda's neck. Don't let them try anything, she thought. Not now. Not when I'm so close to pulling this all off.

And then there was Payne Fletcher, standing right next to her, a beer in one hand. And touching her hair with the other. She recoiled.

'Hey, come on,' said Payne. 'I'm just being friendly.'

Yeah, said the others. You got something against being friendly? But Miranda told them to leave her alone. She was working. Payne didn't move away. He put his beer down and placed both of his hands on Miranda's head, tried to turn her towards him.

'Stop it!' she said. Still in the chair, she tried to pull away, but Payne, standing next to her, was pulling her face toward the zipper of his jeans.

'How about a lollipop?' he asked.

Miranda had sworn to herself that she would never let this happen again. It was this promise to herself that allowed her to keep coming to work at the Kickstart, to share space with the men who'd assaulted her a few months earlier. It was part of the plan.

But she knew, if she was to be certain that it would never happen again, she'd have to be ready. Which was why she now always carried the gun that Eldon had taught her to use. The one she swore she'd never carry. She didn't like guns. Too dangerous to have on you, she'd thought.

But you had to adapt.

'Come on,' Payne said, still holding on to Miranda's head. The other two were making whooping noises. Someone said, 'Me next.'

'Okay,' Miranda said. 'But you have to let go of me.'

That sounded promising to Payne, and so he did. Miranda pushed back with her feet, the wheels of her computer chair sailing her over to the far end of her desk, where she'd left her purse.

Miranda reached into it, her fingers hunting for the weapon. She slipped her hand around the gun's grip, felt the trigger under her index finger.

'What you doing?' Payne said. 'You don't need no condom for this.'

No, she thought, bringing the gun out of the purse. She didn't.

TWENTY-EIGHT

I guess I was nine years old when my friend Jeff Conklin, who, two years later, would find a dead guy, stole two Milky Way bars.

Most days, walking home after surviving another day with our Grade 4 teacher Miss Phelm (we referred to her as Miss Phlegm, given her habit of clearing her throat every twenty seconds), we would pop into Ted's, a small corner store. We'd buy a bottle of Coke, maybe split a package of Twinkies. Ted had an excellent variety of snack foods. Potato chips, Fritos, licorice, dozens of different candy bars.

One day, Jeff told me to go over to the shelf of Hostess cupcakes, then call over to Ted at the cash register, and ask whether I could buy just one cupcake, even though they came in packages of two.

'Why?' I asked Jeff.

'Just do it. I dare ya.'

Well, that was all I needed to hear. So Jeff hung back as I went deeper into the store to the display of mass-produced pastries, examined the offerings, and then said, 'Mr Ted?'

We didn't know his last name, but knew it was a mistake, at our age, to call him just by his first name.

Ted, a man in his sixties, round-shouldered, wearing an old cardigan and wire-rimmed glasses, had been

267

reading the *Enquirer*. He looked up, peered over the glasses in my direction, and said, 'What?'

'I haven't got enough money for a whole package of Hostess cupcakes, so like, can I buy just half a pack?'

'You outta your mind?' He went back to reading his paper.

I met Jeff back outside on the sidewalk. 'That was great!' he said. 'You were perfect! I almost peed my pants laughing, but I held it all in!'

'Why did you ask me to do that?'

Jeff produced a Milky Way from each jacket pocket. 'Look what I got! When Ted looked over at you, I grabbed these.' He handed me one, and at first I tried not to take it, but he forced it into my hand.

'You stole these?' I asked.

'Jeez, could you say it a bit louder so Ted can hear?' Jeff said. He grabbed me by the arm and led me down the sidewalk, walking briskly. 'It was so easy!'

Once Jeff felt we were a safe distance from Ted's, he dragged me into an alley and ripped the wrapper off his Milky Way. He bit off a huge chunk, his cheek bulging out like a chipmunk's.

'Aren't you gonna eat yours?' he asked.

I handed my bar to him. 'You eat it. I'm not hungry.' Not only did I not want to eat it, I didn't want to hold on to it.

'Go on, eat it! I got it for you!'

'I don't want it.' I felt short of breath and a bit nauseous. Sweaty. I thought I might throw up right there, in the alley. I was not cut out for a life of crime.

'God, you're such a baby,' Jeff said, grabbing back the second Milky Way and stuffing it into his pocket. 'Oh well, more for me.'

'You have to go back and pay for those,' I said. 'You could say it was like a mistake, you picked them up and then walked out, like you forgot to pay and you remembered when you got down the street.'

I peered around the end of the alley, expecting to see Ted, accompanied by the riot squad, charging down the sidewalk. I was listening for sirens. But there was no one looking for us.

'Yeah, right,' said Jeff, trying to talk through a mouthful of Milky Way. He seemed determined to dispose of the evidence as quickly as possible. 'Shoulda got a Coke too, wash it down.' I couldn't believe Jeff had done this. I wouldn't have thought him capable of such a thing.

I'd never had a thief for a friend before. It was a new feeling, and not an exciting one. It took more than a week of sleepless nights for me to realize that Jeff and I, his unwitting accomplice, were going to get away with this. We were not going to be caught.

I never went into Ted's again.

This thing with Trixie, well, I'd have to say this was bigger than the Milky Way incident. I couldn't recall anyone ever confessing to me that they'd shot, and killed, three people. I'm sure I'd have remembered something like that.

'Say something,' she said as we stood out there, alone, in the field. A light breeze blowing from the direction of the Bennet farmhouse carried the smells of chicken and the sounds of a child's laughter.

'I'm sort of at a loss for words,' I said.

Trixie placed the palm of her right hand on my chest. 'You need to know the whole story.'

'Will that make me think it's okay that you killed three people?'

Trixie pulled her hand away. 'Probably not. But I'd like to tell you anyway. All that I've put you through the last few days, I think you're entitled to the truth, no matter what you think of me after hearing it.'

'Sure, then. Go ahead.'

She slipped her hands into the pockets of her jeans, turned her back to me, and took a step away. 'You heard a bit, inside, from Claire, about what it was like. With Merker and the rest of them.'

'I got a taste.'

'I didn't turn tricks for them. Some of the dancers, they hooked too. Made a lot of money that way. Guy sees you onstage, wants a piece of you real bad, he's willing to pay. And a lot of the girls, they were happy for the extra cash. I won't tell you I never did things I shouldn't have. I'd be lying. Especially at first. But I was good, taking clothes off, doing the moves, and I was still a good warm-up for the business upstairs, even if I wasn't one of the girls going up there. I was still good for getting them in the mood, you know?'

'Sure,' I said.

She turned back to face me. 'But once I started giving Merker suggestions, how to make more money, worked my way into the back room and started helping with the books, I didn't have to flash my tits anymore. But the thing is, with that crew, no matter how smart you are, no matter what other talents you might have, when it comes right down to it, if you're a woman, you're just a whore.'

I closed my eyes for a second.

'After Eldon, Katie's dad, died, they started looking at me differently. No one would have touched me as long as he was around. He'd have beat the shit out of them, killed them, probably. But once he was gone, there'd be comments, little cracks, like "Hey, ledger lady, I've got six inches for you to calculate." Or, "Let's multiply." Clever stuff, you know?'

And then she told me about the night of November 18, 2001. The night they took turns.

'They held me down. Like fucking dogs. Everyone except Leo. He just stood off in a corner, shaking his head, whimpering like. Fletcher was first, then Gary, then Smith and Heighton. One after another.'

She waited, wondering whether I wanted to react, whether I had anything I wanted to say, but all I could do was listen.

She told me about Gary's visit to her apartment two days later. Finding her with her eleven-month-old girl in her arms. Hands her a 'Come Back to Work Soon' Hallmark card with $110 inside.

I listened. Out of the corner of my eye, I saw the hawk circling.

'You know the part I can never figure out?' she said, looking at me again. 'The ten bucks. A hundred, and *ten*. Was that the tip? Was the ten bucks for expenses? What the fuck do you think the ten was for? Baby formula, maybe?'

All I could offer was a shake of the head.

'But you know what I did? I went back to work. Went back and did my fucking job. I'd already been planning my move, I was moving the money around, into accounts, skimming off cash where I could, and I wasn't done yet. I still needed more. I was putting together getting some new ID, in the name of Trixie Snelling. I was putting things into place, to make a new life for myself and my daughter. But I didn't have enough. So I had to go back there, go back and sit in that room, day after day, putting on my smiley face, with a pack of rapists.'

Softly, I said, 'I don't know how you could do that. It must have been . . . I don't know. I can't imagine.'

'And I carried on, making like nothing happened, like a hundred and ten dollars and a Hallmark card was all it took to make the memory of a gang bang go away. And for a while, they were even a little sheepish. Getting me tea, being real sweet, you know? Like, hey, sorry about turning you inside out, but here's a cup of Earl Grey.'

'So,' I said, 'that wasn't the night it happened.'

'No. Gary, round about this time, I thought maybe he was starting to get suspicious. I was scared shitless that he'd start asking questions, about the books, questioning the totals. The club owed money everywhere, but he didn't know. But I did my best to snow him, buried him in numbers. So he'd buy it for a while, but I knew I was running out of time.

'I could have used another week at least, but things sometimes have a way of unraveling. Gets to be April 9, 2002. Gary and Leo, they're out getting pizza.'

And the ones left behind, Heighton and Smith and Fletcher, decide it's time for a repeat performance.

'No matter how much money I'd stashed away, even if it wasn't enough, I'd made a vow to myself that what happened that other night, that was never going to happen again.'

Back at the house, Claire was on the porch, waving to us. 'Five minutes!' she shouted.

Trixie waved, turned back to me.

I said, 'Your sister and Don. You've told them this story?'

Trixie nodded. 'They know.' She ran her hands through her hair, gave her head a shake. 'Fletcher puts his hand on my shoulder, spins my chair around, puts my face up to his crotch. The others, they're starting to laugh.'

She rolled the chair back so she could get her purse, get the gun.

Fletcher took a couple of steps back, couldn't believe it, barely had a chance to say 'What the fuck' before the first shot went into him.

'Then Smith and Heighton, they were on their feet, not sure whether to get the hell out of the room or come at me, but I was between them and the door, so they pretty much had to run at me regardless. I fired again, got Smith, then Heighton, and they both fell, almost on top of each other. I'd managed to shoot all three of them square in the chest. Eldon, he'd taught me a few things, and one of them was how to use a gun, and how to aim it. They were moaning, telling me to call an ambulance, but I knew that wasn't going to happen. I knew I had to get out of there as fast as I could, pick up Katie from the sitter's, get out of town as fast as I could. Gary and Leo, they'd already been gone half an hour, they'd be coming back at any moment, and someone might have heard the shots, already called the police.'

She put her hands on her hips, took in a deep breath. I saw the hawk swoop down; a moment later it was back in the air, something small and lifeless in its talons.

'But you weren't quite done, were you?' I said.

Trixie's eyebrows went up a notch.

'There was something about the way you shot them,' I said. 'Something . . . distinctive.'

273

Trixie smiled. 'Fletcher was already on his back, so it was easy to shoot him in the balls. Payne was on his side, so I had to push him over with my foot, and then I shot him there too. Heighton, he was crawling for the door, reaching up for the knob, and then he just kind of flipped over on his own. And I shot him in the balls too. And then I walked out, thought I could hear Merker and Leo coming up the stairs, and I snuck out the back way, down the fire escape.'

'Jesus,' I said.

'But I feel bad, you know?' Trixie said.

'Sure,' I said. 'Of course you do. Even though it was self-defense, even though they deserved it, even though they had it coming, you can't take people's lives away from them and not, I don't know, live with the regret, one way or another.'

Trixie smiled at me, patted my shoulder. 'Oh, Zack, you're just so sweet. That's not why I feel bad. I feel bad because I didn't get Gary. I play it over in my head, over and over and over again, and I see myself shooting him, then leaving a little get-well card for him, with a hundred and ten dollars tucked into the envelope.'

Those stolen Milky Way bars didn't seem like that big a deal anymore.

TWENTY-NINE

Heading back to the house, I said, 'A couple of years back, when I came to your house unexpectedly one night, in a bit of a pickle, you sent me to a neighbor when I needed a gun.'

'I remember,' Trixie said.

'But I'm guessing you already had one.'

'Yeah. And if you'd used it, and if they ever matched the bullets you fired to the ones that killed those three in Canborough, by now one of us would have already served a year or two in jail for that.'

'Well, thanks for that, then.'

Katie was on the porch, cupping her hands around her mouth and shouting, 'Dinner!'

Trixie smiled. 'Coming!'

'It's chicken!'

'Okay!'

Katie ran back into the house.

'She's beautiful,' I said.

'Yeah. I might be able to take some of the credit for her looks, but it's Claire and Don who are raising her. And they're doing a hell of a job. She's in kindergarten now, smart as a whip.'

We were taking our time walking back, allowing ourselves more time to talk things out. But I didn't know what to say. I was feeling a little shell-shocked.

'So, now what?' Trixie asked.

'I don't know.'

'You still think I should go to the police, tell them everything?'

'I don't know.' I paused. 'But you can't keep running. You can't live this way. Maybe, I don't know, you've got something to trade? What do you know about the drug trade, that other biker gang in Canborough? Maybe, you tell the cops everything you know, help them clear some cases, you can cut some sort of deal.'

'Yeah, well, I'll have to give that some sort of thought. Regardless, I have to move on. I stay here one more night, and I'm gone.'

'Trixie,' I said, stopping and taking her elbow, looking her in the eye. 'Face up to it. Do what you have to do, try to start over.'

She pulled away from me, gently. Katie burst out the door, jumped off the porch, and ran towards her mom, shouting, 'Chicken chicken chicken chicken!'

Trixie scooped her up into her arms, rubbing noses with her daughter, and the two of them disappeared into the house, the screen door slamming behind them. I stood outside a moment, alone, wondering how this would all play out.

I took the couch.

Trixie had a double bed in the third bedroom upstairs, and she'd whispered to me that if I wanted to share it with her, she'd be a perfect lady if I could be a perfect gentleman.

I thanked her for the offer, but told Claire the couch would be fine. She got out some sheets, even though I told her not to bother, tucked them into the sofa cushions and found me a cushy pillow. I was upstairs, coming out of the bathroom, when I heard Trixie in Katie's bedroom. The door was open an inch, and the room was dark but for a bedside lamp, and Trixie was sitting on the edge of the bed, up close to Katie, who was under the covers, her head pressed into the pillow, her eyes wide.

'Tell me more about the princess,' Katie said.

'Well,' said Trixie, 'once upon a time, there was a princess, with very curly hair, who was only five years old, and she could do anything she wanted.'

'Even stay up late to watch TV?'

'Not that sort of anything. Anything that was hard, that took a lot of work, anything that the other princes and princesses thought would be too much trouble, that was the sort of anything she could do. Like, if she wanted to be a scientist, she could do that. Or if she wanted to be a doctor, or a painter, or a dancer, whatever she wanted to be, she could do it.'

'Was she magic?' Katie asked.

'Some people thought so, but mostly, she was just special. And she was special because so many people loved her.'

'How many people?'

Trixie thought a moment. 'Seventeen,' she said.

'That's a lot,' said Katie. 'So what did the princess decide she wanted to be?'

'What do you think she decided to be?'

Katie mulled this one over. 'I think she decided to be a dog doctor.'

'Really?' said Trixie. 'A dog doctor. You mean, she wanted to be a dog, who becomes a doctor, or she wanted to be someone who took care of sick dogs?'

'She wanted to be someone who wanted to take care of sick dogs.'

'That makes sense,' said Trixie. 'I think that's a good choice.'

'I like dogs,' said Katie. 'But I don't like dragons. If a dragon got sick, I wouldn't try to make it better.'

'Dragons are scary,' Trixie agreed.

'I don't want there to be any dragons,' Katie said.

'Neither do I,' Trixie said, and leaned over to give Katie a kiss goodnight.

I slipped away down the stairs.

'Zack.'

When I opened my eyes, it took me a couple of seconds to realize where I was. On the couch, in the living room of the Bennet house. Trixie, in a robe, the sash knotted in front of her, was kneeling over me in the darkness. I could smell her hair as it hung down her face towards me.

'Zack,' she said again, whispering.

'Yeah, Trixie, it's the middle of the night.' Instantly, I wondered what her intentions were. Here we were, alone, Trixie in a robe, me mostly undressed, in a darkened room.

'Shhh,' she said.

'What is it?'

'I think there's someone out there.'

I blinked hard, several times, getting the sleep out of my eyes and getting them adjusted to the dark. 'Out where?'

'Outside. Around the house.'

'What? How, what, you probably just heard something. An animal or something.' I'd swung my legs out from under the covers and was in a sitting position, in socks, boxers and a T-shirt.

'I came down to the kitchen,' Trixie whispered, 'for a glass of water, and I thought—' She stopped abruptly, put her index finger to her lip. Neither of us breathed.

I thought I heard a board creak. On the porch, at the front of the house.

'Did you hear that?' she asked.

I nodded. Merker, I thought. Somehow, I'd fucked up, led him here. But how was that possible? How could Merker have followed me through the countryside without my noticing? Even an amateur detective like myself would have picked up a tail.

'Have you woken up the others?' I asked. Trixie shook her head. 'Get them up, get Katie.'

Trixie didn't have to be told twice. She disappeared, padding back up the stairs on bare feet. I stood and moved silently to the front door. The door window was curtained, but there was enough of a slit to peer outside. Out on County Road 9, a van with high beams on drove past. I couldn't make out anything between the house and the road, no people, no unfamiliar vehicles, no—

Someone moved past the window, momentarily blocking my view.

My heart nearly burst out of my chest, but I managed to stay very still. I moved away from the door, pressed myself up against the wall. I inched my way towards the stairs and mounted them as noiselessly as possible.

A dark figure met me at the top.

'Zack?'

It was Don. No one, wisely, had turned on any lights.

'Yeah,' I said. 'There's at least one. I just saw him move past the front door.'

Claire and Trixie were behind him. 'Stay with Katie,' he told them, and they both slipped into the girl's room. 'Who is it?' he asked.

'I don't know. But he was going around the south side of the house.'

'I've got a rifle, but it's in the back of my pickup,' Don said. 'Shit.'

I thought of the small garden shovel by the front door, the one Claire had swung at me, but we'd have to go outside to get it, too.

'There's an old baseball bat in the basement,' Don said. 'If I can see to get down there.'

We both went back down to the first floor. I tapped Don's arm, pointed to the front door. The shadow was moving the other way, past the door and then the living room window. Then it crouched down, disappeared below the frame.

'Call the police,' I whispered.

'But if they, if they come and find Miran . . .'

'Don.'

'Jesus, I know.' I followed as he crept into the kitchen, took hold of the receiver from its wall mount, and put it to his ear. 'Oh God,' he said.

'What?'

'There's nothing. No dial tone.'

I took the receiver from him, put it to my own ear, then hit the receiver button a couple of times. I hung the phone back up.

'My cell,' I said. I tiptoed back into the living room, found my jacket draped over the back of a chair, fumbled around in the pocket until I had my cell phone out. I flipped it open, but because I'd left it on for so long, and had neglected to hook it up to a charger on the drive up here, it was dead.

'Are you kidding me?' Don whispered.

'Do you have a cell phone?' I whispered. Don shook his head. 'Okay, go find your bat. I'll stay up here, you see what you can find.' I trained my sights on the living room window and saw part of a head rise into view. Then another shadow moved across the window in the door.

'Oh no,' I said to myself.

I could hear Don bumping into things in the dark basement. Then footsteps coming back up. I could make out what appeared to be a bat in one hand, and a length of two-by-four in the other.

He handed me the bat.

'There's at least two,' I said. 'One by the window, one by the door. He must have brought Leo with him.'

'We get on either side of the door, when they come in, wham,' Don said.

It was as good a plan as any.

We got into position. Standing perfectly still, we could hear the board creak under the two men – it sounded like they were both out there – as they shifted their weight from one leg to another.

Four men, all within a few inches of each other, two on one side of the wall and two on the other, doing their best not to make a sound. All poised, waiting to strike.

Don stood across from me, holding the four-foot section of lumber over his shoulder. I had the bat at the ready.

And then, a good thirty feet away from us, the back door burst open.

My mouth dropped. Don's probably did too, but I wasn't looking at him. I was looking at the four men storming into the living room by way of the kitchen, arms raised, weapons pointed, handheld lights blazing.

And then the front door burst open, and three more men came barreling in, similarly armed.

They were all screaming: 'Police! Freeze!'

Just like in the movies.

Lights got flicked on. Don and I were pushed to the floor by two cops while others ran upstairs. I heard Claire and Trixie scream. Katie crying.

I tried to crane my head around to see what was happening, but a boot came down on my head and held it to the carpet.

I lay that way for a while, listening to the crackle of police radios, and then someone was told to let me up. I got to my knees, and standing there, waiting for me to get up, was Detective Flint.

'Mr Walker,' he said, smiling and taking off his fedora.

And then it hit me. Why he'd let me keep Trixie's car. Its built-in GPS system not only helped a driver figure out how to get around.

It could be used to track a missing car.

They'd let me lead them to Trixie.

Nice one, Zack.

THIRTY

They led Trixie away in handcuffs, but before they slapped them on her, they allowed her to change from her robe into some clothes. While she was getting dressed, I said to Flint, 'I told you about Gary Merker. You told me about the stun gun marks on Martin Benson. Merker was there, he left Trixie a note. I can get it for you.'

Flint looked tired. He was a long way from home, and it was the middle of the night. But he still looked better than the rest of us.

'Mr Walker, a man was murdered in her house. She fled the scene. She left you handcuffed so you wouldn't be able to stop her from getting away. That's what we in the police business call suspicious. Maybe even incriminating. Tell your friend to get herself a good lawyer.' He gave a tip of his hat. 'And thanks again, for leading the way.'

'You called the car manufacturer,' I said. 'You knew where I was all the time. I was being tracked by satellite.'

Flint smiled, but not as devilishly as he might have been entitled to. 'So sorry to have disrupted your evening.'

Upstairs, Trixie was saying goodbye to her sister, to Don. And especially Katie. As Trixie came down the stairs, one officer walking in front of her and one behind, Katie stood, bleary-eyed, on the landing, clutching a yellow blanket and watching, baffled and sad. 'When are you coming back?' she asked.

Trixie glanced at her and said, 'I might be gone a while, sweetheart, but your other mom will take good care of you.' At the bottom of the stairs, they cuffed her.

'I'm sorry,' I said to Trixie. 'It was your car. They used the GPS thing to find it. I led them right to you.'

She smiled tiredly. 'It's okay, Zack. I'm going to make it clear to them that you came up here to get me to turn myself in. Don't worry.'

'You need a lawyer.'

'I told you about Niles. He handles all my difficulties.' She shook her head. 'This one's right up there.'

'We have to go, ma'am,' said one of the cops.

'See ya, Zack,' said Trixie, and Candace, and Miranda. 'Maybe now you'll catch a break. How much trouble can you get into with me locked up, right?'

I was on the road by six in the morning.

Trixie was right, there was something wrong with the Virtue. I tried to start it, but the engine, or the batteries, or whatever it was that made the damn thing go, failed to make a sound. So I hung on to Trixie's car. If Detective Flint wanted to put the space shuttle and all the other resources of NASA into keeping track of my movements, he was welcome to. I no longer gave a rat's ass.

I plugged my cell phone into the cigarette lighter. Long before I was home, it would be recharged, plus I'd be able to make or receive calls during my journey.

I called no one, and no one called me.

There was a lot of time to think on that drive home. And as I reached the city of Canborough and took the bypass, I felt a twinge of guilt. I probably should have driven into the downtown, parked outside police headquarters, and gone in to see Michael Cherry. I had some vague recollection of a promise I'd made to him two days earlier, that if I happened upon any information that would help him with the Kickstart massacre investigation, I'd pass it along.

It was fair to say I had a few new details he might want to have. I'd have a source for life in the Canborough Police Department, helping him crack a triple murder.

Moral dilemma time.

Maybe, for most people, this would be a no-brainer. Trixie had admitted to me that she'd shot and killed three men. Three men who'd raped her before, and were about to do it again. If her claim of self-defense was legit, she could tell it to a judge and jury. He might well agree. So might the jury.

But I could see the prosecutor – and in my mind's eye he looked a lot like Sam Waterston – approaching the witness box. He was saying, 'So tell us, Ms . . . whatever your name is at the moment. Is it Chicoine? Is it Snelling? So these men, they allegedly attacked you, allegedly sexually assaulted you, on this earlier occasion, you claim, and, let me just check my notes here, and then you went back to work with them? Just a couple of days later? And then, when they allegedly did this again, *that's* when you decided to kill them? I'm just having a little trouble with this. Isn't it more likely that the reason you killed them was because you were ripping them off for half a million dollars? And that this first incident, that this never even happened?

That it's just a very good story to justify what you did? I mean, do we have anything but your word?'

I composed Sam's entire summation in my head as I drove.

It seemed unlikely that Gary Merker, the only one left alive who'd participated in the rape, would be called to support her testimony.

There was a good chance, I thought, that the evidence would exonerate Trixie in the death of Martin Benson. But if the cops ever knew what she'd told me about that night at the Kickstart, well, I didn't like her chances of beating that one. Trixie was classic 'blame the victim' material, by virtue of the choices she'd made, her line of work, her use of multiple aliases.

They'd tear her apart.

But was it up to me to keep Trixie from having to answer for the things she'd done? Or to at least explain them? Was I responsible for Trixie's future? And what of my obligations to the *Metropolitan*? To my profession? If I had any intention of actually writing about this — assuming Magnuson put an end to my suspension, and that was quite an assumption — how could I tell only part of the story? If I couldn't do the job properly, I had no business doing it at all.

I needed to talk to someone about this.

And the only person I could think of was Sarah.

I reached for my cell, started dialing our home number, glanced at the dashboard clock and realized Sarah would be at work by now. So I started punching the numbers for the main switchboard, since I had no idea what Sarah's extension was in the Home! section. But when I got to the second-to-last digit, I stopped, and tossed the phone onto the passenger seat.

Maybe later.

There was no one home when I got there mid-morning. Paul was at school, Angie at college. It looked as though everyone had fled in a hurry, dirty dishes still on the kitchen counter, the cream not put away. I opened the fridge, poured myself a large glass of orange juice, downed it and trudged upstairs.

I dumped my travel bag on the bed, walked into the bathroom, turned on the radio that sat next to the sink.

I looked in the mirror. I hadn't yet shaved, my eyes were bleary, my hair a tousled mess. I reached into the shower, turned on the taps, started unbuttoning my shirt.

It was the top of the hour and the news came on. The morning rush-hour traffic had thinned; it would be overcast with the odd sunny break. And then:

'Police have made an arrest in the grisly murder of an Oakwood newspaper columnist who was found dead, his throat slit, in the basement of a dominatrix earlier this week. Charged is Miranda Chicoine, who ran a sex business from her suburban home in Oakwood. Police arrested Chicoine outside of the village of Kelton, at the home of her sister and brother-in-law, Claire and Don Bennet, early this morning. They had been led to her location by Zack Walker, a reporter for the *Metropolitan*, who had been trying to track down the woman, hoping to talk her into turning herself in, according to police. In Washington—'

I turned off the radio.

I was undoing my pants when the phone rang. I walked back to the bedroom, picked it up.

'Yeah,' I said.

'Well, I'll be damned, you're there.' It was Dick Colby, the paper's odiferous crime reporter. 'You're quite the man.'

'What can I do for you, Dick?'

'This story about you and the hooker just broke, police issued a statement, it's already on the radio—'

'I know.'

'And you didn't call us first? Fuck, Zack, what's with you?'

'I just got back, Dick. It's been kind of a long night.' I glanced into the bathroom, saw steam escaping from around the shower curtain.

'Okay, look, the radio, other papers, all they can get is the basics. We need the good shit, the color, from you. So how did you track her down, this Chicoine chick? That her real name? Because she was going by Snelling, right? Let me check these spellings with you.'

'Dick, I got nothing to say. I'm gonna have a shower. The water's running.'

'Zack, hello? This is *your* paper calling. I know you probably think you should write this one up yourself, but you ask me, you're too close, you've got a conflict, just like with those other big pieces you did, but fuck, that was okay with them then, but this time, I don't think so. So you're going to have to tell me what you've got, I'll write it up, but you'll look good just the same.'

I thought I caught a whiff of him over the phone.

'No comment, Dick,' I said. 'I'm on suspension.' I hung up.

I was almost back to the bathroom when the phone rang again. I picked up. 'Dick, I mean it, I have nothing to say.'

'Zack.' It was Sarah.

288

'Oh,' I said. 'I just finished hanging up on Cheese Dick. I thought it was him.'

'It's all over the newsroom, the thing about you and Trixie,' Sarah said. 'Are you okay?'

'Yeah. Tired.'

'What happened?'

'I found Trixie. Police were following me. They raided the place in the night, took her away.'

'She did it? She killed that man? The reporter?'

'No,' I said, thinking, not *that* man. 'The cops'll probably figure that out eventually.'

'Are you in trouble?'

'I don't know. I don't think so. Trixie said she was going to tell them that I went up there to tell her to turn herself in, and that's the spin I just heard on the radio. I guess we'll see.'

'Do you want me to come home?'

I shook my head, then realized that Sarah couldn't see me. 'It's okay. I'm going to shower, maybe go to bed. How's everything here? Kids okay?'

'They're fine. Worried about you.'

'And you? How are you doing?' What I really was asking was how *we* were doing.

'Okay,' she said. 'I'm . . . I can't stand it here. Working with Frieda. Every day, it's like we're planning a church supper instead of a newspaper. I can't swear here. It's driving me fucking crazy.'

I let out a small laugh. I couldn't recall when I'd last done that.

'Is it over, Zack?' Sarah asked.

I wasn't sure what she was referring to. Us? Was it over between us? 'What do you, I mean, I don't, what?' I said. The steam was still pouring out of the shower.

289

'All this trouble,' Sarah said. 'Is it over? Can you promise me that it's over?'

I breathed a sigh of relief. 'Yes,' I said. 'It's over. It's going to be up to Trixie now to figure out what she's going to do. I . . . I thought I was doing the right thing, figuring out where she'd gone, finding out what really happened, and maybe that was stupid. But now that she's been arrested, it forces things to a head. She's got a lawyer, she'll have to work things out. I guess,' and I paused a moment, and then said, 'I'm done with it.'

Quietly, Sarah said, 'You have to be.'

'I know.' I heard her say 'Fuck' under her breath. 'It's Colby, coming this way. I'm surprised he could find his way to the Home! section.'

'He probably caught the scent of cookies.'

'He looks pissed.'

Then, in the background, I could hear Colby asking, 'That him? I want to talk to him. He can't jerk me around this way.'

'I'll see you tonight, okay?' Sarah said.

'Yeah, that'll be nice,' I said.

'Let me talk to him,' Colby demanded.

'Bye,' Sarah said, and hung up.

For the first time in a very long time, I felt good, as though a weight had been lifted off my chest. I took a couple of deep breaths, then thought about how to welcome Sarah home. I'd pick up some steaks, buy a bottle of wine, give the kids some cash to go out for pizza and a movie and—

The phone rang.

The shower was still running, waiting for me. I wondered whether there was any hot water left by now.

I grabbed the receiver and said, 'Hang on.' I ran into the bathroom, reached past the curtain, and turned off the taps. The mirror was completely fogged. I ran back to the phone, put the receiver to my ear, and said, 'Sorry, hi.'

'Mr Walker?'

'Yeah, I just had to turn off the shower.'

'Where've you been? There was something on the radio. I've been trying to reach you.'

'Excuse me?' The voice seemed familiar, but at the moment, I couldn't place it.

'I've been calling you for a couple of days now. Haven't you listened to it? Did you get it?'

'Look, I'm sorry,' I said, 'but who is this?'

'Brian Sandler. Oh my God, are you kidding me? Haven't you listened to the file?'

Sandler. From the health department. The one who wanted to roll over on the Gorkins and the ones he worked with who were on the take.

'Mr Sandler, of course, I'm sorry. You wouldn't believe what I've been through in the last couple of days.'

'Yeah, well, you wouldn't believe what *I've* been through the last couple of days, either.'

'Okay, look, just start from the beginning. What's this about a file? What are you talking about?'

'Is your phone secure?'

'What? What are you talking about? Of course my phone's secure.' But then again, I thought, it might not be. Flint might have had the line tapped, thinking Trixie might call me, tell me where she was.

Fuck it. 'It's fine,' I told Sandler. 'What is it?'

'I e-mailed you a file. A recording, of a conversation.'

'What conversation?'

'Me and my boss. Ellinger, Frank Ellinger. I got this digital recorder, left it on in my jacket pocket, went in and saw him, got him to say stuff. I've got him admitting to the payoffs from the Gorkin lady and others, letting shithole restaurants stay open even when they don't meet minimum standards, that kind of thing. It's all there. Listen to it. You'll see. You just have to make it clear that even though I make it sound like I'm going along with it, it's me trapping him, you understand? You have to make that clear when you do your story.'

'Hold on, Sandler. I'll check it out. I'm sure it's good stuff. Let me have a listen and we'll go from there.'

'Let's meet again, at Bayside Park. We can meet there at nine tomorrow morning. You listen to it, you come and see me, we'll get these fuckers.'

'Okay, okay, that sounds fine. Let me get some numbers from you.' I opened up the bedside table drawer, found a pen and a piece of paper. 'Where can I reach you?'

Sandler gave me his cell, work and home phone numbers. 'Just listen to it, okay? It's legit. You need to get these guys, and these crazy Gorkin women. I can't live with this shit anymore, you know?'

'I hear ya.'

'Ellinger, I think he was suspicious at the end, you know? Like he thought I was up to something, so you gotta move on this fast. He might talk to Mrs Gorkin or something, you never know.'

'Okay, okay. Just calm down. I'll listen to the file, meet you in the morning.'

'Just listen,' Sandler said, and hung up.

I sat on the edge of the bed a moment, then went into the bathroom and turned the shower taps back on.

Just as I figured. No more hot water.

But there was plenty more waiting for me.

THIRTY-ONE

Shirtless, I went down the hall to my study and sat down at the computer. I didn't spend as much time here as I once did, when I was writing science fiction novels. I still had the room decorated with SF toys and souvenirs – I'd recently put a framed *Fantastic Voyage* poster on the wall: orange with yellow lettering, some people spilling out of a guy's eye, pretty cool, really – but they weren't proving to be as inspiring as they once were. Someone being mischievous, Angie probably, had left a Batman action figure sitting on my keyboard. A Post-it note had been stuck to Batman's chest, and written on it were the words 'Make up with Mom.' The handwriting, I realized, was Paul's.

I set Batman aside and fired up the e-mail program. I had a couple of dozen messages, most of them offering various services to enlarge my penis, drugs to enlarge my penis, or Rolex watches that would allow me to time, to the millisecond, how long it would take my penis to reach its full potential (i.e., become big enough to wear a Rolex, if some of the other e-mails were to be believed). Also, some businessmen in Nigeria were seeking my assistance in helping them transfer millions of dollars to North America, and if I could supply them my bank account information, thereby allowing them a place to hide their cash, I could keep a healthy percentage for my trouble.

And then there was one from Brian Sandler.

I clicked on it. His note read, 'Dear Mr Walker: This is me and my supervisor Frank Ellinger talking about the situation. I believe you will agree that it is very damaging for him and also for me, but I am playing a role here to get him to say what he does, which you should make clear in your story. I'm the whistleblower here, you understand. Brian Sandler.'

I opened the attached file and clicked on the tiny triangle pointing to the right. There was a small delay, and then the conversation began. It took only a moment to figure out who was who.

Ellinger: Yeah, sure. Grab a chair. Want one? *(sound of rustling bag)*

Sandler: No, no, well, sure. *(more bag rustling)* You got a sec?

Ellinger: Yeah. You see that game last night? Fuck.

Sandler: Yeah, that was something. Talk about coming from behind.

Ellinger: Fuck, yeah. Wassup?

Sandler: Oh, same old. You know. Busy.

Ellinger: Yeah, busy. Things good at home?

Sandler: Oh yeah, sure. You?

Ellinger: Just got a hot tub. You should come over. Fuckin' awesome.

Sandler: Sure, that'd be fun. Listen, you got a sec?

Ellinger: I said yeah, sure, you gonna sit down or just stand there?

Sandler: Yeah, thanks. So, about Mrs Gorkin.

Ellinger: Oh yeah. Some hunk of woman. *(laughs)*

Sandler: And those daughters of hers. The twins.

Ellinger: In Russia or Kanuckistan or Fuckistan or wherever the bejesus they come from, they'd be beauty contest winners. Over here, they look like they should be wearing an Amana box.

Sandler: Yeah, well. They're strong, no doubt about that. Anyway, I just want to check with you, that we're okay with them.

Ellinger: Sure, yeah, we're okay. What are you talking about? Everything's fine.

Sandler: I mean, I wonder if maybe I should be getting a little more than I'm getting. Like, I'm not really taking anything right now. I just, you know, I look the other way because I don't want them, I don't know, hurting my family or anything.

Ellinger: Jesus, Brian. Don't be such a pussy. They've got money. How you think I got my fucking hot tub?

Sandler: Well sure, that's what I was thinking. I mean, how much did they give you anyway? If I start hinting around, what should I be looking at, for them to give me?

Ellinger: Shit, they usually gave me a hundred any time I dropped by. They'd get pissed, right, thinking I was dropping by too often, but I explained, hey, if I don't come by, it's gonna be someone else, and just how many people do you want to put on the payroll? So once, every couple of weeks, I do a walk-through, tell them some things maybe they should clean up, stuff anybody could see, but the stuff you can't see, that's not a big problem.

Sandler: Okay. So, I go in, I say, you know, I want the same deal you had when you inspected Burger Crisp, before you got shifted.

Ellinger: You want, I can make a call to them. Pave the way, you know? I mean, they got the money, they're doing a lot more on the side than selling burgers. You want me to do that?

Sandler: You don't mind?

Ellinger: Fuck no, no big deal. You ever eat there?

Sandler: No, never.

Ellinger: Yeah, well, that's a plan to stick with.

Sandler: So, Frank, you don't mind my asking, how much, you figure, they paid you altogether?

Ellinger: I don't know. Seven, eight grand maybe. But that was over a couple of years. Can't buy a hot tub that way. Got to have a few Burger Crisps, you understand.

Sandler: Eight, ten grand. That's great. Really helps out, right? We all got a lot of bills. So, how many other places you got an arrangement with?

Ellinger: Brian, what is this? You want to know whether I'm declaring this on my income tax?

Sandler: *(laughs)* No, shit, no.

Ellinger: It's just, you've got a lot of questions.

Sandler: This whole thing, it still makes me nervous, you know? And those twins, they did hold my finger in the fryer, remember.

Ellinger: Yeah, that's gotta hurt.

Sandler: So I'm just sayin', I want to feel my way carefully with this. I got bills too.

Ellinger: Okay. I just need to know you're not fucking around with me. Right?

Sandler: No, man. I'm not.

Ellinger: I just need to know.

Sandler: I told you. You don't have to worry about me.

Ellinger: Because there'd be a shit storm, you started fucking around with me. And it wouldn't be just me, right? Mrs Gorkin, those little darlins of hers, you don't want to go pissing them off.

Sandler: No, for sure.

Ellinger: You hot?

Sandler: Huh?

Ellinger: You hot? You look hot. You're all sweating, like.

Sandler: No, I'm good. Listen, I'll let you go. I got stuff, you know.

Ellinger: I'll make the call. Maybe tomorrow. Okay?

Sandler: Yeah, good. That's fine. Whenever.

That was it.

I listened to the entire exchange a second time. I had to hand it to Sandler. It was good stuff. I could see the entire conversation, reprinted nearly word for word, at least those that the *Metropolitan* would print without dashes, as a sidebar to a main story. People love reading those kinds of things. Brings a story into focus more quickly than a lot of exposition.

I'd have more questions to ask him the following morning when we met in Bayside Park. I decided, for safety's sake, that maybe it was wise for at least one more copy of this audio file to be out there, so I forwarded it to Lawrence Jones, marked it 'FYI' and included a short explanatory note. Lawrence does a lot of surveillance work, and might have some words of wisdom on just how incriminating this exchange was for Frank Ellinger.

I exited the mail program and decided to give the shower another try. There was enough hot water. Just.

Paul was home shortly before four, and Angie appeared not long after that.

'Why don't you guys go out and get some dinner, give me and Mom some time alone tonight,' I said. 'Things have been a bit rocky lately, and I'm hoping maybe I can smooth things over a bit now that this whole Trixie thing is over with.'

'Okay,' Paul said. 'But we're going to need some cash.'

I dug a twenty out of my wallet and handed it to Angie, who was closer. She examined the bill in my hand. 'Is this some sort of a joke?' she asked. She had that wry look in her eye, the one that said *You know I'm kidding, right*? I dug out another ten and handed it over. 'I suppose we'll be able to get something with this,' she said.

'Jeez,' Paul said to his sister as they walked away. 'I thought twenty was good. Nice going.'

There's an Italian place down around the corner where Sarah and I sometimes go for a sit-down dinner. But they do a bit of takeout and delivery on the side, so I ordered two veal *et limone* with sides of pasta and arranged to have them delivered at seven.

I put on some Errol Garner (the Lawrence Jones influence), set the table with a cloth and napkins and everything, turned down the lights, lit some candles, and awaited Sarah's arrival.

Her car pulled into the drive at six-thirty, and I met her at the door with a glass of wine.

Her eyes darted about, caught the candles, the elegantly set table in the dining room off the kitchen.

'Well,' she said, dropping her purse and taking the glass of chilled wine from my hand.

'I love you, Sarah,' I said. 'I'm a dipshit, a pain in the neck, a busybody, an asshole of the first order. Ask anybody. I can supply references. I'm sorry for the things I've put you through. God knows how I do it. Up until three years ago, I'd barely had a parking ticket, and then, it's like, I don't know, I got cursed with catastrophe. And the only thing that's gotten me through all this has been you. I love you more than anything in the world, Sarah.'

She studied my face, took a sip of her wine. 'Is this whole speech just designed to get me into the sack?'

'Not specifically, but if it works out that way, I won't pretend that I'm sorry.' I set my wine down and took a step towards her, put my hands on the sides of her shoulders. 'I want to start over. This is the night where my life, where our life together, takes a new turn. No more troubles. No more craziness. From here on, we're going to lead the most boring lives in the world. Want an adventure? I'll take you to Home Depot. That's as wild as it's going to get around here from now on.'

Sarah put her wine glass next to mine and slipped her arms around me. 'I love you.'

And we just stood there for a couple of minutes, until Sarah whispered, 'Let's go upstairs.'

'But,' I said, 'the food's going to arrive in twenty minutes.'

She moved back, smiled at me. 'How much time do you think you're going to need, really?'

I nodded, took her hand, and turned her in the direction of the stairs. 'You've got a point,' I said.

She reached up and lightly touched my forehead. 'What happened to your eyebrows? There's, like, half of them missing.'

'I'll tell you all about it over dinner,' I said, and took her upstairs.

And over veal and pasta, I did. She said very little, stopped me only a couple of times to ask questions.

'Jesus,' she said when I finished.

I had left a couple of parts out. I did not give Sarah the details of Trixie's confession. I hadn't decided what to do yet with that bit of information.

And I also left out the part where Trixie opened up about her fondness for me. There was no need to get into all that, either.

Later, sitting with Sarah on the couch, I said, 'I think I may quit the paper.'

Sarah turned and looked at me. 'What are you talking about?'

'Well, I don't even know if Magnuson'll take me back, take me off suspension, but if he does, I don't know whether it's right for me. And my being there, it's not working for you, either. You're going places. I mean, you lost the foreign editor thing this time, because of me, but there'll be other opportunities. You've got more of a future there than I do.'

'That's not true.'

'The thing is, Sarah, I don't know whether I have

what it takes.' I paused. 'I don't know whether I can tell the whole story.'

'What do you mean? About what?'

'About . . . anything. To be a half-decent journalist, you have to be willing to let all the secrets out, to tell everything. I haven't been doing that. Not with some of the stories I've already done, not with the one about what happened up at my father's place, and not with what's happened this past week.'

'You're just too close to these things. They've all been too personal. It's different.'

I shrugged, looked down. 'It'll all sort itself out. As long as I've got you, it doesn't matter to me what I'm doing.'

We hadn't planned to make a dramatic entrance, but when Sarah and I walked into the kitchen, my arm hanging lightly around her nightshirted shoulder, her arm loose around my waist, thumb tucked into the waistband of my pajamas, I guess we made quite a picture for the kids, who were sitting at the table, eating toast and drinking coffee.

'Ooohhh, check it out,' Angie said.

'I'm gonna be sick,' Paul said. 'Guys, get a room.'

'Where do you think we just came from?' I said.

Paul grimaced. I poured coffee for Sarah and me, opened the cupboard looking for cereal.

'How about eggs?' Sarah asked. Sarah makes great eggs.

'Won't you be late to Home!?' I asked. She was the one heading off to work, not me.

'Fuck Frieda,' she said.

'But my heart belongs to you,' I said. Paul and Angie exchanged glances.

Sarah was leaning into the open fridge. 'You want eggs or not?'

'Yes,' I said. 'I want eggs.'

And so she made eggs. With cheese, and Canadian bacon, and toast and jam.

'I won't be around for dinner,' Angie said. 'Late lecture, then I'm hanging out with some friends.'

'Me neither,' said Paul. 'After school, a bunch of us are going to this thing, and then we're getting something to eat, and then we're doing this other thing. So like, I could use a bit of cash. 'Cause I don't have a job anymore, you know.'

The kids vanished. Sarah and I sat across from each other at the kitchen table, ate our breakfast, drank our coffee, glanced at the headlines in the *Metropolitan*. I didn't even read Dick Colby's story about me and Trixie and her arrest in Martin Benson's death. Instead, I went to the comics page and read *Sherman's Lagoon*.

We were alone, together, and things just seemed so right. That morning seemed like the dawn of something much more than another day. It had the aura of a new beginning. Handcuffed in a basement with a corpse, duct-taped in a barn in Kelton, tossed about by cops in a dead-of-night raid – all these things seemed like distant memories.

Things were good.

I should have savored the moment even more. It wasn't going to last.

THIRTY-TWO

Once I'd seen Sarah off to work and was dressed, I hopped into Trixie's car (I had to sort out this business of getting my car back from Kelton, maybe on the weekend) and drove to Bayside Park. I pulled into the same spot I'd been in three days earlier. I didn't feel the need, this time, to put Lawrence on alert. The first time, I didn't quite know what to expect from Brian Sandler, but felt confident now that he posed no personal risk to me.

I looked out over the lake, switched on the radio. It was a phone-in show, where everyday nincompoops got to sound off on important political matters because it was considerably cheaper to produce a radio show that relied on nincompoops rather than people who actually knew what they were talking about.

We'd agreed to meet at nine, and I'd arrived five minutes early. I'd brought along a notebook to take down more information from him, as well as the scrap of paper on which I'd jotted down his various phone numbers.

I wondered what the hell I was doing.

I was on suspension. I wasn't even sure I was going back. Yet here I was, waiting to meet with a man who had a hell of a story to tell, a story that couldn't help but end up getting splashed across page one. Provided, of course, Bertrand Magnuson allowed me to write it.

My original thinking had been that I could use this story as leverage to get my job back. And not just any job, but my feature-writing job in the newsroom.

But there was another person who could use some help restoring a reputation and getting back into the newsroom. I could take all this stuff I was getting from Brian Sandler and hand it over to Sarah. Let her write it, take the credit, get the hell out of Home!

I'd have to tell Sandler, of course. I didn't want to mislead him. I'd tell him about the suspension, but not to worry, my wife was a seasoned journalist. She'd been an investigative reporter before moving up the ranks and becoming an editor. She'd do a better job putting this story together than I would, truth be known.

That's what I'd tell Sandler.

If he ever showed up.

I glanced at the digital dashboard clock. It was 9:15. Okay, not really late. There were any number of reasons why he might be fifteen minutes late.

But it was harder to explain being thirty minutes late.

At 9:31 a.m. I dug out the slip of paper with Sandler's phone numbers on it. With my own cell phone, I tried his cell. It rang four times, then went to his voicemail. I didn't leave a message. Next, I tried his line at the city health department, and again, I got his voicemail. I wasn't interested in leaving a message there, either. The only number I had left for him was home, and I punched it in.

After three rings, I figured no one was going to answer, but after the fourth, someone picked up.

'Hello.' Quiet, sullen. A young voice, it sounded like. Male.

'Hi. I'm looking for Brian? Brian Sandler?'

'Who's calling?'

Should I say? Had Sandler told anyone he was talking to me, that he'd made arrangements to speak to a (suspended) writer from the *Metropolitan*?

'Just a friend,' I said.

'Well, he's not here. This is his son. Can I help you?'

'Maybe you could tell me where I could reach him. I have his cell and office numbers, and tried both of them, but he's not picking up.'

'He's in the hospital,' the son said.

'What? When?'

'Yesterday afternoon.'

'What happened? Is he sick? Was he in an accident?'

The boy paused. 'He got all burned.'

My stomach felt weak. 'I'm so sorry. Listen, is your mother there? Could I speak to her please?'

'My mom's at the hospital. Me and my sister are waiting for my uncle and then he's going to take us to see him.'

'Which hospital?'

'The Mercy one?'

'Okay. Listen, I hope your dad gets better real soon, okay?'

'Okay.'

I put the phone in my pocket, turned the ignition, and drove from Bayside Park to Mercy General Hospital. I parked in one of the short-term metered spots near the emergency entrance and ran into the building, approached the information desk.

'Brian Sandler,' I said. 'He would have been admitted yesterday?'

I was directed to the west wing of the third floor, room 361. When the elevator doors opened, I got my bearings, saw which way the room numbers were running, went down the end of one hall, hung left down another, and found the room. It would have been difficult to miss.

It was the one with a cop posted at the door.

'Is this Brian Sandler's room?' I asked the officer. He gave me half a nod. 'Look, my name's Zack Walker, I'm with the *Metropolitan*. Technically, at the moment I'm sort of on a leave, but Mr Sandler and I were supposed to meet this morning, and when he didn't show up I called his home and found out he was here. What's happened to him?'

'Sorry,' said the cop, 'but I'm not authorized to make any comment, I'm just keeping out visitors.'

'Why are you here? They usually put you guys on the door if you think the patient's going to try to escape or you think someone's going to come in here and kill him.'

'Look, pal, if you need a quote or something from somebody, you'll have to get it from the detective in charge or public relations.'

'Is Sandler's wife here?'

'She's off talking to the doctor someplace. She'll probably be back in a bit.'

I glanced through the half-open door, saw a pair of hands that looked like they were inside enormous white oven mitts. Half of Sandler's face was shielded by the privacy curtain, but the half that was visible was covered in bandages, except for one eye, which was closed.

'Jesus Christ,' I said. 'What did they do to him?' The cop kept his lip shut. 'Just off the record, what the hell happened to him?'

The cop considered whether to speak, then said, 'Someone put this guy's face and hands into a goddamn fucking deep fryer. It's a wonder he's still alive. When they get the bandages off his face and he has a look in the mirror, he'll be sorry he survived.'

'Is he able to talk at all?'

'Be a lot easier if he had lips. They haven't been able to get much out of him so far.'

'Who's in charge of the investigation?' I said. 'I need to talk to him, or her, or whoever it is.' I didn't have much doubt who was behind this, and I was more than happy to tell all.

The cop dictated a name and number, which I scribbled into my notebook. I thanked him and headed back to my car. Driving home, I dialed the number he'd given me.

'Hi. This is Detective Herlich. Leave a message and I'll get back to you.'

'Yeah, hi, my name is Zack Walker and I think I can tell you what happened to Brian Sandler. Look, I'm heading home, I'll give you that number.' Which I did, and broke off.

Sandler's instincts were right. His boss, Ellinger, must have suspected Sandler was up to something after he'd dropped by his office and asked all those questions. And then, and I was guessing here but it all seemed to make sense, Ellinger put in a call to the Gorkins, who brought Sandler in for a visit with the deep fryer.

I imagined Mrs Gorkin and her girls must have had a few questions for him before they dunked him into the sizzling grease. Like what he was up to, whether he was going to play along, whether he was going to the police.

Whether he was going to the media.

Shit.

I decided that when I got home, I would put in a call to Lawrence Jones. Get a few tips on how to watch my back. Maybe drop enough hints, act frightened enough, that he'd come over and babysit me until I told Detective Herlich everything I knew about the Gorkins and Sandler. Herlich was welcome to hear the audio file as well. Wouldn't take long, once he had all of that, I figured, before arrest warrants would be sworn out for the Gorkins, they'd be in custody, and I could let Lawrence go home and listen to his jazz collection or surprise philandering husbands in motel rooms.

I parked Trixie's car in our driveway, got out my keys as I mounted the front porch steps, and opened the front door.

The twins were on me in an instant.

I spotted the one on the stairs first, and would have turned to run, but her clone had been hiding behind the door and slammed it shut once I stepped inside. She came up behind me and encircled me in her meaty, pasty white arms while the other one came at me like I was in a bullring waving a red flag.

I tightened the muscles in my stomach when I saw the fist coming, but I am not exactly a hundred-crunches-a-day kind of guy, and when she drove her hand into me I turned into a rag doll. The one holding me let go and I dropped to the floor, desperately trying to catch my breath.

'Oh God oh God oh God,' I said.

It took a moment before I was able to breathe again, but even once I had air going in and out of my lungs, I didn't have the strength to get back up. I rolled over onto my back and saw that the twins had now been joined by their mother, who looked down contemptuously at me.

'Where is file?' she asked me.

'Give me a sec,' I said, still gasping. 'I can barely breathe.'

'Give him minute, Momma,' said one of the twins.

I had a moment now to take them all in. The three of them standing there, looking like a trio of linebackers without the helmets. All short and squat and one of them getting on a bit in years, but no less threatening than the other two. Mrs Gorkin, gray hair brushed back, hook-nosed, a bit of hair on her upper lip, wore a drab dress that would have showed its grease stains to more advantage if it weren't black.

The twins, both around five feet, about four hundred pounds between them, had short, bristly blonde hair. They were both in jeans, one in a red sweater, the other in blue.

I sat up, waved a finger at the twins. 'So, who's who here?'

The one in the red sweater said, 'I am Ludmilla.'

The one in the blue sweater said, 'I am Gavrilla.'

Ludmilla said, 'We are twins.'

I nodded. 'Ludmilla. Gavrilla.' I turned and looked at their mother. 'And Mrs Gorkin. Nice to see you again.' I took another breath. 'I'd just like to say, right now, that I'm really, really sorry about what happened at your place the other day. My son, he seemed to think there might be something wrong with the burgers, and some people heard us talking, and, well, you know the rest. So I can totally understand you being upset about that. Believe me, if I had it to do all over again, I'd just forget about it.'

Mrs Gorkin said, 'We are not here about dat.'

I feigned bafflement. 'Well, I don't suppose you're here to offer my son his job back.'

Mrs Gorkin said, 'Stop being stupid!'

'I'm not trying to be stupid. I'm just trying to figure out what it is you want.' I'd always thought playing dumb came naturally to me, but Mrs Gorkin didn't seem to be buying it.

'Momma wants the file,' said Ludmilla.

'I don't know what you're talking about,' I said. The thing is, I didn't care if they had the file. I was more worried about what they might do to me if they knew I'd heard it.

'The man,' said Gavrilla. 'The man who was going to talk to you. He sent a file to you. That you could hear.'

'Where is computer?' Mrs Gorkin asked.

'My computer?' I said. 'It's up in my study. Upstairs. Help yourself to it.' It wasn't like I had a nearly finished novel sitting in it. Cart it away, I thought.

'Upstairs,' Mrs Gorkin said, 'you take us.'

I shook my head like I didn't know what she was talking about but was happy to indulge her little whims. Once I was on my feet, I took another couple of breaths. I realized now it was Gavrilla who'd held me, and Ludmilla who'd thrown the punch. It felt as though her fist was still in my stomach.

'This way,' I said, leading them up the stairs to the study. 'Honestly, I don't know what it is you're going on about.'

'Shut the mouth,' said Mrs Gorkin, giving me a shove from behind.

'Who's running Burger Crisp?' I asked, just making conversation. It wouldn't be long before the lunchtime crowd showed up. 'Shouldn't you be there? You want, I could bring the computer by.'

'We have people,' said Ludmilla. 'Better than your stupid son.'

I led them into the study and took a seat in front of my computer. Mrs Gorkin had her eyes on me, but the girls took a quick look around the room, taking in my various items of SF kitsch.

'Look!' said Ludmilla. 'Wonder Woman!'

'Neat!' said Gavrilla, taking the busty superhero from the shelf. 'Look, her arms move. She even has a little lasso.'

Mrs Gorkin was not interested in Wonder Woman. 'Show me where you have da files,' she said.

'I've got all kinds of files,' I said. 'What kind of files did you have in mind?'

Ludmilla came up behind me. 'Open your e-mail. Momma wants to see the e-mail.'

I did as I was asked, Ludmilla peering over my shoulder. She smelled of fries. 'Go to Inbox,' she said, and I did. 'There it is,' she said, pointing to the one labeled 'Brian Sandler.'

'I don't hear anyting,' said Mrs Gorkin.

'Click on it,' said Ludmilla. 'Momma doesn't understand computers very well.' I clicked on the e-mail, and then, at Ludmilla's instruction, the attached audio file.

And a moment later, the conversation between Brian Sandler and Frank Ellinger was coming out of the speakers.

'Dat is it!' said Mrs Gorkin. 'You say you not know what I'm talking about!'

'I didn't know you meant *this* file,' I said. 'Do you have any idea how many files I have?'

'Okay, kill da file,' she said.

'I'll do it, Momma,' Gavrilla said, dragging me out of the chair and taking my place at the keyboard. I hoped she wouldn't notice the tiny arrow attached to Sandler's message, indicating that it had been forwarded to Lawrence Jones.

Gavrilla highlighted the e-mail, hit Delete, and it disappeared.

'Is gone?' Mrs Gorkin said.

'I have to empty all the items in the Trash file,' Gavrilla said, switching to the Trash box. She high-lighted all the items, hit Delete again, and they vanished from the screen. But she'd neglected to go to Sent Items, where the message to Lawrence sat.

'There we go, Momma,' Gavrilla said.

'Okay, now we smash it,' Mrs Gorkin said. 'So no one ever sees it.'

'Uh, we don't have to do that, Momma,' said Ludmilla.

'I smash it!' Mrs Gorkin said, and grabbed a stapler off the desk and used it to shatter the computer monitor. Shards of glass littered the top of my desk.

To me, Ludmilla said, almost apologetically, 'Momma doesn't understand that it could still be there in the computer. She thinks, you smash the screen, it's gone.'

I smiled. 'That's sweet,' I said. 'So, you've done what you came to do, the file is gone, so don't even worry about the monitor, I can get another one of those. Don't worry about it.'

'You come,' said Mrs Gorkin. 'Come to restaurant.' She smiled, showing off a brown, crooked tooth. 'We make you lunch.'

'Listen,' I said, 'that would be great, but I have this thing I have to go to. Maybe, later, I could drop by. Love to get an order of fries. Honestly, terrific fries.'

Gavrilla had hold of my arm. 'Momma wants you to come with us.'

I had a mental image of Brian Sandler, the twins dipping his hands in first, then pushing his face into the fryer. If I could just break free of Gavrilla's arm, get out the study door and down the stairs, I could be out the front door in a shot. The girls were strong, but they didn't look as though they were built for speed. I was sure I could outrun them.

Then Mrs Gorkin pulled some sort of short-barreled pistol from the bag hanging over her shoulder. 'You come back with us,' she said, pointing the weapon at me. I could outrun the twins, but a bullet was something else altogether.

The phone rang.

I looked at Mrs Gorkin. 'I should answer that,' I said.

'No, it can ring,' she said.

'But there are people who are expecting me to be here, who might wonder why I'm not coming to the phone.'

'The bullsheet,' said Mrs Gorkin. 'You could be in bathroom, having crap. Let it ring.'

And it rang. Once, twice, three times. And then it went to the machine.

'Hi, Mr Walker? This is Detective Herlich returning your call about the Brian Sandler investigation. Feel free to try me again, or I may try you again, too.'

The message ended. Mrs Gorkin looked very displeased with me. 'So you don't know anyting. But you call police to tell dem what you don't know?'

I couldn't think of anything to say. Especially with the pistol pointed at me.

'We go back,' Mrs Gorkin said. 'Ludmilla, go down street and bring up car.'

We were going down the stairs, Gavrilla in front, then me, followed by Ludmilla and Mrs Gorkin, when there was a knock at the front door. Everyone froze.

'Sheet,' whispered Mrs Gorkin.

It couldn't be Sarah, I figured. There was no reason for her to come home late morning from work. Paul was at school, Angie at college. But whoever it was, it presented an opportunity. Maybe, if the Gorkins allowed me to answer it, I could mouth 'Help!' Roll my eyes, nod my head back into the house, somehow indicate that I was in a great deal of trouble.

'I should see who it is,' I said, turning and looking at Mrs Gorkin.

Another knock. Harder, more insistent. Maybe it was Detective Herlich. No, that made no sense. He'd only just called. Unless he'd called from his car. Maybe he was out front.

Yes. Let it be Detective Herlich.

'Really,' I said. 'Just let me answer it. I'll get rid of them.'

'You girls,' Mrs Gorkin whispered. 'You get on sides of door.' To me, she said, 'I stay up here on stairs. Have gun. You be stupid, I shoot you.'

'Of course,' I said.

Gavrilla cleared the way for me to get down the rest of the stairs, then she and her sister hid on either side of the door.

There was another knock. Whoever wanted me to answer it was banging it with his fist now. Would a cop bang a door like that?

I approached the door, my heart pounding. I took hold of the knob, turned it, and opened the door wide.

It took me a moment to recognize him. Even though I'd heard so much about him, I'd only seen him once in person, at the stun gun demonstration.

Gary Merker. Arms down at his side, one hand, his right one, held slightly behind his back. Beyond him, in the driveway, I could see an old Ford pickup with one adult in it, on the passenger side, and possibly a child in the middle.

'You Zack Walker?' he said.

'Uh,' I said, wondering how much crazier things could get. 'Yeah, that's me.'

Then Gary Merker raised his right arm, and I saw that there was something gun-like in it, but not a gun exactly.

Okay, now I knew what it was. A stun gun.

Merker squeezed the trigger, and then I had, and I hope you'll forgive me for this, the most shocking experience of my entire fucking life.

THIRTY-THREE

I dropped to the floor.

I went down without any accompanying theatrics. This was no Broadway death scene where I clutched my chest and staggered across the stage in tiny steps whimpering that the end was near.

I simply dropped. Like a Thunderbirds puppet with the strings cut.

All the little messages my brain had been sending to my legs to keep me standing, to my hand to keep holding the doorknob, to my mouth to keep asking questions I hoped would buy me some time, all were abruptly interrupted.

Fifty thousand volts has a way of doing that to you, I guess. When the charge from Merker's stun gun hit me, the effect was instantaneous, and I don't believe there are words to adequately describe the sensation. It was like my entire body was a tooth with a filling, and it had just bitten into the world's biggest piece of tinfoil.

So I hit the floor, and lay there a moment, and was only vaguely aware of the commotion going on around me. But there was plenty of it. As best as I can recall, Mrs Gorkin was the first to start shouting.

'Drop it!' she screamed.

'Fuck are you?' Merker shouted back.

Then one of the twins – like it matters which one – appeared out of nowhere and slammed Merker up against a wall. He took another shot with the stun gun – it being one of those newfangled ones, he was able to fire it more than once – and caught the other twin, who screamed and dropped to the floor as quickly as I had, but, and I'm not just saying this to be nasty, with a much more resounding thud. Then Merker fired the gun a third time, but failed to connect with anyone.

There was another shot, but from a real gun. It had come from Mrs Gorkin, who fired wild, sending a bullet into the wall next to Merker.

'Be frozen!' Mrs Gorkin shouted.

And then everything went quiet, except for some whimpering from both me and, as it turned out, Ludmilla. We were the two stunned ones.

'Okay, let's everyone just calm down here a moment,' Merker said, catching his breath. For all he knew, these three lovely ladies were members of my family, and the Walkers were just waiting for someone like Gary Merker to show up so we could toss him about and fire bullets at him.

But he must have also been able to sense that something was amiss here. That he'd actually walked in on something out of the ordinary.

'Who are you?' Mrs Gorkin said, keeping her gun trained on Merker but moving across the room to check on Ludmilla, who was struggling to her knees. 'You okay, sweedie?' she asked.

'Who the fuck are you?' Merker said.

'Listen,' I said, trying to sit up. 'Give me a second here and I'll try to introduce everyone, shall I?' Merker glanced at me, surprised, perhaps, that I would be able to introduce him. I wasn't certain he recognized me from the stun gun demo he'd done for the cops, and it occurred to me after I'd offered to do introductions that maybe it was a mistake for me to let on that I knew who he was.

The fifty thousand volts might have interfered with my mental processes.

'Gary Merker, this is Mrs Gorkin, and her daughters Ludmilla and Gavrilla, and they run the Burger Crisp across town, and it seems that if they haven't come here to kill me, they certainly intend to cause me a great deal of harm. And ladies, this is Gary Merker, who's trying to unload a bunch of stun guns to the police, and who also seems bent on doing me some sort of harm too.' I took a breath. 'I guess you'll have to fight over me.'

'What do you want with him?' Merker asked Mrs Gorkin.

'He had file. We come to get it.'

'What fucking file?'

'About health inspection.'

'Health inspection?' Merker said. 'What fucking health inspection?' He was twitching his nose about, like it itched. He stuck a pinky finger in one of his nostrils, dug around a bit.

Mrs Gorkin looked taken aback by Merker's blatant display of nasal inspection. It was nice to know that even she had standards. 'You don't know about dat?'

'Lady, I don't know what the fuck you're talking about.' He pulled out his finger, examined what was stuck to the end of it, and wiped it on his trousers.

'Den why are you here?'

'Because this son of a bitch' – he pointed down at me – 'is going to help me get back some money that was stole from me.'

'Dat's too bad, because we're taking him with us,' Mrs Gorkin said.

'Why do you need him?' Merker said.

'Because we have to make sure he make no more trouble for us,' Mrs Gorkin said.

That didn't sound good. I was wondering whether I should start rooting for Merker, who had his finger back in his nose to get what he missed the first time.

'You shouldn't shoot my daughter like that,' she said. 'What that thing?'

'It's just a stun gun,' Merker said. 'She'll be fine. Be glad I didn't use my real gun on her. And Jesus Christ, lady, you nearly shot me with that thing.' He was pointing at Mrs Gorkin's weapon. 'That some sort of Soviet piece? Looks kinda different.'

Mrs Gorkin didn't answer him. She was helping Ludmilla get up.

Gavrilla said, 'Maybe we can work something out. What's this money you got stolen from you?'

Merker thought a moment. 'This guy knows someone stole some money from me, and I think if he talks to her for me, I can get it back.'

'There's nothing I can do for you,' I said.

'Really? According to the news, you know Candace, or Trixie or Miranda or whoever the fuck she is this week, very well. Went all the way up to farm country to try to get her to come back before the cops got her. Am I right?'

I nodded wearily.

'So I need you to talk to her, explain to her the situation, and I think once you've done that, she'll tell you where you can find the money, and you and I can go and get it.'

'Are you crazy?' I said. 'She's in *jail*. If you listened to the news, you know that.'

Merker nodded his understanding. 'You'll have to go visit her. I can't do it. People might be looking for me. Last place I want to walk into is a prison. They might not let me out. But I bet you can get in to see her.'

'So I'm supposed to just walk in, *into the jail*, and say hey, where's that money, and she tells me, we go find it, and you walk off with it.'

Merker smiled, delighted that I had grasped the concept. 'Yup.'

Gavrilla interrupted. 'How much money did she steal from you?'

'A lot,' Merker said. I knew it to be about half a million, but clearly he didn't want to tip his hand.

'Then here is a deal,' Gavrilla said, glancing out the front door. 'We let you take him to get the money, but we get a, what do you call it, a cut.'

'Yeah, right,' Merker said. 'That's a plan.'

Mrs Gorkin turned her gun on me. 'We kill him now then.'

'Whoa, hang on, wait a minute,' Merker said. 'Let's not get crazy.'

'Who's that man in the truck?' Gavrilla asked.

'That's Leo,' Merker said.

'Okay, so you leave Leo with us,' Gavrilla said, her mom watching her curiously, 'and we let you take this guy to get your money, then you come back with the money, you give us our cut, Leo can go and you give us back this guy.'

'What, Leo's, like, a hostage?'

321

'No, no. He just stays with us.' Gavrilla shrugged. 'We'll hang out.'

Ludmilla, on her feet now, said, 'I could stay here.'

'There's somebody else,' Merker said. 'In the truck, with Leo. She'd have to stay too.'

'How much money?' Mrs Gorkin asked.

'Like I said, a lot,' Merker said.

'Don't give me this sheet, a lot,' she said. 'We not letting you walk off with him we don't know what's in it for us.'

'The thing is,' Merker said, 'I don't know exactly how much she's got. I know what she took, but she probably spent that, but she's probably made some back. I'm betting she's got it stashed away someplace and I want it back. With fucking interest too.'

'How much she take?'

Merker didn't even hesitate. 'A hundred thousand.' I couldn't see any advantage, at the moment, in pointing out that he was underreporting potential income. I was not the tax man.

'Whoa,' said Mrs Gorkin. 'Okay then, we want thirty per cent.'

'Thirty per cent?' said Merker. 'You fucking joking? What's fucking thirty per cent of a hundred thousand?'

Trixie hadn't been kidding when she said Merker wasn't very good at numbers. I said, 'I think that would work out to about thirty thousand dollars.'

Merker shook his head disapprovingly. 'That's just ridiculous. I'll give you five. Five thousand bucks.'

Mrs Gorkin pointed her weapon at me again. 'You must not need him very much.'

'Okay, okay, ten. Ten thousand. That's as high as I'm willing to go.' Mrs Gorkin's gun was still trained at my head. 'Fuck, all right, what about twenty-five thousand? That would work out to, that would be . . .'

'Twenty-five per cent,' I said.

'Okay, how about that?'

Mrs Gorkin lowered the gun. 'Dat okay.'

Gavrilla was smiling proudly. This had been her strategy, after all. 'That's good. That's great. So, you should call Leo in.'

Merker went to the open door, made a waving motion. I heard a pickup door slam, and then Leo Edgar was walking up the porch steps.

He was leading, by the hand, a child. A little girl, probably no more than five years old. Curly haired. Quiet, walking as if in a daze. Dried tears visible on her cheeks.

Katie Bennet. Trixie's daughter.

THIRTY-FOUR

I was back up on my feet now, the residual effects of a punch to the gut and fifty thousand volts to my entire body momentarily forgotten as Katie Bennet stepped into the house. She looked at me with a glimmer of recognition, but no joy.

'Katie,' I said, moving towards her and going down on one knee. 'Are you okay, sweetheart?'

She half-nodded. I put my hands on her shoulders, and she tensed. I pulled them away. 'It's going to be okay,' I told her, but they were only words. If she was here, with Gary Merker and Leo Edgars, there was no way that things were okay.

I looked up at Merker. 'What the hell's going on?'

'You didn't think her mother would just *give* us the money, did you?' he asked. 'We need a bit of leverage.'

'Are we almost done here, Gary?' Leo asked. 'I could really use a bite.'

'Leo, fuck's sake, I got a situation to deal with here,' Gary said.

Leo, somewhat dimly, took in everyone else present. His eyes bounced off Mrs Gorkin and then her two daughters. Ludmilla stepped forwards, extended a hand. 'Hi,' she said, smiling. 'I'm Ludmilla. Aren't you a handsome one?'

324

Maybe, to someone like Ludmilla, Leo was a prize specimen. Gavrilla insinuated herself between Leo and her sister, extending her hand as well. 'I'm Gavrilla, Ludmilla's younger sister,' she said. By what? Fifteen seconds? Five minutes?

'Hi,' Leo said. 'What's going on, Gary?'

'I'm gonna need you and the kid to stay here with one of the girls while this guy' – he waved his stun gun in my direction – 'helps me get that bitch's money.'

'Why I got to stay here? I need to get something to eat.'

'Fuck, Leo, would you relax? I've worked out a deal with the ladies here. You stay here with – which one are you?'

'Ludmilla,' said Ludmilla.

'You stay here with Ludmilla.'

'I could stay,' Gavrilla said. 'Why don't you go back to the restaurant?' she said to her sister.

'I already said I would stay,' Ludmilla said. 'Didn't I, Mom?'

Mrs Gorkin wasn't going to tolerate this for a minute. 'Gavrilla, you come with me. Ludmilla, you stay, make sure this man stay till *this* man here comes back with the money. Here.' She handed Ludmilla her gun.

'Hey,' said Leo. 'What's she need a gun for?'

'To shoot you,' Gary said offhandedly. 'If you try to leave before I get back with the money.'

'Oh,' said Leo.

Ludmilla took the gun and ran the barrel down the side of Leo's arm. 'Don't worry, honey. It just keeps everyone honest.'

'I guess,' Leo said. 'Why do I have to keep the kid?'

Katie had gone over to our couch, sat down. She looked ahead vacantly. I wondered whether she was in some sort of shock.

'Look at her,' Merker said. 'How much trouble can she be?'

'Well, okay. How long you going to be?'

'I don't know. That depends on shithead here,' he said, pointing at me. 'You gotta get us into that jail to see what's-her-face. You know her as Trixie, right?'

'Yes,' I said.

'So start setting it up.'

'How on earth am I supposed to do that?'

Merker shrugged. 'Maybe you should figure something out. If you can't, we can always have some fun with the kid.'

I swallowed. 'Let me think,' I said. Trixie had mentioned the name of her lawyer when she'd been arrested at the Bennet farmhouse. I closed my eyes, tried to think of it. It had something to do with a dog. Something dogs do. Not bite, not sniff, not—

Wag. Wagland. Niles Wagland.

'I have an idea,' I said. 'I can call her lawyer. Maybe he can get me in. Let me go check on the computer, I can probably find an office number online—' I stopped myself. 'No.'

'What?' asked Merker. 'What do you mean, no?'

I tilted my head toward Mrs Gorkin. 'She kind of disabled my computer.'

'What the fuck did you do that for?' Merker asked her.

Mrs Gorkin, untroubled by Merker's attacks, shrugged. 'Computer was bad.'

'I can check the phone book,' I said. Merker followed me into the kitchen, where I pulled a thick Yellow

Pages out of a cupboard below the phone. I thumbed through the pages until I found dozens of pages for law offices.

'Hurry up,' said Merker.

'Just give me a second,' I said. Not taking my eyes off the pages, I asked him, 'What about Katie's folks? The Bennets? Do they know you have her? They must be worried sick about her. You should at least call them. Let me call them. Let me tell them that she's okay.'

When Merker said nothing, I looked at him. He grinned. 'Be kind of hard to reach them now,' he said.

A chill ran through me. 'What are you saying?' I asked quietly.

'I'm just saying, they ain't taking calls anymore.'

'They're dead? Are you saying they're dead?'

Merker's grin disappeared and he leaned in to me, putting his mouth close to my ear. 'The kid'll be joining them, and you too, if you don't find this fucking lawyer and get in to see her.'

I turned my eyes back to the phone book, and found my hand shaking as I turned the pages. I needed to pull myself together. I was unable to focus. I blinked a couple of times, gave my head a shake.

I could find no listing for Niles Wagland.

'I'm going to have to call information for Oakwood,' I said. 'Her lawyer may be out there. It only makes sense she'd pick one in her own town.'

'Just don't do anything funny,' he said.

I picked up the phone, dialed, got a number for a Wagland law office in Oakwood. Once I had the number, I punched it in, and a woman answered on the fourth ring.

'I need to speak to Mr Wagland,' I said.

'I'm sorry, but Mr Wagland is in a meeting. Who's calling?'

'My name is Zack Walker. I'm a friend of Trixie Snelling. Make that Miranda Chicoine.'

'If you'd like to leave your number, I'm sure he'll get back to you when—'

My voice went up a notch. 'This is very important. I *must* speak to Mr Wagland right now.'

'I'm sure it is, Mr Walker, but I'm sure you can understand—'

'No! Right now, you have to understand that I must speak to Mr Wagland immediately. This is a life-or-death matter concerning his client Ms Chicoine.'

'I see.' She paused. 'Just a moment please.'

I was put on hold. 'That was good,' said Merker, who'd been holding his head close enough to the receiver to listen. 'You were very good.' I did not acknowledge the compliment.

A click. Then a voice. 'Niles Wagland.'

'Mr Wagland, this is Zack Walker.'

'Yes, Mr Walker. I'm in the middle of a meeting here, but my secretary indicated your call was very urgent.'

'I need to see Trixie. Miranda.'

'Ms Chicoine is in custody, Mr Walker. I would have thought that you'd know that. My understanding, from speaking with her, is that you were present when she was arrested. She's already indicated to me that if anyone asks, you were trying to persuade her to turn herself in, so I don't think you have any cause for concern.'

'That's not what I'm calling about. I need to see her. I don't even know which facility she's being held in. But I need to get in and speak with her.'

'What about?'

328

'It's very important, to her.'

'I'm her attorney, Mr Walker. Anything that concerns Ms Chicoine you can discuss with me.'

Merker shook his head.

'I'd like to, Mr Wagland, but I have something I must tell Ms Chicoine, in person. If she decides to share that information with you, I guess that would be up to her.'

'This is highly irregular. And I can't just pick up the phone and arrange for you to visit someone in a correctional facility.'

'I figured that a call from you to the facility might carry more weight than one from me. Mr Wagland, I wish I could be more specific, but if you can't get me in to see Trixie – Miranda – then something very, very awful might happen.'

Wagland was quiet a moment. 'What sort of thing?'

'I can't say.' I paused. 'So Miranda has spoken to you of me?'

'Yes.'

'Has she said anything to indicate that I'm less than trustworthy? That I'd have anything but her best interests at heart?'

'No.'

'You have to trust me on this.'

'Give me your number. I'll see what I can do and will call you back.'

'Thank you.' I gave him the number and hung up.

As I turned to face Merker he grabbed the front of my shirt and shoved me up against the wall. He had his face in mine, and I could see a small booger half hanging out of one nostril. 'You were supposed to get in and see her.'

'Jesus,' I said, trying to back away with no place to go. 'He said he's going to see what he can do and call back. Weren't you listening? You think I can get in to see her just like that?'

'Fuck,' Merker said, turning away. 'How long before he calls?'

'I don't know. We'll just have to sit tight and see.'

Mrs Gorkin appeared at the kitchen door. 'What is happening?'

Merker said, 'We're waiting for a call back.'

In the living room, I could hear Ludmilla and Leo chatting like old friends. 'What kind of food do you like?' she asked.

'I like everything,' Leo said.

'I am a good cook.'

'Yeah, of crap,' said Gavrilla. Mrs Gorkin went back to the living room and yelled at her girls to shut up.

'So let's say I get in,' I said to Merker. 'What do you want me to do?'

'You ask her where the money is. You tell her we got her kid. She doesn't tell, we kill the kid. Do you need me to write it down?'

'No,' I said. 'What if there is no money? What if whatever you say she took from you is all gone? What then?'

Merker considered that. 'Then we got a problem.' He wandered over to the fridge, where a few family snapshots were held on with magnets. There was one there of me, in a tux, with Sarah, decked out in a black gown, taken at a newspaper awards dinner a few months ago. Neither of us had been up for anything, but a reporting team Sarah had overseen had been nominated for an investigative series on city hall contract rigging. Merker studied it.

'Who's the broad?' he asked.

'My wife,' I said.

'Nice rack,' he said. I didn't feel like acknowledging that, either.

I decided to change the subject. 'What led you to me?'

Merker said, 'I listen to the news. They had the story about Trixie getting caught up in Kelton, they mentioned your name, that you worked for the paper, that you tried to talk her into turning herself in, and I figured you'd be a good guy to talk to.' He paused and studied my face. 'We've met before, haven't we?'

'Only briefly,' I said. 'I was there when you were trying to get the cops to buy your supply of stun guns.'

'Fuck, yeah. That really pissed me off, you know? That was you, right, who did the story for the paper? That fucked up everything. Once that ran, the deal went queer. People start asking questions, cops start taking heat about buying my merchandise.'

'Because it's hot,' I said.

Merker grinned at me. 'Where you hear that?'

'One of your old friends back in Canborough. Michael Cherry. That was his guess.'

'Fucking Mikey. You were talking to him?'

'Yeah. I talked to a lot of people, trying to track down Trixie.'

'What'd Mikey tell you?'

'About what?'

'About me.'

'You ran the Kickstart. Some bad things went down. You lost some people, got out of town.'

'He tell you about that?'

'A little.'

'He tell you who did it? Who killed my boys?'

331

'No. He doesn't know. I think he thinks it might have been you. That you cut a deal with the other gang in town, they paid you off, you wasted your own guys.'

'He thinks that?'

'It's a theory.'

'It's pretty fucking wrong,' Merker said. 'It was that bitch, that friend of yours, did it.'

I said nothing.

'You don't even look surprised,' he said. 'She tell you? She tell you what she did?'

'She told me what *you* did. That you killed the father of her child, that the bunch of you raped her.'

Merker shrugged. 'She was a stripper.'

'I thought she did your books for you.'

'Okay, she used to be a stripper, but what's your point? She's just a bit sensitive, you know? I'd a been a lot smarter, let her keep stripping, instead of looking after the money. Talk about getting fucked in the ass over that one. She robbed me blind.'

The phone rang. I grabbed it before the first ring had finished. 'Hello?'

'It's Wagland. It's set up. Eleven o'clock.'

'Where?'

'Clayton Correctional Facility.'

'That's an all-women's prison, right? North Oakwood?'

'Yes,' Wagland said. 'Mr Walker, I had to pull in a couple of favors there to set this up, and that wasn't easy, when I don't have the foggiest notion why you have to see her.'

'I know. I appreciate that. You're doing the right thing.'

'I better be, Mr Walker. For your sake, I better be.' He hung up.

'Perfect,' said Merker. 'We better saddle up, pardner.'

Mrs Gorkin returned to the kitchen, followed by Leo and Ludmilla, who was dragging Katie by the arm. 'Well?' she said.

'It's set up,' Merker said. 'Walker and I are going to pay a visit to the bitch who owes me. We find out where the cash is, we get it, we come back, I give you your share, we're done.'

'And then you give him' – she pointed at me – 'to us.'

'Yeah. And I get Leo back.'

Ludmilla, still holding the gun in one hand, squeezed Leo's arm. 'I might decide to keep him.'

Leo chuckled, and then his eyes landed on the fridge. 'You got anything to eat here?' he asked of no one in particular.

He opened the door, leaned down, examining each rack. 'Fuck, there's nothing in here to eat. Haven't you got – hang on, what's this?'

He brought out a white Styrofoam container. Written on top, in black marker, were the words 'EAT THIS AND DIE – PAUL.'

Leo flipped open the lid, saw the old burger and fries, and smiled ear to ear. 'Fuck you, Paul,' he said. 'You'll have to find some other leftovers. This is mine. Where's your microwave?'

THIRTY-FIVE

I told Merker I needed a moment with Katie before we left.

She'd moved from the couch and was standing at the living room window, peering through a gap in the curtains, as though waiting for someone who'd never arrive. I knelt down beside her, but it was like I wasn't there.

'Katie,' I said. 'Katie, look at me. I need to know that you're listening to me.' She turned her head slightly. 'I know things may look bad right now, but I'm going to see if I can make things okay. Maybe not as okay as they were before, but better than they are now.'

Katie sniffed.

'I promise you I'll do the best I can,' I said.

Katie sniffed again, and she opened her mouth. 'Are you going to get me my other mommy?' she asked.

'I'm supposed to be going to see her now,' I said. 'I hope I can get in to see her.'

'Can you tell her something?' Katie asked.

'What's that, sweetheart?'

'Tell her my other mommy can't be my mommy anymore, so I need her to be my mommy all the time instead of just once in a while.'

I nodded. 'I'll tell her that,' I said. I reached my hand tentatively towards her, not sure whether she'd pull away. She did not, and I pulled her head towards me and kissed her forehead. 'For sure, I'll tell her. I'm sure she'll be very worried about you and will do everything she can.'

'Also,' Katie said, 'I need a daddy. I didn't have an extra one of those.'

Was she simply in shock? Was she traumatized? Or was she the bravest little five-year-old I'd ever encountered? Or was it a bit of both?

'I'll tell her,' I said.

'Let's hit the road,' Merker said behind me. I touched Katie softly on the head, looked one last time into her sad eyes, and turned to face him. He had a real gun in his hand this time, not the one he'd used to stun me. Fifty thousand volts were bad, but they were preferable to one real bullet.

He led me out to his blue pickup, a rust-eaten twenty-year-old Ford that sat up high on oversized tires. Four-wheel drive, by the look of it. I hauled myself up into the passenger side as Merker settled in behind the wheel. He slid the keys into the ignition, turned it, and I wondered if I'd misread the nameplate on the side, and that we'd actually climbed aboard a John Deere. He tapped the accelerator a couple of times and the engine roared like an oversized tractor. He put the column shift into reverse, but held his foot on the brake and gave me a look.

'Let's just be clear,' he said. 'You try anything stupid, you try to run, you try to get the cops, I call Leo, and that kid dies. Do you understand?'

'Yes,' I said.

'We're going to do this thing, we're going to find out where my money is, and when I get it, stop by a playground, let the girl go.'

'But not me. You hand me over to Mrs Gorkin and the Westinghouse twins.'

Merker shrugged. 'I made a deal with her. What can I say?'

'You're going to give her twenty-five thousand? Like you said?'

Merker's cheek poked out as he moved his tongue around, maybe trying to keep himself from grinning. 'Sure.' He wiggled his nose some more. 'That one, Luddite or whatever her name was, seemed to take a fancy to Leo. He's never been that great in the ladies department. This'll be a nice treat for him.'

He let his foot off the brake, backed the truck onto the street, leaving Trixie's car in the driveway. 'So where are we going?'

I gave him directions to the highway that would take us west out of the city. Once we took the Oakwood exit, I'd be able to get us to the Clayton Correctional Facility. I'd never been in it, but had driven by it enough times when we lived out that way to know where it was.

Once we were on the highway, and I didn't have to navigate for Merker, I was quiet. I glanced over occasionally, but Merker was usually preoccupied with wiggling his nose or conducting digital explorations of it. He almost never had both hands on the wheel. I could see, sticking out of his front jeans pocket, what looked like the handle of a knife. A switchblade, most likely.

I was surprised when, after ten minutes or so, he actually spoke. 'You ain't got much to say,' he said.

'Just thinking,' I said.

'Oh. About what?'

'I guess I'm wondering what kind of person would kill a little girl's parents.'

'They weren't her *parents*,' Merker corrected me. 'That was her aunt and her aunt's husband.' So there.

'But they were raising Katie like she was their own child.'

'Yeah, well, that wasn't my decision, now was it,' Merker said. 'That was your friend Trixie's decision.' He shook his head derisively. 'She has an awful lot to answer for, you know.'

He looked up the highway. 'Fuck.' Traffic was bunching up. Brake lights were flashing on ahead of us. 'What time is it?'

I glanced at my watch. 'It's only ten thirty-five. We have lots of time.'

But Merker wasn't a patient man. He made a fist out of his nose-picking hand and bounced it angrily off the steering wheel. 'Do you see an accident? I don't even see an accident. Everyone's just fucking slowing down.'

'The Oakwood exit is just up ahead,' I said. 'Take it easy.'

'Take it easy? Does somebody owe *you* half a mill? Maybe if they did you'd be a bit tense too.'

'Half a mill?' I said, innocently. 'You just told Mrs Gorkin it was a hundred thousand.'

Merker blinked. 'Yeah, well, I forgot a bit of it,' he said. He steered the truck over to the right lane without signaling, cut some motorists off. Someone laid on the horn and Merker held up a finger to the window, then reached into his jacket, where I knew he was touching the grip of his handgun, wondering whether to pull it out and use it as a traffic calmer.

Never again would I honk at anyone.

The exit was a couple of hundred yards up, so Merker rode the shoulder until we reached the ramp. 'When you get to the light at the end,' I said, 'hang a right.'

Merker's face was full of fury. He wanted his money, and he didn't appreciate anything, like other drivers and traffic lights, that delayed our arrival at the prison and moving forwards with his plan. At the light, we waited behind a white Civic, its right blinker going. I couldn't make out the driver, sitting up high as I was in the pickup. But it was a timid one. Several times, there was enough of a gap in the traffic for the Civic to go, but the car held back.

'Fuck! Come on!' Merker shouted, gunning the accelerator while he held his other foot on the brake. The moment he let his foot off it, we'd shoot ahead like a rocket.

'Just take it ea—'

I didn't have a chance to finish. Merker let his foot off the brake, trounced harder on the gas, and rammed the rear right corner of the Civic, shoving it out of our way.

'Christ!' I shouted, throwing my hands forwards and bracing myself against the dashboard.

'Stupid bitch!' Merker shouted, even though he couldn't see into the Civic any better than I could.

The car lurched forward into the street, forcing an oncoming SUV to slam on its brakes. Merker steered the truck around the Civic and headed north, the pickup's shattered exhaust system sounding like a round of gunfire.

'Honest to God,' Merker said. 'Some fucking drivers. How many chances did she have to pull out but she just sat there?'

I craned my neck around, saw a man get out of the Civic, a woman stepping out of the SUV, both of them pointing as we vanished into the distance. What if Merker got us both killed before we even got to the prison? Who'd tell Leo to let Katie go then?

I dropped my hands from the dash and gripped the door handle with my right one. The fingers of my left hand dug into the vinyl upholstery, unable to get a secure grip.

'So how far up here?' Merker asked, his nose twitching.

'Uh, three lights up, turn left. The prison's up on the right.'

Merker scratched his nose, glanced over, grinned. 'You sure are a nervous passenger.'

'Yeah,' I said. 'That's me.'

I glanced back again, expecting to see a police car in pursuit, but no one was coming after us. At least not yet.

'Let me ask you something,' I said.

'Shoot,' Merker said.

'Martin Benson.'

'Who?'

'Benson. The man in the basement of Trixie's house.'

'Oh yeah, yeah, I remember him.' Like he was an old acquaintance, someone from his school days. Not someone whose throat he'd slit.

'What happened there?'

'Well, after I got word from one of my old buddies that our friend Trixie had been spotted, Leo and I tracked down her house and we find this guy there, snooping around, peeking in the windows. We thought maybe he was her boyfriend or new husband or something, didn't know at first that he was the guy what wrote about her in the paper. So we zapped him, got into the house. That little basement business Trixie has going, it had all the equipment we needed to conduct an interrogation, if you know what I mean.'

'Sure,' I said.

'So we tried to find out from him where Trixie was, when she was coming back, where she had my money. That kind of thing.'

'But he didn't know, did he? All Benson knew was that she was running a little S&M parlor.'

'Yeah, so it seems. He was actually pretty useless.'

'So why'd you kill him?'

Merker shrugged. 'I dunno.' He pointed. 'This where I turn?'

I was so dumbfounded by his response that it took me a moment to register where we were. 'Yeah,' I said. 'Turn here.' There were no other motorists blocking our way, so Merker didn't have to bulldoze any cars out of the way. He even signaled.

'Benson's death was a warning, wasn't it?' I asked. 'A way to let Trixie know you were serious about getting your money back.'

'Well, yeah. Now that I think about it, that is why I did it. Do you ever find, as you get older, you start forgetting little things?'

'But killing Benson, that backfired, didn't it? Because you killed him in Trixie's house, left him there in her mock dungeon, that made Trixie an instant suspect with the police, and she took off. She disappeared. Made it a bit difficult to get the money from her.'

Merker shrugged again. 'Okay, so maybe it wasn't a perfect plan. I generally know what I'm doing, you know, but even Einstein made the odd slip-up.' He brightened. 'Shit, there it is. This is it, right?'

The Clayton Correctional Facility. It looked like a community college behind high barbed-wire fencing.

'Yeah,' I said. 'This is it.'

THIRTY-SIX

Of course, some of this I've already told you. We're back to where we started.

My first time walking into a prison. Putting my phone and change and car keys into a locker. Walking through the metal detector. Being brought to the place where you talked to inmates through the glass using a couple of phone handsets.

And now I was sitting in the chair, waiting for Trixie to be brought in. The door on the other side of the glass opened, and Trixie, in jeans and a pull-over shirt, was ushered in. The female guard retreated to the other side of the door to give Trixie some privacy.

She sat down opposite me, picked up the phone.

'Zack, Jesus, what are you doing here?'

'Hi, Trixie.'

'I get this message, my lawyer's setting up a meeting with you, very urgent. What's going on?'

I took a breath. 'I have some things to tell you, but I need you to remain cool when I do.'

'What?'

'Are you listening? You have to stay calm and listen to what I have to say.'

Her eyes danced momentarily. 'Okay. What is it?'

'It's bad,' I said, lowering my voice as I spoke into the receiver. 'They've got her.'

Trixie's mouth opened slowly in a silent scream. I didn't have to say anything else, at least not yet. She had to know who 'they' were. And I had no doubt she knew whom I was referring to when I said 'her.'

She looked as though she'd lost the ability to breathe. She closed her eyes a moment, closed her mouth, breathed in through her nose. When her eyes opened, she asked, 'Is she okay? Have they hurt her?'

'She's not hurt,' I said. 'Right now, she's with Leo. Gary's parked outside the prison, in his truck, waiting for me to come back.'

Trixie looked at me with eyes that were losing hope. 'Claire? And Don?'

The Bennets.

I shook my head from side to side, no more than a sixteenth of an inch each way. Just enough to convey the message.

'Oh my God,' Trixie whispered. 'Oh my God.'

I couldn't help myself – it's the way my mind works – but I thought of that scene in *Invasion of the Body Snatchers*, the remake with Donald Sutherland, when the real Brooke Adams, after she's been taken over by her pod replacement, collapses like a withered corn husk.

She was crying, but trying not to attract attention to herself. Even in her grief, she knew that she didn't want to draw the guard over. That might lead to questions. She found a tissue tucked up in her sleeve, dabbed her eyes.

'Trixie,' I said, 'I need you to focus for me. I'm here—'

343

'I know why you're here,' she said. A tear ran down her cheek. She sniffed, wiped her nose with the tissue. 'He wants his money.'

'Yes.'

'And he'll kill Katie if he doesn't get it.'

'Yes.'

'How much does he think there is?'

'Half a million.'

'There's not that much. There's just under three hundred thousand.'

'I'm sure he'd be happy with that,' I said. 'He might be angry at first, but if he can really get his hands on that kind of money, he'll take it.'

Trixie swallowed, tried to pull herself together. 'I can tell you where it is, but I don't know how you're going to get it. They'll have to let me out, I can't imagine any other way . . .'

'Trixie, they're not going to let you out. There's no way. Why would they have to?'

'It's in a safety-deposit box. They'll have to let me out, just for an hour.'

'Trixie, the only way they might let you out is if you tell them what's going on, that your daughter's life is at stake. The moment Gary finds out you've been released, he'll know you've told them what's going on. And then I don't know what he'll do.'

More tears now. But even though Trixie was in a panic, she was also thinking. For Katie's sake. 'Okay,' she said. 'I'm going to have to tell you what to do. You'll need to write this down.'

'They took my pen,' I said. 'Just tell me.'

'You have to go to my house. Break in, whatever you have to do. Go to the upstairs bathroom, the medicine chest, take out the shelves, then you take out the back.'

'The back comes out?'

'It's a false back. There's a small storage area behind that. You'll find a safety-deposit key and a set of ID. For Marilyn Winter.'

Christ. Yet another name.

'The box is registered under Marilyn Winter. There's a color photo with the ID. It's not the clearest picture in the world of me, but I'm wearing a red wig in it. You're going to have to get somebody to go into the bank, with that ID, with a red wig.'

'Where do I find a red wig?' I whispered into the handset.

'In the basement closet. Along the wall with the straps and ropes and things, there's a set of folding doors. In there, there's a bunch of Styrofoam heads, each one has a wig on it. You'll find a red one there.'

'Okay,' I said. 'The wig, the key, the ID. I got it.'

'The box is downtown. I didn't want it in the same town where I lived and did business. Might run into people who know me as someone else. It's SunCap Federal. On Kingston, near Bellview. You know where that is.'

'I think so. I mean, yes. I can find it.'

'Okay, it's box number 2149. You go in – well, it can't be you. But whoever it is, you show your ID if they ask for it, but they might not if you've got a key, you tell them the box number, you sign in, they take you into the safety-deposit box room, you use the key to open the box, you take it into a little booth. The money's in there.'

'Trixie, I don't know where—'

345

'I know. You'll have to find someone. Zack, you have to find someone who can pass as me.'

I was feeling overwhelmed. I couldn't begin to imagine how we could pull this off, how we could give Merker what he wanted, how we could keep Katie alive.

'Maybe Gary knows someone,' Trixie said. 'He knows hookers and dancers all over the place. He can find someone to be me for fifteen minutes. Someone who can wear the wig, do my signature. She has to sign in. They usually check my signature against the one they have on file.'

'Shit,' I said. 'I can't believe I'm even considering this.'

'And I can't believe they're gone,' Trixie said, wiping her nose again. 'I did it all. I'm responsible for all of this. Gary didn't really . . . they're not really gone, are they? Claire and Don?'

I nodded.

'How . . . Did Katie see?'

'I don't know. I couldn't ask her that.'

'You've seen her?' Trixie brightened. 'You've seen Katie?'

'Yes. She's okay. But she's pretty shook up.' The truth was, I didn't want to know whether Katie had seen Don and Claire murdered. 'She asked me to tell you,' I paused, having a hard time getting it out, 'that she needed you to be her mother all the time now.'

Trixie dropped the phone, put both hands to her face. Her body shook. The guard took note but didn't move. Inmates getting bad news, of one kind or another, had to be a pretty regular occurrence.

'Trixie, listen to me,' I said, the handset still resting on the counter. I rapped the glass. She pulled her hands

346

away, her eyes red and raw, and picked up the handset. 'Trixie, you can tear yourself up about this later, but right now, we have to get this money to Merker.'

She nodded, pulled herself together. 'It's in the box. He can have it all.' She paused. 'I need you to let me know when it's done. When they let go of Katie. I need to know that she's okay.'

'I'll let you know,' I said. If I was alive to, I thought.

The guard opened the door, the signal that Trixie's time was up. She touched her fingers to the glass. I put my hand up, mirroring hers.

'I gotta go,' I said, looking into Trixie's eyes. 'I gotta do this thing. It's going to be okay.'

She looked away. She had to know I had next to no faith in my own words.

'You were quite a while,' Merker said when I got back into the truck. 'I hope you didn't do anything stupid.'

'You're still here, aren't you?' I said. 'Don't you think the cops would have surrounded you by now if I'd told them anything?'

'Maybe you're up to something funny, but it hasn't gone down yet.'

'Okay, why don't we sit here and wait and see, forget about getting the money. Why don't you call Leo, see if everything's okay there.'

'I did. It is.' He paused. 'So what's the deal?'

'It's in a safety-deposit box,' I told him. 'Downtown. But we have to go to her house first. Get the key, some ID.'

'Yes!' He banged his fist on the wheel again, but not in anger this time. 'She say how much is there?'

'Just under three hundred thousand.'

'Fuck! Are you shitting me? What happened to the rest?'

'I don't know. She had to set up a new life. I guess that cost money.'

'That's just totally fucking unacceptable.'

'Then why don't you go in there' – I tipped my head towards the prison – 'and discuss it with her.'

'Shit,' he said, more quietly, thinking about it. 'I guess three hundred thou is better than nothing.' He turned the truck around, headed south, to the neighborhood where Trixie and I were once neighbors. I hardly needed to give him directions to her place. Surely, even if you can't remember why you killed someone, you can remember how to return to where it happened.

'So hang on a sec,' Merker said, his nose twitching. 'How the fuck we supposed to get into her safety-deposit box?'

'You're going to have to find somebody. A woman with some passing resemblance to Trixie. Once you put a red wig on her, almost any woman will do.'

'Red wig?'

I told him about the ID with the color photo of Trixie in the wig. That whoever played Trixie, as Marilyn Winter, would have to sign in. Merker was thinking.

'There's this one chick, I don't know. Her boobs are about right, and she might pass if she's got the wig on.'

'Where is she?'

'She works this bar, Leo and I popped in there a couple of times this week. Used to know her up in Canborough, she danced at the Kickstart. Now she waits tables, that kind of shit. Annette, her name is. She could do this.' He grinned. 'She can't say no to me.'

The old neighborhood was coming into view. Merker found his way to Trixie's house, pulled into the empty driveway.

'Ah, the memories,' he said.

He tried the front door, wasn't surprised to find it locked. 'Let's go around back,' he said. The sliding glass doors off the kitchen were locked as well, so Merker kicked one of them in. I waited for an alarm or something to go off, but nothing did. Merker reached through the opening, unlocked the door, and slid it open wide enough for us to get inside.

'Let's find the key first,' he said.

We went upstairs, into the bathroom. I opened the medicine chest, started to carefully remove items from the two glass shelves – deodorant, toothpaste, bottles of aspirin and Tylenol. 'Who are you, Mr Tidy?' Merker said, and shoved me aside, grabbed hold of the two shelves, and ripped them out of the cupboard, tossing them to the floor, where they shattered amidst everything that had been on them. The few pill bottles and cosmetics that had fallen to the bottom of the chest Merker swept out with his hand.

The rear panel was now totally accessible. It was not immediately obvious that it was fake. A nail file had fallen into the sink, and I used it like a screwdriver to pry out the edges of the panel.

'It's not coming out,' I said. I rapped on the panel with my knuckles. It sounded solid. 'I don't think this panel moves,' I said.

Merker's face went red. He made a fist, pounded on the panel. It was drywall, and it dented only slightly from the force of the punch. 'Son of a bitch!' he said. 'What did she really tell you?'

He grabbed hold of my jacket lapels and shoved me. I lost my balance, went into the bathtub, grabbing the shower curtain as I toppled, snapping it off its rings. My head hit the tile wall. Merker had one foot in the tub, his fist ready to pummel me.

'Stop it!' I screamed. 'Stop it! I'm telling you the truth! That's what she told me! She said the medicine cabinet had a false back! It has to be there! She wouldn't lie about this, not where her kid is concerned!'

Merker was breathing like a bull ready to charge.

'Unless,' I said, thinking of the floor plan of the house we used to have two doors down, 'there's another upstairs bathroom.'

Merker was gone, running down the hall. I'd nearly crawled out of the tub when he shouted, 'Down here!'

He already had everything out of the medicine chest in the second upstairs bathroom by the time I got there. He rapped on the rear panel, and there was a satisfying hollow sound.

With the same nail file, we had the back off in seconds. And there was the key, and the phony ID.

Merker looked very pleased. 'Okay,' he said, pocketing the key and the document. 'All we need now is the wig.'

I tried not to look at the rack in the basement where Martin Benson's life had come to an end. I found the set of folding doors next to a wall display of handcuffs, whips, gags and other paraphernalia, and opened it.

There were half a dozen wigs there in a variety of shades. Merker grabbed the red one.

'We're in business,' he said. 'Now we just have to get hold of Annette and we go in and get my fucking money.'

I turned to head up the stairs, and Merker called to me. 'Hey, look,' he said.

I looked back. He'd slipped the red wig onto his head and was holding one of the whips that had been hanging on the wall.

'Whaddya think?' He grinned. 'Am I not fetching?'

THIRTY-SEVEN

The bar was called Hank's, and it sat a couple of blocks north of the dockworks. It attracted local workers, but it also bordered a tourist district and was three blocks west of a community college, so there was an eclectic mix of clientele. Muscled stevedores, young kids with piercings, a middle-age out-of-town couple loaded down with shopping bags and a video camera.

The whole way back downtown, I considered my options.

If I got a chance to get away, I could call the police. But between the time that I got hold of them and the time they arrived at my house, Merker'd be able to get in touch with Leo. They'd be able to make good on their threat against Katie before the police arrived.

So that wasn't a good plan.

If I could somehow get the drop on Merker, put him out of commission before he could make a call to Leo, then I could call the police, fill them in on the situation, and they could surround my house, with Leo and Katie and Ludmilla still inside. Once Leo and Ludmilla knew they were trapped, there wouldn't be any point in harming Katie.

So that was a plan.

The only problem with that was that it involved subduing, somehow, Gary Merker, who, in addition to being a psychopath who could beat the living shit out of me without breaking a sweat, was in possession of not only a knife and a stun gun, but a real, honest-to-God gun that shot bullets.

Could I get hold of my friend Lawrence Jones? I'd seen him deal with bad guys with a certain degree of efficiency. And they didn't scare him the way they did me. But how, with Merker watching me all the time, was I supposed to reach him?

And so here I was, in a bar with Gary Merker, trying to locate a woman named Annette who Merker thought, with the help of a red wig, could pass herself off as Miranda Chicoine as Trixie Snelling as Marilyn Winter. The only signature she'd have to forge convincingly would be that last one.

Merker approached the bar, which was hosting a late-lunch crowd, more interested in chowing down on chicken wings than getting plastered, and called the bartender over.

'Annette around?' he asked.

'Not in till six,' the bartender said.

'Oh shit, that's too bad,' Merker said. 'I had some money I owed her.'

I thought, No, surely this old ruse won't work.

'Oh yeah?' said the bartender, a tall, bearded man with a bent nose. 'Whatcha owe money to her for?'

'She helped, on her day off, at a party I was giving. A work thing. She ran the bar for me, but I couldn't pay her then, so I was dropping by to make it right.'

The bartender scowled. 'We got party facilities here. You could have had it right here, you know?'

Merker laughed nervously. 'Yeah, well, that woulda been good, but there was a bit of other entertainment, the kind you don't offer here, you know what I mean?'

The bartender smiled and nodded. 'Okay.' He tipped his head towards me. 'Who's your friend?'

'Hostage,' I said.

'Listen,' Merker said. 'You got a number for her, or a home address, I could take care of this?'

'We don't give out addresses or numbers for the staff,' the bartender said. 'Sorry.'

'Oh,' said Merker. ''Cause I'm heading out of town today, won't be back for three weeks, and I wanted to get this money to her before I left. But fuck it, I'm sure she can wait. Can you tell her I was by, that I'll try to get back in a month or so to pay her what I owe her?'

Now the bartender was reconsidering. Maybe this was going to work. He didn't want Annette blaming him when she didn't get what she was owed. He didn't want to listen to her whining for a month, or till whenever this guy came by again. 'Shit,' he said. 'She could probably use the dough, what with the kid and all.'

Merker shrugged, like it wasn't up to him anymore. Don't push too hard, he was thinking.

'Hang on,' said the bartender, and he disappeared to a back room. He was back two minutes later with a piece of paper. Written on it were an address and phone number. Merker glanced at it, folded it once, and shoved it into his pocket. 'Thanks,' he said, and the bartender saluted.

Back in the truck, we headed for Galveston Street, a low-income neighborhood of semi-detached homes with sagging porches. He ran the truck up onto the curb out front of 18 Galveston, a two-story house with a tattered stroller by the door. 'I didn't know she had a fucking kid,' Merker said. 'Bring the wig and the ID and shit.'

We'd put everything into a plastic grocery bag that sat on the seat between us. I grabbed it and followed him to the front door. The bell didn't work, so he knocked.

A moment later, a woman, who no matter her age was probably at least five years younger than she looked, came to the door. She was thin with short black hair and large breasts, and had a child of about two balanced on her bony, jean-clad hips.

'Jesus, Gary,' she said, not sounding entirely pleased to see him. 'What are you doing here?'

'Hey, Annette,' Gary said. He forced his way inside and, despite how wrong it felt to me, I followed.

'Hey, Gary, like, you couldn't have called first?' Annette said. 'Do you mind?' She swung the child, a boy, over to the other hip. The inside of the house was a mess of children's toys, dropped clothes, empty food containers.

'Nice place,' Merker said.

'How'd you find me?' Annette said, placing the child on the floor in the midst of some multicolored oversized Lego-type blocks.

'Listen, Annette, I got a chance for you to make some money,' Merker said. 'How'd you like to make a grand for the afternoon?' That got her attention.

'What are you talking about?' she said. Baffled but interested.

Merker grabbed the bag from me and pulled out the red wig. 'Try this on.'

Annette shook her head. 'Oh no. I don't do that no more. What's this, for your friend here?' She looked at me scornfully. 'This guy likes redheads? So what else you got in the bag? A little schoolgirl's uniform?'

Merker shook his head. 'It's nothing like that. Jeez, that you would even think that of me.'

Annette's eyes went wide. 'Are you kidding me? The stuff you used to have me do at the Kickstart—'

'Forget that shit,' Merker said. 'Just try this on.'

'What's it for?'

'Would you just do it?'

Tentatively, she reached for the wig, inspected it as if it might be infested with head lice, and pulled it on. She didn't have that much hair to tuck under it, and it fit pretty well. Didn't look cheap, either. I figured Trixie was able to afford the best when it came to this sort of thing. Maybe that was why there was only three hundred thousand, instead of half a million, left over.

'Ooh, you look good,' Merker said. Annette went to check herself in a front hall mirror. She cocked her head from side to side, watched the way the wisps of hair fell across her face.

'So like, what's this about?' Annette said.

Merker invited her into her own kitchen to sit down and listen to what he needed her to do. First, Annette shoved a *Finding Nemo* tape into an old VCR, then joined the two of us at the table. Merker had the ID and the key out on the table for demonstration purposes.

'I need you to go into a safety-deposit box,' Merker said.

'Huh?' Annette said.

356

'You wear the wig, you use this ID, you sign this name, and you're in. You take everything out of the box, put it in the bag, and you come back out. Simple as that.'

Annette looked at him open-mouthed. 'Huh?' she said again.

I was starting to have doubts about whether Annette was the best candidate for this operation.

'Listen,' she said, 'I'd like to help, but I got no one to watch the kid.'

'Fuck, Annette, I'm going to give you a grand. Hire a fucking babysitter.'

'Who'm I gonna find in the middle of the day? You ever try to find a babysitter like that?' She snapped her fingers. 'It's not easy.'

Merker was thinking. 'We could drop the baby off,' he said, and looked at me. 'We could leave the baby at your place, with Leo and the fat Yugoslavian chick and the kid. They're already looking after one kid, they could handle another one.'

'I don't think she's Yugoslavian,' I said. I suddenly felt very tired.

'But we could do that. So getting a sitter is no big deal, Ann—'

'Jesus!' she said. 'Are you still doing that?' She pointed at Merker, who had slipped his index finger into his nose. 'That is the most disgusting habit! You were doing that in Canborough. You haven't fucking cleared things out in there yet?'

Merker's nose-picking hand dropped to his side. 'Leave me alone,' he said, suddenly an eight-year-old. 'So, you've got a sitter. You'll do this thing?'

'Is it illegal?' she asked.

Merker, who had not been one to share his feelings with me up to now, gave me a look, as if to say, *You see what I have to deal with?*

'What do you think, Annette? You're going into a fucking bank, pretending to be someone else, and walking out with a bag full of cash, you want to know whether it's illegal?'

'I was just asking is all. How much cash?'

'Enough. Anyway, it's sort of partly legal, because the person who has the box says it's okay for us to do it. She's given us permission.'

'Written permission?'

'Fuck no, Annette, I don't have written permission. You think this is the sort of thing people put in writing?'

'Well, why can't she just do it herself? Why does she need someone else? Did she break a leg or something?'

'Because she can't, okay?'

Annette shrugged.

'When did you have a baby anyway?' Merker asked.

'Two years ago.'

'You married? This baby got a father?'

'That any business of yours?'

'Sounds like a no,' Merker said, tsk-tsking. 'That's not good, bringing up a baby without a father. I know a little something about that.'

'Yeah, well, he was a son of a bitch and I'm better off without him.'

Merker slid the fake Marilyn Winter ID, which happened to be a driver's license, towards her. 'You see the signature there? When you get into the bank, you have to be able to sign it like that. They've already got a signature on file, and they're going to compare. That's how they do things.'

'Yeah, well, I don't know if I can do that,' she said.

'Just practice a few times, you'll be fine. You got some paper and a pen?'

Annette reached over to a table by the phone, found a scratch pad and a pen. Merker was twitching his nose, wanted to touch it, but kept his hands on the table. 'Okay,' Annette said, looking at the ID and taking the pen in her left hand.

'Jesus, you're left-handed?' Merker said.

'Yeah. That some sort of crime?'

Merker looked at me. 'What's Trixie?'

I tried to picture her with a pen in her hand, doing anything. 'I'd guess right-handed,' I said.

Merker shook it off. 'Doesn't matter. Long as the signature matches, doesn't matter which hand it's written with. Go ahead, try it.'

Annette had already written 'Marilyn Winter' three times on the notepad. Even looking at it from where I sat, across the table, the signatures bore no resemblance to the Trixie version.

'Is this a joke?' Merker said, yanking the pad away from her. 'This looks like it was written with a fucking stump.'

'It's hard,' Annette whined.

'Look at your *M*. It's all roundy. It's supposed to be pointy at the tops. Jesus.'

'Let me try again.' She really concentrated this time, her tongue sticking out of the corner of her mouth, and carefully mimicked the original signature, as if she were tracing it.

'Oh, that's good,' Merker said. 'That won't arouse any suspicion. Taking fifteen minutes to sign your goddamn name.'

'You're making me nervous,' Annette said. 'Maybe if you was paying me two grand instead of one, I'd be motivated to do it better.'

'I could be giving you Donald fucking Trump's platinum card and you still wouldn't be able to do it,' Merker said. 'Okay, just calm down and try again.'

'It's just that my fingers are delicate,' Annette said. 'It's hard for me to make them go another way.' In the living room, with the *Finding Nemo* soundtrack playing in the background, the baby started crying. 'Hold on!' Annette snapped.

It was hopeless. We all knew it. Annette kept trying, and Merker kept badgering her, but if anything, her attempts to copy the Marilyn Winter signature were only getting worse. Once, she wrote 'White' instead of 'Winter.'

'I forgot,' she said.

Merker was sweating. To me, he said, 'What are we gonna do?'

'I don't know,' I said. 'Maybe we should get Ludmilla to do it.'

Merker squinted. 'Very funny. We might as well go down to the zoo and see if we can fit that wig onto a fucking hippo.' Fed up, he reached across the table and yanked the wig off Annette's head. He'd caught one of her own hairs, and she yelped. She pushed her chair back angrily and went to get the baby, and Merker's finger went to his nose. He grabbed Annette's pen to try to get at something that was buried pretty deep. I couldn't look.

'This is just fucking fantastic,' Merker said. 'She'd of been perfect, too. She's got the same kind of tits and everything.'

I didn't feel it was worth pointing out to Merker that the bank officials, unlike him, might not reduce a person's legitimacy to a bra size, that there might be other criteria.

My cell phone rang. Merker wiped the end of the pen on his sleeve, dropped it onto the table, and eyed me warily as I took the phone out of my jacket. 'Who is it?' he asked.

I glanced at the number. 'It's my wife, calling from work.' Sarah did seem to be developing a habit of calling at the most amazing times. Tied up in a barn, held hostage by a homicidal maniac. But it was always nice to hear from her.

'Don't answer it,' Merker said.

'She'll just call again,' I said. 'I can handle this.'

He shook his head in frustration. He was having a very bad day. 'All right, take it.'

'Hello,' I said.

'Hey,' said Sarah. 'Where are you? Are you home?'

'Not at the moment,' I said.

'I tried to call home, and I think there's something wrong with our number. I called and I got this other person. I asked for you and he said there was no one there by that name.'

'Really,' I said. Leo, maybe. Or Ludmilla, who didn't sound particularly feminine.

'So then I called back, and there was no answer. But since you're not home, I guess that makes sense. Maybe the lines got crossed the first time.'

'Maybe.'

'Listen, that was nice, last night, and breakfast.'

'It was,' I said.

'It hasn't been nice, being angry with you,' Sarah said. 'I don't like it. But I think, with this stuff with

361

Trixie behind us, I think we can start over, you know what I mean?'

'Sure.'

'What are you doing today, anyway? I thought maybe you'd be home. Although, I guess, with this suspension thing still going on, it's hard to know what to do with yourself. I was thinking, maybe you should get started on another book. Maybe, I don't know, maybe you have to see this as an opportunity, to get back to your novels. I mean, maybe the other ones didn't take off, but lots of successful authors, their first few books, they don't do that well, and then all of a sudden, they have a bestseller.'

'Sure,' I said. 'I just thought I'd go out, get a coffee or something.'

Merker was giving me a hurry-up sign, but then, suddenly, he stopped, as though something had occurred to him. He was waving his hand at me, like he wanted to say something.

'Listen, honey, can you hang on a sec?' I said. I smothered the bottom half of the phone with a fist. 'What?'

'This is the broad, on the fridge?' Merker asked.

'It's my wife.'

'The one in the picture, with the nice rack?'

Was my wife's honor worth protecting at a moment like this? Did I tell Merker to go fuck himself and run the risk of him pulling out his gun and shooting me through the head?

I thought about it, briefly, and told him, 'Just give me a sec. I'm just about done.'

Sarah said, 'Zack? Are you there?'

'No, no!' Merker said. 'She can do it.'

'What?'

'We put the wig on her. She can do it.'

'You're out of your mind,' I said, and unwrapped my hand from around the phone. 'Sorry, honey. There was just someone going by.'

'Where are you?'

Merker was whispering. 'How's her handwriting?'

'Hang on, Sarah,' I said, again, and covered the phone again. 'Shut up. It's not happening. I'm not dragging her into this.'

He snatched the phone from me. 'Hey!' I shouted.

Just as suddenly, Gary had the gun back in his hand – the real one – and was pointing it at me while he put the phone to his ear with his left hand.

I could hear Sarah say, 'Zack? Zack?'

Merker said, 'Hey, Mrs Walker?'

'Zack? Who's this?'

'This is Gary, Mrs Walker. I'm a friend of your husband's.'

'What happened to Zack? The phone went all funny.'

'Listen, we kind of need your help with something. Can I ask you a kind of personal question?'

'What?'

'How would you describe your breasts? I saw your picture, that one on the fridge where you're wearing that gown? At your place? I know you can't tell everything from a snapshot, but I'd say they're pretty nice.'

'Put my husband on the phone.'

'Well, I'd like to, but I've got a gun pointed at his head right now, and if you don't help us out, I'm gonna give his brains some fresh air.'

Annette came back in with the baby on her hip. 'Even if I can't do this thing, I should still get something for my time.'

THIRTY-EIGHT

We were parked across the street from SunCap Federal. Merker behind the wheel of the Ford pickup, me on the passenger side, Sarah between us. She had the red wig on and was practicing her Marilyn Winter signature a few more times. I'd dug a tattered old owner's manual out of the glove box, and Sarah was writing out her new name in the margins of pages that described how to check oil levels and properly install a hitch. She scribbled into page after page, glancing up at the fake ID resting on the dashboard for guidance.

'That's pretty good,' Merker said. 'I think the *W* is off just a tiny bit, I think it should slant a bit more to the right, but really, you're good.'

Sarah, normally fairly polite, did not respond to Merker's praise. I looked at her last two forgeries, and they were pretty much dead on. The situation seemed too unbelievable. Here was my wife, pretending to be Marilyn Winter, the phony name of Trixie Snelling, who was actually Miranda Chicoine, also known as Candace.

'Even if I get the signature right, what if someone notices that I'm not her?' Sarah asked.

'You got the hair, you got the key, you can sign the name, the boobs are close,' Merker said, full of confidence. 'You can do it. Although you could of dressed a little sexier.' Sarah was wearing a black blouse, tan skirt, sensible, flat shoes. 'Can you at least hike the skirt up a bit?' His eyes narrowed. 'You have to get this right. You fuck it up, bad things are gonna happen.'

Sarah glanced at me.

'So we'll be sitting out here,' he reminded her. 'I see anything funny going down, first thing I do is shoot your husband here. Then I call Leo and get him to kill the kid. A cop car comes screaming up, people come running out of the bank, anything like that, and the shit hits the fan.'

'I'll do it,' Sarah said. 'You don't have to worry.' I believed her, but I didn't know whether Merker was convinced.

He patted her bare knee encouragingly. Sarah tried to pull it away, but there was no room to move. 'That's a good girl,' he said.

I so wanted to kill him.

'Let me out,' Sarah said. I opened my door and stood on the sidewalk. I held out a hand for Sarah, but she made a point of navigating her descent from the raised truck without my assistance.

'Don't forget this!' Merker shouted, tossing out a small blue zippered gym bag. He'd asked Annette if she had something he could carry a bit of cash in, and she'd offered him that. If Merker ever did get Trixie's money, it was going to smell like old socks and sour towels. Sarah grabbed the bag by the strap and stood next to me.

'It's a bit crooked,' I said.

'What?' said Sarah.

'The wig. It's just a bit off to one side.'

She used the oversized mirror bolted to the passenger door to take one last look at herself, made a minor adjustment.

'That's perfect,' I said.

She wouldn't look at me. Maybe there was no point worrying anymore about whether I might get out of this alive. Even if I did, I was still a dead man. But all that really mattered to me now was that Sarah survive this.

I had no idea how things would play out. Would she get into the safety-deposit box? Would the money Trixie said was there actually be there? Would something tip off the bank officials that she was not who she claimed to be? Would they call the police? Would Merker kill me when they showed up, and call Leo to tell him to do the same to Trixie's daughter?

After Sarah walked into SunCap Federal, would I ever see her again?

As if reading my mind, Sarah reached out and touched my arm and looked at me.

'I can do this,' she said. 'I don't want anything to happen to Katie.' She'd never met the girl, but she didn't need to set eyes on a five-year-old girl to be concerned for her.

'I'm sorry,' I said. 'I'm sorry for everything.'

She looked as though she wanted to say something, but I knew she wasn't ready to forgive me for the mess I'd gotten us both into, nor did she feel this was the time to tell me what a complete and total asshole I was.

I could only hope there'd be a chance later.

'Wish me luck,' she said.

And I watched her, in her red wig, gym bag in hand, stride across the street, open the door of SunCap Federal, and disappear inside.

It had taken less time to lay it all out for Sarah than I might have expected. At Annette's place, after Merker had asked Sarah about her breasts, he handed the phone back to me.

'Zack, what's going on?' Sarah said.

I had to concentrate a moment and employ what journalistic skills I had to boil everything down to point form. 'The guys who've been after Trixie found her sister and brother-in-law up in Kelton. They killed them. They took Trixie's daughter Katie. They want the money Trixie took from them, or they're going to kill Katie. I went to see Trixie in prison. She has a plan for how we can get into her safety-deposit box, get the money, give it to these guys. One of them is holding Katie at our house. If anything goes wrong, he gets the call and kills her.'

I waited for Sarah to say something, but then heard another voice.

'How's the linoleum thing coming along?'

Frieda, the Home! editor.

Then Sarah. 'I'm on the fucking phone, Frieda. Zack?'

'I'm here.'

'Where are the kids?'

'Not at home. Angie's downtown at a class, Paul's at school, both of them said at breakfast that they weren't going to be home after school today.'

'Most of the time, they don't show up when they say they're going to. Not the other way around.'

'That's what I'm hoping.'

'Are you okay?'

'I guess you could say I'm a bit rattled. But otherwise, yeah, I'm okay. But once this is over, if it goes off as planned, there's a deal to hand me off to another set of bad guys. Or bad gals, actually.'

'What?'

'Let's not worry about that now. The immediate problem is getting into the safety-deposit box.'

'How are you going to do that without Trixie?'

I paused. There was no easy way to do this. 'Gary wants you to do it. He saw your picture on the fridge, when we were at the awards dinner, and he thinks you can pull it off. We have Trixie's red wig, which is part of her Marilyn Winter persona. That's the name she used to get the safety-deposit box. You'd have to go in, pretending to be her, with the key, sign in as her. Then you get into the box, transfer all the money into a bag, and bring it back out. Give it to Gary, Katie gets released.'

Sarah said nothing.

'Honey?' I said.

'I'm here.' Another pause. 'Tell me about Katie.'

'She's scared to death, Sarah.'

'Do you think they'll actually let her go?'

I felt a wave of hopelessness wash over me. 'I'm just going along for now, Sarah, hoping this works out the way it's supposed to.'

Merker said, 'Can we get this show on the road? Tell your lady we're coming to pick her up. Where's she work?'

'The *Metropolitan*,' I said.

'Where's that?'

'Sarah,' I said into the phone. 'Don't do it. This has all gone far—'

Gary Merker snatched the phone back. 'Hey, lady, you don't do it, he's dead, the kid is dead. You in?'

'I'm in,' I heard her say.

Twenty minutes later we picked her up out front of the paper. And now Merker and I were sitting in the Ford pickup, waiting, wondering how it was going for Sarah inside the bank.

As I sat in the truck, I spotted something just barely sticking out from under Merker's seat. It was a handle for something.

It was the stun gun. The one he'd used on me and one of the twins at our house.

He had his real gun sitting in his lap, his right hand resting on it, but without a finger looped around the trigger.

'She smart, your woman?' he asked me.

'Yes,' I said. 'A lot smarter than I am.'

'Yeah, well, that I can believe. How long she been in there now?'

'Only a couple of minutes,' I said. 'It just seems like a long time.'

'How long should it take? You go in, you show them the key . . .'

'Just hang in. Maybe the bank is busy. Maybe it's taking her a while to get someone to help her.'

Merker fidgeted nervously, scratched his nose, but, mercifully, stuck nothing in it for once. 'She has to get the signature right. If she can do that, she'll be fine.'

'She's been forging mine for years,' I told him. 'She can do this.'

But it was torture, sitting out there in the truck, having no idea of how it was going inside.

'Maybe I should go in,' I said. 'Just watch from a distance, see that everything is going okay.'

Merker snorted. 'Yeah, that's a great plan. I sit out here all by myself, let the two of you just run off.' Merker turned on the radio, twisting the dial from station to station, then, deciding there was nothing interesting enough to take his mind off his current situation, turned it off.

'Shit,' he said, looking up the street. A police cruiser with two officers was approaching. 'Shit shit shit,' he said. 'She fucking told.'

I glanced down again at the handle of the stun gun. 'Relax,' I said. 'They're just driving down the street. It's not like they're slowing down or anything. If they were—'

The police car slowed down.

'Shit!' Merker said through clenched teeth. He slammed his fist into the steering wheel. 'She's blabbed, I know it.'

'She won't have done that,' I said. Unless, of course, she was unable to pass herself off as Marilyn Winter and had to confess to what she was up to, what was at stake.

The cruiser came to a stop in front of the bank, and the cop on the passenger side got out. He said something to the driver, held up two fingers, as if to say he'd only be a couple of minutes. Unless, of course, it meant to send for two more police cruisers.

Merker got out his cell phone, punched in some numbers. 'Leo?'

'Jesus!' I said. 'Nothing's happened yet.'

Merker waved at me to shut up. 'Just checking in, man. How's it going there?' Merker listened, nodded, looking back and forth between me and the bank across the street. The cop had the door open and was going inside. It looked as though he was reaching into his back pocket.

'He's going for his wallet,' I said. 'He's just going to the ATM.'

Merker was listening to Leo. 'Okay, good, yeah, well, we're just waiting on this end. What?' Leo was telling him something else. 'Well, take some Pepto or something. Fuck, I got bigger things to worry about than your stomach. I'll call you back if anything goes wrong here.'

He put the phone back into his pocket.

'Where's the cruiser?' he asked.

'It kept on going. I think he's doing a loop around the block. If there were a problem, he wouldn't waste time looking for a parking spot.'

'Yeah, maybe.' He looked in his mirror, checking to see whether the cop car was still visible. 'Hang on,' he said, opened the door, and stepped out so he could get a better view down the street.

I leaned swiftly across the seat, reached down and grabbed hold of the stun gun. I was back in position, holding the gun down by my right side, between my body and the door, by the time Merker was getting back in.

'I think he's doing a slow drive around the block,' he said. 'Maybe you're right, maybe he's just using the money machine. He better be.'

His eyes were trained on the doors of the bank. 'Come on. Come on. I want to see somebody come out of there. Your wife, or that cop, and not together.'

I'd been waiting for my moment, some way to get the drop on Merker, and now it was at hand. Stunning him would only put him out of commission for a few seconds, but it would be long enough to wrest the gun away from him, to get his cell phone, to smash his goddamn fucking head in if I had to. Then I could wave down either the cop as he came out of the bank, with or without Sarah, or the other one doing a loop around the block. Once Merker was subdued, police could surround our house, get Katie out safely.

My mouth was dry, my heart was pounding in my ears.

There was nothing to say to Merker. No need to give him a warning. No need to tell him to freeze or drop his weapon.

I could just stun the bastard.

And so, while he sat with his back to me, focused on the bank doors, I steadied the stun gun in my lap and pointed it at him.

And pulled the trigger.

The gun went *bzzzt*.

Merker did not suddenly go into spasms. He did not crumple into his seat or fall against the steering wheel. He did not scream in pain.

All he did was turn around and ask, 'What was that?'

And then he saw the stun gun in my hand. Fear flashed across his face briefly, but then he smiled. 'You dumb fuck. Once you've fired that thing three times, it has to be all reset.'

He reached across the seat, grabbed the stun gun out of my hand, and hit me across the nose with it. Blood sprayed out onto my shirt.

'You're really starting to fucking annoy me,' Merker said. 'I've already got enough on my mind without having to worry about you trying to be some sort of fucking hero.' He shook his head in disgust and shoved the stun gun back under his seat.

I cupped my hand under my nose to catch the blood. There was a steady trickle. I didn't think he'd broken anything, but it hurt like a son of a bitch.

'Hold on,' Merker said. He was looking at the bank again. 'It's our cop.'

I wiped my bloody hand on my pants, dug a tissue out of my jeans pocket, and held it gently around my nose. I looked across the street to see the police officer come out, alone, walk out between two parked cars, and look down the street to flag down his partner when he reappeared.

'Yes!' Merker said. 'You were right! Probably just getting some cash. So they can go buy some doughnuts.'

The cruiser appeared, slowed, and the cop got back in. It drove away, taking away not only the two officers, but my immediate hopes of being able to get us out of this mess.

'Yes,' said Merker gleefully.

My tissue was soaked with blood. I tossed it onto the floor, found one more in my other pocket and held it to my nose. 'Hey, don't make a mess,' Merker said, glancing over.

The moment he looked at me, Sarah came out of the bank, clutching the gym bag. 'There,' I said.

Merker whirled around. 'Oh my God, I don't believe it. This is fucking fantastic.'

Sarah checked the traffic and then crossed, coming around the back of the pickup and then up to the passenger door. I opened it and stepped out so she could get back in between us.

She saw the blood on my pants and shirt immediately. 'Jesus, Zack, what happened?'

'Just get in,' I said, and she climbed up into the truck with the bag and slid over, but she kept looking at me. I was a bit of a mess.

She turned on Merker. 'What did you do to him?'

'Oh, he's fine,' Merker said, grabbing the bag out of Sarah's hands. He unzipped it, opened it wide. 'Motherfucker,' he said.

I almost said it myself. The bag was jammed with cash, made into bundles with rubber bands. Most of it, it appeared, in tens and twenties.

'Is it all here?' he asked Sarah accusingly.

'No, I left half of it in the safety-deposit box,' Sarah snapped. 'Of course it's all there.'

'Okay, okay,' Merker said. 'Sheesh.' He took out one packet of cash and handed it to Sarah. 'For your trouble.'

'No thank you,' she said.

He tossed it back into the bag. 'Okay, but don't forget I offered. This is amazing. Did you have any trouble? They didn't ask for more ID? They were okay with the signature?'

'I was in and out,' Sarah said. She went to touch my nose, but held her hand an inch away when I recoiled. 'Are you okay? What did he do to you? What happened?'

'I had a plan,' I said. 'It didn't work.'

THIRTY-NINE

Merker was ebullient. So maybe he didn't have half a million dollars in the bag. Maybe it was only three hundred thousand. Of course, he'd have to count it to be sure, but the thought that he had this much of his money back had planted an enormous grin on his face.

He was rocking back and forth behind the wheel, as though listening to the beat of a rock song, but the radio was off.

'The living's gonna be easy from here on,' he said. 'I think me and Leo'll go south. Get a place in Florida or something. Or maybe we'll go to Europe, one of those countries over there.'

'South of France is nice,' I said, not really knowing why.

Merker made a farting noise with his lips. 'Fuck no, I hate the French. I'm gonna stick with Europe.'

'Definitely not foreign editor material,' I said to Sarah, who had taken off the red wig and tossed it down on the floor like a dead rat.

'What's that?' Merker said.

'You'll have to get some foreign material,' I said. 'Like travel books. Read up on the places you want to go.'

Merker nodded. 'That's not a half-bad idea. Where would you find books like that?'

'I'd probably try a bookstore,' I said. I touched my finger to my nose, checked it for fresh blood. My wound seemed to be drying up, but I still looked as though I'd walked into a bus.

'So all I gotta do now is pick up Leo, turn you over to the beauty queens, and we are on our way.'

'You forgot to mention giving them their share,' I reminded him.

'Well, sure,' Merker said slowly, like a kid who'd been asked whether he had his homework done. 'Just sort of slipped my mind for a second.'

'Listen,' I said. 'You've got what you want, right? This all worked out, I helped you out, I got my wife to help us, we're good, right?'

Merker glanced over. 'You mean, not counting when you tried to fucking zap me?'

'Aside from that, yeah.'

Merker thought a moment. 'I suppose. So what's your point?'

'First of all, we pull over and you let my wife go. She went in, she got you the money. The Gorkins don't know or care about her. Just let her go.' Sarah listened intently as I argued for her release, and momentarily reached over and squeezed my knee.

'Well, shit, I don't know about that,' Merker said. 'Maybe once Leo and I are on our way and this is all over.'

The thing was, how could he let us go? Look at what we knew. Particularly me. Merker knew that I knew he'd killed Benson, the Bennets, the biker who'd fathered Trixie's child. And for all he knew, I'd passed all this information on to Sarah.

If I were him, right about now, I'd be thinking about how I was going to get rid of two more bodies.

And that didn't even count Katie.

Jesus. What would he decide to do about Katie?

My mind started working again, looking for another way out of this. I wasn't confident of my ability to leap from a moving pickup truck, and even if I could, I wasn't about to leave Sarah with Merker.

I knew Sarah was doing the same thing, calculating the odds, looking for an opening. If she'd come up with anything, she certainly hadn't found a way to communicate it to me. Merker was using one hand to steer so that he could keep his other hand on the gun. The only bonus for us from this arrangement was that it meant he was leaving his nose alone for a while.

There was no need to tell Merker how to get back to our house from the bank. He seemed to know where he was going, and he was driving with great purpose. I noticed he had not bothered to ask me where Mrs Gorkin's Burger Crisp establishment was. We could drop by there on the way and give her the twenty-five thousand dollars he'd promised her for not taking me away before I could get his message to Trixie in prison.

Perhaps, if he really did plan to give the woman and her twins the money, which I seriously doubted, he was going to present it to Ludmilla at the house, who could then call her mother to report that everything had gone as planned. Then, presumably, Mom would drive back over and pick up her daughter, and me.

I did not want that to happen.

I suspected a fate similar to Brian Sandler's – a deep-fry experience – awaited me. It's hard to tell the authorities about a health department payoff scam, and other illegal business operating out of the back of a restaurant, when your lips have been melted off.

I had to ride this out, hope for something to go wrong for Merker, the smallest distraction, anything.

I had to get Katie out of this.

I had to get Sarah out of this.

If I could manage those two things, I'd start looking for a way to get myself out too.

Merker wheeled the truck around a corner, paying no attention to the stop sign. If only there'd been a cop in the vicinity. If he wasn't careful, Merker would finally have his money, be set for life – or at least a good chunk of it – only to lose it all over a stupid traffic violation.

We were back on our street, Crandall. Merker slowed, not familiar enough with the street to know our house instantly. 'Just up here,' I said.

'Oh yeah,' he said, and pulled in behind Trixie's GF300, blocking it. 'Okay, kids, we're home. Everybody out.'

He was out first, his truck keys looped onto a finger of his left hand, which was carrying the bag of cash, the gun in his right. He came swiftly around to the other side, watched me and Sarah warily as we stepped down out of the Ford.

He ushered us along in front of him, up the front porch steps. Before we'd reached the front door, he shouted, 'Leo! Hey, Leo!'

The door opened, but instead of being greeted by Merker's partner, it was Ludmilla letting us in. Her eyebrows went up a notch when she saw Sarah, evidently surprised that there was a new guest coming to the party.

Katie was lying down on the couch, but not sleeping.

As soon as Sarah saw her, she went to her. 'Hey, you must be Katie. I'm Sarah.'

Katie looked at her with tired eyes and said nothing. She'd met too many bad people in the last twenty-four hours to trust anyone new right off the bat.

'I'm Zack's wife,' she said, her voice full of reassurance. 'How are you holding up? Do you need something to eat? Have they been feeding you?'

There was no sign of Merker's associate.

'Where the hell is Leo?' he asked Ludmilla.

'Upstairs,' she said. 'In the bathroom. He is not feeling well.'

'What do you mean, not feeling well?'

Ludmilla shrugged. 'He is throwing up, and he is having trouble at the other end too, I think. I think it is maybe something he ate. That burger in the fridge. I think maybe it was bad.' She looked at me accusingly. 'You shouldn't keep bad food in your fridge.'

I held back from telling where it had come from, that we'd been holding on to it in the hopes of turning it over to the health department.

Merker went to the bottom of the stairs, set down the gym bag, his keys resting on top. He shouted up the stairwell, 'Leo!'

Edgars shouted back from behind the closed bathroom door. 'Gary?'

'Leo, get down here!'

'I can't! I'm sick! I think I'm gonna die!'

Merker rolled his eyes. 'Honest to God,' he said, more for our benefit than Leo's.

Ludmilla said, 'Did you get the money?'

'Yeah,' said Merker, annoyed. 'We got the money.'

'You give me our share, and I'll go.'

'Already taken care of,' Merker said.

Ludmilla's eyebrows went up again. 'What do you mean, taken care of?'

'On the way back,' he said. 'Didn't you get the call?'

'What call?'

'From your mother. She didn't call?'

'No, she has not called.'

'That's funny. Well, she was pretty busy. Maybe she's still counting it.'

'You gave her the money? You were supposed to bring our share here, then I call her and then we are done.'

'Fuck, sorry about that,' Merker said. 'I got confused. But anyway, you can go. Take off. We're all done. I dropped by, gave your mom the twenty-five grand. Oh yeah, actually, she told me to tell you to come on back. I don't think she was going to call you anyway.'

Even if English had never been Ludmilla's first language, she knew bullshit when she heard it.

'Leo!' Merker shouted again. 'We gotta get out of here!'

Sarah had knelt down next to Katie. 'Come on, honey, talk to me. Are you okay? Has anybody hurt you?' Katie shook her head no. 'Would you like a snack or something? A drink of water?'

Leo shouted back, 'I can't get up yet! I feel terrible! Can you come up here for a second?'

Merker got a look on his face like he'd just bitten into a lemon. This was not his idea of a good time, having to go up and check on a friend suffering from a catastrophic intestinal disorder.

'Just finish up and get down here as quick as you can!' Merker said. 'We got a few things to deal with.'

380

'I'm going to call my mother,' Ludmilla told Merker. 'I will just check that she got the money.'

'Sure,' said Merker, his eyes dancing. 'That's what I'd do too, I was you. But your mom said she was having phone trouble, which is why she told me to tell you that everything was totally okay and—'

'Gary!' Leo sounded like he was going to die.

'Ah, fuck,' Merker said and bounded up the stairs, two steps at a time, to see what was wrong with his friend.

And suddenly, for the first time in hours, Gary Merker was not watching over us. He was out of the room. Sarah and I exchanged glances. Katie's eyes went back and forth between us. Even she seemed to sense that there was an opportunity here, and we might be the ones to help her take advantage of it.

Ludmilla, however, was looking at the gym bag. She must have had a pretty good idea what it contained.

Upstairs, Merker shouted through the bathroom door, 'Pull up your pants, we're getting out of here!'

'Could you come in here?' Leo said. 'I think I'm done, but I feel kind of weak.'

'Jesus, no,' said Merker. 'Clean yourself up and come on.'

Ludmilla advanced on the gym bag, picked up the keys on top, and pulled back the zipper. Just a couple of inches, but enough to see the mountain of cash. She was turned away from me, so it wasn't possible to see her expression, but I could imagine it.

But the sight of all that cash wasn't enough of a shock that she forgot how to react. She kept the keys to Merker's truck in one hand and grabbed hold of the bag's straps with the other. She was out the front door without another word.

I made no move to stop her. This was my opportunity to escape not only Merker, but the Gorkins as well.

To Sarah, I said, quietly but with great urgency, 'Go.'

She grabbed Katie by the hand. The girl seemed suddenly alive, swinging her legs off the couch and planting them on the floor.

'Just run,' I whispered. 'Anywhere.'

Upstairs, Merker said through the bathroom door, 'Smells like you died in there. I'll be waiting for you downstairs.'

'Come,' Sarah said to me, her eyes full of pleading, already heading with Katie to the kitchen so she could sneak out the back door.

'Right behind you,' I said.

Out front, I heard the door slam on Merker's truck, the engine turn over with a great roar. While Sarah and Katie slipped out the back way, I took a moment to peek through the glass in the front door to see Ludmilla backing out of the driveway.

It turned out to be a stupid thing to do. It was a moment I could not afford to take.

Merker came bounding back down the stairs. It took him a second to register that the bag was gone. 'What the—'

Then he looked at me. He had the gun out, and while he was waving it around, it was pointed more or less in my direction.

'Where is it?' He'd become instantly maniacal. 'The bag! Where is the bag?'

I made a motion with my thumb, like a hitchhiker, pointing out front. 'Ludmilla,' I said. 'I think she wanted to be sure Mom got her share.'

He ran straight into me, shoved me up against the wall, and opened the front door. He stepped out onto the porch, looked down the street in time to see his truck receding into the distance, and got off a shot.

I started running back through the house. I got as far as the kitchen, saw that the back door was still open from Sarah and Katie's escape. Then there was another shot. Ahead of me, the kitchen window that looked out onto the backyard shattered.

'Hold it!' Merker shouted.

I froze. He ran, caught up to me, put the barrel of the gun to the back of my head.

'Where are they? The kid? Your wife?'

'They're gone,' I said.

Merker pushed the barrel harder against my skull. 'Jesus! Goddamn it!'

I could feel his hot breath on the back of my neck. This was it, I figured. He was finally going to blow my brains out. Part of me wished he'd just get it over with. I felt strangely at ease. The two people I most wanted to save were on their way to freedom.

They were safe.

'Fuck them,' Merker said. 'I want the money. We've got to go after the money.' He took a couple more breaths. He was trying to pull himself together. 'You know where they hang out? Where the twins and the mother are?'

'It's a burger place.'

'Show me. Take me there.'

The cold steel against my head made the decision a bit easier. 'Sure,' I said.

Leo, coming into the kitchen, was doing up the belt on his pants and walking like he'd just ridden in on a horse. He was white as a sheet. If he was surprised to see Merker and me alone in the kitchen, Ludmilla and Katie gone, and a gun to my head, he didn't show it.

He asked me, 'You got any, like, Alka-Seltzer or anything?'

I pointed to the pantry. 'Bottom shelf,' I said.

Leo opened the pantry door, found the tablets, ran some water into a glass and dropped two of them in.

He squinted at the bubbles as they rose off the water's surface, then drank it down in one gulp. He wiped his mouth with his sleeve and said to Merker, who was still holding the gun to my head, 'Did you count the money yet?'

FORTY

'Ludmilla left with the money?' Leo said. He seemed genuinely shocked. 'Are you sure, Gary?'

'Am I sure?' Merker said. 'You see a bag of money around anywhere? I left it at the bottom of the stairs, and not only did she take that, she stole my fucking truck.'

Leo was perplexed. 'She seemed like such a nice person. We talked about all sorts of things while you were gone. Did you know that someday she wants to open her own beautician's shop?'

Merker looked at Leo, dumfounded.

'I know she's not what you'd call a beauty herself, she could stand to lose a few pounds, but she has a nice way about her,' Leo said. 'I don't see why she couldn't make a go of it.'

Merker, who still had a gun at my head, said to me, 'Keys.'

'What?' I said.

'Car keys.'

The only car left in the drive was Trixie's, and if he wanted to take it and find his way to Burger Crisp on his own, that was fine with me.

'In my pocket,' I said, reaching in and dropping them onto the kitchen counter. Merker snatched them up.

Then he grabbed me by the back of my jacket and started leading me to the door. 'Just take the car,' I said. 'What do you need me for?'

'Navigator,' Merker said. 'Leo, come on.'

Leo said, 'I feel like I might have to go to the bathroom again.'

'Leo!' Merker said. 'We're going! We're picking up three hundred fucking thousand dollars. If you shit your pants, you can buy a new pair.'

Leo still looked uneasy, but followed as Merker and I went out the front door. He hit the remote button on the key to open the doors of Trixie's sedan. 'You,' he said to me, 'up front with me. Leo, you take the back.'

I got in the passenger side, Merker slid in behind the wheel, and Leo got into the back seat. He got in gingerly, favoring his ass.

'Take off your belt,' Merker said to Leo, who was just buckling up.

'You don't want me to wear my seatbelt?'

'No, on your pants. Take off your belt and tie his head to the headrest.'

'Aw, come on,' I said.

Merker looked at me and pointed. 'I don't want you trying anything. I'm tired of getting fucked around. Letting your wife and the kid leave, letting that bitch run off with my money, that was wrong.'

'Sorry,' I said. 'I didn't realize I was working for you.'

'You see? That's the sort of thing I'm talking about. It's your attitude. Leo, what are you doing?'

'I'm just trying to get my belt off, okay?' I glanced back, saw him slip it out of the last loop of his jeans. 'How am I supposed to keep my pants from falling down, Gary?'

'I'll buy you a new belt this afternoon,' Merker said. 'I'll buy you a hundred belts.'

The belt went over my head and down to my neck. Leo looped it around the two aluminum posts that supported the headrest.

'It's kind of loose,' Leo said. 'I got it on the last hole.'

That, thankfully, was true. While the belt prevented much mobility on my part, it didn't keep me from breathing. As long as I didn't lean forwards suddenly, it wasn't touching the front of my neck. I sat rigidly in the seat, pressing my head back against the cushioned headrest.

'All comfy?' Merker said. When I did not reply, he put the car into reverse and backed out of the drive. 'Which way?' he asked me.

I pointed. Merker headed north. 'Second stop sign, hang a right,' I said.

Merker put his foot to the floor, listened to the engine's powerful surge. 'Nice wheels. This is yours?'

'Trixie's,' I said.

'No shit. Hey, Leo?'

'Yeah?'

'Like this car?'

'Yeah. It's really nice. Nice upholstery.'

'We're gonna keep this car. Make up for the fact that we got short-changed on the safety-deposit box.'

'Okay,' Leo said without much enthusiasm.

'You don't mind, right?' Merker asked me with mock consideration. 'It's not like it's your car.'

'Be my guest,' I said, pushing my head back against the headrest.

Leo called to me. 'Hey, mister, that burger? I think there was something bad about it.'

'You were warned,' I said.

'Huh?'

'It was written right on the box.'

Leo didn't have anything to say about that.

'Here?' Merker asked. We had come to the stop sign. I nodded and he turned right. The car surged forwards again.

'At the light, a left on Welk,' I said. 'It's up five or six blocks on the right. Burger Crisp.'

'Gotcha.'

'You going to let them keep twenty-five thousand dollars?' I asked.

Merker smiled. 'Oh, I'm going to give them something. I'm definitely going to give them something.'

'Maybe when we get there I could use the washroom,' Leo said.

'You'll be staying in the car, watching this asshole,' Merker said. 'We can stop somewhere else, after.'

'Okay,' Leo said, but he sounded pretty uncertain.

And that was pretty much how I felt too. A few minutes earlier, I'd felt good that Sarah and Katie had managed to get away. But now, I was, literally and figuratively, feeling my neck. I was, once again, looking for an opportunity, a way out. It was something that I had shown myself, so far, to not be very good at.

My cell went off. This, I knew, would be Sarah. She'd have gotten Katie and herself someplace safe, and would want to know where I was.

'Give me that,' Merker said, and I reached into my pocket and handed him my still-ringing phone. Merker punched his power window button, tossed the phone out the window.

Merker pointed ahead and to the right. 'That it?'

'Yeah,' I said. 'That's it.'

Merker pulled into the Burger Crisp lot. There were three other cars there, and, best as I could tell, business was light. It was midafternoon, the lunch crowd had thinned.

'Check it out,' Merker said.

Parked down around the side of the restaurant was his Ford pickup. 'We gonna get the truck back?' Leo asked.

'Fuck the truck,' Merker said. 'We're keeping this.' He had his left hand on the door handle, the gun in his right. To Leo, he said, 'Keep an eye on him. Hang on to the belt. I'll be back in a couple of minutes.'

Leo grabbed the belt and pulled it taut as Merker got out of the car, leaving it running, and strode towards sthe Burger Crisp, the gun down at his side and slightly to the back.

'I can't breathe,' I said, the belt cutting into my neck.

'Okay,' said Leo, loosening it only slightly. 'I just don't want you doing anything dumb. Gary'll be really mad at me.'

'Leo, listen to me,' I said. 'This is your chance. Let me go, and just walk away. The police are going to be after you guys, but especially Gary. He's the one killed Martin Benson, right? He's the one cut his throat.'

'Gary's better at those kinds of things.'

Gary Merker opened the door of Burger Crisp and disappeared inside.

'Exactly,' I said. 'You're not like him, are you? He's the violent one. The police will understand that, especially if you go to them, tell them what he's done.'

'He's my friend. He looks after me. I was riding with him one time, on his Harley, and he turned too sharp and I fell off and I hit my head and he's been real good to me ever since then because ever since then things have been a bit cloudy, you know?'

'He's a friend that's getting you into a lot of trouble. You don't kill people, do you, Leo? I'll bet, when you and he found Katie, I'll bet you didn't kill those people who were looking after her.'

'I waited outside the barn when Gary shot them. I had Katie with me. I put my hands over her ears.'

'There you go. That was good of you. You see? You're not like Gary. You're actually a pretty gentle guy, am I right?'

'I like animals,' Leo said, still holding on to the belt but not quite as tightly. 'I like all kinds of animals, but probably dogs the most. You like dogs?'

'Oh sure,' I said. 'Who doesn't like dogs?' To be honest, I had some bad, fairly recent memories concerning dogs, but I didn't see much sense in getting into that. 'Dogs are great. And I think I know something else about you, Leo. You wouldn't even join in, would you, when Gary and others, back at the Kickstart years ago, were raping Candace. The woman I know as Trixie.'

'That was mean,' Leo said. 'She's actually pretty nice, you know?'

'I know. And her daughter, she's nice too, don't you think?'

'Yeah. So where did she go, exactly?'

'She went off with my wife. She's going to be fine.'

'That's good.'

I felt I didn't have much more time. 'Leo, you have to let me go. It's the right thing to do. And you should go too. Just get out of the car and get out of here.'

'Gary'd be really pissed if I did that. He'd say—'

And then we heard the shots from inside the Burger Crisp. Five, it sounded like, in quick succession.

Bang. Then *bang bang*. And then one more. *Bang*. There were screams inside the restaurant, people throwing themselves to the floor, it looked like, through the window.

And then the door burst open and Gary came running out, gun in one hand, gym bag in the other.

Looking like a crazy person.

He set the bag on the roof, opened the door, grabbed the bag and tossed it into the back seat with Leo, got in and closed the door.

'Whoa!' he shouted, nose twitching. 'Holy shit!'

I didn't want to ask what had happened.

In the back, Leo said, 'There any chance I still might be able to use the washroom?'

FORTY-ONE

Merker slammed the console shifter into drive and sped out of the Burger Crisp parking lot without considering Leo's request for a pit stop. As the car fishtailed onto the street, I tried to keep my upper body from whipping about too severely to avoid being choked by the belt around my neck. I had one hand gripped onto the door armrest, my nails digging into the plastic, the other onto the edge of the leather bucket seat. It helped a bit that once Merker got back into the car, Leo released his grip on the belt, so I had a bit of slack.

I turned my head enough to see a few people running out of the Burger Crisp, screaming. I did not see, however, any of the Gorkin ladies among those fleeing.

'Did you see Ludmilla?' Leo asked.

'I saw them all,' Merker said, weaving from one lane to another, trying to put a lot of distance between us and the Burger Crisp as quickly as possible.

'I know this is crazy, after being sick and all,' Leo said, 'but all of a sudden I feel a little bit hungry.'

'Look in the bag,' Merker said. 'That'll take your mind off food.'

I heard the zipper of the gym bag, then Leo say, 'Holy shit. There's lots and lots of money in here! Like, even more than I thought!'

'Pretty good, huh?' Merker's nose was twitching.

My last-ditch plan, to turn Leo Edgars against Gary Merker and persuade Leo to let me go, had failed. I had pretty much run out of ideas.

But there was something in the back of my mind. Something Trixie had mentioned. When we'd first gotten together and she'd told me about her problems with a reporter from the *Suburban*.

Somewhere behind us, I thought I heard sirens.

'Hey, Gary, you hear that?' Leo said.

'Yeah, I hear it. Nobody's going to catch us, buddy. We got ourselves a kick-ass getaway car here today.'

I wondered just how many witnesses there were to Merker's misdeeds, other than myself. Sarah and Katie, the customers at the Burger Crisp, the other drivers out in Oakwood who'd seen him bulldoze another car out of the way with his pickup truck. And that was just today. The evidence and eyewitness testimony that could be used against Merker and Leo – clearly not a couple of rocket scientists – had to be overwhelming. You didn't have to be a genius to bring misery to a great many people. The question was how many more people's lives they'd ruin before it all caught up with them.

'What are we gonna do with all this money?' Leo asked.

'Retire,' Merker said, reaching down into the console for Trixie's yellow wooden pencil. 'We're going to retire.' He turned the pencil around so the eraser end was pointed away from him. An extraction aid. I couldn't look.

'I like the sound of that,' Leo said. 'I don't have much of a pension, you know.'

The sirens were getting louder. Merker glanced into the rearview mirror. 'Leo, I can't take my eyes off the road. Whaddya see behind us?'

'Nothing much,' Leo said. 'Nobody's coming after – hang on.'

'What?'

'I can see a flashing light way back there.'

Merker turned abruptly down a side street. The car was made to corner. He'd only gone a block when he turned again. The belt cut into my neck as the tires squealed. I made a hacking noise.

We'd been having coffee, Trixie and I, in one of those joints where if you order just a regular coffee they look at you like you just got off the boat. She'd just picked up her mail. Said something about how, in her line of work, a post office box was the way to go. The less mail coming to your actual house, the better.

'I think you lost him,' Leo said. 'Nice going.'

But Merker wasn't slowing down. We'd wandered into a residential area, and he was taking a left and then a right and then a left. I don't think he had any idea where he was – I certainly had no idea where we were – but as long as he wasn't being followed, that was all that mattered.

There were a number of envelopes Trixie had dumped onto the table. One of them, I remembered, was from a car company. The words 'Recall Notice' had been stamped on the front.

German cars, Trixie had said derisively. Great to drive, but they were always having little things going wrong with them. Fuel injection, power seats—

The sirens, having faded briefly, were getting louder

again. It almost sounded as though they were ahead of, instead of behind, us.

'Hear that?' Leo said.

'Shit!' Merker said, wheeling the car down another quiet residential street. 'I don't even know where the fuck we are.'

I've never been a very good passenger. Not with Sarah, not with friends, certainly not with Angie when she was learning to drive. I spend a lot of time pressing my right foot into the firewall, thinking that maybe, if I press hard enough, a brake pedal will miraculously appear, the car will slow down.

Riding with Merker, the belt around my neck, whizzing past other cars at high speed, pedestrians jumping out of our way, I thought I'd break my ankle, I was pressing so hard. A van backed out of a drive into our path, and I slipped my hands up between my neck and the belt, seeking to mitigate its strangling effect when we collided.

I closed my eyes.

When another two seconds went by without an impact, I opened them.

'Close, eh?' Merker said, twirling the pencil in the air.

Trixie had mentioned something else about her car. Another problem, something she'd been notified about in the mail.

Air bags. That was it. Something about the air bags. That they were extra sensitive, that the slightest bump on the front bumper could set them off.

If Merker hit something, even nudged it, and if that set off the air bags, maybe that would provide enough of a distraction that I could turn the belt around, bring the buckle to the front, loosen it enough to get my head out, and bail out of the car. Merker didn't have the gun, Leo did, and I wasn't convinced he'd be as quick to use it. And it would take a few seconds to hand it to Merker in the front seat.

Merker made another turn, slammed on the brakes. He'd taken us into a dead end. He threw the car into reverse, backed up so quickly he couldn't control the steering, and the front end of the car whipped around so that we were facing the other way immediately. Back into drive, and we were off again.

'Just like Jim Rockford,' Merker cackled.

'Hey, Gary, this isn't very good for my stomach,' Leo said. 'I was just starting to feel better, like I could eat something.'

'Jesus, Leo, enough.'

Up ahead, at the next cross street, a police car went screaming past from left to right.

'Yikes!' Merker shouted, and slammed on the brakes. I didn't have time to get my fingers in between my neck and the belt and I lost my breath, gagged, as the belt cut into my windpipe. I closed my eyes a moment, wondering whether I'd pass out.

Maybe, I thought, keeping them closed was a smart idea. If we did have an accident, there might be flying glass.

But curiosity prevailed, and I opened them. We were approaching a stop sign. A small car – it looked like another Civic, not unlike the one Merker had rammed with the truck on our way to the prison – was waiting to make a right turn.

Merker might ordinarily have driven around the car, to the left, but there was a brown UPS truck there. Not enough room to get through. On the right, our path was blocked by a metal pole supporting a stop sign.

Our car screeched to a halt behind the Civic. 'Jesus Christ, lady, let's go!'

This time, his prejudice against lady drivers was at least accurate. The person behind the wheel of the Civic was an elderly woman, her hair tinted a light shade of blue.

Behind us, we could all hear the approaching sirens.

The lady's right turn signal continued to blink while she waited for a break in traffic.

'Maybe,' I said, wanting to sound as helpful as I could, 'you need to give her a bit of a nudge.'

'Fucking right,' Merker said.

And again, I closed my eyes and waited for the impact.

The car bolted forwards, but we only had to go a foot or two before the bumper of the GF300 would connect with the rear bumper of the Civic. Merker wouldn't be able to get the car up to much speed.

But it was enough.

I scrunched my eyes shut as hard as I could, threw my hands up to my neck to get them around the belt, and then we hit.

There was a soft explosion as I was jerked forwards. Not that I could go that far, with Leo's belt and all. The explosion was loud, but muffled at the same time. I felt the fabric of the passenger-side air bag brush, only momentarily, against my face.

For the few milliseconds my eyes were closed, I plotted out my moves. Move the belt back to front. Hunt for the buckle. Slip out. Open the door.

Run like hell before Merker could grasp what had happened and tried to grab me, or worse, shoot me.

I opened my eyes. My air bag, and the one that had exploded out of the steering wheel, had already deflated. I started twisting around the belt, my heart pounding, but fingers fumbling for the buckle.

But the sense of urgency seemed to have passed.

Merker was not moving.

His head was tilted forward, and there was blood dripping from his face onto his shirt and pants.

His eyes were still open, but they seemed lifeless.

Then I noticed something silver and pink and rubbery under his nose.

It was the yellow wooden pencil. The force of the airbag had driven it clear up Gary Merker's right nostril.

The only thing left sticking out was the eraser. He had six inches of pencil in his brain.

FORTY-TWO

'Gary?' said Leo, who'd been tossed to the floor of the back seat and was getting himself reoriented.

I had my hands on the buckle, was pulling the belt through it. Once I had enough slack, I pulled it over my head.

'Gary, you okay?' Leo leaned forwards between the seats and tapped Merker on the shoulder. Leo saw the blood, then saw the end of the pencil sticking out of his nose.

'Gary!' he shouted. He burst into tears. 'Gary?'

I opened the door and stumbled out of the car. I could hear sirens coming from different directions. The elderly woman in the Honda had gotten out too, and was standing next to her car, shouting back at us, 'Where'd you get your license, asshole?'

I took three steps over to the curb, crossed the sidewalk, and collapsed onto the perfectly cut yard of a two-story brick house.

Leo, gun in hand, got out of the back seat and opened the front driver's door. His beltless pants were slipping down and he tugged them up with his free hand. 'Come on, Gary! Wake up! Come on! Wake up.'

Gary Merker was not waking up. Not with a lead pencil through his head.

A police car barreled up the street from the direction we'd come, and a second one was screeching to a halt in front of the Civic. A cop jumped out of each, weapon drawn.

There were tears running down Leo's cheeks. 'Come on, Gary, jeez, come on.' He saw the cop approaching from the rear vehicle, and waved the gun at him, not intending to use it menacingly, I thought, but gesturing the cop to come up, to give them some help. 'He's hurt!' But the cop wasn't reading it that way.

He screamed, 'Put the gun down!'

But Leo was too busy crying and yelling to get the message. 'He's hurt, man, you gotta help him.'

'They ran into my car!' the old lady shouted, pointing, seemingly oblivious to the guns that were being waved about.

'Ma'am, get down!' the officer from the second car shouted.

'On purpose!' she said. 'They ran right into me!'

'Ma'am, get down!'

The old lady stopped shouting, but she did not get down. She turned and started walking over to where I was. 'Were you in that car?' she asked me. 'They ran right into me!'

But instead of talking to her, I was back on my feet, shouting at Leo. 'Leo! Do what he says! Put the gun down!'

Leo, however, overcome with despair, was still waving the weapon around. Everyone was shouting. The cops were shouting at Leo to drop the gun, I was shouting at Leo to drop the gun, and Leo was shouting that his friend needed help.

From my vantage point on the lawn, it seemed that all the clichés were true. It's like it was happening in slow motion. Like a dream.

The cop shouted again for him to put the gun down. The other cop was braced against the open door of his cruiser, his weapon bearing down on Leo.

'Can't you see he needs help?' Leo pleaded to the first cop, and waved the gun in the officer's direction. Not pointing. It was more like he was making gestures of hopelessness, and forgot that he had this thing in his right hand that could kill people.

If I'd been the cop, I probably would have done what he did.

He fired. Leo went down.

Just like that.

Even before the massacre at the Burger Crisp – Merker had walked directly behind the counter, fired two shots into Mrs Gorkin and one each into Ludmilla and Gavrilla – the police were hunting for us. Sarah, Katie in tow, had gone to a house on the street behind ours and called 911. She'd directed them to our house on Crandall, and when she heard the sirens approaching, had left Katie with the neighbor and run back. But by then, we were all gone. Sarah gave them a description of Trixie's car and the hunt was on.

I spent the rest of that day explaining things to the police. Detective Flint from Oakwood was brought in so he could hear it too.

I told them they'd find the Bennets, dead, in their barn in Kelton.

I told them about Merker's plan, to use Katie to extort money from Trixie. About our trip to the prison. How Sarah had been coerced into going into the bank to empty the contents of the safety-deposit box.

I told them Merker had also told me, in the course of our conversations, that he'd killed Martin Benson. That he and Leo, while hunting for Trixie, had encountered Benson looking for more evidence of Trixie's operation. That Merker had killed Benson in his bid to get information out of him.

And then I did something I suppose I didn't have to do. I'm not even sure that I should have done it. But it seemed right.

I mentioned, more or less in passing, that Merker had alluded, at one point, to the deaths of the three other bikers at the Kickstart in Canborough.

How he'd taken care of them too.

The police wondered whether he had told me why. I said no. Best to play dumb. But when they got in touch with Detective Cherry in Canborough, he'd tell him his theory that maybe Merker had worked out some sort of deal with the opposition, that he'd already been the prime suspect in the death of his former second-in-command.

The thing was, they were already able to tie half a dozen murders to Merker. Why not throw in another three for good measure?

Other stuff happened later.

Trixie was released from prison. They'd been holding her as the chief suspect in the Benson murder. There wasn't much point in that anymore.

She let me know, quietly, that the gun she'd pointed at me in the basement of her house, the same one Eldon Swain had given her and which had the potential to connect her to the killings in Canborough, had been dropped into a river from a highway overpass on her way up to Kelton. She'd been scared to hang on to it.

Brian Sandler, the health department inspector that the Gorkins dumped into the fryer, didn't die. But his recovery will be long and difficult. He was soon well enough to communicate everything he knew about corruption in the health department. About his boss, and others, who'd turned a blind eye, either for money or out of fear, to a number of establishments' health violations, as well as other illegal activities that were being conducted on the premises.

Sarah wrote the story for the *Metropolitan*. I put her onto Sandler and turned over to her everything I had, all my notes, the audio file that Lawrence Jones found in his e-mail.

I thought if it was her story, it would get her out of Home! and back into the newsroom. After all, I was already on suspension. Better to rescue a career that still had a chance to be redeemed.

It worked. And Sarah's version of the story was better than what I could have done.

Managing editor Bertrand Magnuson did call me, however. He'd had some sort of change of heart, given everything Sarah and I had been through. He said he was willing to rescind the suspension and let me write about tracking down Trixie Snelling, her subsequent exoneration, the Gary Merker affair, the biker massacre in Canborough – the whole nine yards, as they say. A first-person exclusive.

I said Dick Colby could do a good job with it. I'm too close this time, I said. Let someone with a bit of distance write about it. The thing was, I didn't see how I could write a story that I wasn't prepared to tell in full. I didn't want my byline on a story I couldn't write honestly.

I knew who'd really killed those three bikers that night at the Kickstart. And I wasn't feeling fully committed to the public's right to know.

What business did I have being a reporter for the *Metropolitan* with that kind of attitude?

'Well,' said Magnuson over the phone, 'if you change your mind and want to come back to work for us, let me know.'

I told him I would think about it.

To the best of my knowledge, Frieda never did get anyone to write a series on linoleum. I never saw it in Home!

So many stories that go untold.

Things could be better on the home front.

I had failed to keep my promise – make that promises – to Sarah that I'd stop getting mixed up in these kinds of messes. It's a knack I seem to have developed of late, and I'd like very much to lose it. Sometimes, you make one mistake, and it's like knocking over that first domino. I'd already allowed a couple of dozen to tip over, and had no idea how far down the row I was.

Lawrence Jones phoned. 'You should have called me,' he said.

'Believe me, if it had been possible, I would have,' I said.

'How's it going?'

'Sarah mentioned the other night that maybe we should . . . that maybe we should try some time apart.'

'Jeez,' Lawrence said. 'Seriously?'

'Yeah. I mean, I think she loves me. But look at what I've done, Lawrence. Look at the things I've fallen into.

I'm a menace to my loved ones. Maybe I'll just go back to writing science fiction novels. Keep to myself. Lock myself in a room someplace, where I'm not going to get into trouble, drag my family in with me.'

'I'd offer to let you bunk in with me for a while, but I think you'd drive me out of my mind.'

I couldn't help but laugh. 'I guess we'll see how it plays out,' I said.

'Good luck, man,' Lawrence said.

A couple of weeks after the dust all settled, and we had our own car back, and Sarah had returned to work every day and I was home, still trying to figure out what to do, Trixie – she'd actually gone back, legally, to Miranda Chicoine but I still have a hard time thinking of her by that name – dropped by with Katie.

It was after Sarah had gotten home from work, and we both got to the front door at the same time.

When Sarah saw who it was, she began to retreat into the house. 'I'll let you two talk,' she said.

But I took Sarah's hand and pulled her, gently, to my side, preventing her escape.

'We just came by to say goodbye,' Trixie said.

'Where you off to?' I asked.

'Out west,' Trixie said. 'Seattle, maybe San Francisco. I'm looking at a few things.'

Sarah and I stepped out onto the porch. Katie slipped away from her mother and ran her fingers along the posts in the railing.

'How's she doing?' Sarah asked.

Trixie smiled sadly. 'She's been through a lot. She sleeps with me. She's afraid to let me out of her sight. It's going to take a long time for her to ever feel secure again. Everything I do now is going to be for her. I'm starting over, with Katie. I'm selling the house in Oakwood. And there's Claire and Don's estate to settle.' Her eyes were moist. 'My lawyer, Niles, is trying to get my three hundred thousand back. The police still have it, they retrieved it from the car after the accident, but they're holding on to it as evidence. Niles says eventually we'll be able to get it back. They can't prove that I'm not entitled to it. But you know what? Even if we don't, we have plenty to start over with, get another house somewhere, close to a good school. I want to always be there for her, so I might try to get some sort of job that allows me to work from home.' She smiled again. 'But something different this time. That other job, that's over.'

Trixie's GF300 car was parked at the curb. Sarah and I walked with her to the end of the driveway. Katie wandered in dizzying circles in the front yard, arms extended, like she was an airplane.

Trixie looked at Katie. Her lip trembled slightly, and then she looked at us.

'I came here to thank both of you. For saving Katie. For saving my daughter's life.' She hugged Sarah, put her arms around her and held her close, and then hugged me, whispering into my ear, 'Thank you for explaining things to the police. About what happened in Canborough.'

'Sure,' I said as she pulled away.

Then Trixie turned back to Sarah. 'I'm sorry. I'm sorry for all the trouble I've brought into your life.'

Sarah started to say something, but Trixie, tipping her head towards me, continued, 'I know you want to kill him.'

Sarah made no protests.

'If he were my husband, I'd probably want to kill him too. He's very possibly one of the biggest pains in the ass I have ever known. And I envy you every day that you've got him.'

Sarah swallowed.

'If this helps,' Trixie said, looking right into Sarah's eyes, 'I'm going to make you a promise.' Trixie took a breath. 'You're never going to see me again.'

Neither Sarah nor I said anything. Trixie watched Katie playing in the yard, wiped a tear that was just starting to make its way down her cheek. 'She's my little girl. I hope, if I do right by her now, she can forgive me for all the mistakes I've made.' She clapped her hands together. 'Katie! Let's go!'

Trixie led her daughter to her car, buckled her into the safety seat in the back.

'Goodbye, Miranda,' I said as she got into the car.

As we watched the car disappear down Crandall, Sarah said to me, 'She killed those three bikers, didn't she?'

'Yeah,' I said.

Sarah thought about that for a moment, then said, 'I would have too.'

As the car rounded the corner at the end of the street, Sarah turned to me and said, so softly I almost didn't hear her, 'I think there's a bottle of Beringer chilling in the fridge. I could pour a couple glasses.'

It felt to me like the entire world was holding its breath.

'That would be nice,' I said. I tried to smile. 'Are you going to put something in mine that'll kill me?'

Sarah looked at me very seriously. 'It could go either way,' she said, and took me inside.

They drove until it got dark, then found a motel alongside the interstate. Miranda figured, why rush it, no sense driving all through the night. They'd take their time, make an adventure out of it.

Katie didn't want to sit in a restaurant to have dinner. She felt scared when there were lots of other people around. Miranda said, 'Why don't we get some pizza, and some ice cream, and we'll take it back to our room and we'll sit on the bed and we'll eat it right out of the box and then we'll eat the ice cream right out of the container with two spoons.'

Katie liked that idea.

They went to bed early. They were tired from driving all day. So they got undressed and got under the blankets together and turned off the lights and listened to the trucks on the highway go by and disappear into the night.

'Tell me about the princess,' Katie said.

'Well,' said Miranda, 'once upon a time, there was a princess, with very curly hair, who was only five years old, and she could do anything she wanted.'

'Even stay up late and watch TV?'

'Not that sort of anything. She could do anything that was hard, that took a lot of work, anything she set her mind to, she would do that thing.'

'Could she be a movie star?'

'Yes.'

'Could she be a hot dog person who sells hot dogs?'

'Yes, she could.'

'And would there be any dragons? Would there be dragons chasing her and trying to get her?'

Miranda wrapped her arms around Katie, brought her in close to her, felt the rhythm of her heart coming into beat with her own, her curls against her cheek, and she put her mouth to Katie's ear.

'No dragons,' she whispered. 'No more dragons.'

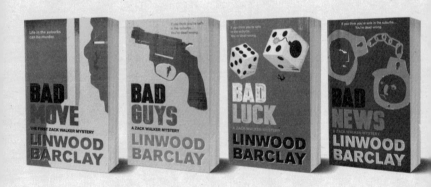